Felicity in Marriage

Jane Austen's *Pride and Prejudice* continues…

Part One

C. J. Hill

Other books by this author

Prudence and Practicality: A Back-story to Jane Austen's *Pride and Prejudice*

Wickham's Wife: A Back-story to Jane Austen's *Pride and Prejudice*

"I am the happiest creature in the world. Perhaps other people have said so before, but not one with such justice. I am happier even than Jane; she only smiles, I laugh."

~Pride and Prejudice~

Chapter 1

"Oh, Mamma!" Elizabeth sighed as she scanned the spikes and flourishes conveying her mother's irritation. She turned over the letter and grimaced.

"My dear? Is it very bad news from Longbourn? I'm sure there was nothing more than is usually amiss when I left; nothing that had outraged your mother unduly." Mr. Bennet turned the page of his paper and coughed unconcernedly. "What perplexes her now, I wonder, as I am not there as the source of it?"

"Father!" exclaimed Elizabeth as she looked up from her letter. "I do hope you informed Mamma of your departure and intended length of stay with us? From her letter it almost seems as if you disappeared in the night and no one knows where you have got to."

"It is, of course, the usual nonsense, my dear. How could I possibly have left Longbourn with no one knowing where I was going? I may not be the most communicative of persons but I hope I am not so thoughtless as to leave without word, although it is debatable if anybody marks that word.

"It is true enough; your mother was most displeased when I announced my intention of travelling into Derbyshire for a surprise visit, but, as she was still suffering from a recent bout with either a cold or her nerves - I forget which specifically - and determinedly confined to her bed, she could not possibly have accompanied me. In her fragile state of health it would have done her no good at all. The state of the weather and the roads precluded it, but she was most animated on the unfairness of it all, I assure you, accusing me of all manner of subterfuge and favouritism."

Elizabeth laughed again and returned to her letter. "Well, she is certainly most vexed at your 'high-handed attitude' as she calls it, but hopes that you will not suffer too many aches and pains from such a lengthy ride; although, I do not think that sentiment is quite meant in the manner it is written, Father. She is, however, very concerned that Darcy and I think badly of her for not accompanying you and wishes to explain the extent of her illness, which she does, for several lines, in great detail."

"It is nothing but her usual imagined nervous disposition with which you are perfectly familiar, and a trifling cold, the likes of which she has dismissed in others on more than one occasion, but which served its purpose for my escape. I think it perfectly natural that your father should be the first visitor in your new home, with or without the added impediment of an ill wife. But, are not you glad to see me, Lizzy?"

Elizabeth rose and hugged her father where he sat, crumpling his paper in the process.

"We are both delighted to see you – I can speak for Darcy in his absence - and hope you are able to spare several weeks to spend with us, if you think Mamma will manage without you."

"There, there, Lizzy! No need for that; get along with you! Manage without me, indeed. She has done so to great effect these twenty years at least and will continue to do so quite admirably for some time to come, I have no doubt. I believe I shall stay just long enough to feel rested from the journey and able to consider the return aspect of it with equanimity, but not so long that you are both wishing me long gone. It is a delicate balance for a guest, but do not concern yourself, my dear, I would not wish to impose where I cease to give pleasure.

"I am, however, most conscious of needing to impress your new husband; we must improve his view of our family, Lizzy, and I hope that this visit will promote that. It is another reason, perhaps, that your mother's illness was so well-timed."

Elizabeth returned to her breakfast and letter, when she let out a sudden gasp.

"Oh, how wonderful that she feels so well! Charlotte is to leave Meryton tomorrow, Father, with baby William! Apparently the Barouche box has arrived from Hunsford and is even now parked in Lucas Lodge's stable. Ah! Mamma says Lady Lucas is making the most of it, telling everyone how kind Lady Catherine has been to her grandson and daughter, 'quite revelling in the situation' apparently. I am so happy for Charlotte that she will have a comfortable journey home. Lady Catherine must have improved her opinion of Mr. Collins after his perceived involvement in my *disgraceful* marriage to Darcy. I am glad of that at least. I wonder if the Barouche box will soon be sent here as a peace offering?"

"I would not count upon it, my child, if I were you. I think it will be some time yet before Lady Catherine accepts you back under her roof. Mr. Darcy will have to do some serious mollification before you set foot again in Rosings. But I would not let the situation dismay you; she is behaving as the lesser person in all of this. If she cannot concede defeat magnanimously and wish you both happy, then so be it. Let her rot in her grand house – what is that to you? She can have no effect upon you or Mr. Darcy, or your joint happiness. Do not dwell upon it my dear, all will be well."

"It does not bother *me* so much, but I think, perhaps, that her attitude towards us does rankle more with Darcy. He does not mention it but she is still his nearest relative, his mother's sister. He cannot bear that she thinks so ill of me, particularly: her opinion of him has less effect than she would wish and so she will have to make amends to me before he will soften towards her, I think, but I do hope all will be mended before he must make his usual visit to Rosings in the Spring or it will be awkward for everyone."

Her father grunted as he laid the paper on the table and rose stiffly from his chair.

"I am sure you will exert your influence upon your husband and make him the better person in all of this, Lizzy, and that Lady Catherine will soon see the error of her judgment. I think I will take a turn about the Park in a while to loosen up these stiff joints your mother so kindly enquired after; would you care to join me and show me the delights of Pemberley on a Winter's morning?"

"Of course! I do so hate being cooped up inside; we must make the most of this sunshine. I will join you shortly after I have spoken to Mrs. Reynolds about some household matters."

"I should not think being cooped up in such a house as this can be anything other than extremely pleasant, my dear, it is so peaceful and comfortable; no quarrels or doors slamming as you are used to having. Although, much of that has abated now your sister is in Newcastle.

"Will Miss Darcy join us, do you think? I should like to get to know her a little better, now that I am here."

"Oh, Georgiana prefers to stay inside when it is cold; she is not a great walker. I try to convince her but she will not be moved from her fire and instrument. She is perfectly happy as she is."

Mr. Bennet smiled and slowly took the stairs to his room as Lizzy sailed away down the hallway to the housekeeper's quarters. How satisfying it was to find her so happy and content, relishing her new situation in life. Everything about her displayed a talent and ability for her new role as mistress of Pemberley which could not be feigned; her ease of manner commanding respect and affection already from her servants. He would have much to report upon his return and, so far, nothing of concern.

As they took a turn about the lake, Elizabeth pointed out her favourite sights: the woods across the bridge, now bare of leaves but still impressive in their stands of oak and beech; the walled garden, the river with its trees scattered on its banks, and the winding valley as far as the eye could trace it. Although her father had first expressed a wish to explore the entire Park, upon hearing of it being more than ten miles around, resolved to follow his daughter's suggestion that they enjoy her accustomed circuit through the woods bringing them down into a small glen comprising of a small stream and a narrow walk amidst the coppice-wood. Elizabeth loved this particular section of the property with its windings and secrets and, since her arrival, had done her fair share of exploring the hidden nooks and crannies to be found there. Every time she passed through there was something new to be seen, and today was to prove as interesting for her father. His attention was caught as he passed close by the stream and noticed the fish moving sluggishly along the river bed.

"You have some admirable trout in your stream, Lizzy. It is a pity it is not the season for it or I would take advantage of my leisure and spend some time terrorizing those inhabitants!"

Elizabeth laughed. "Indeed; uncle Gardiner could hardly stay away last Summer when we visited and Darcy was kind enough to supply him with fishing tackle and point out those parts of the stream where there is usually the most sport. I do not think that any other part of our holiday compared for Uncle with those few happy days. Of course, their visit at Christmas merely renewed the early friendship between my aunt and uncle and Darcy; they think very highly of each other. Darcy and I, of course, cannot thank them enough for bringing me into Derbyshire and allowing us to see each other in a new and improved light!"

"Ah, yes; but your mother was not so pleased that her brother should have been the first to visit, you know, confined as she was to Meryton and your sister, Jane's, for Christmas. She was quite put out, as I am sure she mentioned."

"Oh! Have no fear, Father. Mamma made her feelings quite plain upon the matter, but as I reasoned with her, Jane is so convenient, and the weather so bad, it was only sensible for her to remain where she would be the most comfortable and not put undue stress…

"…on her poor nerves! Yes, my dear, you are quite right and sensible as always; and of course your mother had a most enjoyable time at Netherfield behaving as she always does, blithely discussing her latest letters from Mrs. Wickham and yourself. The vicious sisters smiled and bore it all as best they could - their comments were an admirable exercise in civility under pressure - but it was easy to see how it galled them, especially Caroline, having to entertain those of us with such dubious manners and connections! I quite enjoyed their discomfort.

"No, coming here would not have been as entertaining for me, so I applaud your and your sister's arrangements, and hope they will continue for a few more years yet or until Mr. Bingley's sisters decide they have other places to be when we visit."

They turned back towards the house and paused on the stone bridge to admire the setting and its surroundings.

"You have certainly gained a fortunate situation here, Lizzy. I hope you will always be as happy and contented as you are now. Marriage certainly is no guarantee of happiness but I think you should be fairly on your way to that state, as is your sister. You both deserve it. I am relieved to find you able to respect your partner in life, as I know you could be neither happy nor satisfied unless you truly esteemed your husband. Your lively manner would place you in the greatest danger in an unequal marriage."

Elizabeth squeezed his arm. "He is truly the best man I ever knew and I believe I shall always love and respect him, Father. There is no danger of it becoming an unequal marriage; I try to improve his serious nature and he regulates my impulsive desire to judge everybody! It is a perfect combination, I assure you."

"Then I shall leave here content, my child, knowing you are in good hands and well-loved by someone who deserves you.

"It turns cold; let us return to the house and a warm fire. Perhaps Miss Darcy will be downstairs by now and we shall have some conversation to look forward to."

Chapter 2

Glad to be returned out of the chill of the morning, Mr. Bennet retired to the library – a place about which he had heard a great deal - to satisfy himself of it being one of the most impressive in this part of the country.

He was not disappointed. The room was large and well-furnished with leather armchairs and sofas set in sensible places with reference to available light coming in from the wide floor-length windows, allowing an expansive view outside while also taking into account the proximity of the fire when necessary, and necessary it certainly was this morning. The remaining walls were almost exclusively covered in shelves of books: large, leather-bound volumes in various rich hues.

Mr. Bennet was immediately satisfied with the state of his son-in-law's library. Here was a place not merely for show as was the general way, but a place where, it was perfectly clear from the wear upon both the books and the seating, persons who enjoyed extensive reading loved to sit and peruse the written word at length.

Selecting a book, Mr. Bennet settled himself with great pleasure into one of the deep chairs placed at such an angle that his view from by the fire was unobstructed through the windows to the parkland beyond, and opened a page at random.

And there he remained.

Elizabeth meanwhile had gone straight back to speak with Mrs. Reynolds about another matter she had just considered and then made her way upstairs to her sister-in-law's private sitting room where, Elizabeth knew, Georgiana would be perfectly happy at her work for an hour before coming downstairs to her instrument and filling the house with music for another hour or two. Elizabeth tapped quietly upon the door and entered at the sound of Georgiana's voice.

"Good morning, sister!" Elizabeth smiled. "I hope I am not disturbing you at your work? Oh! That is very fine stitching indeed, Georgiana, it progresses very well. It will be a splendid piece when you are finished with it."

Georgiana smiled at the compliment and put her work aside.

"And how is your father this morning after his long ride yesterday? Did he sleep well? Is he quite recovered?"

"Oh, yes indeed, he is quite refreshed, thank you. He joined me for breakfast, I shared a letter from my mother which arrived in the first post, and then we took a quick walk about the park together. He was most interested to see Pemberley in all its glory, even in the middle of Winter, and is now perfectly happy, ensconced in the library. He expressed a desire to become acquainted with you, my dear, if you feel like some company this morning."

Georgiana sighed, glancing at her work. "It is most unfortunate that my brother is in Town this week; I am sure your father would much prefer his company to mine. But, if he wishes it, then I shall try to entertain him, although I am sure I do not know what I shall say to him."

"Oh, my father is perfectly able to lead a conversation himself, when others can think of nothing they believe will be of interest, but I am sure he would not wish to inconvenience you, Georgiana and he will be perfectly content left where he is. I will tell him you are otherwise engaged."

Elizabeth left the room, slightly piqued at Georgiana not wanting to interrupt her morning routine, but she was not very surprised; she had learnt that Georgiana's claim to shyness and discomfort in company was, like her brother's, quite real.

The little her husband had imparted about his sister's adventures in Ramsgate the Summer before last had surprised her once she had become better acquainted with Georgiana. But very young girls, like her own sister, Lydia, when left to their own devices for the first time generally adopted the opinion that the entire world revolved around them and their construction of reality. It was not until they were severely corrected in that view that they even began to consider other possibilities.

So it had been, apparently, for Georgiana. Darcy had spoken of her almost-elopement with Wickham in the most affected terms in his letter to Elizabeth, a letter which had had the power to reveal her own true nature and inclination to pre-judge everybody upon the merest acquaintance. Elizabeth still cringed when she remembered the words contained therein; although she had disposed of it the instant Darcy had requested her to do so, its remembered contents still made her more aware of her thoughts and actions even this far from the reading of it.

Elizabeth made her way back downstairs to speak with her father before attending to her letters. She heard a door slam and footsteps running quickly behind her.

"Elizabeth! Wait! Do not be angry with me. I will come and meet with your father, of course I shall! My brother would never forgive me if I was so ill-mannered, even though it is a great strain to me. Come, please introduce me."

"Pray, do not concern yourself about how your behaviour will be perceived by your brother; I shall not be one to tell him of it, I assure you. You may meet my father now if you sincerely wish it, or when it is more convenient for you; it makes no real difference to him."

"No, indeed, I assure you. I am most interested in meeting any of your family; I only wish that he had brought your younger sister – Kitty, is it not? – I should dearly like to have been allowed to meet her."

Elizabeth nodded, slightly mollified, and led the way into the library where they came upon Mr. Bennet as expected, entirely engaged in his book with a pot of chocolate and a single cup on the table beside him.

"Ah, my dear! What a delightful place this it! So comfortable; so thoughtful – look, Mrs. Reynolds has quite foreseen my needs! - and so quiet. Oh," he rose quickly from his chair, "and this, I presume, is your new sister?"

He bowed and smiled at Georgiana who curtsied and sat upon the nearby chair.

"I am very glad to make your acquaintance, sir. Elizabeth has told me much about you, and my brother speaks most highly of you. He will be very glad that you have visited so soon to see how Elizabeth has settled in her new home."

"Indeed! The admiration flows both ways, I assure you. How could it not? And the longer I spend in his house, the more I feel the need to approve of everything about him. Of course, his choice of wife cannot be faulted as she, along with everything else he seems to acquire, is the most elegant and charming there is to be had! Naturally, as his sister, you are well aware of his natural superiority and good taste and have long grown used to it, I am sure."

Georgiana laughed at the thought of her brother being admired principally for his choice of wife and heritage.

"Oh, I am very aware, I assure you, of my brother's superiority in everything. But, more than that, he is the kindest and most thoughtful person, especially to me, and takes prodigious care of me."

"Well, naturally he would; he cannot be too careful where you are concerned! Have you always remained here at Pemberley, Miss Darcy, or have you been to London, perhaps, for a change of scene?"

Elizabeth drew in her breath, anxious that Georgiana not feel embarrassed by her father's innocent enquiry.

"Indeed; I have had the fortunate opportunity to visit both London and Ramsgate, the Summer before last, sir. My brother allowed me to venture into the outside world a little, understanding that all young people wish to see new things."

"And how did you find London, may I ask? Truth to tell, it holds little interest for me, with all the rush and noise and bustle; I only go when I must, or to visit relations. But I am sure for a young person who has never seen it, it must be something enjoyable?"

"Yes, at first it was all new and exciting and enjoyable, but it did not take long for me to tire of just what you have mentioned, young as I was, and for me to wish to be somewhere else entirely. But I did not wish to merely return to Pemberley once I was out on an adventure. It would have been such a disappointment. And so my brother then arranged for a visit to Ramsgate; perhaps you know it, sir?"

"No, not at all. I travel as little as possible, although now I am bound to be drawn oftener from home if I wish to have sensible conversations and quieter company with my daughter. This house's gain is a serious loss to mine, as you can imagine."

"Father!" Elizabeth interrupted. "You still have Mary and Kitty at home; and Jane is close by. Do not work upon my conscience. I am perfectly happy in my new situation and you should be happy for me and not wish me back. Come, Georgiana, let us leave him now before he makes me feel even worse for no reason other than his own amusement!"

"Yes, yes, please do leave me to my delightful solitude. It is possible I may be in sufficient need of company in a few hours and so will seek you out then!" Mr. Bennet returned to his book, smiling with satisfaction at his daughter's discomfiture.

"Your father misses you a great deal, I think, Elizabeth. It must be a comfort to you to be the object of two men's affection; to be able to make them both content just by your presence. He certainly seems to be a man who enjoys his privacy, is not he?" enquired Georgiana as they made their way around to the larger room at the front of the house in which sat her pianoforte, given her as a present several years before by her brother.

"He seems perfectly content with a good book and fire. He must have been a reasonable man to live with at home, Elizabeth?"

"I have always found him to be eminently reasonable where I have been concerned, but I feel he has always treated me and my sister, Jane, with more affection than perhaps he has shown to my other sisters. And he takes great delight in vexing my mother whenever he can manage it; it is his amusement. He means no harm by it and she rarely takes offence, but, I confess, sometimes it has pained me in the past to hear it."

"Is that where you learned your lively discourse, sister? I have many times been surprised at the teasing manner with which you deal with my brother. I had not known that it was possible to tease him and live to tell the tale!"

"Well, perhaps, a sister may not take as many liberties with an older brother as can a new wife, but I find that your brother softens a great deal when encouraged not to take himself quite so seriously all the time. A little self-deprecation can never hurt when one is confident of one's position and regard, but I would never wish to hurt his feelings through anything I might say in jest."

The women entered the room which, although it got the early morning sun, was still rather cold and unwelcoming.

"Oh!" shivered Elizabeth. "I had no notion that this room was so cold – where is the fire?"

Georgiana sat down unconcernedly at the instrument, pulling her shawl about her shoulders and opened her music.

"It is of no consequence, I assure you. Once I begin to play, I do not feel the cold. My fingers soon warm up as does the rest of my body. It is as good as a walk outside for circulating the blood. Will you stay and listen, Elizabeth?"

Lizzy gathered her own shawl about her shoulders and shivered again.

"I will sit for a while, Georgiana, as I do love to hear you play, but if I leave, know it is the cold that drives me away not my disinterest in your playing. Remember that I do not have the benefit of playing to warm me."

Elizabeth managed to stay a quarter of an hour and then crept away without being noticed, so involved was her sister in her music. She made her way into the morning room, glad to see her usual fire burning brightly in the grate and her writing desk awaiting her. She would mention to Mrs. Reynolds about lighting a fire in the music room for Georgiana; it was a wonder she had not become ill before this.

She settled herself and began her daily correspondence. It was a job she had at first rebelled against: all of the letters to merchants and suppliers, local dignitaries and new friends, lamenting the time spent when she could have been engaged much more happily elsewhere. But she had come to realise very quickly that her daily correspondence was an important part of her new role and one she should take seriously and perform with grace and style. However, her greatest pleasure was always to read and respond to her friends' and family's letters, and she quickly settled down to reply to her mother's letter, knowing her father had no intention at all of informing that lady of his safe arrival, what he had encountered already, nor of the date of his intended return.

After that note had been addressed, she pondered whether to send a letter to Charlotte. Mamma had said her friend was to leave Lucas Lodge imminently for the journey with her son back to Kent, but she desperately wished to write to her friend and so began:

Pemberley House
January ~

My dear Charlotte,

Mamma has informed me that you are to travel back into Kent within the next few days – she did not know exactly when – and so I shall send this to Hunsford to greet you upon your return. I do hope that you were not disappointed in the mode of travel you were forced to endure. A Barouche box offers nothing to the excitement of travel by Stagecoach and I am surprised you did not insist upon the latter as befitting your designated sphere in life! Beware, dear friend, that you do not become accustomed to such luxury and expect it for every small trip into

Hertfordshire. Little William, may, of course, become as accustomed to spoiling as he pleases for I am sure there is no other child so loved and doted upon as is that small person. Do I dare to hope that we shall be allowed to darken the doorsteps of Rosings Park in the Spring? I shall wait with anticipation and try very hard to convince my husband to soften his hard line against his aunt so that we may, indeed, meet again in Hunsford and continue our happy friendship.

Darcy is currently in Town for a week at least on business, and Georgiana and I have been very quiet by ourselves, but yesterday, to my very great delight and surprise, my father arrived late in the afternoon, horse-weary, but undaunted. But perhaps you already knew of it? No matter, it is a very great pleasure to have him visit and I shall show him everything that I love about my new home. He is already quite delighted with the Park and the library and I expect he will continue to praise everything about Pemberley until he leaves. I think his greatest pleasure is the peace afforded to him; he has mentioned it at least three times to me already and we are not yet past the twenty-four hour marker of his visit! Mamma accused him in her letter of leaving secretly and against her will but I will believe very little of her story, knowing as I do her propensity to enlarge everything for greater effect.

I must close now in the hope that you will write very soon, once you are re-settled in your home, and tell me of everything you have experienced since becoming a mother. Both Jane and I hope to follow in your example as soon as we are so blessed; how wonderful it would be to have all of our children become friends just as we have always been! But even more exciting than that, will be to read of your distinguished ride home and the commotion you caused as you passed by in the Barouche box!

Yours affectionately
Eliza.

Chapter 3

Elizabeth was as good as her word and ensured, before many days had passed, that her father had walked every path and road that had become as dear to her as the walks around Longbourn. The gardens and woods had a stark beauty of their own in the dead of Winter, but she enjoyed describing the splendour she had seen on her visit the year before when they were all adorned in their Summer foliage. Her father was an avid listener and surprisingly keen walker - far more than he ever had been around his own estate - and Lizzy felt the compliment of receiving his full attention. However, privately, they were both awaiting the return of Darcy: Elizabeth, because with each day that passed she felt his absence more acutely, and her father because he wished to know his son-in-law better and to see how comfortable his daughter was with her husband by her side. He could not, in all good conscience, leave before he could report honestly to his wife that he had witnessed true happiness in marriage for their second daughter.

On the third morning, a conversation ensued between them regarding Georgiana; Mr. Bennet was curious as to her contentment with remaining closeted away in the country, since she had experienced her freedom before.

"For surely she must wish to spread her wings a little – the age she is now. Does her brother intend introducing her at court this year?"

Elizabeth smiled as she side-stepped a muddy track. "I do not believe he intends to do any such thing. He cares very little for that nonsense - parading before the Prince - and for what reason? No, if she wishes, we shall take her into Town for a few weeks and have the oversight of her amusements ourselves. Much as he dislikes the society there, I believe it is another idea to which he will have to become accustomed."

"Yes, I fear it will be the case, and he has my sympathy in the matter. I did not like to ask too deeply, but there was a definite impression that things had not gone very well for Miss Darcy the last time she was in London. Are you at all acquainted with the facts, my dear, or are you sworn to secrecy?"

"Oh, I think she was just too young for such freedom and not well-managed. Darcy thought he had been cautious enough, but as we have learnt to our cost, allowing a very young and inexperienced girl her head before she is wise enough to manage her behaviour can never end well."

"Indeed! Indeed!" laughed her father, ruefully. "You never need to remind me of the cruel lessons learnt from your sister and her behaviour. And, as you know, I absolutely bow to your good sense and advice which I was too stubborn and disinterested to contemplate then, to my cost, and will happily advise your husband not to make the same mistake. But, I may assume that Miss Darcy's outcome was much more favourable than that of your sister?"

"Well; she is not married to Wickham and living in Newcastle, Father, so I think you can safely assume that! But it was a troubling and most affecting time for my husband. He has told me a little of the matter but I am certain that much has been kept secret. Clearly, Georgiana's self-importance was given a severe setback during her travels which accounts for her contentment at remaining in safety at Pemberley, however dull it may be for a young lady.

"But, Father, speaking of favourable outcomes, is Lydia content, do you know? I have not heard from her in many weeks, but when last I did she said they were moving lodgings *again*. It seems they move lodgings rather too frequently for my liking."

"I have no particular reason to think her discontent, but I have no doubt they must be living beyond their means to ensure her happiness. They are both of them foolish and profligate - we knew that when they married, and before - but they must make the most of what they have created for themselves. Thus far they have not approached me for assistance, and they should not either; they will get short shrift if they do."

Mr. Bennet brooded silently to himself before adding, "And you must not listen to their pleas for help, either, Lizzy. Not that I have any influence over your generosity now you are married, but I have no doubt that they will importune you regularly if they think they can gain anything from it. They must learn to survive by themselves. Your youngest sister, I hate to say it, has no scruples and will expect help from both you and Jane as you are both so fortunately situated. I have already spoken with Jane and Bingley but they are too easy-going to see the detriment of their kindness. You and Darcy, however, are made of sterner stuff and understand the futility of misguided kindness."

Lizzy nodded while secretly cringing at her father's words. Not because she disagreed with anything he said but that he had so astutely pin-pointed the exact content of several of Lydia's letters to her since she had become the mistress of Pemberley. Lydia had conveyed her delight at her sister's marriage mainly because she was now so rich, and rather hoped that she would think of them in Newcastle when she had time. Already, Lizzy had been appealed to for help to pay bills when they moved to a new situation, and she had managed, secretly, through making some economies in her own private expenses, to send a little to smooth her sister's path. But it was worrying indeed, and for all his bluster, she knew her father was also concerned about the fate of his youngest daughter so far away from family and friends, and under the so-called protection of a man like Wickham.

"But surely *you* would not let her suffer, Father, if you had it in your power to ease her suffering?"

"Yes; your sister I would help, but it is that worthless, good-for-nothing husband of hers that it pains me to think of inadvertently assisting if I should help her. Every penny I would give her indirectly pays his bills and whatever other debts he may have. He must learn to regulate his behaviour and mode of living before I could be prevailed upon to assist *him* in any way, and I do not think him capable of such a change without experiencing something very shocking. Perhaps they must reach the absolute bottom before they will see the error of their ways, but they will never experience that unless we leave them to their fall.

I warn you Elizabeth, as I warned your sister; do not be tempted by the ties of sisterhood to help Lydia every time she asks for it. Leave them to suffer at least a little so they may have some regard for their situation and perhaps learn from it and improve their ways.

"Oh – look yonder! A rider coming at us at great speed across the hill there! You must have a visitor, and one in great haste, it would appear. It must be a matter of great importance. Shall we return to the house, my dear and await him?"

Elizabeth's heart leapt, the rider easily recognisable even from this distance, and she was filled with a great warming joy. Darcy! Darcy was come back! Already!

Turning to her father she beamed at his confusion.

"It is Darcy, Father! We must make haste to beat him back to the house. Oh, how I have missed him."

And with lightning speed she set off back through the woods, her father keeping up as best he could, both of them panting and well-warmed by the time they arrived at the house. Elizabeth frantically looked about to see if Darcy was already there, but could see nothing. She left her father in the hall and rushed outside to the stables, only to see his horse being led into a stall by one of the stable boys.

Darcy was still nowhere to be seen.

Frustrated, she gathered up her skirts and ran around the side of the house and in through the back entry to see the exact person she had been looking for calmly removing his dirty boots in the boot room. His back was towards her.

She crept up behind him and wrapped her arms about his waist in delight. He turned about, astonished, and there they stood; he with one boot on and one off, she still in her muddy boots, coat and bonnet, locked in each other's arms, not a word necessary between them. After a while he put her away from him and smiled tenderly.

"Elizabeth, my dearest!" he murmured, "I do not recall ever being so warmly welcomed back from a journey, but I believe I shall quickly become used to it. Do not you think it rather an unorthodox use of this room? I am certain it has never seen such tenderness before."

"And why should it not? Now I know where to find you the minute you return home, this room will have to get used to such behaviour. Why should I wait until you are ready, when others will be in our way, may I ask? I am so happy and relieved to see you home safe and sound, my darling man; I have missed you terribly, more than I even expected. It is unfair to abandon a new wife in such a way, when she is only just becoming used to being your wife. Next time you go away, I insist upon coming with you."

"I pained me no less to leave you, my dear," he smiled, "and, I confess, my thoughts have been only partially on business whilst I have been gone, constantly straying as they were back to you and wondering what you were doing and what you were wearing, and whether you could sleep without me!

"I contrived to finish my business quickly and be out of London; my sole purpose being to return to you as soon as possible. I think you will have your wish. I shall not leave you behind again; it is too distracting!"

Elizabeth stole a quick kiss and then backed away as his became more ardent.

"Wait, my dear! Much as I would like to reciprocate this very instant, it is not quite the right place nor time; we must be patient a little longer as I have not told you my news." She smiled as she removed his arms from her waist, and moved away a little.

"It was fortuitous that I remained at home this time, at least, as we have a visitor, my dear: my father! He arrived, quite unexpected, three nights ago and has been so very content with his new surroundings that no mention has been made of his intention to return to Longbourn. He finds everything about Pemberley to his satisfaction; it only wanted your presence. He will be here to stay if we are not careful."

"Your father? He is here? Then I am glad indeed that I curtailed my business early. I should not have liked to have missed him. And your mother; did she accompany him?"

Elizabeth laughed quietly. "You may rest easy on that score, my dear, even though I see your valiant attempt to hide your dread.

"Mamma is slightly unwell - or exceedingly unwell - depending upon whose interpretation you wish to depend, and so was unable to manage the journey in all this weather. She wrote a long letter explaining her absence and assured me that my father had planned his journey to coincide with her illness just to spite her."

Darcy smiled and reached for her. "Then I suppose there is no choice in the matter? We must go and greet him immediately?"

Darcy kissed her tenderly again and brushed a stray hair back from her forehead. Elizabeth closed her eyes and allowed herself to melt against him. The warmth and strength of his body, the now-familiar smell of him - the mixture of saddle leather and the muskiness of his horse - and the Winter cold that still permeated his jacket, combined in her senses making her the happiest of women; she could have remained there, in the boot-room, forever, so long as he was with her. She reached up to return his kiss and then they smiled quietly at each other. They had plenty of time.

"Come, Mrs. Darcy. This is no place for you to linger; the servants will think you are inspecting their work, or doing your own shoe cleaning. Let us greet our guest and Georgiana before we attend to our own needs."

Reluctantly, leaving their private desires behind, they made their way out of the lower room, along a rather dark corridor, through a heavy door, arriving in the entrance hall where Grant was waiting to greet them and receive his master's riding coat and hat, clearly perfectly used to his master appearing unshod from the servant's quarters.

"It is good to have you back, sir," he bowed. "A pleasant and successful journey, I hope, sir?"

"Thank you, Grant, yes, very successful. I believe I shall require a change of clothes before meeting with our guest, if you would be so good as to alert Allum to my return."

"He is already awaiting you, sir, in your dressing room. Is there anything else you require, sir?"

"No, that will be all. Thank you, Grant. Excuse me Elizabeth; I will return as soon as I can."

Elizabeth smiled and turned towards the music room where she knew Georgiana would still be playing, utterly oblivious to the arrival of her brother, or any other event happening about the estate.

It was a happy company that finally met in the drawing room. Georgiana, delighted to have her brother back, could not refrain from questioning him about London: Whom had he seen? Who had asked after her? Where had he been? Were there any interesting shows being performed? Her questions came thick and fast as from a person starved of sustenance; her exile in the country evidently more wearing than even she had thought it. Old friends such as the Stantons and Mr. Jardine were enquired after and sadly dismissed when Darcy assured her that neither had been in Town at the time. However, one person Darcy did mention was Mrs. Younge, Georgiana's former governess-companion. Apparently he had made a point of visiting her establishment in Edward Street but had discovered that she was in America.

Georgiana's interest was piqued, as he knew it would be, but had to be controlled in favour of her brother's attention to Mr. Bennet who appeared in the room at the exact moment of Darcy revealing the information, with pleasantries following to such an extent that even Elizabeth began to wonder at her husband's loquaciousness.

"Mrs. Younge has gone to *America*, brother?" broke in Georgiana at the first opportunity, utterly incapable of restraining her curiosity any further. "Surely not! Mrs. Younge has several businesses to oversee; she could not have managed to visit America, surely? I cannot believe it. She had trouble enough leaving them when we went into Ramsgate; how can it be possible that she could manage America? And, why, brother? Were you able to discover her purpose?"

Darcy looked coolly at his sister. "Perhaps, Georgiana, if you had kept in contact with Mrs. Younge, as she hoped you would, you would not be so surprised at my information. It is unfortunate indeed that you have never chosen to contact her and offer the hand of friendship, as she offered you."

Silence descended on the room as Georgiana blushed at her brother's words. Elizabeth, startled, looked from her husband to Georgiana in confusion. Was this the Mrs. Younge who had conspired with Wickham to try to convince Georgiana to run away with him, and thus gain Georgiana's inheritance of thirty thousand pounds? The woman in whose character Darcy had been most *unhappily deceived*, as he had claimed in his letter last year explaining his connection to Wickham? The woman he was now calling on at her home and speaking about to his sister with affection? It was all most intriguing indeed but Elizabeth put her questions aside for the moment and quickly sought a new line of conversation.

"We have been kept quite busy ourselves, have not we, Father?" She turned to Darcy smiling. "It would appear that my father is an excellent walker when out of Hertfordshire. He has walked every path that I have discovered thus far, several times, and has even once ventured out with the gamekeeper to walk the Park into areas too rugged for my boots. I believe him to be quite content at Pemberley, my dear."

Darcy smiled, pleased at the compliment. "You must stay as long as you can be spared, sir. I know we are both delighted to have your company. I am sure Elizabeth would not wish you gone too soon."

Mr. Bennet nodded comfortably. "I confess, the idea is tempting; I have mentioned more than once how quiet and comfortable this house is; a balm to the senses. And your library, sir, is such that should I wish to venture nowhere else in my life; I could happily occupy it every day. It quite puts my own meagre book-room to shame. I have, with Elizabeth's permission, of course, made good use of the volumes which I have not as yet been fortunate enough to peruse – but there are so many of them! It is rather bewildering to be so spoilt for choice, I assure you. I do not know how you get anything done, sir; your strength of will must be greater than mine."

"Then you must feel free to take some with you upon your return to Longbourn, sir. It is gratifying to know another who enjoys extensive reading and appreciates fine writing. We shall have some interesting discussions, I hope.

"But where did you go with the gamekeeper, Mr. Bennet? Was there a problem in the Park while I was gone?"

"No, indeed; not at all. He merely wished to take a turn about to see how effective the fox hunting had been; he was concerned that the season had not been as successful as it could have been. We saw some evidence of them about, dens and such, but not as many as he had feared. It was a thoroughly enjoyable morning in all respects. The woods are very fine here about; they have clearly been planned and planted through the foresight of several generations."

Elizabeth watched in quiet contentment as her husband and father found similar areas of interest as landowners to agree upon while developing a mutual respect for each other. Indeed, her own opinion of her father, long over-shadowed by his behaviour towards her mother and her younger sisters, was steadily improving now he was away from that environment and she could appreciate another, more worldly side of him. She glanced over at Georgiana who appeared to have recovered her equanimity, and smiled.

"Come, sister, let us leave the gentlemen to their discussion about books and foxes and trees. What was that beautiful sonata you were playing earlier? I would like to hear it again, if you would be so kind. I am at your disposal as a very competent page-turner."

Chapter 4

The sisters walked along to the music room where a fire now burned brightly giving it a much more welcoming feel than it had previously. Georgiana went to her instrument and began to play while Elizabeth sat beside her in a chair, watching her fingers move dexterously across the keys. The piece, she knew, was of a difficult nature and testament to Georgiana's dedication to her practice, but after a few minutes, Georgiana's hands fell away from the keyboard and she bent her head, silently weeping.

Horrified, Elizabeth moved beside her on the bench and put her arms about her, waiting for the sobs to subside. Presently, Georgiana sniffed, pulled away from the embrace and delicately wiped her nose on the handkerchief Elizabeth proffered.

"I am sorry, Elizabeth. I have no reason to make such a spectacle of myself. It is childish; please forgive me."

Elizabeth looked closely at her sister, noticing the sadness in her eyes and wished to know more without imposing herself without permission. She shook her head, smiling gently.

"There is no reason to ask for my forgiveness, Georgiana, but I am troubled that you are so sad when I thought you were happy here at home. Has something happened which causes you such distress? Is there anything that I can do to help you? I know your brother would be deeply troubled to know you are so unhappy."

Georgiana drew further back in alarm. "No! You must not tell my brother; promise me that you will not, Elizabeth. He would immediately know the reason for it and be disgusted with my weakness. He must not know."

"If that is your wish, then, of course, I shall not betray your trust. But will not you tell me, at least? I may be able to see that whatever it is that troubles you is not as important as it seems. We all can contemplate a problem until our imagination grows it into something intolerable. I will not insist upon your confidence, but I believe it may relieve your suffering a little."

Georgiana rose from the piano stool and walked to the chaise in front of the fire, wringing the handkerchief in her hands, still in a most agitated state.

Elizabeth sat in another chair and looked at her sister. She was young, barely seventeen, beautiful, accomplished, and a very eligible match with her great inheritance. She was everything, and had everything that Elizabeth had not enjoyed or imagined at her age, but she was certain all of those benefits were nothing to her sister right now. Something had upset this young woman terribly and it pained Elizabeth to see it. She supposed it had something to do with Darcy's mentioning of his visit to London and his curt response to Georgiana regarding Mrs. Younge.

Eventually, Georgiana had control over her emotions; she sighed and faced Elizabeth, looking her squarely in the eye.

"You must, I suppose, be wondering about my earlier reaction to my brother's visit to Mrs. Younge's establishment while he was in London, and his remark to me, accusing me of unfriendliness to that lady?"

Elizabeth held her gaze and nodded.

"I do not know how much my brother has told you of my stay in London and Ramsgate almost one and one-half years ago; from your surprised look at him, I presume you understand that it ended badly, that I was removed from the so-called clutches of Mrs. Younge and Mr. Wickham, and returned to the safety of Pemberley where I have remained ever since. Most of what you know, then, is true, and my brother's intervention prevented me from making a very great mistake and an even greater fool of myself. The only thing harmed was my self-respect; a necessary lesson to teach me the foolishness of an inexperienced girl at the hands of an experienced gentleman."

"You speak of Mr. Wickham, I presume, Georgiana?"

Georgiana sighed and looked down at her hands. "Wickham; Bingley; Jardine: what does it matter? I foolishly took every one of those gentlemen's attentions as proof of their regard for me. Mr. Jardine, I think, was the only one in earnest: the other two gentlemen were merely being polite and assuring my protection from other suitors in the absence of my brother."

Elizabeth gasped. "Mr. Bingley, I can believe that to be true of his character, but George Wickham? You imagined Mr. Wickham was *protecting* you? But I thought…your brother led me to believe…

"Mr. Wickham is not an honourable man, Georgiana, as *our* family learnt to our almost disgrace. Had not your brother known where to find him, he would have left my poor sister without a second thought. There is *nothing* good to be said about George Wickham, I assure you, and I have great difficulty in believing that he *ever* had your best interests at heart. What could you have been thinking that you thought yourself in love with such a man as you must have guessed him to be?"

Georgiana smiled sadly at that. "*Such a man*, Elizabeth? What did I know of him other than what I remembered from my childhood when he took great trouble to entertain me when he could? He was my brother's playmate and greatest friend until they left for Cambridge. But I knew nothing of their subsequent falling out: how could I? My brother never confided in me about it; there was no reason he should have. So, when Mr. Wickham appeared in London, of course I was delighted to see an old acquaintance; we had so many memories in common and he is so charming and handsome and attentive. On what could I have based my opinion of him, other than what I already knew and what I saw before me?

"But, in retrospect, I know his attention to me was merely for my security and amusement, just as Mrs. Younge had warned me. Mrs. Younge should not have been blamed for collusion, as she was. I was angry at her at the time; I believed her to be jealous of, what I perceived to be, Wickham's feelings for me. But I think she and Mr. Wickham had some previous attachment – they were always talking in corners and very comfortable with each other - she trusted him with her business while we were away in Ramsgate, relied upon him entirely, and so why should not I have done the same? It was not until she tried to warn me from him that I realised this, and angry as I was, I preferred to ignore her warnings and instead accuse her of jealousy.

"She wrote to me upon my return to Pemberley, regretting the incidence of our parting and hoping to be remembered with affection, but I refused to reply; I held her responsible for my embarrassment, my loss of Wickham, my ignominious return to Derbyshire. Even after I had reflected on the situation and informed my brother of the truth of the matter – that I was the one who had manufactured feelings and intentions that were not there and cleared Wickham of any devious intentions towards me - I could not find it within myself to forgive Mrs. Younge. And now my brother speaks so gently of her, visits her on his trips into London, and makes me feel guilty for my treatment of her."

Georgiana's voice quavered as she stumbled into her last words and fell silent. Elizabeth waited a few moments before gently enquiring:

"And why is it that you have not made any attempt to heal the misunderstanding between you, especially now that you have accepted the truth of the matter? Perhaps your brother is trying to encourage your better feelings towards the lady in question; he certainly believes her to be of merit to go so out of his way while he is so busy about his business in London. Now I know more of the situation, I feel that I should also thank that lady, unknown as she is to me, but the assistance she must have given Darcy in his search for my poor sister last year shows her selfless behaviour in discarding Wickham to the obvious detriment to her own happiness and future with him. Oh! The trouble and heartache my sister has caused to others through her thoughtlessness continues to be uncovered."

Georgiana smiled weakly, "Yes, I believe she did give up Wickham for the sake of your sister's reputation. I recall my brother mentioning that he had managed to arrange a marriage, a union that had to be brought about to protect the reputation of the lady, but that in doing so would cause severe unhappiness to another lady undeserving of such cruel treatment."

The two women looked at each other slowly piecing the story together in their minds.

"But why would not he have mentioned this to me? My aunt Gardiner is the person to whom I owe the greatest thanks; she informed me of Darcy's tireless effort on my sister's behalf, of his travails through London, of his insistence in taking the blame for my sister's shame upon himself through his misplaced pride, but she, at that time, believed him to have been *assisted* by a woman whom he had known previously in connection with you and in whose character he had been sadly deceived. It is only now that I learn that this woman is quite raised in his opinion.

"Oh! Why have I never asked further about this matter, happy as I have been to leave it alone, happy in my own situation? To think that my sister has been the cause of misery for another, unknown, person is intolerable. No wonder Darcy makes a point of visiting her when he is in Town.

"But we must not dwell upon mistakes of the past, Georgiana; we must make amends as we can and decide to improve our behaviour in the future. I, more than anyone, know what it is to judge upon first impressions and appearances. You cannot be blamed for being entirely taken in as any young impressionable girl would be when faced with the likes of George Wickham."

Georgiana blushed, looked away, and then enquired diffidently, "What were your first impressions of him, Elizabeth? You must have suffered similarly to me, from what you say."

"Indeed I did! As did every young lady in Meryton; we all were quite taken in by his manner and good looks. I foolishly thought myself particularly fortunate when he focused his attentions upon me to the almost exclusion of all others; my sister, Lydia, as I remember, was quite put out about it which, I confess, gave me some satisfaction. She was always so wild, so insistent upon being the centre of attention everywhere she went, that for her to feel second best was good for her, and also for me!" Elizabeth laughed ruefully.

"But, after receiving such damning intelligence from your brother, in his most eloquent and open-hearted letter, I began to see Wickham in another light entirely. I began to see that the man he was portraying himself as was not the man he was, and this was substantiated after rumours of his behaviour about the village became common knowledge, and then, of course, his actions concerning my sister entirely sank his reputation into depths from which it can never be salvaged.

"I had the most difficult time maintaining my composure with both him and my sister when they visited Longbourn after their marriage and could barely tolerate their company while they remained with us. Their leaving for the North was a dear relief, I can assure you.

"But now he is my brother-in-law and I am forever attached to him through this connection, but it will be a long time before I can ever forgive either of them for their foolish and selfish actions, all the more so since now I hear of another person who has been hurt by them."

"I am glad to have discussed this with you, Elizabeth; it has been a matter that has been cloaked in darkness and hung heavy upon me for these past months. Perhaps I will write to Mrs. Younge as my brother suggests, and proffer my sincerest apologies for not having done so sooner; I know now that she was a caring and kind person, concerned only for my welfare and I would not have wished her further unhappiness on any account."

The sisters embraced and made their way into the morning room where the late Mrs. Darcy's desk had been repositioned, at Elizabeth's request, to a place by the window where she could see her beloved woods and fields as she conducted her household and personal correspondence.

Elizabeth sat and began one of several letters to her family, the first of which, as always, was to her sister, Jane. Georgiana took her place at a side table and began a letter to her old governess-companion in whose character and designs, she now wished openly to acknowledge, she had been entirely mistaken.

Chapter 5

And so, it was this happy domestic scene that greeted Darcy upon his entrance into the morning room a while later, intent upon spending as much time as he could in the company of his wife whom he had missed terribly during his absence. He had felt quite at a loss when apart from her and found it disconcerting that anybody could affect him so thoroughly and in so short a time; her suggestion that she should accompany him on any future trips was one with which he agreed wholeheartedly.

The ladies turned and smiled at his entrance, both delighted to see him and have him back in their midst.

"Ah, there you both are! I have settled your father in the library – apparently he already has a favourite chair – with several volumes which I recommended. We shall have some thorough discussions very soon once he has absorbed some of their contents, I wager. But what keeps you so busy writing? You both look very serious indeed."

"No, not very serious, brother, but I am writing to enquire after Mrs. Younge and ask her forgiveness for my silence over the past year and would request her address, if you would be so kind. I am sure it can be forwarded to her in America. Elizabeth and I have been having a very interesting discussion concerning several matters from last year, and before, which we have discovered relate to us both. Had you permitted me to know more, I would have never continued so distant from Mrs. Younge. My knowledge, it seems, has been severely limited indeed.

Darcy raised his eyebrows and looked quizzically at his wife. Elizabeth shrugged.

"We finally had cause to put two and two together, Darcy, and with both of our information we have now pieced your involvement with Wickham, Mrs. Younge, and my sister together; would you care to hear it, sir?"

Darcy smiled. "Naturally I would enjoy hearing your suppositions, and your discovery of my actions, but why has this been such an urgent discussion, today, pray? You have known each other for many months now; I cannot imagine what has caused this interest in the history of those people."

"I believe the announcement of your visit to Mrs. Younge and your altered opinion of that lady surprised both of us, my dear. The last time *I* heard that name referred to was contained within a delightful letter from my aunt Gardiner when she laid out your involvement in my sister's rescue last August, an involvement even I should never have known if she had not been so candid upon my request. But that opinion did not signal approval at the time. So imagine my surprise to hear you had recently visited this lady, regarding her highly enough to rebuke poor Georgiana for also misunderstanding your opinion of her. You are too unkind, Darcy, to allow everybody to continue with false impressions, when one word from you could have altered them greatly."

Darcy had the grace to look slightly ashamed under his wife's gentle reproach. He looked at his sister whose eyes had widened at Elizabeth's speech, astonished once again at how freely she offered her opinions about anything, and to anybody.

"I should not have accused you of cruelty to that lady, Georgiana, and I apologise for my thoughtless words. Of course you could not have known my changed opinion of her since I had not thought to inform you of it."

Georgiana rose quickly and hugged her brother and sat beside him. "Will you tell us now, brother? We should like to know the truth, if you think it suitable."

Elizabeth laughed gaily, "Aye, husband dearest, for we may have allowed our imaginations to over-reach themselves in our attempt to piece the puzzle together. Do tell us the truth, for

I am sure it will be an interesting story, but, I fear, will still not improve my opinion of the other two actors in it."

Darcy smiled and nodded his agreement. He began slowly.

"Well, Mrs. Younge, as you know was employed as a governess-companion to Georgiana a year and a half ago when I allowed my sister her first taste of freedom because I was too lazy and disinterested to take on the task myself."

"Oh, do not blame yourself for *my* foolishness, brother! I was too young to understand the attentions of the men I met. And Mrs. Younge truly did try to make me understand and was not to blame in the slightest."

Darcy smiled, "Yes, of course I know that, I knew that very soon after I removed you from Ramsgate. You insisted upon those very same commendations once I informed you of Mr. Wickham's true nature, which you also tried to refute. However, I shall never go so far as to give *that* man the benefit of the doubt. You may claim that you encouraged his attentions and that he merely wished to protect you, but believe me, Georgiana, he is not the type of man who would ever consider protecting any woman unless there was something to be gained from it, and in your case, there was a great deal to be gained. He will always remain in my opinion as an opportunistic charlatan, and that opinion will never be altered.

"However, of Mrs. Younge, I *will* speak more favourably. I know that upon leaving Ramsgate I had falsely accused her of leading you astray, of encouraging you in your delusion of being in love with Wickham, believing at the time that *she* was intending to profit from the match should it have come about. But I began to suspect that all was not as it appeared with this lady and when I met her again, in great anxiety, seeking your sister last year, Elizabeth, I found a lady in possession of a quiet dignity and a desire to put things right even knowing it meant she would ruin her own chances of happiness with the man she loved.

"Mrs. Younge helped me find Wickham and your sister and, through her selflessness, I knew I had left her broken-hearted, without any hope. She is a sensible, resourceful person who has triumphed over adverse conditions all her life. As you know Georgiana, she has many business interests both inherited from her late husband and also from her own hard work and foresight, and should be commended for those instincts which have brought her so far. Her only failing, and one she agrees is her greatest failing, is her love for that scoundrel, Wickham. Now that I have experienced the power of being in love with a person," he looked gently at Elizabeth, "I cannot blame her for falling in love. I am only sorry that she was not able to bestow her affections upon a more deserving person."

"And was Wickham in love with her, do you think, Darcy?" asked Elizabeth. "Or was her success to be his security, just like that of Mary King?"

"Oh, I believe that the affection must have been mutual, judging from the way they behaved together when I knew them," broke in Georgiana. "I was too self-involved to really notice it at the time and merely thought they talked together when we were out as a distinction to me so I would have some freedom amongst my new friends. But actually, they *wanted* to be in each other's company as much as possible. The affection was real, I can see that now."

"I do not judge: after all, there are those in high society who behave in a less than respectable manner, but I know that Mrs. Younge believed herself to be the rightful owner of the title and position your sister now holds; that it was only a matter of time before Wickham would change his ways and prove himself to be a responsible person, and one she could entrust with her future happiness."

Elizabeth started. "You do not think she might still intend to remove him from my sister, Darcy? You would not approve of that, surely?"

"No, indeed, I do not think that to be her plan at all; after all, she has removed herself onto another continent, a move, I understand, that occurred immediately after my meeting with her last year. It is a sad story that does not have a happy ending.

But I think she will appreciate a kind letter from you, sister, and when she returns to Town, I intend to visit her as an interested friend. It is all she wants or needs from us, I assure you."

"Your opinion of what makes an accomplished woman has expanded, my dear!" laughed Elizabeth, "I recall the long list proclaimed by Miss Bingley was increased by you regarding the necessary improvement to a woman's mind through extensive reading; you must now add astute business acumen to that list. 'Tis not fair! I can never compete."

"You know very well that is not true, my dearest. You will always be the epitome of an accomplished woman. But where there is need, as in Mrs. Younge's case, one cannot help but admire such fortitude and determination."

Georgiana once again hugged her brother before standing and moving back to her table.

"I shall re-write my letter, in an even more friendly style after what I have just heard," she announced, "and I will take great care never to mention that despicable Wickham ever again. How cruel he has been to her, and him pretending to be so affectionate and charming."

Darcy looked at Elizabeth. "How close was *your* estimation of these events, my dear?"

Elizabeth laughed, "I believe we had contrived most of it, but your first-hand account cannot be improved upon, I assure you, and I now find myself even angrier at my sister and her foolishness. She has caused grief and loneliness for another of her sex, although without any knowledge; but, indeed, if she *were* to be told, she would not care in the slightest. Until something similar happens to her, she will never have the compassion necessary to understand another's feelings. But Wickham does not escape my anger, either. He is the most to blame in all of this. He is the one who has failed the woman who loves him and he cannot be forgiven for that. Running away from whatever happened in Brighton with my sister only compounds his sins. He is truly the most despicable of men and my greatest wish is never to see him again."

"Believe me, my darling wife, I second that wish, most ardently. Unfortunately, as in the past, I have no doubt that Wickham will continue to cause me embarrassment and expense for the rest of his life, and I must accept that as incontrovertible. You would not wish to see you sister starve because of her profligate husband, would you?"

Elizabeth guiltily thought of the money saved from her own household accounts folded in with her last letter to Lydia, and shook her head.

"No, I could never allow that to happen, but it is frustrating indeed to know that whatever he does, he drags down everybody connected with him. Lydia is destined to live a life of uncertainty with a man who likely is already regretting his hasty escape with her - which they have only brought upon themselves - and Mrs. Younge suffers because of it. It is concerning indeed, but my father is quite determined they must be allowed to feel their situation with all of its difficulties before *he* will be induced to assist them."

Darcy smiled. "That is sound thinking on your father's part, and I admire his fortitude. He cannot be blamed for feeling such animosity after their behaviour almost ruined his good name. But they will always find friends who *can* be induced to help them; they both have engaging manners and will survive well enough. Do not concern yourself unduly, my dear. I have dealt with Wickham for many years now; he is a survivor and Lydia will emulate that fighting spirit. In that manner, they are both well-suited for each other."

He glanced over to his sister at the other side of the room where she was busily composing her second letter to Mrs. Younge and murmured:

"I would not be quite so sanguine had Georgiana's infatuation for Wickham, and his interest in her, been greater eighteen months ago. To have Wickham married *directly* into my family would have been intolerable; to see my own sister miserable, unbearable indeed. At least your sister believes herself to be in love and loved. Let us hope that she continues to feel that way for some time yet before the ugly truth about her husband becomes apparent, even to her."

"I believe Georgiana is still quite chastened by her experiences from that time," Elizabeth murmured back. "She feels embarrassed and unable to shake off that embarrassment even though I have tried to alleviate her concerns. Her inexperience, her immaturity in such situations as she found herself has quite left its mark. She does not go out visiting with me, you know, and she was most reluctant to meet my father when he arrived. She prefers to remain here, alone, in the house every day. It is not natural to be so retiring for a young lady. Perhaps you would advise her, my dear, as she attends to your opinion much more than to anybody else. She must see that it is all in the past and to use the experience as something to be learnt from, not paralysed by."

Darcy looked into his wife's concerned face and quickly bent down to brush his lips against hers. He smiled at her discomfiture and nodded as if concluding a discussion about another matter entirely.

"You are absolutely right, my dear; we have been derelict in our duties," he announced in a loud voice, causing his sister to turn around curiously. "Georgiana will give you a list of everyone with whom we are acquainted in the neighbourhood, and we shall give a ball. It is time we entertained and introduced everyone to the new mistress of Pemberley. Georgiana; you are to assist Elizabeth in every way to make this a success. It is time Pemberley reclaimed its place in local society."

And with that astonishing announcement, he swept out of the room.

Chapter 6

A ball!

Elizabeth looked at Georgiana in confusion. Georgiana looked at the empty space that had been her brother leaving the room, and then raised her eyebrows at her sister.

"My brother has never had a ball here; he detests them. Why would he suddenly decide upon one now? What on earth did you say to him to put such an idea into his head? And why would he imagine that *I* would be able to help manage such a thing with you? I have no experience of entertaining and he knows even the smallest of formal occasions cause me discomfort. Perhaps he is tired from his journey and talks nonsense."

"No, I believe he is in earnest, sister, and of course he is correct; since the first flurry of activity when I arrived before Christmas, and some limited morning visits, we have been keeping very much to ourselves. We *should* be entering into the social round more vigorously; I am sure there are a very great many families hereabout who are still wondering what kind of person the new Mrs. Darcy is!"

"Well; I do not think it a very great neglect of your duty as you have only been in residence a mere month or so, Elizabeth. People cannot expect much more than you have managed if they consider the very great responsibilities connected with your position. And my brother does not help the situation, absent as he has been this last week. But a *ball*, Elizabeth! Perhaps no one will be able to attend and then we can resume our quiet lives with a clear conscience."

"Well, that would be a failure indeed!" laughed Lizzy, "but I rather think that a ball announced at Pemberley, where there has been none for so long, will attract everybody from miles around; even those in Town might be persuaded it would be worth their while. When Mr. Bingley gave his first ball at Netherfield, in honour of my sister's recovery from her illness, it was the event of the season and everybody attended, especially those who generally do not like balls, much to my mother's annoyance, as I recall - there was barely any room to move – but it was a night to remember in many respects."

"Why so, Elizabeth? Why was it so memorable?"

Lizzy smiled ruefully. "Well, let us just say that it marked the time when your brother was fixed as being the rudest, cruellest, proudest person I had ever met, and I could not imagine a worse fate than having to spend much time in his company. I had met him four times by then and he had not endeared himself to any of our family nor neighbours by his manner or opinions. I was perfectly sanguine about the accuracy of my opinion, I assure you!"

"And now you love everything about that same person, Elizabeth! How strange that your view of him was so different, then."

"Yes, indeed. It does not do to listen to others' opinions and allow them to cloud your own, Georgiana; I have learnt that at least, almost to my cost.

"But, we have a ball to arrange, my dear. I think our first call should be upon Mrs. Reynolds; she will have a great deal of advice, I am sure, and will know what is to be done."

And with that, the two sisters proceeded to spend a great deal of the rest of the day with Mrs. Reynolds, whose eyes had lit up at the mention of such an event as had not been seen at Pemberley since the death of the late Mrs. Darcy. Within an hour, Elizabeth had been shown the leather-bound guest book, with all of the names and addresses written in a very fine hand, had been advised about the usual arrangements – which were the particular favourites of the late mistress – all also contained within a log of

Mrs. Reynolds, and had been given a list of the usual suppliers for approval.

Elizabeth sat back down in her desk chair in the morning room and looked through the guest book, at names of people with whom she would have to become acquainted very soon. A date must be fixed and she would need Darcy's approval for that. She rose and made her way into his study where he always could be found at this hour working on estate matters with his steward. The two gentlemen stood up at her entry and the steward bowed most courteously, made his farewells, and left the couple together. When the door closed behind him, Darcy moved to take Elizabeth in his arms and they embraced quietly before he put her away from him with determination.

"We cannot keep meeting in private, my darling, it is too distracting!"

Lizzy laid her head against his chest and laughed. "Is that not what a wife is for, pray? To distract you from your work and lead you to your inevitable ruin? But I merely came to enquire about suitable dates for this ball which you have so thoughtfully announced and then left to be arranged without a further thought as to the inconvenience to your distracting wife and retiring sister! Or was it merely a passing thought which should be ignored, as Georgiana claims, knowing, as we all do, how you detest such occasions?"

"Indeed I do, but, as a married man with the loveliest wife in the county, I feel it incumbent upon me to share my good fortune with as many of my neighbours as possible, and a large gathering is the best way to accomplish that in a short space of time. Everyone will have the opportunity to discuss your attributes behind their fans…"

"… or openly discuss my defects with their friends, within my hearing!" laughed Lizzy.

Darcy coloured and kissed her forehead. "That was unforgivable of me, but, in my defence, I did not know you could hear my comments to Bingley. I would never knowingly give offence without reason and you had not done anything to deserve such treatment other than being the person upon whom I unfortunately decided to vent my discomfort at being thrust into that situation. I do not perform well in front of strangers, as you already know, my dear."

Lizzy returned his kiss and, this time, was the one to remove herself from his embrace. He was right; being alone together was very distracting indeed and she almost felt like forgiving him for his shocking early treatment of her.

"Well, if that is the case, then you must peruse the guest book with me and remove any whom you consider to be strangers, my dear; we cannot have you insulting guests in our own home, can we now?"

Smiling, he once again took her in his arms and they were oblivious to anything other than each other for the passage of quite some time.

Eventually, the guest book was returned to and perused at length, with Darcy explaining the names within it and their connections to the estate or the family. He increased the list by the same number as he decreased it, including those of new acquaintance and excluding those whom he knew no longer lived in the neighbourhood or for various other reasons. A date was decided upon for a fortnight hence, but the menus from the last ball given by his mother – a distant memory for him – were discounted in favour of Elizabeth's choice; whatever she wished to serve as befitting a more modern situation was agreeable to him, and left her to the onerous task before her. But it was a task she faced with greater composure than when she first heard of it; she reminded herself that her sister, Jane, had already had her first ball at Netherfield, under the guidance of the sisters Bingley no doubt, but every answer for Lizzy's questions could be furnished from that familiar quarter. Elizabeth immediately wrote to her sister, enclosing an invitation in the fervent hope they could manage to get away.

Her father, utterly unaware of the excitement developing around him, continued his perusal of the texts given him by his son-in-law; he meant to do them justice and not appear ignorant of their content when next they met. His reception of the proposed ball, at nuncheon that day, displayed his usual distaste for such entertainments.

"I rather think that I shall endeavour to be away from here by that time, my dear. Two weeks should see me quite resigned to making the journey home to Meryton and to leaving this most delightful spot here in Derbyshire. A ball, as you know, is not for me but I shall have great pleasure in informing your mother of all preparations made before my departure. It will make her quite envious I dare say, but any news of her least-favourite daughter is preferable where none other is to be had."

"Well, of course I shall send an invitation to Mamma and Kitty and Mary, Father. Do not you think that they might wish to join you here for a week or two, if Mamma's health permits it? We would be happy to receive them," Elizabeth lied, quietly crossing her fingers under the tablecloth. She knew the embarrassment that their visit would entail and the annoyance to her husband, but family must be invited.

Her father laughed, rightly guessing the truth behind her statement.

"I think not, my dear. I am quite sure that the roads North will remain impassable for some time yet, and you know very well how much your mother detests travel and the effect it has upon her nerves. No; I think we will allow you to entertain your new neighbours without our help."

With that out of the way, Lizzy lost no time in perusing the guest list supplied by Mrs. Reynolds and her husband, and embarking upon the writing of invitations, assisted by Georgiana. It was to be a rather large affair, judging by the growing stack of cards on the desk, and when she entered the kitchen area the following day to speak with Mrs. Reynolds, Lizzy found a hive of activity already started and great excitement accompanying the extra preparations.

In the midst of the flurry of activity, a letter arrived from Jane which broke into Lizzy's focus upon her own affairs.

January 20th ~
Netherfield Hall

My dearest sister,

Mamma is all grievous agitation here due to our father's continued absence. I believe poor Mary bears the brunt of it: Kitty spends a great deal of her time with me or with Maria Lucas and does not seem to be the worse for it. I have assured Mamma of our father's return, but I would beg you to write and confirm this; she imagines he will stay away for an entire year at least. Why this should be of concern, I do not know as he is perfectly capable of managing his affairs from the comfort of Pemberley, I am sure. But remind him that he must return, Lizzy, very soon!

We are all great happiness here, regardless of the cold and the damp that surrounds us at this time of year; my delight with my situation can only be eclipsed by yours, I suppose, but we shall have to compare our experiences to determine who is the happiest! Charles is a most attentive husband; nothing is too much trouble or expense. His sisters both remain here for the present and they make a great show of how much they like me and how happy they are for their brother. What they say when I am not within their hearing is very different, I have no doubt, but I confess to being quite unperturbed at their insincere friendliness; their slyness and falseness does not affect me as they wish it would. I have only to say how I feel about their attitude towards me, and Charles will dismiss them from Netherfield without compunction. He has said as much, although I still think he believes them to have had a complete change of heart. You brought their character to my attention and I have taken note; however, they shall not spoil my happiness through their disagreeableness.

You see, I am quite strong, Lizzy; you would not recognise me after so short a separation! And as for directing the servants – I am quite the firm lady of the house, proving my father wrong in my ability to do so when he imagined me to be so compliant that I would be cheated by them all!

But how do you get on Lizzy? How do Father and Darcy get on, I wonder? I am sure it was a great surprise to have him visit so soon and without any warning. He takes great pleasure in calling upon us here – he goes further abroad than ever he used to do – and remains a great while with Charles, advising him, apparently, when asked, on certain aspects of good estate management. Poor Charles feels rather overwhelmed, I think, being left his father's estate and having to live up to both sisters' expectations of buying a property for the family. Of course, Darcy has been a great comfort and source of sensible advice when he is here, and I am glad indeed that our father is able to offer assistance also.

I expect to hear from you very soon, Mrs. Darcy; I expect to hear all of your news, starting with that of my father's return. The sanity of the family at Longbourn depends upon it, I assure you.

With greatest affection,

Jane.

Elizabeth smiled over her sister's letter a great deal, imagining vividly just how her mother was suffering the absence of her husband; a husband who, before, had never moved far from his book-room, now showed little inclination to return to that book-room after his discovery of another, superior one in the Pemberley library.

She later relayed the message from Jane, and Mr. Bennet smiled at her over the cover of the book he was reading.

"Indeed? Misses me already, does she? I am sure she enjoys having an excuse to create drama and would not thank me for curtailing it with an early return. No, I think that I shall adhere to my original plan – that of remaining until just before the ball – to enable me to relate in detail all of your preparations which will, I am sure, be of sufficient interest to distract your mother from her excitement at my return.

"May I enquire how the plans are proceeding, my dear? I have noticed a very great deal of activity on the part of the servants; I had to wait some considerable time before my ring was answered today, and it was not Mrs. Reynolds who came, either, but some lowly young girl who had no notion of my expectations of chocolate appearing at my elbow at that precise minute! Everybody is distracted, but I am glad that you appear confident, at least."

Georgiana, who was listening in on the conversation as she quietly worked at her table, broke in, "Oh, indeed, yes, we have been very busy the past two days, have not we, Elizabeth? We have addressed a great many invitations for all the families round about and we hope to begin receiving responses within the next day or so. It is very exciting."

Lizzy smiled at her sister, pleased at how much more animated and friendly she had become; her husband had guessed correctly the manner with which to bring his sister out of her self-imposed solitude. Georgiana had barely played her pianoforte since the planning had begun.

"We do indeed; it will be well-attended, I am sure, if only for the opportunity to stare at me from a great distance and pass comments to each other about my appearance. But I shall endure it as best I can. And you, Georgiana, must always be by my side, for your brother will hide away somewhere, I have no doubt; I have seen how he behaves at balls!"

"Well, he is a sensible man indeed. Avoiding an evening of nonsense and gossip is always to be wished for in preference to the quietness of books and sensible conversation. But you ladies must have your entertainments, much as we men dislike them, and we accommodate you as we can!" her father opined.

"He has no reason to avoid this evening, Father; he cannot complain about anything as it was his own notion that a ball should be given. He has given me permission to design it myself and I shall not allow him to call it an inconvenience to him now that it is to happen. Not all men dislike balls, Father, indeed some men, your other son-in-law, for instance, likes nothing so well as a country dance."

"Then we shall agree to differ on the merits of such evenings, my dear, but I shall make certain that I, for one, shall not be here to suffer through it. Now, if you will excuse me, I have an hour of serious reading to accomplish before my walk about the Park; if you are not too busy with your plans, I would dearly enjoy your company, Lizzy."

A letter was duly sent to Jane with requested information, and another letter arrived from Jane who expressed her relief at the news of her father's imminent return and declared herself perfectly delighted that her sister was already carrying out her duties as befits the lady of the estate, giving her best advice with regards to same, and she then continued:

…but we cannot possibly attend ourselves, unfortunately, as Charles intends to be in Town for a few days that week on business and I am to accompany him! I took your advice, my dear Lizzy, and declared myself unable to remain here alone without him. He did not argue the point, nor the fact that I should not be here alone, but now his sisters have decided that they, too, must come to London; that the countryside begins to pall and they require greater society. They certainly gave *your* invitation some serious consideration when they thought I could not hear them, but even that diversion paled when they heard their brother's plan for Town. Now they cannot wait to see their old friends again, go to the theatre, &c., &c..

Naturally, Charles has no argument against their coming - they have always accompanied him wherever he has gone - but can I admit to feeling a little grieved that I am not allowed to be his sole companion? I shall attempt to hide it as best I can. At least I shall be able to invite my aunt and uncle for company whilst we are there; they will prove to my new sisters that not all of my family are worthy of their contempt.

Meanwhile, my dear sister, I expect every detail of your plans in your next letter and hope that the small service of information I have offered is useful to you. Kitty sends her best love; she sits at my elbow as I write and giggles at some parts of it. I have suggested that she spend some time writing to you and Father but she claims to be entirely taken up with her correspondence with our sister in Newcastle, which causes me some consternation, I have told her.

Write to me at our house in London where I shall be certain to receive it.

Take every good care of yourself and I wish you great success at your first ball at Pemberley.

Yours affectionately,

Jane

Chapter 7

Plans proceeded apace, Mr. Bennet left as he designed, and the day of the ball was upon them. Decorations had been ordered and arranged all week, suppliers had made deliveries, and extra help sourced from the village. Now all that could be wished for was a fine evening and healthy guests; a sudden snowstorm or outbreak of a cold could disrupt any entertainment no matter who was providing it. Elizabeth was sure she held her breath leading up to the day as she gathered the replies from the mails.

Everyone was to attend, the rooms would be full, and she checked several times with Mrs. Reynolds with regard to the catering; it would not do to appear wanting in that area. Finally, there was nothing left to do; the evening was at hand and Lizzy was dressed in a new silk gown as Darcy looked on in appreciation while the maid finished arranging her hair; he was already attired in a handsome blue coat but constantly ran his finger about the collar of his shirt accompanied by quick turns about the room.

"Why must these be made so uncomfortable, pray? You must enquire of Mrs. Reynolds what can be done with these collars, my dear."

Lizzy laughed and dismissed her maid. She sat beside him on the couch and reached out to settle his collar which had folded over itself with all of his fidgeting.

"There; is not that better? Now; sit, relax, if you please; we will soon have a houseful of guests and you need to be at your most charming, not your most disagreeable, my dear. Why are you so anxious, pray? It is not such a very great strain for someone who is used to being in the public eye, surely? Calm yourself; all will be well."

Darcy rose from beside her and paced once more about the room as she returned to the dressing table and fixed her gold chain with its simple cross about her neck. Without a word, Darcy immediately left the room leaving Lizzy gazing into the mirror at the empty couch, puzzling at his odd behaviour and then shrugging as she held up the hand mirror to view her hair arrangement from behind, patting a few stray strands into place, when Darcy re-appeared in her view once again. In his hand he held a long box, which he abruptly opened and silently presented to Elizabeth. A delicate lacework of diamonds and pearls lay shimmering in the candlelight against the dark green satin in which it nestled. Elizabeth let out a quiet gasp of admiration.

"This belonged to my mother – my father bought it as a wedding present for her – and I was reminded of it as I watched you preparing for your first ball in her stead; I was also reminded that I have not replicated my father's generosity by giving you a similar token of my affection upon our wedding day. I am appalled with my neglect of you. Please accept this as a continuing token of my esteem for you, esteem that I know would be shared by both my father and mother were they both here to know you. My mother, indeed, left me with the strictest instructions that this was only to grace the neck of a lady, other than her, whom I should admire for the rest of my life.

"Please do me the honour, my dearest Elizabeth, of replacing that which you have always worn with elegance and pride, with this token of love; it would give me the greatest pleasure to see it worn again."

Elizabeth, for once, was quiet; she permitted the removal of her simple chain and gasped when the weight and coldness of the gold lay against her skin. Darcy closed the clasp and kissed the spot where gold met skin. She clasped his hands in hers.

"It is a most beautiful piece, my dear. I am astonished and delighted; thank you! I shall wear this with pride tonight, and everybody will admire it because of its beauty, and the memory of your mother whom they will remember to have often worn it. But allow me to return to my usual retiring sort of adornment tomorrow, if you please; too much finery may go to my head and make me think more highly of myself than appropriate."

"You must wear it to all of our future engagements until such time as I am able to replace it with one that reflects my level of esteem for you; I only wish I had thought of such a thing sooner, but my happiness swept away such thoughts of material evidence. Can you ever forgive me, my dear?"

Elizabeth laughed. "Naturally such an omission speaks very ill for the rest of our life together; I should think, had I considered it, that you had not covered me with precious jewels because you wished to save yourself the trouble and expense!"

Darcy smiled at her and caught her up in his arms. After a while she pulled away, smoothing her hair and straightening her dress, and then adjusted his collar which had, once again, folded itself over in a most uncomfortable manner.

"Come, my dear; we must go downstairs to greet our guests. They will soon be arriving and I would like to watch for the carriages as they come up the drive – I wonder who will be the first."

The couple descended the stairs to general applause from the servants who broke off from their duties about the hall and throughout the great rooms to welcome them; the musicians could be heard tuning and the final touches were being made to the tables of refreshments. Flowers cast their scent from multitudes of vases, candles blazed from every wall and table, and the polished woodwork on the floors and walls glowed warmly.

Elizabeth squeezed Darcy's arm in nervous excitement as they processed through the rooms, checking the readiness of everything with Mrs. Reynolds and Grant. All was in order as they heard the crunch of gravel under the wheels of the carriage of their first guests.

Suddenly, Elizabeth gave a groan of despair; she had forgot something! She gripped Darcy's arm and hissed:

"The horses; the *carriages* and the horses, Darcy! Where do they go? I did not consider them. Oh! How many there will be tonight, and no thought given to their comfort and care. I have always left the carriage that brought me and entered the ball or party without a moment's thought for where they went afterwards. Please tell me that someone who knows what they are about has seen to this? Look! They have all arrived together – the drive is positively blocked with carriages - I can barely see where they end."

Darcy smiled gently at her agitation and patted the hand clutching his sleeve.

"Naturally *someone* has taken care of it; you cannot blame yourself. It is, after all, the domain of Grant and the groom although, I confess, I did ensure that they would open the top field, provide all horses with a bucket of warm oats, and the coachmen a hot meal and drinks. It is all perfectly in hand, I assure you; watch where that lead carriage goes. See? All is as it should be. Now it is your turn to calm yourself and enjoy the evening; I intend to make a valiant attempt at it, as I promised, and if you remain by my side for the entire evening, I am almost certain such a thing might almost be accomplished."

Elizabeth, greatly relieved, watched as, after depositing their load of finery, carriage after carriage disappeared from view around the side of the house towards the field which, she knew, was a very sheltered place away from any wind that might be blowing and appreciated the thoughtfulness of her husband. However, she could no longer concern herself with the goings on outside the house as her attention was re-directed to the arrival of their guests and she happily greeted their neighbours and friends beside her husband and Georgiana.

When there came a break in the receiving line, Georgiana leant over and whispered:

"I am delighted to see how Mamma's necklace becomes you, Elizabeth. I never saw her wear it, but I knew of its existence and enquired of my brother only recently what had become of it;

it is the one she wears in her portrait in the gallery upstairs. She would be very glad to know the wearer of it now, I am sure."

Elizabeth smiled at her sister as she lightly touched the beautiful object weighing gently around her neck; she had no doubt it been noticed as she greeted the guests but none had felt intimate enough with her to comment upon it.

"It is a beautiful piece indeed, Georgiana, and although your brother claims he is intent upon purchasing another especially for me as a belated wedding gift, I do not think that anything could surpass this one, do you?"

Georgiana's reply was deferred as she turned to greet some of the final guests before they were all free to enter the main rooms for dancing. Darcy hung back, reluctant as ever to participate in so exposing an occupation, but Elizabeth, knowing his nature, pressed him forward and smiled at him as they took their place at the head of the line.

"This will be one of only two dances we shall enjoy together this evening, my darling man," she whispered as they passed back-to-back before peeling out into another formation. His reply came at their next meeting:

"Is that a promise, or do you merely tease me because you will insist upon dancing every one, knowing as I do your love for such activities?"

"Well, naturally, I intend such a thing, but I shall not insist upon more than two *with you* all evening. But I expect to be asked to dance with every gentleman here and so that is all I can afford you!"

"By that, I suppose, you hint that I must dance with any available ladies, all evening?"

"Well, I presume that will be the way of it, my dear. I do hope you are prepared and ready to carry out your duty; it would be very shocking if you do not. You had much better dance! For you cannot expect to stand about in a stupid manner - and I merely quote a very good friend of yours speaking at a dance you attended in the past, you know – where, in your estimation, there was not *one* lady who could tempt you. What a notion, indeed!"

Elizabeth laughed gaily at his astounded expression as she wound away from him.

She was as good as her word: he was permitted only one other dance with his own wife – the person with whom he most wished to dance – and was then forced to endure a lengthy procession of neighbourhood ladies - some agreeable, some not - until it came time for refreshments when the musicians could stretch their tired fingers and arms and go downstairs to partake of their own meal.

Darcy could now perfectly recollect the reasons no balls had been given at Pemberley whilst under his ownership. He broke away from a particularly determined neighbour and crossed the room to where Lizzy was happily engaged with several ladies, discussing who knew what with great animation.

He stood by Lizzy's elbow for several minutes before begging leave of the group to remove his wife due to an urgent matter that required her immediate attention. Guiding her through the throng, his hand firmly upon the small of her back, he succeeded, eventually, after several attempts by barbarous neighbours to detain them, to gain the peace and quiet of his study. He closed the door, immediately pulling her into his embrace.

Elizabeth sighed and released herself without restraint to his desire and it was he who finally recollected himself and pulled away. He held her face in his hands and searched it hungrily.

"What is wrong with me that I am unable to survive one evening away from you?"

"But I am not away from you, my darling: I am across the room. Is not that close enough?"

"Having you so close, yet so distant is not enough! If you insist upon leaving me anymore this evening, I shall go mad, of that I am certain. You must stay by my side. I cannot dance with anyone else, nor do I wish to. Surely you must feel the same; tell me that you do, Elizabeth."

"Ah! There I cannot agree with you; I have enjoyed the company of *several* delightful partners this evening. I am not so attached apparently; indeed, I almost forgot you were in the same room!" she laughed. "Perhaps it is because I have become so used to your glowering at me from the corners of many different rooms that I am able to blot you from my consciousness!"

She reached up and kissed him lightly on the cheek. "Come; we must return to our guests, but I promise I shall dance only with you, and talk only with you for the rest of the evening. There! Is that acceptable?"

He placed a light kiss on her lips and they retraced their steps towards their guests, the music, and the dreaded dancing but Elizabeth was as good as her word; any requests to dance were politely refused with a smile and vague excuse. Her husband's warm hand on her back or squeezing her hand was all she needed to make her the happiest of women that night; no request by another gentleman to dance could tempt her.

Georgiana continued to enjoy herself far into the night, dancing every dance until she, too, could exert herself no longer. She came to where her brother and sister were standing, observing all that was going on with proprietary interest and quiet comments, and sank into a small chair by their side.

Immediately, she was inundated by several young men who wished only to be allowed to bring her something: a glass of punch, perhaps? A small titbit from the side tables? Her fan? Georgiana laughingly refused them all and begged only for a few minutes of rest, which they could not refuse, but realised put them in the way of entering into conversation with Mr. Darcy and his new wife, standing so closely by the object of their attention.

However, they soon discovered that any attempt to entertain Mr. Darcy with foolish observations generally thought to be highly amusing, fell flat upon his ears; with Mrs. Darcy they had slightly more effect but not enough to encourage them to remain. They gradually returned to their groups, chastened but undaunted in their quest for Miss Darcy's interest and attention.

The ball continued quite happily into the small hours of the morning; apart from the Darcys – whose unwavering detachment was noted and discussed - everybody was determined to enjoy themselves for as long as possible, and it wasn't until the final drinks and cakes were brought around as sustenance for the journey home - and as a hint that that journey might be considered very soon - did the revellers sadly begin to make motions of departure: making their thanks and invitations to dine and to visit very soon to their hosts; ordering their carriages be brought round to the door, and their wraps, coats and hats brought from the music room; noticing how cold the evening had become and the hopes that the ride home would not be complicated by ice or wind; clapping each other on the back in a jovial fashion in the custom of men unused to such intimacies with their neighbours, whilst their ladies yawned quietly behind their fans and murmured about the evening and their respective levels of exhaustion.

Finally, the last guests had said their farewells; Mrs. Reynolds had ushered in several of the staff to begin a quick sweep of the rooms and to deliver the dirty plates and utensils and glasses to the scullery as an early morning treat for the poor scullery maids, and Grant had barred the doors and was extinguishing the candles already burnt low in their holders.

Darcy, Lizzy and Georgiana climbed the stairs, too tired to speak more than wish each other a good night with a quick kiss for Georgiana. When they were safely inside their room, and Elizabeth had immediately dismissed Baxter, Darcy gathered Elizabeth in his arms.

"You are to be congratulated, my darling, dearest Elizabeth, as hostess of a ball that everyone will be talking of for weeks and months to come. My only misgiving is that we shall now be expected to attend any others we are invited to – and I anticipate a deluge of those infernal cards – as now we have entered local society, we cannot hide again. That is unfortunate indeed. But Georgiana certainly came out of herself, did not she?"

"And as that was the reason for the whole evening, as I recall, my dear, it is you who should be congratulated for a very successful evening. But I cannot talk anymore; I am very happy but utterly exhausted. Help me out of my pins and buttons, and this gorgeous necklace, and come to bed.

"I warn you," she yawned, bending her head to allow his fingers to undo the clasp, "I intend sleeping shockingly late into the morning."

Chapter 8

Lydia sighed in utter contentment, stretching languorously across the full width of the bed, her eyes scanning the four corners of the apartment she had been allocated upon her arrival. The elegant furnishings, the pale green damask drapes, the soft rugs all spoke of unlimited money. She was not certain, but she believed that this just might be the grandest guest apartment at Netherfield and it was - of this she was certain - at least four times as large as her rooms in Newcastle, and far exceeded them in comfort.

How delightful to be safe amongst her family and away from the fears that arose every time there was a knock on the door. Indeed, how delightful to know that any knock on the front door would not be heard or have to be dealt with by her, but would be taken care of by one of the many Netherfield servants.

She sighed again and reached out to pull the bell. Within minutes there was a quiet knock on the door, which opened upon her call, and admitted a small girl of perhaps thirteen, who bobbed a curtesy.

"Yes, madam?"

Lydia smiled with all the satisfaction that address brought her and ordered her breakfast to be brought up immediately. The girl hesitated.

"I believe … madam … that Mrs. Bingley is delaying her own breakfast until you come downstairs. Shall I tell her that you are indisposed, madam?"

"*No!* I am not *indisposed.* I merely wish to take my breakfast in my room. Kindly tell my sister that I shall join her afterwards. I am still very tired from my journey and need to rest, that is all."

The girl bobbed another curtsey and closed the door behind her.

Lydia sank back down into the pillows, biting her nail angrily. Why must she be questioned at every turn? All she wanted was to rest in this house for a while, out of the way, without having to explain herself. She needed some time to think, without interference or unwanted opinion, that was all; to think of what was best to be done.

Her sister had been most astonished and alarmed at her arrival in a hired carriage, late yesterday afternoon, just as Lydia had anticipated she would be. Jane's anxiety had stemmed firstly from concern that Lydia may have found no one at home, thanking Providence that she and Bingley had returned early from Town; and then secondly, regarding the propriety of her sister travelling alone.

This latter concern had been easily allayed; a friend of Lydia's had been travelling with her husband from Newcastle in the same direction as far as the last Stage, and had been good enough to procure a seat and see her into it. Of all her sisters, Jane was the only one to whom she could go knowing there would be no insistent probing of her reasons, or her intended length of stay, or demands for solutions, and, true to her character, she had welcomed her most warmly after her first shock, and ensured she was made comfortable.

Jane was kind to, and thought well of everybody, sometimes even in the face of evidence to the contrary, and Lydia desperately needed someone who would not judge her decision and force her to make another one in haste. However, that did not mean she had any intention of informing her sister about the truth of the matter. No, indeed; the truth of this matter would not sit well with anybody, and especially not with Jane who would feel all the pain involved and wish to solve it equally for everyone involved.

Lydia pulled herself upright against the pillows as she heard footsteps and the clink of china approaching her door; pulling her shawl around her shoulders, she called out in answer to the knock. Delicious smells accompanied the two servants carrying trays piled with covered plates and a steaming pot of coffee. Following behind came Jane, who nodded to the servants and thanked them when they had set up the small table in the corner of the room, and then smiled at Lydia as she poured out two cups of strong coffee.

"Come along, Lydia; as you are not indisposed - although even if you were I should have come - I decided to take my breakfast with you since you felt unable to join me downstairs. Come! You would not wish it to get cold after waiting all this time."

Deeply displeased at the interference but driven by hunger, Lydia swung her legs out of bed and walked slowly to the table, dreading what conversation would ensue and how she could avoid it.

Jane smiled softly and handed her a plate. "I hope you do not mind but I have sent a message to Longbourn; I know Mamma and Kitty would like to know you are here. I should not be surprised if they are downstairs already."

"La! Kitty rises much later than this, Jane. And I am sure since I have been gone, and with only Mary for company, she has wished to spend the entire *day* in bed, for why would she wish to get up and face one of Mary's sermons?"

Jane looked at Lydia with the glimmer of reproach in her eye.

"I think you will find that since you have been in Newcastle these past six months, Kitty has improved her society beyond that offered at Longbourn. She is very firm friends with several young ladies in the village, including Maria Lucas - who grows everyday into a sensible and lovely young woman - and Kitty has also been introduced to other, very respectable people at small parties we have hosted here, at Netherfield. Perhaps she has mentioned them in her letters to you?

"So, she has no reason to stay in bed with her life so very busy and happy. I believe, also, she is working on our father to take her with him the next time he plans a surprise visit to

Pemberley; she would be very welcome there, I should think. Lizzy would enjoy the company, and Kitty could be introduced to Mr. Darcy's sister, Georgiana. Lizzy believes they would get along very well, indeed she is concerned about Miss Darcy's retiring nature and wishes for nothing more than to see her out in society more, and happy once again."

"Ha! Yes, I suppose Kitty *must* be enjoying being the youngest daughter, since I am now gone away. She *might* have mentioned such things in her letters but I am so busy with my own life, I hardly have time to take in what she writes to me. But I hope our father refuses to take her into Derbyshire, just as he refused to take me to Brighton; it would be most unfair if he did not. I do not see why he should treat Kitty any better than he treated me."

She bit into her muffin angrily, remembering the suffering caused by her father's refusal to take her into Brighton; she would have lost Wickham if she had not gone. But she had got herself there through her own connections, and everything had worked out as she planned – well, almost as she planned, anyway - and she had won him.

"*Lydia!* That is an unkind thing to say about our father, and after everything he went through for you last year; he was thinking only of your safety, and considering the outcome, he was right to do so. You should be grateful for his concern; he was terribly worried about you, as were we all.

"Tell me; are we to expect another surprise arrival soon? Does Mr. Wickham intend visiting us also?"

Lydia glanced at her sister; she smiled and said airily:

"Oh, dear me, no, Jane! Wickham is much too busy to visit at this time of the year. He is so busy that I am entirely neglected in Newcastle, even though I have many new friends, you understand, but there is something very serious afoot, something very secret and exciting – he and all of his men are sworn to silence on the matter, you know – but they must meet until late every evening. I told him only recently that such a workload cannot be good for them, but he merely laughed and told me that it was man's work and not to trouble my pretty head about it! He is such a wonderful husband, Jane; I hope yours is as good."

Jane looked sceptical at this but agreed that Charles was, indeed, a wonderful husband in every sense of the word, and they were perfectly happy together. Lydia smiled in a superior manner from her experience of being a married woman longer than her sister.

"Ah, yes, it is generally the case in the first months of being married, Jane. It is exciting discovering each other: everything is new; everything they do or say is amusing and different; everything we do or say is charming and delightful. They only grow more handsome, and we only improve in beauty. That is the way of being newlyweds, I assure you. Let us hope it continues longer for us than for some, sister! That our husbands continue to look only at us, and we wish only for them to do so."

Jane, flustered at the turn the conversation was taking, blushed a little and refilled her cup.

"I am sure that when people marry a partner they love and respect it can only produce happiness for both of them. Of course, when two people live in close proximity to each other, there are bound to be some vexations – it is not possible to always be in accord over everything – but these will work themselves out if both partners are respectful and loving towards each other."

"Yes, indeed! Wickham and I are just that way. We have mutual respect and consideration, and that is why, when he noticed how dull I was feeling, he proposed this journey to see my family and home; he knew just what would bring me back to my former gaiety."

"That is certainly very thoughtful of Mr. Wickham, considering the very great expense it must have been to arrange for your transportation all the way from the North East corner of England. Your finances must be greatly improved since last you wrote, and I am very happy to hear of it.

"Of course you are welcome to remain with us for as long as you can be spared by Mr. Wickham; if he is as busy as you say, perhaps it is best you are here with us enabling him to fully concentrate upon his business, knowing you are happy with your family. Yes! I think it a very thoughtful and generous gesture on Mr. Wickham's part, and I commend him for his concern about your happiness.

"Now; if you are finished, why do not you join me in the morning room where there is a large fire blazing and more-comfortable chairs for us to continue our discussion?"

Smiling at her sister, Jane left the room, not at all convinced that the story she had been told was one of fact. It was only a month ago, very soon after her own wedding that Lydia had written in apparent desperation, needing money for some undefined emergency. For Mr. Wickham to have recovered his finances in such a rapid manner was beyond credibility; for him to agree to spend vast amounts of that sudden income on travel was also unbelievable, unless he had started gaming again, as he was known to do.

Sincerely worried now, Jane hastened downstairs to her desk where she quickly penned a letter to Lizzy; without her sister's sensible advice, she did not know how to deal with her unexpected visitor at all. She managed to give the letter to the maid just before Lydia strolled into the room and flopped down upon the chaise closest to the fire.

"Ah! How pleasant all of this is, Jane! You are certainly fortunate indeed to have all of this at your disposal, and a house in Town, too. I hope that very soon Wickham will be able to find a comfortable house for us; of course, it will have to be somewhere around Newcastle for there is his occupation, but it is not such a bad place for all of its isolation from everything that the South has to offer. We have just as many parties and dances and assemblies as do you, I dare say. We are kept quite busy, the other wives and I, designing entertainments for the officers and surrounding families. There are several young ladies who are anxious to meet the officers, and we introduce them as we see fit.

"I have invited Kitty to come and stay, to experience life in the North and perhaps introduce her to an eligible young man, but thus far she has made every excuse, and now I understand why if she is kept constantly busy, here with you. Although I cannot but suspect our father of keeping her here also, in fear she might never return, or may return a married woman like her sister!"

Jane drew in a breath at Lydia's careless allusion to her own shocking behaviour; clearly her sister still did not understand the enormity of her almost-disgrace, nor the great good fortune in escaping that disgrace through the generosity of their uncle Gardiner.

"I am sure you are quite correct, Lydia. Father certainly would *not* like to have a second daughter attempt to bring his good name into disrepute, as did you. Forgive me for speaking plainly, but you seem to have no remorse about your behaviour of last year and the repercussions it might have had upon our entire family. The potential ruination of our good name along with your own was too horrific to consider. Yet here you are, again accusing our father unjustly for doing everything in his power to recover you before such a terrible event happened, of keeping his remaining daughters safe from being able to make the same mistakes, and of stopping Kitty from enjoying herself 'like her sister'.

"It is all nonsense; you must see that everything that has been done was done in the name of protection: of you, of our family, of our futures. I refuse to listen to any more of your selfishness. You should consider yourself to be a most fortunate girl; you have gained everything that you set out to, and by your own accounts are very happy with your life. Let us have no more recriminations against our father, Kitty or Lizzy, while you remain with us, if you please."

Jane had become quite heated in defence of her family. It was most unusual for her to accuse anybody of anything, much less her sisters, and she instantly began to feel regret at speaking so harshly. One look at Lydia's shocked and pouting face, however, relieved her of any compunction at her words; clearly they had merely angered her sister, not produced any remorse for her behaviour as had been the intention.

"I am sure I do not know why you are angry about things that happened so long ago, Jane. Whatever happened, however it happened, whoever was involved in the outcome, it should not still be preying on *your* mind. Truly, I hardly ever think of it myself except as a most exciting and enjoyable time! And since nothing terrible happened to anybody in our family, I see no reason for you to speak so cruelly. All ended well, did not it? You got your Mr. Bingley, and Lizzy got her Mr. Darcy – so what is there to regret from my actions?"

Lydia punched the sofa pillow with a vengeance and then threw it down on the seat as she stood, angry herself now.

"If you are quite finished lecturing me, I have a letter to write. I must let Wickham know I am here safely, if not entirely welcome, it would seem."

Jane nodded silently. It was hard to see her sister so angry but she was unable to muster the reassuring words she knew Lydia was waiting to hear, because those words, she knew, would be lies, and they were lies she would not say for the benefit of Lydia's self-regard. How she wished Lizzy was seated there right beside her. Faced with both of them, Lydia would display much less bravado and would, perhaps, attempt some self-reflection. Jane sighed as Lydia flounced out of the room, slamming the door behind her.

Chapter 9

Elizabeth awoke late the morning after the ball and sleepily reached out to Darcy, only to encounter a cold and empty space where he had been. She rolled over and saw a note propped against the pillow, smiling as she read the few words contained therein. Her eyes glanced over at the bell pull – how tempting to pull it and have breakfast brought up to her! – but resisted the utterly decadent urge, pushing back the covers and pulling on her robe.

She had never had the luxury of servants at her every beck and call and could not get used to the idea now. She was perfectly capable of carrying out her own immediate dressing and ablution needs. Her eyes lighted upon the necklace, resting where Darcy had carefully lain it last night amongst the green satin of its box. Dreamily, she held it against her skin and marvelled at the delicate workmanship and glow of the jewels; Darcy had set himself a challenge indeed to surpass this particular love gift!

She replaced it along with the longing to have another reason to wear it very soon and rang the bell for Baxter to assist with her final dressing and hair, who brought her a cup of tea along with the first mails of the morning and some information gleaned from the servants' quarters.

"It is all the talk this mornin', madam, of how particularly well last evenin' went; all the servants are saying as how they can't remember the last time the house was so happy and alive. It was quite a wonderful evenin' was not it, madam?"

Elizabeth nodded, smiling. "Yes, indeed. I believe everything went extremely well and I must thank Mrs. Reynolds for her superior arrangements that made it so. I know Mr. Darcy was very pleased that it was such a success after a long period of no entertainments; he does not particularly enjoy such events but he must become more used to them from now on, I think. I hope you were able to see some of the evening, Baxter, and enjoyed what you saw?"

"Oh, yes, madam! It was a beautiful sight, to be sure, with all them ladies in their finery and jewels! It felt like we was at the Court in London, indeed it did!"

Elizabeth smiled again and turned her attention to the writing on the letters. Her mother, Jane, *and* Lydia appeared to have written all at the same time. A strange foreboding started in her stomach and remained there until Baxter vacated the room, leaving her alone.

Quickly, Elizabeth slit open the letter from Jane who could always be relied upon to send the most sensible version of any drama that might be unfolding in Meryton or at Longbourn.

Netherfield House
February 2nd 18~

Dearest Elizabeth,

I know you will be recovering your strength after what I hope was a successful first ball at Pemberley and I would not normally trouble you at such a happy time but something has happened about which you must be immediately informed.

Our sister, Lydia, has arrived at Netherfield, without so much as a by-your-leave, and is even now sitting in the drawing room, quite at home, seemingly without a care in the world, but refusing, absolutely, to inform us of the reason for her strange and unexpected visit. Of Wickham, she will not say a word other than he was in good health when she left him. She seems perfectly unconcerned about having left her husband alone in Newcastle as she assures me he is entirely taken up with his business interests – whatever they may be - and leaves her to her own devices much of the time. She claims he insisted upon her making the visit and was quite happy to provide the funds to do so; but I am afraid that this information does not sit well with me, knowing as I do how precarious their finances were only a month ago.

Our mother will, of course, be delighted to have her youngest daughter back with us, but even she must be concerned at the suddenness of it, so soon after their departure last year for their new life in Newcastle. I have tried to press Lydia for more information but she insists there is no cause for concern.

I am sorry to say that her attitude regarding certain events of last year has become even more careless. She is still the same: unrestrained in her views on life and happy to cover her actions with the blame of others, and I found myself forced to remind her of her disgraceful behaviour of last year, which she appears to have dismissed entirely from her memory. I grew quite heated in my accusations and upset at being forced to speak in such a manner.

Dear Charles seems perfectly composed about it all; he believes she will leave when whatever the current disagreement between her and Wickham has been resolved, and even mentioned that her solitary visit was to be preferred over one that consisted of them both, which is a most uncharacteristically pointed remark for him to make, as you know.

Perhaps you would be so good as to inform me if you become aware of any reasons for our sister's flight, and I shall, of course, inform you should anything come to light here.

Otherwise, please know we are all well and longing to hear about the success of your ball.

With fondest love,
Jane

Elizabeth put the letter aside, perturbed that her usually calm and generous sister had been so provoked, and opened the one from Lydia herself; perhaps the information Jane sought was contained there. As usual, it was written in an indifferent hand, full of blotches and crossings out, and apparently at great speed.

Dear Lizzy,

Do not be angry with me. I am come to Jane's where I supposed myself to be the most welcome and safe. I thought to stop in Derbyshire as I travelled down from the North but dared not bring my news in person to those who understand my husband the best.

I now understand the extent of Wickham's feelings for me; or lack thereof. It has become clear that, even though my affection for him is not diminished in the slightest - he remains as the dearest person in the world to me – any affection he might have had for me appears to have all but died. He spends all his time in Newcastle with his friends – discussing business, he calls it – but I call it by what it is: drinking and gambling away our small resources.

Even worse: we have no money, Lizzy! Even though both you and Jane have been most kind in response to my pleas for help, we have again been forced to remove ourselves – this is for the third time already since we have been in Newcastle – for want of the required rent. Our other creditors are all ferocious in their demands that we repay our credit with them, but we cannot. I am very frightened, Lizzy, you cannot imagine how unpleasant life has become. When I confronted Wickham about our situation, he only laughed and advised me to go to my sisters' if I did not like our life; and so here I am.

Do not tell Darcy, Lizzy. He will be furious, I know he will, both with me and with Wickham; and Wickham will be angry with me for telling you everything, but what am I to do? Am I to be blamed for our situation? I cannot be, Lizzy.

Oh! It is so unfair, indeed it is, and I do not know what I shall do if you and Jane do not continue to be kind to me. I cannot return to Longbourn – Father has made that very clear - much as I would like to. How I long to return to my former life where everything was so carefree and easy. But I cannot; everyone will want to know why and then they will condemn me or be pleased at my failure.

But I must get this to the mail secretly before Jane writes to you, as I know she will. I have told no one else the truth of my situation, Lizzy, and you must not either – especially not Mr. Darcy. I rely upon your sensible advice: I cannot ask Jane or Mamma, and certainly not Father. You are my only guide, Lizzy; take pity upon your poor sister.

I shall remain at Netherfield until I hear from you, as I do not know what else to do.

Write quickly,

Lydia Wickham

Shocked and angry, Elizabeth threw the offending missive away from her. Really! Such news so early in the morning, after a late and very enjoyable evening and before she had taken breakfast, was not to be borne.

She shook her head in disbelief. Lydia, whose determination to get Wickham for herself had caused such pain to so many, was now regretting her decision and wished for her, Elizabeth, to advise how such a thing was to be re-arranged?

It was insupportable!

That Lydia had always been a selfish and headstrong girl with naught in her head but men and frivolity was something that had concerned Elizabeth for many years; indeed, she had warned her father on that very subject before the ill-fated trip to Brighton last Summer and all that had eventually entailed both for her family and for Darcy's. And now; now that Lydia had everything that she set out to have – a husband, an entertaining type of life albeit one that could no longer be afforded, and some adventure – but none of which had worked out as she hoped, Lydia desired an easy escape from her situation, a return to her former life.

Elizabeth recalled her father's now-prescient warning of a week ago about showing restraint before helping Lydia; how she must be made to appreciate the situation she had made for herself and truly repent and feel the trouble she had caused through attaining it before he would ever consider helping her.

At the time, Elizabeth remembered, she had considered his reaction to be a little harsh towards a daughter who had never been forced to consider anything before doing it, much less repent of any actions she had taken. But now, in the face of this letter which was so clearly a request for somewhere safe to hide before, undoubtedly, recovering sufficiently to recommence her old behaviours and forgetting the consequences of her actions, Elizabeth felt her own heart hardening towards Lydia. Even more so when she recalled what she had learnt not only of Darcy's painful involvement in effecting the marriage between Lydia and Wickham but also of the intolerable hurt inflicted through her sister's machinations upon the one person who had truly loved Wickham and who was probably the only person he had ever loved more than himself.

Before leaving the room, Lizzy opened the third letter and quickly scanned the irrational nonsense contained therein: delight at Lydia's sudden appearance; curiosity as to the extent of Lizzy's knowledge; a demand that she divulge any information immediately; the anticipation of dear Wickham joining them all shortly when they would, certainly, need a house in the neighbourhood, and a hope that the shock would not have any lasting effects upon her nerves. Sighing, Lizzy cast it aside with the other two letters and left the room, hoping not to meet anyone in the breakfast room.

She was in luck. The servants informed her that the master had already eaten and left with the steward, and Georgiana was still in bed. After taking only a small cake and some tea, Lizzy quickly left the room and donned her walking cloak and boots. If ever she needed the solace of the countryside, today was the day, and she thanked her good fortune that, although cloudy, the weather seemed to offer the chance of a lengthy walk to give her some perspective upon her problem.

If she was to advise Lydia, what should she say? What she really needed to do was discuss it with Darcy - he would know the best solution - but Lydia had begged her not to tell Darcy. But why should she not tell him? He was her husband;

they should not have secrets from each other and he was already closely involved in the whole affair.

No one could be surprised that Wickham had soon tired of Lydia: the difference in age, the lack of anything other than animal attraction, their extravagant wants and heedlessness of the future could only have ended badly, but Elizabeth had hoped that the first flush of matrimony would have lasted rather longer than – how long was it? – slightly longer than six months.

There was the expectation that Wickham would have at least tried, out of respect for Darcy, to make a success of his commission and new life even if he did not love the partner with whom he found himself sharing that life. Many experience similar disappointments upon making the true acquaintance of their marriage partner, and make do. But no; he was as selfish and self-absorbed as Lydia, focused only on what would make *him* happy in the moment without any consideration for the future or how his actions and behaviour would affect others.

Elizabeth felt herself walking faster as her anger towards both people increased. She forced herself to slow down before she became too exhausted to make the return journey. Already, she realised as she looked about her, she had covered far more ground than was her usual exercise – she was far through the woods - and storm clouds were gathering in the distance. If they caught her, she would be soaked through and become chilled and be lain up in bed for days with a red nose and unattractively blotchy face.

She smiled, dismissing her ridiculous vanity and quickly turned about, heading back the way she had come, concerned now that she would not regain the Park before the deluge hit. All thoughts of her sister were put aside in the scramble to beat the storm; frequent glances at the sky behind her confirmed the ferocity of it and the speed at which it travelled.

The sky darkened and the weak sun was obscured behind the black rain clouds. A fork of lightning split the darkness and a roll of thunder overhead announced the arrival of the rain.

Lizzy gave up any thoughts of regaining the house and sheltered instead beneath a clump of smaller trees in the woods, watching as the torrents poured down the leaves and formed rivulets in the ground about her. Soon, the leafy ceiling above could resist the wetness no longer and she experienced the misery of being drenched, all of a sudden, in freezing cold water.

She was wet; she could get no wetter, so she left her hiding place, but immediately retreated as another flash sliced the sky. It was clearly too dangerous to cross the open parkland, conspicuous as she would be, and so determined to make herself as small as possible at the base of the tree where there was still some slight protection from the rain, and wait for the storm to pass.

She had no way of knowing how long she sat there or of assuring anyone of her safety but knew that by now she must surely be missed. She had not informed anyone of her departure, never mind her intended direction - indeed, *she* had not known her intended direction - and they would be concerned about her safety by now.

Darcy would be concerned. She imagined his disquiet, standing helpless at the door, looking out for her, hoping against hope to see her figure appear through the darkness. Her heart lurched with guilt and remorse.

Lydia! This predicament was all to be placed firmly at the feet of her sister and her worthless husband. Anything they touched turned out badly for those around them. It was shocking indeed how two people could cause such chaos, and then regret only how it had affected them. Selfish, careless people!

Anger brought Lizzy to her feet; she felt the storm was easing slightly but she could no longer stay hiding, knowing how others, how Darcy, would be worrying about her. She would make every attempt to return home immediately.

She set off determinedly along the path to the edge of the woods that led into the Park around Pemberley. Her feet slipped inside her boots and her cloak flapped wetly around her, hitting her legs and weighing her down; she considered once or twice the value of removing it entirely, sodden as it was, but knew that it still provided some relief from the cold February weather.

As she came into view of the house, she could feel her limbs trembling from cold and tiredness but she pressed on through the constant driving rain, thankful that the lightning, at least, had passed. Her mind pushed her forward; thoughts of Darcy warmed her, fanned by the simmering anger built up against Lydia and her disgraceful, selfish behaviour.

And so, it was an extremely dishevelled, muddy, soaked, saddened, and furious Mrs. Darcy who stumbled through the front doors of the house and into the waiting arms of her husband who had, as she supposed, been anxiously waiting for his horse to be saddled and brought round in order to start a search for her, after being alerted to her absence by Mrs. Reynolds.

Thoughts had jostled his reasoning: first that Elizabeth was a great walker and would not put herself in danger; then, more concerning, that she had fallen and injured herself; and then finally, which had occasioned the saddling of his horse, the sight of lightning and torrential rain and her exposure to it. He had to find her and bring her back without delay, but here she was already, leaning exhausted upon his arm, soaking wetness through his jacket sleeve. He put his arm about her waist and effortlessly swept her up into his arms, carrying her up the stairs to her bed chamber, calling for Mrs. Reynolds and Baxter as he went.

Immediately, all was uproar. Mrs. Reynolds ordered warming pans and hot drinks; Baxter, clucking around her mistress like an anxious mother-hen, shooed her master out before helping Elizabeth out of her soaked garments and wrapping her warmly in her nightgown and shawl, then tucking the bed covers about her as if she were a small child. The housemaid came to build up the fire, and only then was Darcy admitted back into the room. Mrs. Reynolds bustled in all warm good humour and sensible advice, watching as Lizzy dutifully swallowed gulp after gulp of Cook's best hot soup into which had been added a large measure of brandy.

Once these good ladies were satisfied that everything had been done that could possibly ward off the ill-effects of her drenching, did Mrs. Reynolds and Baxter remove themselves from the room leaving the couple alone.

Elizabeth smiled sheepishly at the fuss she had created and started to apologise to Darcy for it. He shook his head smiling his relief.

"There is nothing for you to be sorry about, my dearest. But what on earth possessed you to stray so far from home, today? Perhaps, in the future, it would be as well to inform at least one person where you intend walking. I know how you love to walk unaccompanied – you are an independent woman – but your safety is paramount to me, and to everyone who loves you."

"I promise I shall try to remember to tell someone where I am going, but I find so many new walks and paths every day that even I do not know where I may be. I am sorry to have caused you pain, my darling man, I knew I had done so even as I stood being drenched under one of your less-than-waterproof trees, and resolved to return regardless of my discomfort because I could not think of you suffering for a moment longer than you already had."

They both turned as the door opened and Georgiana poked her head around it, then entered to sit on the other side of the bed. She had just risen after the lateness of the ball and, therefore, had missed most of the excitement; her maid informed her only a moment ago and she had immediately rushed along to check upon the patient.

"But I see you are in good hands, Elizabeth, and warmed by everyone's affection and care. I will stay with you this morning so that my brother can get on with his work."

Seeing that both were about to protest, she continued to Elizabeth. "You know Mrs. Reynolds will not allow you to get up until at least tonight and only after she has determined you are fit to do so, so you must accept my kind offer or suffer boredom alone all day. Brother; you may leave her with me, we shall be perfectly content. I will not allow her to walk one step, not even across the bedroom. Go on! She will do perfectly well without you."

Darcy smiled and nodded at his unusually assertive sister, kissed Elizabeth unnecessarily thoroughly, and left the ladies to their own devices.

Chapter 10

Elizabeth's chilly soaking resulted in a lengthy stay in bed of several days which grated upon her nerves and challenged those in charge of her care to supply amusements of sufficient interest for their patient. Georgiana gladly forsook all of her usual daily pastimes: her music practice might have suffered but her sister suffered far more from boredom and restraint. No outside visitors were allowed and Elizabeth's only contact was through the mails which brought a flurry of sympathy and advice from both Hertfordshire and Kent. The weather, also, seemed to play purposefully upon her patience having turned unseasonably warm for the time of year; Elizabeth felt it mocked her every time she looked outside and compared it to the storm that had forced her into bed rest. Darcy was as solicitous as he possibly could be but Elizabeth preferred him not to see her in such a state, as a bed-bound invalid, desperately wishing for her strength to return and her nose to regain its pale pink colour.

However, the enforced leisure ensured a response to the letters from her sisters and mother. In her missives to Jane and her mother, she assured them of her complete assistance regarding Lydia, promising to keep them informed if she learnt any truth of the matter. She had almost felt the childish urge to cross her fingers as she wrote such falsehoods.

Her response to Lydia took a great deal more thought, several drafts being cast aside before one conveyed her message clearly enough without resorting to the recriminations and blame that Elizabeth dearly wished to lay right at her sister's door, and was as follows:

Pemberley House
Derbyshire
February 11th 18~

My dear sister,

I am sorry not to have written earlier but, as you may have heard from Jane, I have been unwell after being caught out in a sudden rainstorm last week. You may rest assured that I am perfectly recovered now and merely await the approval of my housekeeper and husband before I am allowed to return to my normal duties.

I was grieved to read the contents of your letter; to be only six months into your marriage and already considering leaving your husband is certainly not something which you can regard with your usual complacency. Marriage is not one of your frivolous amusements to be cast off at whim.

I am glad you had the good sense not to ask personally for help from this quarter; my husband, as you so rightly gauge, would not relish the news that his generosity to Wickham has once again been squandered. But also to beg my help while foisting yourself and your troubles upon poor Jane and Mr. Bingley is more than a little disingenuous. I do not approve of you involving them in your scandalous behaviour and must insist that you leave Netherfield with as much grace as you can muster while continuing to cover your real reasons for being there, catch the first post back up to Newcastle, find your husband, and work out between the two of you what is to be done.

As I understand it, he has not mistreated you in any way; he has not caused you mental or physical harm. Your discovery of your husband's faults is surprising only in that it has taken you this long to do so, as, already knowing the transitory nature of his affections towards Miss King and me you should have been somewhat forewarned. Whilst he is certainly a charming and handsome man - the only attributes you cared to notice last year - those surface features cleverly hide other, less favourable characteristics about which you are now painfully aware.

However, I do not believe you to have been entirely ignorant of these traits, whatever you may claim, Lydia, after spending some time in his company in Brighton, as I know you did. His gambling and drinking cannot have escaped your notice, but perhaps you thought it exciting, as you considered everything to be?

I have the greatest faith in your ability to improve your husband and your manner of living, should you so wish. Reclaim his interest and respect. Respect is the greatest ingredient in a true partnership, and you have it in your power to regain it through your own improved behaviour and patience towards your husband's weaknesses.

Wickham is your husband; he is now solely responsible for your happiness and well-being: your family no longer holds that obligation. However, he also knows that you are not alone in the world, to do with entirely as he pleases, Lydia. If matters deteriorate too far, he knows he will have not only Father and uncles Gardiner and Phillips to contend with but also Mr. Darcy and Mr. Bingley. You are not without friends, sister, but you must attempt some improvements yourself before abandoning everything at the first sign of trouble. You desired nothing more than to become Mrs. Wickham: now you have that title, for life. Accept and begin to live up to the expectations of it.

If this advice seems harsh, so be it, but you are a married woman and married women remain with their husbands through wealth and poverty; through the good times and the bad.

Remember your vows, Lydia, and go home before it is too late.

Your loving sister
Elizabeth

Elizabeth sighed as she signed the final copy of the letter, enclosing a sum of money to ensure Lydia's ability to carry out her advice. But she doubted that advice would be taken, fully expecting the next letter from Jane would confirm Lydia's continued visit, without any explanation.

But the truth had to be stated. For too long Lydia had been allowed to run wild, her faulty assurance and disdain of any restraint had made her an amusing companion for more than one gentleman, but only until they realised her unguarded and imprudent manner placed them at a great disadvantage, at which point they moved on to less unruly ladies who did not cause heads to turn and shocked voices to be shielded by fluttering fans or raised hands.

Lydia had authored her own desperate situation through that lack of prudence; she had gained that which she had set her heart on and now must live with the consequences. With a sickening realisation, Elizabeth understood more than ever, that Lydia would always be wanting more than she had, envying those around her who seemed happier or wealthier or more loved than she, and would never rest until she managed to get what they had.

Unfortunately, she was married to a person who looked around him with the same eyes; who also saw only what he did not have, but it never impressed him enough to try to improve his situation. Both of them were lazy, jealous people who refused to work to improve their lot in life and certainly did not appreciate anything they were given. They took and took and then looked for more when that ran out.

Elizabeth then thought of Darcy and how much he must have suffered over the years dealing with Wickham; he had never said anything more about the two incidents she knew about – he was too reticent for that – but she knew just those two concerning Georgiana and then Lydia must have both involved grand sums being settled upon the covetous Wickham.

Oh! And the generous payment in lieu of the living so many years ago; how many more times had Wickham been the recipient of Darcy family money, and he only the son of the late steward? How many more times would he expect a childhood friend to bail him out when things became too difficult through his own egregious behaviour? It was shocking indeed and Elizabeth felt more and more concerned as she mulled it over, alone with her thoughts during her enforced rest.

The fifth day arrived and she could bear it no longer; she informed her maid she required her dress and shawl and would take her breakfast in the dining room after she had spoken with Mrs. Reynolds. Darcy was delighted to find his wife once again sitting in her usual place, pouring his coffee and appearing none the worse for wear.

"I trust you do not intend walking out, this morning?" he enquired drily, noting her shawl and eyes that kept wandering out of the window at the view. "It is not as warm outside as it seems; I would not want you to compromise your recovery by getting another chill."

Elizabeth smiled, removing her gaze from the enticing greenery and frost-tipped grass glinting in the sun's thin rays.

"No, indeed; much as I would wish it, I believe I shall remain indoors for several more days yet, but I could not stay in bed a moment longer. Will you keep me company, my dear? I should greatly enjoy talking with you."

"I would enjoy that, too my dear for I intend to attempt a task this morning which I have been postponing for some time; a task that requires the greatest diplomacy, and since the subject of it centres around you, perhaps you may wish to assist me, if you would be so kind?"

"*Around me?* Surely not! What must you be diplomatic about that concerns *me*, pray? How intriguing! I will assist you with the greatest of pleasure if only to have you to myself and discover what secret you are about."

Darcy smiled and led the way into his study, waving her to take a small armchair pulled up closely to the blazing fire. Elizabeth snuggled up, pulling her shawl around her, surprised that the effort of dressing and the short walk from the dining room had tired her so quickly. Clearly, she was not as well as she had at first imagined, but she would not let Darcy know of it and smiled brilliantly at him where he was now ensconced behind his father's great desk.

"Now; let us be diplomatic together, my dear. To whom are we addressing ourselves, and why?"

Darcy pulled the ink pot closer to him and dipped the pen into the ink. He looked over at her and smiled as he wrote the salutation.

"Lady Catherine is our subject today, and changing her mind about you and your worthiness of being Mrs. Darcy is our object. It is not something I relish, but you have on several occasions attempted to persuade me that such a reconciliation should be attempted."

Elizabeth laughed disbelievingly. "It was your taking such great offence at her letter regarding our nuptials, and her subsequent abuse of me, abuse which I roundly defended, may I remind you, which has caused such a rift in your relationship, and I do not blame you in the slightest; if any of my relations had dared to call any of your intentions into question, I too, would cast them off forever. But we both know the genuine frankness of her character; she cannot unsay what she has said, and she said what she meant at the time hoping to dissuade you from what she believed to be a most imprudent marriage. It was said in haste and without any thought other than anger. I do not hold it against her, and, as I have said, you must not either. She is someone who has always directed everything within her power and does not like to be gainsaid.

"Come, let us overpower her with kindness and forgiveness; let us invite her to Pemberley so she may see our felicity for herself and realise that the woods round about are not quite as polluted as she imagined they would be!"

Elizabeth laughed again at her husband's quizzical look but refused to explain the allusion. Together they spent a very pleasant and loving hour composing a letter to someone who, both of them doubted, had ever experienced the happiness and love that they felt in each other's company, and for that deficiency, they agreed, they felt sorry for her, excusing her unkind manner and lack of affection towards others.

Chapter 11

A rather chilly air had descended between the sisters at Netherfield for the remainder of the day as they nursed private thoughts against each other although Jane, at least, attempted some degree of reconciliation, unhappy at causing distress to anybody. However, after her conciliatory overture the following morning was rebuffed by Lydia - who privately preferred the silence between them to another lecture on her past failures and faults - Jane determined to keep to herself.

Unbeknownst to her, she had surprised Lydia with her depth of feeling and emotion. Jane's outburst had actually pierced Lydia's usually thick skin and made a pinprick on her conscience. A very small pinprick, fortunately, otherwise she should have to suffer the pain of discovering her character, and Lydia had never managed that feat in all her sixteen years, and easily dismissed any feeble attempt by her conscience to force her to start now. But some of Jane's words still lingered in the corners of her mind and had whispered to her at most inconvenient times during the night.

The next morning Lydia announced that she intended visiting Longbourn. She rested her knife on the plate and looked at her sister; it was as if Jane was deaf.

"Would you arrange the carriage, Jane?" she pressed further, "for it looks like rain and it is a long walk there and back. I do not expect to stay out too long."

Jane glanced at her coolly. "I am sure that could be arranged, but it will need to be put off until tomorrow now; I have need of it for my own purposes today."

"Then you can take me to Longbourn before you attend to your own affairs. Mamma will be delighted to see me, I know, and Kitty too; I have such a great deal to tell. I shall not need to be collected until quite late."

Jane, seeing her silence did nothing to quell her sister's determination, relented grudgingly.

"I suppose that will be the best way, but you must make your own arrangements for your return if you do not know how long you will be. Remember that Father's carriage is not always available for family use."

Her advice fell on deaf ears; Lydia had already excused herself from the table to prepare for her visit. What a lot she had to tell about her life in Newcastle! She rather hoped that Lady Lucas and Maria would both be visiting so they would also have the benefit of her news.

Jane sighed as she watched her sister fly out of the room; she was irrepressible indeed. When she had aired her concerns about Lydia to Charles the previous evening, he had assured her that she was concerning herself unduly; he was certain nothing untoward had prompted this unexpected visit but was merely a desire on Lydia's part to visit her family and home. She had been exiled for a while and it was natural that she should miss it. When Jane mentioned Lydia's tales of happiness in her marriage, he had merely shrugged, declaring that no one can ever really know the truth about any other person's private life and to take Lydia's words as she wished them to be taken. Jane decided to wait for advice from Lizzy, which she hoped would arrive very soon.

Unfortunately, the next missive to arrive was Lizzy's announcement that she had taken a chill and was confined to bed for the next few days; however, she assured Jane, the enforced rest would enable her to communicate with Lydia and discover any possible reasons for her visit, '… and knowing as we do, the character of our poor sister's husband, we should certainly encourage her to return sooner rather than later, before whatever imaginary insult that prompted the visit is magnified into other, more tangible reasons for her disgust at him, and his for her!'

Elizabeth had gritted her teeth when she had responded to Jane's plea for information with such airy nonsense, knowing as she did the true state of affairs between Lydia and Wickham. The very best solution was for Lydia to return immediately, just as she intended advising in the half-formed letter that lay awaiting its completion upon the desk. It was a letter that had to be carefully worded but very clear in its message. There could be no room for misunderstanding by its recipient.

Almost a week later, Lydia received the finished letter in the morning mail and gasped at the contents. She quickly re-read her sister's words and checked the money folded inside. Her heart sank as she stuffed it into her pocket before Jane noticed; it would be sufficient merely for her return travel to Newcastle. Jane, fortunately, was immersed in her own letter from Lizzy and smiled as she finished it. She looked up at Lydia.

"Elizabeth seems to have recovered from her illness; she says she intends going for a short walk tomorrow if the weather holds. She wants to visit the site of a bluebell grove that Mr. Darcy mentioned to her but thinks it will certainly be too early to see anything just yet. Does not that sound delightful, Lydia?"

"Yes; *delightful*. I am sure she will do just as she pleases and that the bluebells will certainly know about it if they are not already blooming early for her. Excuse me, Jane; I must go to my room."

Once in the safety of her room, Lydia re-read her sister's advice. How sensible! How conventional indeed! *He has not mistreated you in any way* - Lydia sniffed angrily - *Go home, Lydia, before it is too late.* Lydia felt her eyes blurring as she read the calm and detached recommendations deemed necessary by her sister in order to regain her felicity in marriage. But how could she return to a life that was not what she had hoped for? There was no security, no stability, not the smallest of luxuries. How would they survive without money or the means to accumulate any?

It was all impossible, indeed it was. Life had become impossible: the never-ending demands for payment; the drinking and the drunkenness; the late night 'meetings', leaving her alone. Bursting into tears of self-pity, Lydia threw herself upon the bed and sobbed uncontrollably for her lost youth, innocence, and dreams until she exhausted herself into a deep sleep.

But the next morning, much to her sister's astonishment and quiet relief, Lydia announced her intention of leaving the very next day if her sister would be so kind as to arrange for an escort. Wickham, she announced, had written to say he could no longer endure her absence and demanded her return to Newcastle immediately.

"I must make one last visit to Longbourn and Lucas Lodge and say farewell to all my dear family and friends before I leave, for who shall say when I may return? I am certain that there are many more in Newcastle who have *long* wished for my return and I shall be hard pressed to fulfil all of my outstanding engagements. Will you come with me to Longbourn, Jane? I am sure they would be glad to see you once in a while, you know."

"Did you ever discover the reason behind the visit, my dear?" enquired Bingley as he stood with his wife waving goodbye. "Was there any great circumstance as you feared, or merely a desire to see her family - a homesickness - that determined it, as I guessed?"

"I have no insight to offer upon the matter, I assure you, Charles. She did not see fit to take me into her confidence, particularly after I reminded her of a few home truths which she had conveniently forgotten. Anyway; let us hope that she does not intend making a habit of it, although I believe she found Meryton rather too confining for her now compared to the freedom and excitement she has in Newcastle. Perhaps this has settled her mind and any homesickness has been quite resolved."

"Then it has been a worthwhile journey, my dear, and we shall enjoy our privacy all the more now we have it back again." Bingley kissed his wife's cheek and smiled at her warmly. "I was happy to arrange the necessary escort for her, of course, as you see, but may I enquire how much you pressed upon her to help with the other aspects of her journey?"

Jane blushed slightly. "Oh - a trifling amount - nothing more than will buy her a meal at the inns as she changes carriages. I could not allow her to travel without sufficient money for her needs, Charles, and I have enough to spare for my sister. But I thank you for the escort, on Lydia's behalf, as I know she will not have thought anything of it and so did not thank you herself."

Bingley smiled ruefully. "There is no need for that, my dear, but it would appear she is *extremely* well taken care of for this journey, as the amount she received from me was for the same purpose and any further expenses she may encounter upon her return home! We have certainly provided more than she expected, I am sure, but I wish her well of it, if it can smooth her way just a little. I do not believe that life with a man such as Wickham can be easy, and I pity her the road she will have to face with him by her side."

Jane hugged him closely. "Then I am glad we both feel the same way about helping those less fortunate than ourselves; we are so happy and blessed. I also fear for her happiness and security even if her situation is of her own making. I hope very much that the money will ease that situation, for a while at least."

Happily knowing they had been duped out of a sizable sum of money, neither person felt the usual anger most would feel at such a deception; neither person thought to enquire why Lydia had not mentioned the other's generosity and forestalled a double gift as both knew the answer, but also knew what drove her silence and did not blame her for it in the slightest. They turned back into the house as the carriage bearing Lydia disappeared from view around the last bend in the drive and the sound of the horses' hooves on the gravel faded into the distance.

The pair parted company at the door to the library where Bingley excused himself to write urgently to Darcy regarding a problem to do with the estate and to request some advice on the same. Jane had similar work awaiting her and hastened to her parlour where she could finally write a response to her sister and enquire about any news from that quarter.

Netherfield House
February 14th 18 ~

My dearest Lizzy,

I was very glad to receive news that you have recovered from your bout of illness and are back to your usual pursuits. I can imagine you exploring the woods around Pemberley and discovering all they have to offer. How I long for the opportunity to visit you; it seems strange that I do not know what your home is like, the views from the windows, the village and the countryside around. Even though you have described it, and I have had some of it from our father, I cannot rest until I have seen everything with my own eyes. What a happy day that will be!

Charles and I have just waved off our sister who is today returning to Newcastle. She seemed in very great high spirits and seemed to wish for nothing more than to be reunited with her husband and friends in the North. It has been a surprising and very peculiar visit. Her manner upon arrival was one of some great secret that could not be shared and she tended to dwell on the past year in a most unforgiving and cynical manner; she even accused our father of mistreatment - which I refuted vehemently – you would have been very proud of me, Lizzy!

But then, she quickly reverted to her usual open self, reminiscing happily upon the shocking events of last year, anxious to visit friends and family and re-instate herself into her old life here in Meryton, flaunting her new position as a married woman. Mamma and Kitty were delighted to have her visit every day and I was most astonished that she did not decide to remain with them, but preferred to return here to us every evening, for which, I suppose, we should take some comfort in being worthy of attention even if we are not as amusing as other company to be had.

She made no mention of wishing to return to Wickham, indeed she did not speak of him at all for an entire week, but then, all of a sudden, almost overnight, she announced her intention of her immediate return on the following day, stating that Wickham had written and requested her presence; that he could no longer endure her absence. It was all very strange - none of the servants recall a letter arriving for her other than yours, of course - it was all we could do to arrange her transport and escort for the ride home in time, she was in such a rush. But Charles managed everything and so she is gone. It is relief to know that all is well between them again as, I confess, I worried a dreadful rift had developed causing the sudden separation.

I have no doubt that my new-found solitude will be of a limited duration; our mother will soon appear and take a great deal of consoling upon the matter of losing her daughter so soon after having regained her. Wish me well for that, dear sister, as none of us can equal Lydia in amusing wit and entertaining stories, as you very well know.

I write in hope that we shall see each other very soon, as even though I know it has been only a short time apart, I find I miss my sister terribly.

Stay well my dear,

Jane

Elizabeth put her letter down at almost the same moment that Darcy did the same. They looked across the table at each other. Darcy grimaced.

"It would appear that Bingley and Jane have had the pleasure of your sister, Lydia's, company for the past few weeks and she has just departed for Newcastle and Wickham. Bingley says that they have no idea of what precipitated her dash South, nor what prompted her sudden decision to return North again. Do you have any light to shed upon their confusion, my dear?"

Elizabeth smiled brightly. "No; indeed! How could I? Lydia's has always been an impulsive nature and once she takes something into her head, she must act upon it immediately. Clearly whatever it was that prompted her travels has been resolved to her satisfaction. Jane did write to tell me of the unexpected visit and Lydia managed a few lines also, but knowing your abhorrence of anything to do with her or her husband, I thought better of apprising you of the details. I have no intention of allowing the antics of my sister to affect your or my peace and happiness. Jane intimates here in this letter that she believes something was amiss with the relationship but she has no certain facts, and so I shall not concern myself, either. I shall advise Jane to do the same and commiserate with her for having had to endure a most self-centred house guest whose consideration is only for and about herself."

Darcy noticed her impatience and glanced back at his letter.

"It is unfortunate that Bingley still has not found his own house to buy – he writes to me about the matter here in his letter – they are still at such close quarters to your family and so will always be inevitably involved in all of their sudden dramas." He smiled. "It is convenient indeed that Derbyshire is several counties removed from Hertfordshire, is not it?"

"Yes, and it is *not* an easy distance, as I recall you once mentioning as a beneficial aspect with regards to Kent and my friend Charlotte." Elizabeth responded, casting him a sideways look to see if he recalled the circumstances of that statement.

He returned her smile with a knowing look which sent warm tingles up her spine.

"I recall very well saying that and stand by my thoughts on the matter. However, as I also remember saying to you, I could not think that you would always wish to be near Meryton, and now you are not. I wished to ascertain that living so far away from your own family would not cause you too much grief, and it would seem that you are perfectly content being several days' journey from them."

He raised his eyebrows quizzically; he knew his wife well enough by now that he was sure this was the case, but did not flatter himself that he knew every thought in her head.

Lizzy nodded and looked at Jane's neat writing lying beside her plate.

"I am truly the happiest of women, of that you can rest assured, my darling, with the smallest of regrets that my dear sister is so far away. That is the only instance where distance troubles me."

"Then we shall have to work upon Bingley and encourage him to view properties I shall seek out for him within an easy distance of Pemberley; he asks for just such assistance here. How would that suit you, my dear, having Jane back within calling distance again?"

Lizzy's eye glinted with sudden tears. "*Oh!* That would be the very thing I could ever wish for to make my happiness utterly complete. And when you find those properties, I will insist upon viewing them with you; only the best will do for my sister."

Chapter 12

February moved slowly by with dark mornings and afternoons, and frosty walks revealing only a few snowdrops that dared to push their heads up through the snow for especial delight; Nature certainly took her time in announcing the advent of Spring this far North.

Every day when the weather allowed it, Elizabeth walked through the woods and lanes, meeting very few other persons in her rambles, and began to have an appreciation of just how secluded Georgiana's life had been living here, secure and comfortable as it was. The poor girl did not appear to have any close friends in the area and Lizzy pondered, as she marched along on her solitary walks, the difference between her own life in Meryton with what her new sister's must have been.

In Meryton there had been a large network of families and friends, aunts and uncles, to call upon and gossip with; Georgiana appeared to have none of those easy relationships. No wonder she relied so completely upon her brother, and in the past, George Wickham, as her only source of amusement. No wonder she was so dedicated to her piano and work; what else was there in that great house to interest her all day? And absolutely no wonder Georgiana had been so overwhelmed by her sudden introduction to the attractions and excitements of London and Ramsgate; any young girl would have had her head turned with so much unfamiliar attention suddenly being directed at her, never mind one who had been so far removed from any sort of society.

Lizzy decided that she would make it her aim to improve Georgiana's social sphere. The ball had given her a glimpse into what could be done if plans were made, and Darcy did not appear averse to entertaining in general, although she believed another ball might be rather too much to expect, but other smaller and more intimate gatherings comparable to those offered at Lucas Lodge or even Longbourn, could certainly be arranged. And, she reflected, if she was honest, it was not all concern about her sister that prompted these plans. Although she delighted in everything her marriage had brought her and regretted nothing, the stillness of the house every day and the lack of society was becoming stultifying.

Darcy did not notice such things, indeed it was astonishing that he had noticed his sister's need and suggested the ball, but he was a man and had many things with which to occupy his days; it was not his duty to entertain either his sister nor his wife, Lizzy reminded herself, so she must arrange her own life and foster her own interests.

There had been many visitors to Pemberley when she and Darcy had returned from their wedding last November; everyone had called to pay their respects and to wish them well in their marriage - and to evaluate the new Mrs. Darcy and discover her good points as well as the bad to fuel gossip around many a Winter fire - but the weather since Christmas had discouraged any further outings either to Pemberley or from. However, blaming the weather for their solitude was not the answer.

Lizzy recalled how her friend, Charlotte, had immediately settled into her new life in Hunsford at the same time of year, with no excuses or problems. She had decided to prove herself useful around the neighbourhood, and, thought Lizzy, why should not she and Georgiana also prove themselves just as useful around Lambton?

Yes, though Lizzy, as she puffed up a rather steep path, it was certainly time to begin the social round within the Pemberley Estate and around Lambton Village and to be seen as an active, useful sort of person rather than a distant and aloof lady of the manor. It was essential for Georgiana, for Darcy, and most particularly, herself.

Entering the quiet house, warmed by her exercise, she heard the muted sounds of the pianoforte and walked towards the music room. Smiling at her sister, she sat next to her and waited while she finished the piece.

"You are very rosy-cheeked, Lizzy, you must have walked far this morning. The heightened colour becomes you, although perhaps the windswept hairstyle is a little unorthodox!"

Elizabeth patted her hair unconcernedly. "Well, who is to see my appearance other than you, Darcy and the servants? I have always had trouble presenting a perfect feminine picture, and I shall continue in that vein, I should imagine. Outward appearance is not everything, you know, Georgiana; it is foolish to place any more than a slight value upon it, as I have learnt to my cost.

"Now, I have a proposal for you which I shall discuss with your brother but I am sure he cannot have any argument against. We, as the ladies of Pemberley, must begin to make ourselves useful. We cannot hide away from society and keep our good fortune to ourselves. We must become acquainted with those of our neighbours whom we have not yet met."

"Oh! But the weather deters anyone but you from venturing out, Elizabeth. I can hardly bear to look out at the grey dullness of it all, knowing how my feet and hands should tingle with the cold if I were to venture into it. But I suppose if we were to use the carriage and lots of blankets and mufflers, we should not mind it so much. With whom do you intend to start, sister?"

Lizzy smiled at her sister's reluctance to endure any kind of deprivation but pressed on.

"I thought to visit Parson Wheeler this afternoon and offer our services to the needy and sick in the village. I should very much like to do some good for our neighbours through visiting and helping to make their Winter endurable."

Georgiana sucked in her breath; visiting the poor! She had not envisaged that. Visiting the long-established neighbours on local estates was bad enough but, at this time of year, this new notion was beyond duty, surely?

Elizabeth waited and watched the thoughts visibly cross her sister's face and then smiled.

"I am sure your dear mother fulfilled such a role in the neighbourhood, Georgiana, a role that has been sorely neglected in the long years since her demise. I do not fault you in this, naturally; how could you ever have known it is something which came under your remit as lady of the house? But now I have thought of it, I shall not be diverted. It is a neglected duty which needs to be revived and I intend doing so, with or without your help. I have no doubt that your brother will encourage me in this and would be glad to see you also taking an active role. We have a responsibility, Georgiana; it is a small payment for the comfortable and easy life we are privileged to live."

Georgiana shifted uncomfortably on her bench. She had an abhorrence of meeting new people and hated forcing herself onto others' attention. Ever since her mortifying escapades in London and then Ramsgate, she had purposefully kept herself to herself, hiding away from anyone who might have learnt of it from acquaintances. She had no desire for company, to be the topic for gossip and criticism, but she could see her sister was in earnest.

"If you think my brother will approve your plan, then I will accompany you as far as Mr. Wheeler's this afternoon," she agreed reluctantly, "but I am sure there can be nothing of great need in our small village; I am sure my brother is already taking care of those who need it, Elizabeth."

"I am sure he is, my dear, but only as far as a man may do; we women have a far superior skill in providing support of another kind altogether."

Darcy, once he recalled the affection with which his mother had been held by all those in the village, due partly to her selfless devotion to visiting the sick and needy, and partly to her charming and unassuming demeanour, agreed wholeheartedly with Elizabeth's plan and the inclusion of his sister in it.

He had long since been concerned about Georgiana's retiring nature and insistence upon solitude, knowing as he did from what events it stemmed, but had been unable to persuade her out of it: not through appeals to her duty, disputing her imagined sense of humiliation, nor his teasing reference to the utter lack of suitable husbands to be found within the confines of the Pemberley Estate, and had eventually thought it best to leave her to her own devices. Now his dear wife had managed what he had failed to do; first the ball, which had been a great success - everyone had spoken of it most animatedly - and now had conceived an idea which was long overdue.

"And when do you propose to begin this activity, my dear?"

"Immediately; I see no reason not to now we have your approval, dearest. We shall call upon the parson directly and enquire how we may begin and with whom. I think that the best way do not you? He will certainly know the needs of his parishioners and will be able to advise us."

"I believe so, and you would be rewarded also by enquiring of Mrs. Reynolds; she has her own sources, particularly regarding those who live immediately on the estate. She would be happy to advise you. But take care; you may find yourself overwhelmed. Very little of this sort has been seen since the death of our mother many years ago; everyone will want a visit regardless of their need!"

"Oh! Georgiana and I have no concerns upon that score, Darcy. I only hope we are not viewed with suspicion, or regarded as having ulterior motives, or considered intrusive, all of which Charlotte warned me happened to her in the first weeks and months of her work in Hunsford."

"Do you think they will not appreciate our visits, Elizabeth?" Georgiana queried nervously. "For if they would rather not, then I am sure I would be the last person to intrude upon their privacy."

"No, no, sister; you do not escape your duty so easily at the first hint of trouble, however imagined it might be," scolded Darcy. "Elizabeth is quite correct; our duty towards the village and estate has been severely lacking and it is essential that it be put right. It does not do to be so removed from one's workers and tenants, and you will both be perfectly pleasant and welcome visitors, I am sure, and will not find many doors closed to you!" Darcy laughed as he got up.

"They would not dare, in any case, but I am certain those you visit will appreciate the gesture and your interest in their welfare. Now, speak with Mrs. Reynolds first; you should start with our immediate family, those who work tirelessly in our service. I am sure there are several who would enjoy quiet consolation and interested enquiry."

And so it was. The sisters quickly found themselves busy every day that allowed it, and even on some when the weather was inclement, their sense of duty over-ruling their regard for comfort. Every morning the carriage was brought to the front steps and the ladies, acting firstly upon Mrs. Reynolds' recommendations, but later upon their own knowledge of need, sallied forth and met and sat, and listened, and talked, and commiserated, and equally importantly, discovered the very great need some families had of extra supplies of food or clothing to see them through the Winter months.

Georgiana's eyes were opened widely; she had not known the extent of her brother's responsibility. Her previous visits into Lambton had been fleeting affairs on minor errands and she had barely left the confines of her carriage. She privately blushed with shame at what everyone must have thought of her behaviour; so fine and grand that she could not even spend some time amongst her neighbours.

And, gradually, over the weeks, she became quite accustomed to visiting the sick, or the elderly and listening quietly to their stories, several becoming her firm favourites and she, theirs; those who managed whatever troubles had been thrown their way with a cheerfulness and determination encouraged her to recognise the very great good fortune she had always enjoyed her entire life. It was a new Georgiana who returned to Pemberley every day, full of stories and ideas of what needed to be done. Elizabeth smiled as she watched her sister's improvement and Darcy more than once whispered in her ear how thankful he was to her for bringing about such a pleasant change in his sister.

Their heightened visibility in the area was not long in being noticed and this in turn brought about a new flurry of calling cards and visits from neighbours who wished to discuss their new sociability over tea and cakes. The whole neighbourhood, it now seemed, was conscious of the fact that since the new Mrs. Darcy had arrived, a breath of fresh air had blown through Pemberley, a place that had long kept its windows firmly closed and its doors locked, and all agreed it was a most pleasant and interesting change.

Chapter 13

Busy as she had become, Lizzy had put Lydia's problems to the back of her mind and was, therefore, surprised to see her sister's hand upon a letter one morning. Not without a slight feeling of dread, she broke the seal and quickly skimmed the contents, surmising whatever was contained therein could not be good news. She was not mistaken.

Newcastle Barracks
March 27th 18 ~
Lizzy,

I hope you are satisfied. I took your advice, cruel and unsympathetic as it was, and returned here to my marriage and husband but found both in the identical state in which I left them. I have struggled these past weeks, Lizzy, remembering your words, to act as you directed. I have tried to speak with Wickham on the matter of our finances; I have tried to appease him in every way, to appeal to his sense of duty, to bring about the lost happiness we had enjoyed together in Brighton and, for a short time, here in Newcastle. I am not innocent of some of our problems and I have curtailed my own amusements in an attempt to display that better behaviour you suggested, but he will not be moved; he has ignored my attempts.

I have tried, Lizzy, truly, I have, but it is impossible. You might think your advice was in the best interest for all concerned but I assure you that it was not. He has become worse in his neglect of me since my return than ever he was before; it is almost as if he had hoped I would remain away and thus relieve him of his obligation.

You say that I must stay with him regardless of what he does, as he is my husband; that others have suffered what I am now suffering, and I can hear your strictures about his and my behaviour being a consequence of our actions. If I did not know better, and that you are happily married to your Mr. Darcy, I should believe you to be jealous of me winning Wickham, Lizzy, and that is why you insist upon my being miserable and suffering the consequences in silence. Well, I have never been one to suffer in silence and I do not intend doing so now.

I write to you now in dire need. He has just informed me that he intends travelling into London upon some business and that I must arrange to stay with one of my sisters, or my parents, as he is giving up these lodgings immediately. He refuses to say why he cannot take me with him to London, a place I should very much like to visit, but it is, of course, for the reason that he cannot afford to rent a house there and therefore must stay in other, less pleasant, lodgings. He did not say as much but I understand more than people give me credit for. I thought that I should arrange to stay with you Lizzy, as you are closer and I have only just been with Jane and enjoyed all that Meryton has to offer.

You must reply by return; my hopes depend upon you being kind to me, Lizzy. Wickham will travel with me into Derbyshire and go on from there. I cannot tell you how long you should expect my visit to be as Wickham is being most uncommunicative about the whole affair, but I can only surmise that his business will be of a protracted nature.

I wait to hear from you soon, Lizzy. It will be so exciting to see your new home - although I am rather apprehensive about meeting Mr. Darcy over the breakfast dishes!

With love,

Lydia

Elizabeth paled as she read the letter and then placed it face down upon her desk before rising and walking about the room, pausing in front of the small fire and watching the flames as she thought of what to do next, and what to say to Darcy. Her other letters lay unopened in a small pile, and she returned to the desk opening them all slowly: one from Jane; one from Charlotte; another from Lady Campion who lived on a neighbouring estate, and one in an unknown hand. Jane and Charlotte's were happy missives, full of gossip and intimate details of their small daily lives and Lizzy smiled as she skimmed over them; she would re-read and respond to them later once she had dealt with Lydia's request. Lady Campion would also have to wait. Lizzy paused before opening the mystery letter; the writing of her address so bold she could only think it to be from another neighbour. She opened it and immediately turned to the back, gasping when she read the signatory: *Yours with affection, Geo. Wickham Esq.*

With a racing heart, she turned back to the beginning and read:

My dear sister,

It has been a very long time since last we met and I hope you have thought gently of me in that time. I hope, indeed, that what passed between us upon my marriage to your sister has diffused sufficiently and enabled you to accept me as your friend, at least, even though I know Darcy will never agree to those terms between him and me again.

I find that business calls me from Newcastle to London very shortly and I would request a favour, if my wife has not already requested it. I cannot say how long this business will take, but it must be attempted; those of us without ready-made fortunes are forced to seek them for ourselves, and if I do not go, your sister's future security will be materially affected.

Unfortunately, Lydia cannot accompany me thither - much as she might wish it - and therefore I request that you offer her your hospitality until I can return with news of my success. I cannot make this request of Darcy, as you know, and rely upon your good nature and the kindness you have always shown me, and not fail me in this instance.

I will write again when I know the exact date of our departure from Newcastle, but it will certainly be within the next few weeks as my business cannot be delayed further than that.

Yours with affection,

Geo. Wickham Esq.

With trembling hands, Lizzy placed the second letter beside the first and sank into her chair.

Why? Why must Lydia's mistakes, her bad choices, always affect everyone else's happiness?

But it was clear; they were to have a guest, and very soon, and Darcy could not be kept ignorant of that fact any longer than it would take to relay the details. She picked up the letters and walked along to the study where Darcy was consulting with his manager. The men smiled at her entry, Darcy immediately noticing her pale complexion and the letters in her hand.

"My dear? You look very shocked; what news has upset you? Is it your family?"

Lizzy mutely handed the letters over to him and sank into a chair, the manager solicitously leaving them alone. She watched as he quickly read Wickham's first, and then Lydia's, the line between his eyes deepening. He slammed the letters down and thrust his hand through his hair, bowing his head for a moment before fixing his eyes upon Lizzy.

"What does your sister mean by *your advice*, Elizabeth? You did not tell me you had given her advice. What advice and why, pray?"

Elizabeth sighed. "Yes, I did tell you, although I did not tell you everything. I wanted to shield you from some of her behaviour and demands; I am not proud of my sister."

"And I am not proud of my former friend but I tell you everything I do with regard to him. I do not need protection from either of them, Elizabeth, and I wish you had not kept this to yourself; divided we are weak against their importunities."

"Well, you did not tell me *everything*, my dear; indeed, you told me very little about certain activities of yours, if I remember correctly; Georgiana and I had to piece things together only recently, and my aunt told me the rest.

"But there you have it; now you know. Lydia wrote to me privately after she had left Wickham and turned up at Netherfield, as Bingley told you. She claimed that she did not feel secure in her marriage to Wickham, that he was involved in some business which kept him out late every night; that he was being inattentive and uncaring. I merely advised her, in no uncertain terms, that she had to endure whatever her husband chose to do, and that she must return to Newcastle and work upon her marriage. I was the only one to whom she told her worries; Jane and Mamma merely imagined her visit to be a result of homesickness."

Darcy looked long and hard at her as her explanation tailed off, as if trying to read if there was any other information she was concealing.

"And now this 'business' calls him to London, and he cannot afford to have his wife accompany him; therefore, he assumes she must come here. A fine excuse! I would like to know how he can be absent from his position in Newcastle for an extended period. But I shall not enquire; I can imagine well enough what his real reason is.

"Write to your sister and tell her that she may come as our guest, but Wickham must not venture closer to Pemberley than Lambton where she will be collected. There is little use in enquiring further about the extent of her visit as she, naturally, will still have no idea, and I refuse to ask that husband of hers. But I have a very bad feeling about this, Elizabeth; it is of grave concern when a husband abandons his wife and cannot explain why or for how long. But we must do what we can, and who knows, perhaps Lydia will learn some decorum during her stay here."

"Yes, perhaps, but I would not expect anything quite as drastic as that. She has managed to evade all efforts thus far so there is little reason to expect her to do so now. But even she will understand her position to be tenuous when she comes here, even she cannot imagine herself entirely welcome, and that may produce some alteration in her behaviour.

"But I will write, as you say, and remind her that Wickham is not to come onto the grounds; that she will be met at the Inn at Lambton. I am afraid it will be a protracted stay, Darcy, and you will not be the first to wish her gone."

Elizabeth rose, brushed a kiss against his cheek before returning to her parlour to find Georgiana comfortably ensconced in front of the fire, reading her own letters and smiling at the contents.

"Elizabeth! Good morning; I have such happy letters from some friends in London."

Elizabeth smiled thinly and sat opposite Georgiana. "I'm glad your correspondence has brought you joy, my dear."

Georgiana looked more closely at her sister. "But what is in your letters, Elizabeth; not bad news, I hope?"

"There are degrees of badness, I suppose. It would seem that you will very soon have your wish to meet my sister; she intends joining us in a week or so for what will probably be a rather prolonged visit."

"Oh, *Kitty*! How delightful. Is she coming with your father; does he intend returning so soon to my brother's books and trees?"

"No, not Kitty; I rather wish it was that sister, for your sake as well as my own. No; it is my youngest sister, Lydia, of whom I speak; Lydia *Wickham*, I am afraid, my dear," Elizabeth added gently.

Georgiana, shocked, looked up at Lizzy and then at the fire. She could think of nothing to say. Eventually, upon regaining her composure, she asked, "And Wickham? Does he accompany her?"

"Good *God*, no! Of course he does not. Your brother would never allow George Wickham to set foot inside the furthest corner of the Pemberley Estate, and nor should he. I never wish to improve my acquaintance with him, either, after all the trouble he has caused my family and yours."

"It is quite alright, Elizabeth. I have told my brother several times that Wickham was never trying to seduce me; I know now that he was entirely taken up with Mrs. Younge. He was merely charming and attentive to me as a friend and wished to ensure I enjoyed my time in London and Ramsgate. He had no notion how his attention would be perceived by a young and inexperienced girl quite out of her depth and willing to impute all manner of romantic designs where none actually existed. I would not have you think so harshly of him on my account. Your sister had the good fortune to win him, even away from Mrs. Younge, and I shall be glad to know her when she arrives. I am sure she will liven up our society here at Pemberley."

"Well, I hope you will not be too shocked by her behaviour and manners whilst livening up our society, and that you will be able to exert some of your refinement upon my sister, Georgiana; she will benefit from any she can get, believe me. Our family has tried to influence her over the years but she has resisted us all."

"I am sure she will behave properly, if not for me, then from fear of my brother! Many people find themselves behaving much better when he is present. I will leave you to reply to your letters, Elizabeth, and I look forward to making the acquaintance of your sister very soon."

Elizabeth nodded doubtfully and went to her desk where she penned two very short letters: one to Lydia instructing her to bring only what she needed, and warning her that any misbehaviour would result in her being sent packing to Longbourn; the second to Wickham, reiterating Darcy's instructions and a fervent hope that Wickham would, indeed, return very quickly with success and fortune at his heels to retrieve his wife and resume their life together.

She re-read both, affixed the seals and sent for the servant to ensure they caught the afternoon mail.

Chapter 14

It was no more than a week before Wickham responded coolly to Elizabeth's letter, assuring her of his expectation that his business would prove fruitful in a very short space of time, at which juncture he would be delighted to whisk Lydia away to a life of riches and happiness such as she deserved. Mrs. Wickham would be in Lambton the day after next on the four o'clock coach.

Lizzy drew a steadying breath and marched her missive down to Darcy who was reading a letter of his own in his study. He smiled as she entered.

"Here is good news indeed; our joint efforts at convincing my aunt that she should come to Pemberley have been effective, Elizabeth. She writes to say she will be leaving Kent in two days and will be with us two days after that. She anticipates she will stay for a month before her return to Rosings where, she says, she expects to reciprocate our hospitality whilst I check the estate in the Spring with Fitzwilliam as I usually do.

"Well, naturally, I did not envisage her taking such a long visit with us – two weeks would have been more than sufficient, perhaps even one – but she mentions her anticipation of being re-acquainted with my dear wife – that, I believe, refers to you, my dear – and my sister, whom she has not seen in many years."

He paused as he re-read another few lines. "Ah, yes; and she mentions that she has every intention of bringing Anne with her this time - health permitting, I imagine - who has expressed some disappointment at always being at Rosings and wishes to see more of the world.

"There! What have you to say to that? It is all you wished for – reconciliation between my aunt and us, and company for an extended visit."

He laughed at Lizzy's astonishment, tailing away as she repeated,

"In *four* days, Darcy? Lady Catherine and Anne de Bourgh will arrive? Here? In four days? Oh, this is not going to go well at all, my dear; is there anything that can be done to delay their visit?"

Mutely, she handed him her letter and nodded as she saw the dawning of realisation grow across his face.

"I see that you understand now that a problem of some magnitude is about to descend upon this house, far removed from the happy reconciliation you envisage, and I do not think that even a house this size will be large enough to accommodate both my sister and the de Bourghs in tranquillity. But what is to be done?"

Darcy shrugged. "What is to be done, indeed? There is nothing at all to be done and we should not attempt to intervene. It seems that Lady Catherine and Anne will have not only the pleasure of making themselves agreeable to you, my dearest wife, but also of extending that courteous behaviour towards your wayward sister; it promises to be an interesting visit at the very least."

"Yes; but I predict an immediate curtailment of her visit. Lady Catherine will certainly decide that a month is far too long in such shocking company, much longer than she can tolerate and something, anything, will call her away early. If there is one thing I know about Lady Catherine it is that she has no tolerance for opinionated and reckless young women, and my sister has never cared about the opinion of anybody; neither of them will be able to bear the other for very long.

"It should be, as you say, an interesting visit, but at least Lady Catherine's opinion of me can only improve when she has Lydia as comparison!"

Darcy caught Lizzy up in his arms, seemingly undaunted at the impending disaster about to strike his house. He kissed her quickly and she laughed up at him.

"Do you see what happens, my dearest man, when you marry such a worthless and disgraceful person against the advice of your aunt? You are forever embroiled in my family's disgraceful behaviour and cannot show your face again in public! Lady Catherine warned you, did not she? And will be very glad to know her predictions were in every way, correct."

"On the contrary; her predictions were in no way correct. I would happily face any trouble instigated by your family if it means I shall always have you by my side, Elizabeth. You know you have made me the happiest man in England; everything else is as nothing to me."

"The happiest man in England, indeed," teased Lizzy as she leant back in his arms to look into his face. "Surely not; I believe that title was claimed by my cousin when he was so fortunate to gain the affection of my friend. Your happiness can never come close to comparing with his, I am afraid."

There was silence for several minutes as the clocks ticked on unperturbedly, the pair only breaking apart at a knock on the study door. Georgiana peeked her head around and blushed when she saw the couple clearly moving out of an embrace. She made to leave in confusion but Lizzy called her back.

"Georgiana! Come in, do. We have even more news to share with you. Not only is my sister to arrive in two days' time, but also Lady Catherine and Anne de Bourgh are to arrive very shortly afterwards. We shall have a very full social calendar keeping them all entertained and, more importantly, out of each other's way. You must accumulate great stores of calm and patience, my dear, for a very large storm is gathering over Pemberley. We must hurry and do as much of our visiting as we can in the next day or so, as we shall have to neglect our duties to attend to our guests and stop them from attacking one another!"

"Well! That is good news indeed; now I shall have two young ladies to become acquainted with. I think that Anne must be quite different from your sister, Elizabeth?"

"Oh, indeed she is!" Elizabeth laughed. "You might say they are on the opposite ends of the spectrum of young ladies;

everything about them will throw the other's behaviour into relief. It will be quite an education for you, Georgiana, to be able to observe and learn. I have no doubt that your aunt will not hold back in voicing her opinions on the comparison, either."

Darcy laughed at Georgiana's shocked expression. "It will be a spectacle indeed, Georgiana, and one worth studying, as Elizabeth says, especially your aunt's reaction to Lydia; there will be power plays, back-stabbings, caustic remarks, mutterings, and threats of dark deeds from both sides, but we must merely observe and ensure we stay out of danger."

"You make it sound like wild beasts are visiting instead of three ladies, brother. It is quite shocking how you speak; I am sure Mamma never allowed such thoughts about her sister to be spoken aloud and with such candour."

"You must blame me, sister," smiled Lizzy as she linked her arm through Georgiana's. "I am the bad influence upon your brother's manners and, have no doubt, they will regress even further after Lydia and Lady Catherine are in residence. Beware! He will become more and more silent and scathing the longer they are here, and more reclusive; we shall be fortunate indeed if we manage to gain a glimpse of him once a day in the far distance. I have witnessed such behaviour before.

"Now, I must inform Mrs. Reynolds of our guests and which rooms should be made ready for them – as far apart as possible, I think - and I leave you, Darcy, to seriously deliberate on your sister's concerns regarding your deteriorating manners and behaviour." She raised her eyebrows at him and laughed as he did his best to look apologetic; he could never entirely manage to hide his true feelings.

In two days the carriage was dispatched in the afternoon and returned within the hour with Lydia and her several trunks. All were ensconced in a bright front bedroom and Lydia plumped herself upon the bed as her sister organised the unpacking of the trunks' contents. Once the servants had finished and left, Lydia smiled at Lizzy and patted the bed beside her.

"Come, Lizzy, sit with me. How pleasant this all is; I had no notion how much grander Pemberley is than Netherfield. This is a very comfortable room indeed; I might never wish to leave it! Oh! Do not look so shocked, I will not overstay my welcome. Wickham assures me he will return when he has arranged a new life for us - I know not where exactly, he gave me no particulars - but I hope him to be in earnest. He has an idea for his future which he is pursuing in London.

"I do hope we shall move to London, Lizzy. It would be a new start for us, and back where we began, really. How delightful that will be, to live in Town and go to the theatre and shows and have lots of elegant friends. You know I did not see anything of London when I was there last year; I was quite kept locked away, first by Wickham - for he wanted to keep me all to himself, he said - and then by our aunt and uncle who were most unpleasant indeed before the wedding, not allowing me any outings of any kind; I was almost a prisoner." She sighed at the memory.

"But now he has returned to London and I hope he will manage everything to his satisfaction. Tell me what Wickham told you, as I know he wrote to you, and you responded. What did he say? Did he inform you of some of his plans?"

"He told me nothing of any import, I assure you. I wish that he had so I could tell you and relieve your uncertainty. Merely that he intended to return after bringing about his business – of its success he seems absolutely certain – and he claims this separation is to be of a short duration, Lydia, his letter was most adamant on that fact, and I pray he is telling the truth."

"Oh, yes, I am sure he is telling the truth, Lizzy, but the truth as he wants to tell it, not as it will be. We have been living on his versions of the truth since we were married, and it is a difficult life, as I told you. I should be very surprised if he came back for me within a six-month if he is to be successful; I cannot think what he has organised in London that will assure him of his future in a shorter time, for if that was the case then we should not have been living as we have been for the past six months.

"Do you know how we managed to pay for our travel this time, Lizzy? No, I shall not tell you the particulars but know it was not *his* business ability or our frugal living that enabled it. Oh no, indeed not. In fact, some others are becoming much more adept than is he at increasing our portion, which is a good thing or we should have been starving before now, even with your and Jane's kindness.

"Oh, do not look so shocked, Lizzy. I have always enjoyed playing cards, as you very well remember, and I have become rather good at it, too. It is only a short step from playing for fish to playing for profit if you are careful, and I am most certainly careful, Lizzy; I have learnt to be. Do not concern yourself about that.

"But now I am here, and there will be nothing to do, no games to play and profit from in Derbyshire to feather my nest, and so I must rely entirely upon your hospitality for the duration. I might teach you something of my skills, Lizzy, as an entertainment for you and Darcy's sister."

"I thank you, no. For my part, I have no interest in card games played for profit and you will most certainly *not* disclose any of what you have said to me to Georgiana or Darcy. Is that understood? You are a guest of my husband's - against his will, I might add - and you will, therefore, take very great care to restrain your manners and behaviour to the expectations of this household."

"Yes, yes, Lizzy, I read your letter; I know how I must behave. But how dull it will be with no company, no parties, no assemblies! It will be worse than Meryton; there at least I had Mamma and Kitty. But you must introduce me to Georgiana immediately, thank goodness for someone close to my age. Even if she has not had my experience of life, we should have some things in common to talk about."

"You will refer to her as *Miss Darcy*, Lydia, until she gives you leave to do otherwise. And no, indeed, I imagine you will find you have very little in common with her, *not having had quite your experience*, as you say, but that is certainly something to be grateful for. She is a charming creature and I will not have you upsetting her in any way, is that clear?"

Lydia shrugged. "Of course not; what could I possibly say that would be upsetting to her? I will be on my best behaviour, I promise, Lizzy.

"Come; let me meet your new sister, and Darcy again, I suppose. Although I admit to some trepidation of that meeting, after the last time I saw him. He was most officious. He became quite heated about the situation when he found us in London and quite insisted upon me leaving Wickham, you know. He claimed it would be for the best, but I stood my ground; I wanted to be Mrs. Wickham and that is how it turned out to everybody's satisfaction."

"No, not to everybody's satisfaction, Lydia, not at all, but it is too late to remonstrate with you over the past. Just know that people were hurt by your actions and not all of them were of your close family. You acted selfishly and irresponsibly and were fortunate that your marriage was brought about without further scandal. That is why I advised you so strongly in my letter and I am glad you have taken my advice; you cannot easily undo past actions just because they do not turn out as you wished. I pray that Wickham has also seen sense and is even now working on a more stable future for you both."

"La! You sound just like Jane! She was quite angry about it, too. I have never seen her so cross, but, of course, crossness in Jane is not a terrifying thing at all, and is over very quickly. Well; I think I should like to tidy myself a little and then I shall join you and Georg... *Miss Darcy* ... downstairs when I am refreshed."

Elizabeth nodded and left the room and her sister's presence, dreading the weeks or months Lydia would occupy that room and the aggravations she knew were in store for both her and Darcy because of it. She straightened her shoulders as she descended the stairs to alert Georgiana of the imminent introduction.

Chapter 15

Wickham stood in the inn's courtyard, relief lifting his spirits as the carriage carried Lydia away to Pemberley. Her previous departure from him in Newcastle had been acrimonious, full of accusations and spiteful truths which he had immediately regretted; regardless of his lack of feeling towards her, it was no reason to hurt someone who had done nothing other than love and trust him. But this departure had an element of hope to it. The pressures of the last six months – the unpleasantness of army life, the unrelenting lack of ready funds, the demands of a spoilt wife, the devastating loss of Julia – had become increasingly unbearable and had begun to tell upon his patience and humour. He felt trapped; he was miserable, unhappier than he had ever been heretofore, and he could no longer endure his life's continual downward spiral.

Now that he had privately made the decision to leave the army - to seek his fortune amongst others with similar interests while re-capturing some semblance of his old life - he watched Lydia's departure with deep satisfaction. At least she would come to no harm at Pemberley; she would experience comfort and luxury unlike anything she had during her months of married life, and he nursed the quiet hope she would be in no rush to reclaim her position as his wife until she could be assured of a reasonable level of comfort being offered. Her casual estimate to her sister - that this separation would be far longer than the month he had predicted - was prescient, for Wickham had no great plan; no successful business awaiting him in London; no reason to believe that his life would be turned around in the short time he had claimed in his letter to Elizabeth.

But this uncertainty was nothing compared to his feeling of liberation as the Pemberley carriage disappeared down the road. He might have nothing particular in his foreseeable future, but he now had one less annoyance in his present and he returned to the inn's parlour with a spring in his step.

Over a tasty meal and several drinks, Wickham became even more optimistic concerning his future, convincing himself that he had only to get situated in London once again and all would be as it had been before: before Lydia; before Brighton; before causing the hurt in Julia's eyes.

If truth be told, if it could be arranged, he would like to replicate the happiest time he had spent in London, when he had been entrusted with the running of Julia's business while she was away with Georgiana in Ramsgate; a time when he had felt honourable, useful, and effective. He had managed to resurrect her business in a small way so that when she returned it had been something to be worked with. That is where he would like to reinstate himself: in business of some description, in London; an interesting business, naturally, one that would engage his mind away from the temptations of the gaming houses and other expensive distractions.

But what would such a business be? he mused, as he sat by the fire in the inn's parlour, engaging with no one for fear of being recognised by an inhabitant of the village. He had never before concerned himself with such thoughts; any work he had done in the past had been forced upon him as a consequence of his dishonourable behaviour. Even his army commission, bought for him by Darcy, had been forced upon him, but he was not a military man when it came down to it. His time in the Militia had been marked by nothing more than entertainments and socialising, which suited him very well, but life in the Regulars had not been so pleasant. It had palled after a very short duration and the remuneration certainly did not provide sufficient motivation to continue.

So he had decided to sell the commission, unbeknownst to Lydia, to get what he could for it – fortunately there were many others who still eagerly sought such a life – and use the proceeds to escape Newcastle before his creditors caught up with him and insisted upon settlement; he must have something with which to sustain his new venture, after all. He had prudently set aside enough for his needs in London, and managed to increase the remainder significantly at the tables in his remaining week in Newcastle. None of this had he related to Lydia whom, he knew, had also become quite adept at increasing her own small finances at the ladies' tables, just as she had begun to do in Brighton. She had actually crowed over him that she was perfectly able to provide the cost of her *own* transport to Derbyshire, and he had quietly allowed her that satisfaction, wanting her to know as little as possible of his plans and situation.

His mind flicked between possibilities for employment but the more he considered, the fewer seemed his choices. He felt his former indolence returning very quickly now that the strains of his life had been removed; nothing presented itself that would do; nothing seemed interesting enough, profitable enough, easy enough. He sighed and finished his drink, rose from the chair and bade the landlord a good night, reminding him that he would expect his horse to be waiting for him at seven o'clock the following morning, and retired for the night still mulling over his future.

A long journey in early April is arduous: while slightly better than November, the roads are invariably still fetlock-high in mud, with deep carriage-wheel grooves lying in treacherous wait for an unwary rider. Add to that a persistent, freezing rain and there is gained a fair indication of Wickham's journey South the next day. His cloak was soon soaked through and by the time he reached his inn for the next evening, he was in a very bitter humour indeed. His hired horse had been slow and uncomfortable, and his exposure to the elements had only increased his self-pity. He believed he would pay the extra cost involved and tomorrow take the coach into London instead. He grunted at the barman as he took his place on a stool and threw his cloak and jacket onto another chair; he was exceedingly uncomfortable and out of spirits.

"I will require a single room for the night, if you please," he said after taking a swill of his drink. "And some hot water and a large meal, for I have not eaten all day."

"That will be arranged for you immediately, sir," the man replied and went behind the bar to speak with his wife about the order. He returned with a plate piled high with food and another drink.

"Now, will you be wantin' to keep on with that there horse you come in on to continue your travels, or shall I arrange another, fresher one, sir?"

Wickham paused in shovelling his food and considered carefully. Now he was warmer and more comfortable, it seemed foolish to throw away money on a coach seat.

"Arrange another for me, but make sure it is sure-footed and fast, if you please, and send that old nag back to the inn at Lambton; tell them it is not a suitable hire for a long journey – I have half a mind to demand a refund. I had all but decided to continue in the comfort of a coach tomorrow, but hopefully the weather will improve before the morning. Would your good woman be so kind as to dry my clothes tonight? I cannot bear to think of wearing them wet again tomorrow."

"Jus' leave them outside your door and they will be taken care of, sir, an' I will ensure your next horse lives up to your expectations, sir, don' you worry about that. But afore you think of retirin' for the night, if you are not too tired, that is, would you care to make up a table that's formin' in the other room? There is a need for another gentleman, and you look as though you are not unacquainted with entertainments of that sort, sir."

Wickham fought the urge to immediately agree to the offer, his straitened circumstances fixed in his mind, asking:

"And what manner of game is being started, may I ask?"

"Oh, merely a small game of whist, sir; an entertainment to pass the evening hours, that is all. Shall I say you will join them shortly, sir?"

Wickham nodded. He could not plead ignorance of so universal a game, and it might be profitable, after all. He went to his room, changed into dry clothes and left his wet ones where the landlord had suggested, washed the dirt from his face and hands, and pocketed a small amount of money. He returned to the bar where he was escorted to a small room behind it where a fire blazed brightly and all was warm and welcoming with a game already in play.

The gentlemen around the table glanced up at his entry, immediately returning their attention to their game. Wickham nodded to them and sat down beside another observer, happy to be given the opportunity to size up his opponents. They appeared relaxed and friendly enough but were clearly all strangers to one another; gentlemen and businessmen passing through the village on their way to somewhere else in the morning. He felt the crackle of the notes in his pocket, pleased he had had the good sense to leave the remainder in his room, and began to feel the familiar anticipation of a pleasant evening's diversion.

Chapter 16

"Now Anne," intoned her mother as the Barouche box made short shrift of the rutted and muddy road it was traversing, "while this visit is a peace-making gesture - healing the breach, as it were; I am not one to hold grudges, as you know - it does not in any manner constitute approval of the match my nephew has made. Although Darcy's letter was conciliatory enough to entice me to make this gesture, the family to which he has attached himself is so far beneath his own that it makes the alliance a disgrace; that fact is indisputable. I cannot but think that we shall bear witness, when we arrive, to the unhappiness of a most ill-matched couple. However, my forbearance shall be such that *I* shall not be the one to remind them of my warning and their determination to proceed regardless." She sniffed and stared at her daughter who was smiling to herself. Mrs. Jennings glanced at them both and then returned her gaze to its habitual observation of her folded hands.

"And what amuses you so, may I enquire?"

"Merely, Mamma, that I do not believe we *shall* see such evidence at all. I believe we shall *bear witness*, as you like to term it, to two of the most happily married people in Derbyshire, if not the entire country. I have it on the highest authority from Mrs. Collins that only days ago she was in receipt of a letter from her friend describing her perfect contentment with everything about her new life."

"*Indeed?* Well, naturally *she* will feel such happiness; *she* has elevated herself far beyond her sphere and presumably congratulates herself on her situation *every* day. I have no doubt about that. But we shall see if that sentiment is held by my nephew, now he has had several months to reflect upon and regret his rash decision. I shall not fault him for it, I shall not speak a word about it, but he must have realised by now just how detrimental his marriage has been to his position in society. I feel for him, truly I do, but he has made his decision and must endure the consequences of it."

"I am sure you are wrong, Mamma. Mrs. Collins informs me that they are both deeply in love and of the same mind in everything; clearly there are no regrets, nor any desperate realisations on either side. You must accept the facts, and not presume that your prejudice against the new Mrs. Darcy and her family carries any weight with my cousin or those of his acquaintance. I, for one, will be very glad to see my cousin and his wife's felicity, and wish them both health and happiness in their future."

The carriage lurched violently at that moment, causing Lady Catherine to clutch at the handle.

"What is that driver doing, almost throwing us from the coach?"

"I am sure the driver is not doing anything of the kind, Mamma; the roads are very bad but you insisted upon travelling them at this time of year and this is the consequence. We feel very little of the motion considering the state of the road; be glad we are not forced to travel by Stage – then we should certainly intimately know every pothole and rut."

"*By Stage*? Oh, what nonsense you do talk, Anne. I do not like your new outspokenness; it is most disagreeable to be contradicted at every turn. And it has come on very suddenly this past year. I blame Mrs. Collins; you never were this forthright about your opinions before she arrived."

Anne laughed easily, acknowledging her mother's accusation.

"Indeed, you are perfectly correct, Mamma. Before Mrs. Collins became my dearest friend, I had no life, no opinions of my own, no real purpose. I was a shadow. But after Mrs. Collins befriended me, I saw that there was no need to be silent on everything, to imagine myself sick at every turn. I do not intentionally set out to annoy or oppose you, Mamma, but why should not I explore my own opinions, too; surely that is not such a terrible thing? You have, after all, always expressed your own opinions quite freely; with you as my model, why should you be surprised that I follow your example?"

Lady Catherine pressed her lips against any further comment while admitting to herself that, irritating as it was to have her opinions contravened by her own daughter, it was a relief for Anne to be so much more confident and at ease in company.

"I look forward to seeing Pemberley again, Mamma; it has been some years since I visited my cousin. Was it much changed the last time you were there?"

"Naturally, it had changed very little at that time. A single man has no idea of making changes to the furnishings unless it is brought to his attention, but I think you may rest assured that, since her occupation, the new Mrs. Darcy will have re-furbished the entire place from top to bottom; there will have been some extensive bills sent to my nephew. I shudder to think how her taste will have tarnished the gracious and elegant arrangements of my dear sister. You must prepare yourself for inferior workmanship and materials all in the name of modernisation, Anne. There will be no quality or style in anything she has bought, you mark my words."

"Oh, Mamma! Mrs. Darcy has hardly been mistress of Pemberley for more than a few months. I doubt very much she has made any great changes or expensive purchases whatsoever in that time. And why do you suppose her to be so lacking in taste and elegance? I did not discern either of those defects in her when she visited us last March. She was all quiet good taste, as I recall; nothing showy or vulgar. You imagine the worst, Mamma, and it does you no credit."

"I merely like to prepare myself before I am faced with a shock. We shall see who is correct, Anne; we shall see."

And with that both ladies turned to their respective windows and swayed in silence for the next several miles.

Meanwhile, the arrival of the two visitors was being anxiously awaited by the ladies of Pemberley: the object of Lady Catherine's pity had already absented himself in the name of some abstruse business about the estate, determined that it would, in all likelihood, engage him entirely until the evening.

Georgiana stayed with Elizabeth in the parlour where there was a generous outlook on the drive and the bridge spanning the lake over which any carriage must pass if it were to arrive at the front steps.

"Will Lydia join us soon, Elizabeth?"

"No, she will not. I have instructed my sister to remain in her room this afternoon. It is better that we meet Lady Catherine and Miss de Bourgh by ourselves before exposing them to Lydia's outspokenness. I do not want Lady Catherine put out and leaving before Darcy returns this evening, not after his reluctant extension of the olive branch. I refuse to have my sister spoil the reinstatement of peace and harmony between two sides of his family."

Georgiana laughed. "I cannot believe that you think your sister to be such a bad influence upon that process, Elizabeth. She has been very quiet and polite since her arrival; I am beginning to think your stories and fears about her must be figments of your imagination. I can hardly encourage her to discuss her life in Newcastle or her husband, or any such thing with me. It is almost as if she is afraid of speaking of anything for fear of offending you and so prefers to stay silent."

Elizabeth looked startled at Georgiana, and then glanced out of the window again.

"I am very glad to hear she has said nothing of any consequence to you, my dear, for I should hate her to offend or shock you. Lydia has never known what it is to consider the effect of her words or actions, and that ignorance has caused several people a great deal of pain over the years; the most recent years, especially. But I think it best for all concerned for her to stay out of harm's way for this first meeting."

"As you think best, Elizabeth. Oh! I am anxious for my aunt to arrive; it has been such a long while since I have seen her. My only recollection is of a very tall and severe lady and being too afraid to speak in her presence. I do hope I shall not feel as frightened of her this time."

Elizabeth laughed as she rose from her chair: the carriage containing the fearsome lady was crossing the bridge as Georgiana spoke.

"You will soon discover your mettle, my dear, for I see her carriage approaching. Brace yourself!"

The sisters made their way to the front steps, gathering their shawls around them against the incoming draughts of wintry air. The light was fast fading and Elizabeth secretly hoped that whatever was keeping Darcy would be curtailed due to the lack of it; now Lady Catherine was actually descending from her carriage, Elizabeth felt her confidence dissipating with every step that lady took down to the gravel.

"Lady Catherine! Welcome to Pemberley; I hope your journey was not too unpleasant? And Miss de Bourgh; how delightful to see you again. Welcome. Please, do come inside in the warm and out of this weather."

Elizabeth felt herself prattling but could do nothing to stop herself. Just one look at Lady Catherine had reminded her of the opinions that had been aired prior to her marriage to Darcy, and, although Elizabeth had promised herself that she had put it all behind her, she rather felt that Lady Catherine had not.

Lady Catherine deigned to give the merest hint of a smile in response to her welcome and looked about her.

"And where, pray, is my nephew? After a journey such as I have had, it is the least he could do to be here to welcome me."

"Lady Catherine; please do come inside. Darcy will join us very shortly; he found he was required in another part of the estate just at this time but promised to return as soon as the situation allowed it. Here, you see, is Georgiana. We must both stand in my husband's stead until he joins us."

And with that, Elizabeth managed to coax her unwilling and disgruntled guest up the steps and into the main hall, where she was divested of her outer travelling cloak and hat, and ushered into the parlour to a chair in front of the fire. Throughout it all, Anne had remained perfectly silent, merely looking about her in interested enjoyment, utterly disconnected to her mother's annoyance and discomfort. Suddenly she spoke:

"How delightful this all is, Mrs. Darcy. Happily, we have had an uneventful journey, I thank you for kind interest, apart from several hard jolts due to the state of the roads. Our comfort, otherwise, was not compromised in any way at all and we are happy to be here. But my first message to you must be from our mutual friend, Mrs. Collins, who bade me to give you her best wishes in the sincere hope that I would find you quite well, and to deliver this note."

Elizabeth smiled warmly at Anne. She had heard from Charlotte that Anne was a changed person since last she saw her, but now she had the proof of it with her own eyes. The shrinking violet who had withered under any person's gaze was gone, and now, instead, smiled confidently at Elizabeth, including Georgiana in that gaze.

The tea arrived and, as Elizabeth poured and offered edibles, Anne rose and went to sit with Georgiana where a quiet conversation ensued. Lady Catherine, as was her wont, continued to outline every detail of every mile she had endured between Kent and Derbyshire, and Elizabeth, being her captive audience, was forced to smile and nod and ask pertinent questions when her ladyship appeared to be running out of complaints. After she had eaten and rested and controlled the conversation long enough, Lady Catherine found the strength to focus her attention upon her surroundings.

"I see that you have done nothing yet in this room, madam; it is much as my sister designed it apart from the desk having been moved to a most uncomfortable spot by the window. It must catch all of the morning sun and will become very hot in the Summer. You will not be able to work there in a month or so."

She glared about the room, inspecting it for other obvious signs of bad taste and management.

"But I much prefer where the desk is placed as it affords me a clear view of the garden and the Park. When I am unable to go out for my customary walk due to the inclemency of the weather, I can look at it from the comfort of my desk while working."

"Ah, yes; your *walks*. You should not be so keen to display your country ways now you are mistress of Pemberley, you know. Scurrying about the countryside is not something that becomes a person in your position; I would strongly advise you against it, now or in the finer weather."

"Oh, Mamma!" interrupted Anne laughing. "I go *scurrying* about the parish with Mrs. Collins every day when we can manage it, and no one think the worse of me for it, I am certain. You must move with the times. Ladies are allowed to walk in their own Park, you know; it is no longer shocking."

Lady Catherine was about to retort when the door was thrown open and Lydia made her entrance, pausing in the doorway as if anticipating being immediately dismissed, and then, in response to the silent stares her arrival had produced, smiled with satisfaction and made her way between the tables to sit upon the same sofa as Lady Catherine.

Lady Catherine shifted herself uncomfortably, regarding her new seat-mate with a gimlet eye and, without removing it from her object, addressed Elizabeth.

"And this, *I suppose*, must be your sister?"

Elizabeth, also glaring at her sister, responded,

"Yes, yes, indeed, Lady Catherine. May I introduce my youngest sister, Mrs. George Wickham. She is also our guest and likely to stay for the next month at least. She has come down from …"

"*Newcastle*; yes, yes; I know all about Mrs. Wickham, as does everybody who had the misfortune of being privy to the disgraceful events of last year. I presume that her *husband* has not been extended a similar invitation?" Lady Catherine allowed her gaze to slide over Lydia until it reached her face.

Lydia held Lady Catherine's eye with absolute control; she would not be brow-beaten, especially not by someone who thought she should behave as if ashamed of her position.

"And how was your journey, Lady Catherine? Lengthy travel is very tedious, is not it? The roads coming down from Newcastle were in an abominable state as, I am sure, were those from Kent. Our carriage was hard put to stay on the roads in places and several times we were forced to offload all of the passengers and baggage to help the horses out of difficulty.

"I thank you for your kind enquiry and can assure you my husband is not here; he is currently in London on business, so I thought to take some time in his absence and visit my sister in her new situation. I find myself very pleased with Pemberley thus far, but of course, I have not been here long. You, of course, know the area and house very well, do not you, madam? How do you find it?"

Elizabeth choked back a laugh that threatened to spill over.

"Lydia? Would you care for some tea, perhaps? Lady Catherine has just been recounting her travels to us; I am sure she has no wish to repeat her stories."

"Well! I am sure that if I had been notified that such a tea party had been arranged, I should have been here to hear it and compare notes on our separate journeys, and commiserate. Yes, I will take a cup, if you please, with lots of sugar. Oh! And several of those little cakes would be delicious; I find the country air makes me quite ravenous indeed! I do hope I shall not outgrow my best gowns whilst I am here. That would be unfortunate and what would Wickham do then with an unattractive wife?"

"Then perhaps you should restrain yourself, sister," Lizzy murmured as she passed the tea and one cake to Lydia.

Georgiana and Anne, who had both been watching the proceedings with interest, looked at each other and Georgiana spoke up,

"Lydia: do come and meet Miss de Bourgh. Bring your plate, do."

Lydia smiled and bowed slightly to Lady Catherine as she gathered up her edibles and went to sit with the younger ladies. Very soon there was quiet conversation and laughs emanating from that side of the room, leaving Lady Catherine and Elizabeth to an uncomfortable silence.

Fortunately, within minutes, the door was thrust open once again and the long-awaited Darcy marched in, smiling a smile that was more grim than gracious. He greeted his aunt and cousin, made the usual enquiries as to their journey and then listened impatiently to Lady Catherine's lengthy re-telling of it. Eventually, he broke in, addressing Elizabeth:

"Would it not be prudent to show our guests their rooms, my dear, now they have been fortified a little after the rigours of their journey?"

"Oh, naturally that was my intention, Darcy; they have only just arrived." She turned to Lady Catherine and enquired, "Perhaps you would like to be taken to your rooms now, as Darcy suggests, to refresh yourselves before dinner? Let me call Mrs. Reynolds. Everything is prepared but if there is anything else you require, you have only to say the word."

"Hmm; it is of no great matter, although a short rest would be acceptable. But, nephew, before you fly off again, what was so important that you were unable to greet me upon my arrival?"

"My dear aunt, there is nothing I would have liked more than to have welcomed you and Anne back to Pemberley, in person alongside my wife and sister but, as with many things, a crisis occurred that required my immediate attention. It could not be forestalled, no matter if the Prince himself decided to visit. But you must forgive me; I shall accompany you to your room now, myself, and make sure you are comfortable. Anne, I am delighted to see you so well. It has been too long since you were able to travel this far. I hope I shall be able to show you something of Pemberley whilst you are with us; I know Elizabeth will enjoy having someone else to show her secret walks to."

And with that voluble outburst, Lady Catherine was entirely subdued and meekly agreed to be shown to her room accompanied by Anne. Elizabeth remained in the parlour with Georgiana and Lydia, and they exchanged glances alternating amusement and relief.

"Lady Catherine does not terrify me as much as she used to, Elizabeth. I think having you here makes me braver than usual."

"Oh! I have no doubt that it is merely a matter of your being almost ten years older than when last she visited; age is a great leveller of terrifying demons. And why should anyone stand in fear of anyone else, pray? Charlotte has certainly never bothered to be and she is well regarded by Lady Catherine. I was very agreeably pleased with Miss de Bourgh's demeanour today; she might almost become the equal to her mother in opinion and outspokenness if she continues on in that way, but hopefully without the inconsiderate manner. Let us hope that dinner will continue with everybody on their best behaviour. I must remind *you*, Lydia, to be especially so after your performance this afternoon; you never will follow instructions, will you?"

"Oh, la! What nonsense you speak; you make Lady Catherine sound like a dragon and yet what do I find? Merely an old lady who thinks she knows everything about everybody and has the mistaken idea that she can say whatever she likes about them. Well; I shall not be afraid of her or her opinions, but I shall be polite as I am your guest."

"I suppose that is something for which I should be thankful, is it? Mark my words, Lydia; neither Darcy nor I will tolerate any bad behaviour or outspokenness from you that could cause Lady Catherine or Miss de Bourgh distress or to consider our family any worse than they already do – is that clear?"

"*Yes*. I have *said*. I shall be on my best behaviour; I *promise*."

Elizabeth glared once more at her sister and then left the parlour, climbing the stairs to the guest apartments where Anne and her mother were already comfortably ensconced, to find Darcy sitting, apparently quite at ease, in a frail chair in the sitting room, whilst his aunt held forth animatedly about certain aspects of Rosings Park that were in need of his attention when next he visited. She broke off as Elizabeth entered and Darcy leapt up eagerly.

"Ah; there you are, my dear. Lady Catherine was just congratulating us on our arrangements, were not you, aunt?"

Lady Catherine paused, "Yes, indeed. Everything is quite comfortable and just how my dear sister would have arranged them; indeed, this is the same room in which I stayed the last time I was here. I congratulate you, Mrs. Darcy, upon anticipating the preferences of your guests."

Elizabeth smiled unconcernedly. "Oh, that is all due to Mrs. Reynolds, of course; she has been a great help to me whilst still learning my duties as mistress. She remembers everything as it should be done or has always been done. I do not take any of the credit yet, I assure you, but I am glad that everything is to your satisfaction. However, I see you are engaged at present and so will leave you to your conversation.

"Until dinner, then."

Chapter 17

There was a certain divide in the drawing room where everyone gathered before dinner: Anne, Georgiana, and Lydia – already firm friends - secluded themselves by one of the windows even though they were beyond the reach of the fire's warmth, willingly enduring the chill of the evening coming through the gap in the drapes rather than endure the stilted conversation that was to be had around the fire with Lady Catherine, Darcy and Elizabeth.

Lydia was proving to be an amusing companion, as Anne had informed her mother earlier, with her wealth of stories and gossip - most of which concerned people with whom neither Anne nor Georgiana were acquainted – tales, told with a frisson of mischief, proving irresistible to both ladies who began to feel their experience of life rather lacking thus far. Lydia, in her turn, had not the slightest compunction at staying away from Lady Catherine and Darcy; she was not about to forfeit what enjoyment there was to be had of the evening by being talked at by Lady Catherine again. She would gladly take the little that was on offer from the other two ladies of her own age and risk the anger of her sister. She had been polite enough to Lady Catherine for one day.

So Darcy was forced to endure his aunt's thinly-veiled critiques upon all and everything she had noticed about the house and grounds, even though she had only driven through the latter and merely visited two rooms of the former. His gaze kept wandering to the door as if conjuring the servants to announce dinner ahead of time, but this inattention served no purpose or effect upon his aunt who was, as always, content to speak without reference to any others' opinion for as long as her thoughts ran upon such matters.

And so it was this evening. She espoused upon the state of the drive – it had caused her carriage to rock violently; the movement of furniture – with every acceptance that such was the new Mrs. Darcy's right so to do, but again voiced her opinion of the short-sightedness of it all; the very great likelihood that the dinner would consist of something that would not agree with her constitution; the concern that Mrs. Darcy might be spending far too much time on visiting and not enough on her duties as mistress; and, finally, eyeing the offensive person standing by the windows with Anne and Georgiana, supposed that some great trouble must have descended upon Mrs. Darcy's sister as to explain her presence in the house and the prolonged absence of that person's husband.

"It is all as I expected it to turn out, and as I explained to Mr. Collins when he imparted the news to me, hasty marriages are always suspicious and fraught with problems: they rarely last and are never happy. I do hope that Mrs. Wickham understands her situation and that it is for her to endure whatever is thrown her way as a punishment for making herself and her family ridiculous."

"Forgive me, Lady Catherine, but you presume too much regarding the situation concerning my sister," retorted Elizabeth, stung into defending her family.

"She is staying here as our guest, as are you and Anne; there is no hidden secret behind her visit, no great scandal involved, and there is no reason to imagine one. After all, many marriages are made in haste, including the marriage of your own clergyman to my friend, and he is not unhappy, is he?

"I realise it is a shock to have my sister as a fellow guest, but I have insisted Lydia act with decorum whilst she is here and I know you will do the same."

Elizabeth was flushed and angry; angry that she had to defend her sister against attack but also that Lady Catherine thought it acceptable to do so whilst in another's home. At

Rosings, she might behave as she liked, and certainly did, but Lizzy refused to countenance such rudeness in her own home, and in front of her husband.

Lady Catherine was shocked into silence and before she had the chance to remonstrate, Darcy chimed in, secretly catching Lizzy's hand as it clenched her skirts, applying warm pressure to it as he spoke.

"Indeed, aunt, it is too bad of you to immediately despise those whom you hardly know and have only heard of through gossip. Elizabeth is right; I will not have you speaking ill of her family or of her arrangements. You are entitled to your opinion of course, and where it can be useful, it will be appreciated, but any attempt to discomfit the residents of Pemberley will not be tolerated. Rest assured, my dear aunt, that when we are in your house and enjoying your hospitality, we shall never utter one word of complaint against any of your arrangements, nor of your acquaintance.

"Ah, here is the dinner announcement. Take my arm, aunt, and let us go into dinner together. Elizabeth, my dear, pray, take my other arm." Smiling at the silence he had produced, he led them into the dining room and saw them both seated comfortably before taking his own.

Lydia placed herself between Elizabeth and Georgiana, while Anne quietly sat opposite them, next to her mother - who seemed unusually restrained - and Elizabeth. The silence during the first course was deafening; only the clink of cutlery against china and the guttering of the candles broke it.

Darcy ate without concern; he had eaten in just this manner for most of his life and had no great fear of silence, in fact he preferred it to the nonsense that usually passed as entertaining chatter. He unconcernedly worked his way through the first course smiling occasionally down the table when he caught Elizabeth's eye.

Eventually, Anne gently cleared her throat, dabbing her lips with her napkin before speaking.

"Miss Darcy; you mentioned that you and Mrs. Darcy generally go visiting each morning when the weather permits. Do you intend such an excursion tomorrow morning? For if you do, I should very much like to join you; Mrs. Collins and I do the same around Hunsford, and I should like to see your village and the work that you do."

Georgiana smiled and looked to Elizabeth. "Shall we go tomorrow, do you think, Elizabeth? Is there anyone who is in need of a visit?"

"I am sure that there will be someone whom we can visit, if only to introduce Miss de Bourgh to the neighbourhood; there does not need to be sickness to visit friends and acquaintance. Otherwise, there is no reason why we should not take a turn about the Park, which is delightful even on the freshest of mornings."

"Oh, be very careful, Miss de Bourgh," chimed in Lydia, "for once my sister discovers another person who enjoys walking, she will never let you alone. I should deny all interest immediately and thus save yourself from days of tedious exercise."

Anne smiled. "There is nothing I like so well as a walk; it is most beneficial even in the coldest weather and certainly improves my health. Mrs. Collins and I believe it to be so and I am so much improved since I have taken some regular exercise, am not I, Mamma?"

Lady Catherine sniffed and raised her eyes to her daughter.

"Indeed; your improvement has been very great, Anne. But you must not force yourself upon Mrs. Darcy's privacy – she may wish to be alone - and there is nothing which you could possibly add to any visits she may make. I would suggest that you curtail your beneficial exercise in favour of keeping *me* company whilst we are here."

Anne looked down at her hands in embarrassment and Elizabeth quickly spoke.

"Of course Miss de Bourgh must accompany us tomorrow and any other day she wishes, if you can spare her, of course. Georgiana and I would be delighted to have her company - as will those we visit - and show her around the grounds and village."

"Then *I* shall keep you company here, Lady Catherine," Lydia declared stoutly, smiling with satisfaction at the various shocked faces that turned at her offer. "I am sure we shall discover a great deal in common if we try."

No one could think of a suitable reply to such a suggestion and again the meal continued in silence, Darcy merely raising his eyebrows at Elizabeth, to which she responded with a widening of her eyes. The idea of Lady Catherine and Lydia having even the slightest common ground between them was sufficient to set the mind spinning with terrible possibilities. Elizabeth determined to mention again to Lydia that she must behave whilst at Pemberley and that even making an offer of company was fraught with unimaginable consequences if she were to speak ill-advisedly to her ladyship.

Lady Catherine, who had clearly struggled to find a suitable response judging by the lengthy pause, eventually managed,

"That is most *kind* of you, Mrs. Wickham, and I am sure that, should I have *no* other engagements to concern myself with, I might be glad of your company where there is none other to be had. However, I do have several dear friends in the neighbourhood upon whom I absolutely must call; they would be distressed indeed to discover I had not immediately paid them a visit. I believe I shall begin with Lady Royston and that will lead to others whom I have not had the pleasure of seeing since my last visit."

Elizabeth hid a small smile behind her napkin and said,

"Oh, yes; I believe there are several who are eager to see you again, Lady Catherine. They say it has been too long since they had the pleasure of your company."

Darcy looked from one lady to the next. Those of the female sex were very confusing; they said and looked one thing at each other, but he was fairly certain nothing that was currently being said and looked was actually the truth. Why could not they just state things clearly so everyone could understand? All this circumlocution only served to confuse and deceive people, and he abhorred deception.

He brought this up once he and Elizabeth were alone, preparing for bed, but she merely laughed at his concerns whilst sitting in front of the mirror so he could loosen her hair from its ribbons and pins, a job she preferred done by him rather than the maid, mainly because it always included intimate kisses on the bare nape of her neck and delightful, nervous fumbling as he tried to gently remove them without pulling a hair.

"It is the way we women work best, my dear. We each of us understand the other without causing any animosity. Lydia has stated her willingness to be a companion to Lady Catherine, which has been acknowledged."

"But that is entirely *impossible*, is it not?" expostulated her husband.

"*Naturally* it is, my dear; neither lady intends to carry out their stated actions, I have no doubt. It is all well understood now that Lydia will stay away from Lady Catherine, and Lady Catherine will ensure that she will be too busy 'out visiting' to allow Lydia access to her. It is all as we planned."

"But that is not what was said, at all. You are saying that Lydia has put Lady Catherine on notice that if they should cross paths then they will have to endure each other's company, and she will not be responsible for whatever transpires?"

"Yes, my darling man," Elizabeth smiled as she turned around to face him, "so we should have a peaceful house for the duration of their visits if everyone adheres to their stated actions. Now; come with me to bed. I am cold with all this sitting and require warming up again."

The following morning produced a clear and crisp aspect and so, after everyone had breakfasted and read their letters, Elizabeth, Anne, and Georgiana declared themselves ready to walk towards Lambton and make some visits on their way. Lady Catherine announced her intention to write several letters in the morning room, and Lydia agreed; she, too, had letters to write to her friends in Newcastle, and her sister, Kitty.

Elizabeth quailed at the thought of leaving the two of them together, alone, in an enclosed space but forbore saying anything, merely indicating the location of the stationery and ink before wishing them both a pleasant morning and joining the other two ladies in the hall. They set out briskly, forced by the steady wind to gather their wraps closely around them and hold their bonnets on with gloved hands, but the air was invigorating and none of them complained.

Lydia settled herself at a small side table, leaving the larger one in its disagreeable location to Lady Catherine, and for a while both ladies worked at their correspondence in silence save the scratching of the nibs against the paper and the clink as they were dipped into the ink pots. The sun shining in was warm, proving Lady Catherine's point very satisfactorily, and so she was eventually forced to gather her writing things together and move to another, smaller table on which she could continue her writing.

Lydia noticed and commented, "Yes, my sister rather enjoys the effect of the sun, especially in Winter when there is so little of it to be had. That poor table shall certainly bear the brunt of her preferences before the year is out. But she has always not cared much for appearances or the opinion of others; she is not vain at all. When she travelled with my aunt and uncle Gardiner last Summer, she returned quite tanned from being so much outside."

"Indeed: Mrs. Darcy is almost evangelical in her insistence upon being outside in all weathers; she walked about a great deal last Easter when she was at Hunsford. Such energy is commendable, I suppose, but not what was considered ladylike behaviour in my day. But even Anne takes to it now, so I must accept it as the way of the future and apparently not condemn it too much within anyone's hearing."

"Oh, I have no such restrictions upon my opinion about it; I never could abide walking too far or for too long. If I could not have the carriage, then I preferred to stay at home until it could be got. My father could never let it go as it mostly was needed on the farm, and so I was forced to remain at home with my sisters. Everyone who knows me knows that I do not walk much if I can help it unless there is a party in the village that is enticing. I would much rather get my exercise through an evening's dancing and I sincerely hope that my sister will arrange something during my stay to relieve the monotony of the days, for I do not know how long I shall be here, and if there is nothing to relieve it, I shall go quite mad, I assure you."

"Yes; I have heard that you are fond of dancing and company, Mrs. Wickham. But now that you are a married woman surely you have curtailed your tastes in such areas, as you should?"

"But why should a married woman not continue to enjoy those pursuits which gave her pleasure when she was unmarried, pray? There is no great disgrace in dancing surely, or enjoying oneself? Why should we all sit at home and spend the rest of our days miserable and focused only on our home and husbands? Why; how boring we should become if that was the case. No wonder husbands tend to leave their home for hours at a time; it is to escape the boring person their wife has turned into. No; I think continuing one's pleasurable entertainments can only improve a marriage and bring other areas of interest into it."

"Hmm." Lady Catherine regarded Lydia with a calculating eye. "And how does your husband like these modern ideas of yours, pray? Does he encourage your amusements every evening?"

"Wickham? Why, he understands my desire for company, just as I do not restrict his desire for it, either. We both of us cannot bear to be shut up away from interesting people. He has his interests and I have mine, and we both enjoy similar ones too, such as dancing and watching games. We are very well suited, you see, and very happy, too," she ended defiantly.

Lady Catherine started to say something, then thought better of it and returned to her letter. A period of silence again ensued as both ladies focused upon their tasks but thoughts were swirling about Lady Catherine's head as she wrote; thoughts regarding the probable truth behind Lydia's assertions and bravado which seemed more than a little too insistent about her happiness in marriage. Surely a husband in a marriage so open and understanding would not have left his wife for an undetermined length of stay in the care of her sister while he enjoyed himself in London without her? Without a doubt, London was a place someone of Lydia's character would desire to be above all other, certainly above being shut away with her sister in the country.

But it was not her concern, and surprisingly, Lady Catherine found herself warming slightly to this wayward sister of Elizabeth's, despite her prejudices. Lydia reminded her of her own younger sister, Sophie, long dead now, who had also grasped every opportunity to enjoy herself without reference to society, her family, or friends. Lady Catherine rather hoped Lydia's life would not follow a similar path to that of Sophie's, and found herself deciding, that she would try to influence this young lady so that she might avoid a similarly unfortunate ending.

Chapter 18

And so this was the unforeseen development over the next few days that caused Elizabeth and Darcy much astonishment. It appeared that far from wishing herself removed from the company of Mrs. Wickham, Lady Catherine was going out of her way to include Lydia in every visit she made to acquaintance in the neighbourhood, and favouring her with her opinions and advice whilst taking a leisurely turn about the grounds.

Darcy came upon Elizabeth one morning, transfixed at a window as she watched a slow promenade occurring around the lake area and, placing his arms about her from behind, also rested his gaze on the incongruous sight.

"What do they have to talk about, I wonder? They are two of the most disparate women with not one thing in common, yet there they are, close in conversation, seemingly of one opinion and with a growing regard for each other. What alchemy have you devised to make it so, my dear? This is not what we anticipated when we learnt their visits would clash; it is unsettling in the extreme."

"Would you prefer screaming and shouting to this amity? Or Lady Catherine leaving in high dudgeon at the perceived insult to her and her daughter? I confess to be as intrigued as are you: Lady Catherine is not only countenancing my disgraceful sister, which is all we could have reasonably expected, but actively seeking her company and introducing her to people in the neighbourhood - people I am not sure *I* would introduce to my sister - is a side of your aunt I had not envisaged and, as you say, exceedingly disquieting."

"Well, if you do not know the cause of it, then we must congratulate ourselves on our unforeseen ability to forge friendships between the most unlikely people, and be thankful for unconsciously averting a disastrous visit."

Elizabeth smiled, quietly turning around in the circle of his arms and rested her head upon his shoulder before looking up into his eyes and speaking of something she had been considering for several days.

"Tell me, my dear; have you had any word from Wickham? I have not and I know that Lydia has not either. It is as if he has disappeared from the world entirely. There has been no letter from London for almost two weeks now. I begin to fear the worst."

Darcy grimaced slightly. "You are not alone in your concerns, my dear. It is certainly suspicious that he has not sent even one letter to announce his safe arrival in Town. I have been contemplating riding there to make enquiries about his whereabouts. It is quite possible that Wickham could have left the country as soon as he rode out of Lambton; I would not put it past him. The sooner we know the truth of the matter, the better for all concerned, but I had not mentioned my concerns for fear of worrying you. And now I discover that you have been worrying about the matter of your own accord." Darcy's face was grim as he spoke, triggering fear in Lizzy's heart.

"*Oh!* But do you really think that was his plan? That his talk of business was all a ruse, a deception to cover his tracks until he could escape without Lydia in tow? But that is shocking indeed, to deceive her into thinking, and me, and you that he would return for her very soon. But perhaps she has received word and we do not know of it."

"You may check with her, but Grant assures me that, as of yesterday, no such letter has arrived from London for Lydia; in fact, the only correspondence she has received has been from Longbourn and Netherfield. I believe I shall have to make that trip very soon before his trail goes cold."

Elizabeth looked anxiously into his face and kissed him quickly.

"You are the kindest of men, my darling. You take the greatest care of those with whom you should no longer have to concern yourself. Marriage to me and into my family has caused you all manner of complications and unnecessary pain, and I am sorry for that."

Darcy kissed her back.

"I will not have you feel sorry for anything. I was never in any doubt what marrying you would entail, my dear, and once I set in motion your sister's marriage, I knew with absolute certainty that I had also arranged for myself a lifetime of attachment to a man whom I would have willingly cast aside without a second thought in other circumstances. It seems that I never shall be free of responsibility for the actions of George Wickham, but it is the exchange I willingly made to secure my own happiness, and I assure you, I do not regret that decision.

"I am shocked, though, that he has not lived up to his duties as a husband; I expected even one such as he is to display greater resolve than this. He has managed to cause your sister to dream of happiness and security where there appears to have never been any reasonable cause for that dream. He was never in love with her, after all, as those finer feelings in him - such as he might own - had already been bestowed upon Mrs. Younge, a lady who has also been denied her happiness through my actions. I confess, I do not like the way things have fallen out. What seemed to be sensible and right six months ago, is now disintegrating before my eyes and I do not know how I can make it whole again. I am the sorry creator of unhappiness in three people."

Elizabeth looked at him tenderly.

"There is nothing for which you should fault yourself, my dear. Any fault lies entirely with Wickham and my sister; they caused their own unhappiness and must deal with it as they can. They will have to work through their difficulties, just as any married couple must. Lydia certainly does not appear to regret her marriage at all, although she now understands it and its flaws a little better; indeed, she still rejoices in her success in having secured the man she set out to and now appears to have convinced herself that his absence is justified while he works towards their future security."

"Yes, but, if he has abandoned her, as I fear, what should I do then, Elizabeth? Hunt him down again and force him back with the promise of more money to sustain his mode of living? – although I dread to calculate just how much would *ever* be sufficient for that - or accept failure, cut all ties with him and send your sister back to Longbourn in disgrace? I suppose we might allow her to live here, if necessary, but I cannot see her being happier here than in Hertfordshire; the gossips' tongues will wag wherever she resides once they catch a whiff of scandal."

"Oh! Do not anticipate trouble before it arrives, my dear; it will not come to that, surely. But your plan is a sensible one; you should go immediately to discover what you can of his whereabouts and activities. It will put all our minds at rest once we know what we are truly dealing with."

She refocused her gaze on the two figures now approaching the house, heads bent together like old companions.

"But, first, I would like to know what it is we are dealing with between my sister and your aunt; it is a conundrum indeed."

Darcy took one look, gave her a quick peck on the cheek and hurried out of the far door muttering,

"Well, that is one subject with which I have no need to concern myself; I leave that entirely in your capable hands, my dear."

"Was that Darcy I just saw racing towards the stables?" enquired Lady Catherine after she had settled herself in front of the fire. "Where is he off to in such a hurry, I wonder? We have seen so very little of him."

"A warm drink, Lady Catherine?" asked Elizabeth and rang the bell. "Darcy recalled an important message for the groom; he will return shortly. May I enquire how you enjoyed your stroll with Lydia this morning? Forgive me if I am being impertinent, but you appear to be getting along surprisingly well, considering your opinion of her when you arrived."

Lady Catherine looked quickly at Elizabeth and then at the flames, holding out her numb hands to their warmth.

"Your sister merely requires taking in hand. She reminds me of my own younger sister at about the same age who also had a careless exuberance and love of life; I would prefer Lydia *not* experience the sadness that my sister was forced to endure due to a lack of understanding and guidance. Thus far, your sister has proved herself to be a quick learner and has impressed those of my acquaintance with her lively manners and quick wit. Yes, I think all she needs is a firm hand and the right example to weather whatever her future has in store for her."

Lady Catherine sipped her drink and smiled at Elizabeth's expression.

"You are surprised, I see, at my changed opinion, and why should you not be? I have always acted in the interest of protecting my family and ensuring adherence to rules - which explains my resistance to your marriage into this family and all that I feared it would entail - but I also accept that that which cannot be averted, must be endured as best one can."

Fortunately, Lady Catherine's gaze was again directed at the fire as she said this and so missed the amused expression of her companion.

"That is very magnanimous of you, I am sure, Lady Catherine, and to have also extended your generosity by taking my sister under your protection and giving her the benefit of your experience is a kindness indeed, but I do hope you have the stamina for it; my parents soon gave up the idea of ever controlling her *exuberance* as you call it, preferring a quiet life, which meant allowing her far greater freedom than she should have been permitted.

"It was a never-ending battle for my sister, Jane, and me, to try to curb her precociousness and demands for entertainment. Fortunately, my aunt Philips was a great resource when we lived in Meryton - she was constantly having parties and Lydia was a regular attendee - and, under my aunt and uncle's protection, Lydia was quite safe. Unfortunately, once away from the protection of her family, her unchecked behaviour resulted in her marriage to Mr. Wickham, as you know. I can only assume that her behaviour since then has been equally unrestrained, as she assures me that her social round in Newcastle has been highly entertaining.

"I am thankful, therefore, for your interest in my sister and hope that your influence may have some steadying effect upon her. It has been a kindness indeed that you have been able to provide some society for her amongst those friends you have here in Derbyshire. I hope Lydia has not embarrassed herself in front of them."

"You wish to warn me about your sister, Elizabeth? Surely that is rather uncharitable of you for someone who prides herself upon taking care of her lowliest neighbours? But do not concern yourself on my account, for I assure you I have experienced everything she believes to be new and amusing, and have already corrected her judgment several times; she takes my advice remarkably well, considering your previous statements.

"My own daughter has little use for my advice now that she quite dotes upon every word of your friend. I do not dislike the idea of Anne having an opinion – it is about time – but a mother still likes to exercise some control over her daughter's decisions."

Elizabeth smiled. "I hardly imagine that Miss de Bourgh, or anyone, would refuse your advice, Lady Catherine, if you are so kind as to offer it, and she must understand that everything you do for her is in her best interests. But is there any decision in particular she has made without your approval?" Elizabeth was eager to know if, since her own marriage to Darcy, Anne had declared herself secretly in love with an entirely unsuitable person, and she smiled inwardly at the notion.

"No, indeed not! But she has assured me of her decision not to marry anyone for the foreseeable future, if at all." Lady

Catherine waved her hand at Elizabeth's expression, "Oh, do not concern yourself - not that you did so last November - Anne was not broken-hearted over losing Darcy; far from it. She informed me in no uncertain terms, even before your wedding took place, that she would never have married him; that he was a terrifying prospect to her and, she was certain, she was an equally tedious prospect to him. It was her declaration against blaming either of the two of you which softened my opinion and paved the way for our visit.

"And so now I find myself with advice to give and no one willing to hear it, away from Kent as I am. Your sister is a challenge and a useful way to pass the time whilst I am here, and if I should do some good, have some beneficial effect upon her, then that is time well spent.

"But she mentioned on our walk about the garden this morning that she has not received one single letter from her husband since she arrived here; that is most irregular. Is this true? It seems negligent in a husband of less than a year, even for one such as I understand hers to be. Perhaps Darcy should do something about contacting him to put her mind at rest, for surely he must know where the man has gone?"

"Unfortunately we do not, your ladyship. The last contact we had with Mr. Wickham was several weeks ago when he announced he had urgent business in London regarding his future plans, but his silence for so long is also causing us some concern. It is possible he may have decided to go where he is unknown and begin another life; he has done it successfully before - he is very plausible and charming and easily believed - and is quite capable of doing so again."

"And have you discussed this with your sister? Is she aware of your concerns? She seemed perfectly content in her conversation with me; although he had not made contact, she believed it to be a good sign, a sign of him busily forging their new life in London."

"We do not see any reason to contradict her illusion just yet. She might be entirely correct in her assertions; indeed, I sincerely hope so. We have no proof, only a worrying mistrust of the person we know him to be. Darcy blames himself for forcing the marriage, for interfering in the lives of so many people."

"But why should he blame himself, pray? Darcy acted in the best interests of the injured party – your sister – who, it seems, is still quite smitten with her good-for-nothing husband. Wickham had to marry your sister before her reputation became the object of vicious gossip. Of course Darcy must go to London immediately and discover what he can; an absconded husband is a tricky thing to manage but if found in time, much easier than the lot faced by an abandoned wife who must lie and pretend but never be quite able to produce him for inquisitive neighbours. No; Darcy must find him and either make him collect Lydia soon, or prove his intentions in London are honourable."

"I believe he has already decided to go tomorrow. He has many contacts in London who will be able to help him in his search and if Wickham is there, he will find him." Lizzy sighed. "It is not a worry we wanted to haunt our lives like this."

"But that is the obligation of marriage and families, Elizabeth; what one partner or member does affects the whole through their actions. It is most unfortunate, but there it is. However, you cannot say that I did not warn either of you of the foolishness of joining your two families. Nothing good could ever possibly come from such an arrangement, and now here is the proof, just as I said."

"I *beg* your pardon, madam! There is everything good in *this* marriage. Neither Darcy nor I have any regrets on that score, I assure you, and I would warn you against airing such opinions within the hearing of my husband. Our concern, which is quite distanced from the felicity of our own marriage, is only for my sister's happiness and security which appears to be in some peril."

An uncomfortable silence descended and was not broken until the welcome appearance of Darcy, returned from his errand. Lady Catherine's rigid posture and his wife's determined turn of head away from her guest told him everything he needed to know.

"Ah, tea! It is exceedingly chilly out in the stables, my dear. Thank you." He accepted the proffered cup gratefully and sipped whilst waiting for the ladies to explain, or continue their conversation.

The silence endured.

"I have told Banks that I shall need my horse ready early tomorrow morning, Elizabeth; I will proceed with what we discussed earlier. I apologise, Aunt, but I am called away from home for a few days. I hope you will still be here upon my return."

"You refer, I presume, Darcy, to your proposed search for your brother-in-law? Your wife has apprised me of your fears about that gentleman and, of course, your response must be immediate. I shall keep the information in the strictest confidence - you may rely upon my discretion - and continue to engage Mrs. Wickham in our usual manner until your return.

"And now, if you will excuse me, I shall seek out my daughter and Georgiana, both of whom I have been neglecting; I am sure they have felt it."

Darcy and Elizabeth watched Lady Catherine as she left the room and then looked at each other questioningly with widening eyes.

"And what, pray, gives my aunt the notion that I require her approval to carry out my plan without delay, other than her usual determination to interfere with and control everyone's lives and everything in them?"

Elizabeth laughed, sitting beside him on the couch.

"Surely that is the only reason she needs, is not it? You will be even more astonished to hear what she has had to say about my sister, my dear. I could hardly believe it myself, and *I* watched the words formed by her own lips. In short, she has very kindly decided to take on my sister as a project whilst she is here, both as a challenge and a diversion, it seems, informing me that a firm hand and experienced guidance will heal all the problems of having a wayward sister. Is not that most thoughtful of your aunt, Darcy?"

"Hmm; yes, but most odd, and entirely out of character to put herself in the way of possible embarrassment and gossip; I am not convinced about her generosity of spirit, it is quite the opposite of what she has always displayed. I confess to wondering about an ulterior motive, but cannot imagine for the life of me what such a motive could be."

"We should not judge her too harshly when she is willing to do good, Darcy! Apparently Lydia reminds her of a sister she lost long ago; a sister, she told me, very briefly, who also had a wildness about her manner and a determination to enjoy life to the full. I did not enquire further but rather imagine that that sister's ending was not pleasant and causes private sorrow and regret for her ladyship, even now.

"But come now, Darcy, we must arrange the necessaries for your journey tomorrow; I shall inform Mrs. Reynolds immediately."

She then stopped in her tracks and smiled at him mischievously.

"Of course, once again you are leaving me here, alone, to go into Town; did not you promise never to leave me behind again? I shall never believe a word you say if you persist in failing to keep it!"

"That is true, but I hope not to be away for long and it is easier for me to stay at the Town house with minimal staff for a few nights than for you; ladies require so much more comfort than do we men. I do not go for entertainment, as you know, and you should be very dull waiting whilst I go about my business.

"And, here, you are not alone. It would not do for you to leave our guests to their own devices – especially your sister – notwithstanding Lady Catherine's good intentions."

"I know, my dear, I only tease you; of course you must manage this alone, and why would I complain when it is all done for the benefit of my own sister? Go; go, now and see to you preparations, as I shall. We must put it about that you are again called away on business; no one needs to know more than that, and when you know more, then we shall know what to tell my sister."

Chapter 19

Darcy left the following morning before anyone was up. Elizabeth contented herself with his promise that she would hear from him upon his arrival in London and determinedly turned her attention to her guests and usual occupations, although, always in the back of her mind, she was travelling with her husband along the roads and byways pointing south towards London. Her delight on the third morning to be in receipt of a letter informing her of his whereabouts was, therefore, profound.

Netherfield Park
April 15th 18~

My dear sister,

Mr. Darcy wishes me to send his very best love to you and his sister. He has just left us to travel onwards towards Town and has taken our father and my husband with him! We were most surprised to see him and very glad that we were not in Town ourselves, as we had previously decided.

The three of them had a long discussion in private, the contents of which were made known to me only after they had decided upon their course of action. I have been sworn to secrecy, as I know have you, but suffice it to say that a flurry of letters left our house that very day, but for only some of them did I see the addressee: they have written to our uncle Gardiner, Mr. Darcy's attorney, and several went to persons unknown to me but all with London addresses. Even more secret was that Charles' attorney was called in for a meeting late yesterday – I can only surmise that it has to do with the legalities of what they intend to set before Wickham when they find him.

I know that I am always too anxious to see the best in everyone, for which you have often derided me, but I cannot believe Wickham to be as malicious and despicable as this! To have no intention of supporting himself and Lydia, is shocking indeed. Charles became rather stern when he discovered that I had been sending extra money to Lydia over and above that which he knew about. But what are we to do when our own sister writes in dire need? We cannot ignore her plight just because she married an impecunious person when we have so much.

I do see more clearly now that not only we here at Netherfield have been taken advantage of, but also our mother - who has little enough - has been pressured into parting with some of her own resources for Lydia. And, of course, all that you and Mr. Darcy have already provided, makes it all add up to rather significant amounts for two people who should be able to live on one half or a quarter as much. My generosity has been subdued by what I have learnt and I shall abide by my husband's wishes and no longer succumb to Lydia's importunities.

Our father and husbands left this morning early and I do not expect to see any of them before the week is out. Mr. Darcy was initially reluctant to involve Charles but he would not be put off, and our father was unusually insistent, and so they are all gone. If you hear anything of them, please be quick about writing all that you know to me, as I shall do for you.

Now I must visit Mamma and hope I shall manage to keep the worst of the situation from her; I am sure Father had no difficulty doing so, uncommunicative as he can be, but I have no doubt he has left her with many questions regarding his sudden decision to accompany both of his sons-in-law to a place he generally abhors.

I will put this in the mails with love. I do hope that your guests are all behaving themselves!

Affectionately,

Jane

Elizabeth smiled as she re-read the letter, comforted to know that Darcy had been able to share his concerns with his friend and taken advice of others both within and out of the family. It was a task much better tackled jointly.

Lydia noisily entered the room, closely followed by Georgiana and Anne. She plumped herself down in a chair and gave a great sigh.

"We have been trying to come up with some sort of amusements, Lizzy, for we are all tired of walking the gardens and talking of the same things to each other. How I wish Wickham would come back, then we would be much brighter and amusing. He always knows what to say to make ladies smile and laugh."

Elizabeth stiffened slightly at the mention of the person causing so much anxiety in her life.

"Well, Georgiana and Anne are to come into Lambton with me this morning on some errands and you are welcome to join us if you wish, Lydia. It will not be terribly amusing but there are shops to look in and it will give us another topic to discuss over dinner."

"I suppose that will be something, although I am sure that Lady Catherine was intending to take me visiting again this morning, but I have not seen her. Has she risen yet, Anne?"

"Oh, no, I think not, Lydia. Mamma rather enjoys those little luxuries which she used to condemn in others not so long ago as being only for the lazy or invalid. Taking her breakfast in bed and remaining there until she is sure the fires have warmed the rooms downstairs is one of her nods to her increasing age and desire for more comfort."

"Increasing age, nonsense!" scoffed Lydia. "Your Mamma has more energy than most ladies her age, certainly more than our Mamma who can barely last the day without several rests and quiet sleeps behind a convenient fan, is that not so, Lizzy? I have become quite attached to Lady Catherine and her opinions upon everything, which I am sure most people find exacting, but I rather like even if I do not always agree with them.

"Last week, for instance, we called upon a very charming lady here in Derbyshire – it was a little way out into the countryside but a most pleasant drive, I assure you – and upon our return Lady Catherine told me that this was a lady who had been *divorced*! What do you think of that? I used to think that anyone who became divorced would be cast out of society forever, but here is this lady, an acquaintance of her ladyship! And Lady Catherine was most pleased to see her and polite and interested in her wellbeing, and nothing in her manner to indicate this lady's difference in society."

"Ah, yes. That must have been Lady Haveringham, over at Gillard Lodge, was it not?" queried Elizabeth. "Darcy introduced her to me upon my arrival and informed me of her situation. I understand she had a dreadful time both during her marriage and her divorce from her brute of a husband. Her divorce was not easy, I understand, because he refused to admit his behaviour, and so she had to hire detectives and lawyers to prove her point. In the end he gave way, partially to stop the gossip mongers and the toll it was taking upon his reputation.

"I admire her indomitable spirit; there are many who would not have been so determined. She refused to tolerate his unspeakable behaviour but she had to suffer everyone knowing of it to ensure her freedom from him. But I am very glad to learn Lady Catherine has not cast off her sister's former friend because of it; the lady does not deserve to endure any further pain from her past."

Lydia listened impatiently to her sister's declamation. She had no interest in the trials experienced by the lady; she had merely thought it to be exciting to meet someone who had been divorced.

"Yes, well; perhaps if she had chosen her husband for love, then she would be married still, would she not now?"

"Unfortunately, love is no guarantee of happiness," Elizabeth spluttered, her mind still engaged with her husband's quest. "It is a very fragile thing, Lydia, as you should be well aware, and it does not take a great deal to turn love into hate or at the very least, disinterest; very little can be done to restore that first flush of feeling if there was no depth in it to begin with."

Lydia flushed, her sister's admonishment piercing even her armour.

"Well, perhaps that is so for some people, but who can gauge any person's depth of feeling upon entering the marriage state? Feelings can grow again just as easily as they can wither away."

Lizzy smiled thinly, thinking of all of the people currently involved in trying to save just such a loveless marriage from withering away. However, she hoped they would be successful in finding Wickham and convincing him to return to his marriage without Lydia becoming any the wiser, depth of feeling or not.

Two days later another letter arrived and Elizabeth, fortunately, was alone in her morning room dealing with household affairs when it was brought to her.

London

April 18th 18~

My dearest Elizabeth,

I know you have been anxiously awaiting word from me but I hope that Jane sent her letter promptly which relieved your mind a little. Your father, Bingley and I arrived last night and already several responses were awaiting us from those from whom we had requested assistance. Mr. Gardiner has offered his every support and had already started to make enquiries, without waiting for our arrival. We are to meet today and discuss what is best to be done. You may have heard that your father insisted on accompanying us when he heard the extent of my concerns and he hopes to be of some use.

We shall begin immediately to make enquiries in all of Wickham's old haunts and I shall call upon both Mrs. Younge – in case she has returned - and Mr. Jardine today as they are those whom Wickham would most likely involve in his plans and seek assistance. I hope and pray we are not too late already.

I miss you, my darling wife, but know that everything I do, and have done, is for you and for you alone.

I will write again tomorrow with, hopefully, some news of our success.

All my love,

D

Elizabeth smiled and kissed the letter before carefully filing it amongst her household accounts to re-read later. This was done just in time as she was startled simultaneously by the door to the room being thrust open and Lydia's jubilant greeting.

"*See here*, Lizzy!" she cried, "What do you think? Wickham has *written*! Look! Oh! A full page and one half informing me of his endeavours and all the wheels he has set in motion in London. He sounds quite happy and positive indeed; he has contacted some of his old friends – he does not say who – ," she scanned the letter again for more details.

Elizabeth stood up and crossed to where her sister was standing.

"I am very glad, for your sake, Lydia. It is good news indeed and I hope that he will soon have everything arranged to your satisfaction. Does he say exactly what he has been doing and with whom? And when he might be able to send for you?"

"Oh, Lizzy! You are always looking for the worst in everyone. No, he has not stated anything *specifically*, it is all rather general, but clearly he has been working hard all this time and begs me to excuse him for not managing to write before this. He writes as if he truly misses me!

"Oh! A new life in London! How exciting that will be, to be away from the countryside and all of its smallness and boredom; back into a life of parties and balls and theatre and everything imaginable that is amusing. I must write to him immediately and enquire how soon I may join him. How lonely I have been; Oh! how I have missed his company!" and she danced off up to her room to write a full five pages of her hopes and desires and expectations with a great deal of meaningful underlining and exclamations.

Elizabeth watched and waited until the bulky letter appeared later that day in the outgoing mails tray in the hall and took it upon herself to copy the address exactly, adding it with a postscript to the letter she had just completed to her husband:

P.S. Here is Wickham's address – or an address where he is receiving his mail. I hope it will help your search and bring it to a quick conclusion. A letter arrived from him this morning and its contents have Lydia convinced that he has been working all this time towards their future, just as he said he would. I hope and pray that is the case when you find him. Good luck, my darling.

She then turned her attention to another conundrum: Charlotte's most recent letter had made enquiries again about the intended return of Lady Catherine – Mr. Collins wanted to be assured of having ample notice - and also the expectation of being blessed with a visit from her dear friend. It had been too long, she said, and she was most anxious to have Lizzy meet her son, William, who was now three months old and growing apace. She had begged to hear soon of their intended visit and, although she quite understood that the Darcys would inevitably be the guests of Rosings Park rather than of the Parsonage, she looked forward with anticipation to daily visits during their stay.

Lizzy stared out into the Park as she thought about what her answer should be. She could not give anything definite until Darcy's return with the result of his undertaking, but she could enquire of Lady Catherine what her plans were for the next few weeks; indeed, it might propel her home faster if she thought her presence was being particularly missed. Perhaps Georgiana might be persuaded to accompany Anne and her mother back into Kent; it would be a pleasant change of scenery for her sister, and would continue the friendship between the cousins.

Rising from her desk and smoothing her skirts, Elizabeth decided to further those plans; it would be to everyone's advantage if a return to Rosings were to be carried out in the next few weeks: Lady Catherine and Anne would be kept unaware of the outcome of the Lydia-Wickham debacle which might possibly turn unpleasant; Georgiana would gain the benefit of travel and new scenery; and Darcy would return to an almost-empty house, depending on what transpired with Wickham and Lydia, which he would relish greatly.

Yes, she nodded to herself; it was time to start planting seeds of departure in her guests' heads. If discreetly done it would appear almost as if they had thought of it themselves. Lizzy smiled with pleasure at the thought of having her home to herself again and left the room to have a discussion with Mrs. Reynolds about the plans for the week's meals.

Chapter 20

Wickham, unaware of being the focus of so many people's attention and concern had finally arrived in London - the only truthful part of his letter to Lydia - feeling rather the worse for wear not only from the rigours of his journey but also as an after-effect of his losses at the inn's table. He had thanked his foresight in leaving the main portion of his money safely in his room that night. Temptation, as expected, had reared its ugly head several times during the evening as he lost everything with which he had started and had been forced to retire, something he previously would never have done. Perhaps this unusual restraint indicated he had learnt a thing or two about responsibility and managing to defeat the urges that rose within him every time he gave in to the temptation of a gaming table.

So he had arrived in London with most of his proceeds from the sale of his commission intact and immediately sought refuge in the familiar: at a certain house in Edward Street. He rang the bell and waited nervously for the door to open, his mind racing while wearing his most disarming smile in the slight possibility that Julia herself would open it.

That smile dimmed considerably when the door was opened by a young, unfamiliar maid who informed him that, no, there was no Mrs. Younge at this address. If the gentleman would care to leave his card, she would enquire about this Mrs. Younge of her mistress and he could call back another day for his answer.

Wickham, shocked and disappointed, shook his head as he turned away.

"No, no, I would not wish to trouble you any further. I was foolish to call, foolish in my expectations. Please do not mention it to your mistress, it is of no consequence. Good day to you."

He wandered about for another hour or so in shock at the realisation that he had no idea where Julia could be or why she no longer had the Edward Street house; he had no other welcoming place to go in the City and no particular friends to visit. After travelling a great distance with great purpose, his lack of preparation regarding his actions now he had reached his destination was immobilising; everything seemed purposeless, overwhelming, confusing.

He did not wish to enter any of the clubs in search of familiar faces, knowing as he did the great temptation contained within them, and he did not wish to spend much money on his lodgings for obvious reasons. He felt like a stranger: an outcast who belonged nowhere and was welcome in almost as many places. It was a sobering realisation indeed. As he tormented himself with the futility of his journey, he finally sank down on a bench in the Park to rest and to think, entirely unaware of the great many interested glances, from ladies in particular, who wondered what such a handsome young gentleman could possibly be looking so downcast about.

He thought long and hard about a solution to his most pressing predicament: comfortable and free lodgings. His thoughts returned repeatedly to whether he could bluff his way into Darcy's house, claiming him as his brother-in-law, but each time quickly dismissed that notion. Or, he supposed, he might call upon his one good friend, a friend who had helped him out in the past and who may be able to help him again: Mr. Jardine. Jardine was a successful gentleman of business and had discovered all of Wickham's failings several years ago. It was he who had forced Wickham to honour a debt to him by working it off in his employ; an employment which had evolved into a grudging respect and then into friendship.

If only Jardine was in Town and not off on one of his business trips abroad, but again, Wickham stopped himself. He hated to have to admit his regrettable situation to his friend; it would certainly cause a loss of that hardly-earned respect. The last time he had seen Jardine, Wickham had been about to travel with the Militia into Brighton for the Summer; he had managed to disengage himself from his many embroilments in Meryton before he left, and everything had promised well for his future.

No; he could not approach Jardine and risk exposing all of his current problems.

It began to grow dark and the Park was clearing quickly. Wickham rose slowly to his feet and his steps took him once again back to his old haunts around St. Clement's parish, a place where he had enjoyed much happiness with Julia in their first years together in London: he, living the wonderful life of a gentleman and she, as always, quietly developing her own business interests.

He had been attracted to the area because of its proximity to the clubs and entertainments and had certainly lived the life he had envisioned for himself – until the funds dried up. Wickham smiled ruefully to himself; *dried up?* No, of course they hadn't dried up; he had managed to lose everything in those clubs of which he was so fond. He had also managed to lose the good opinion of the one woman he had ever loved - would ever love - through his dishonourable and thoughtless behaviour.

He walked, slower now, past his old lodgings which tonight were brightly lit and welcoming; how he wished they were his lodgings still and the light in the window was for him. He walked further down the street and turned right off Sheer Lane where Julia had had her little employment agency and pulled up with a start: there was light showing inside the shop. A female figure could be seen moving about, and, as he strained to read the sign above the door in the gathering gloom, he saw with a rush of joy, the familiar inscription: *Younge's Employment Agency – exceptional household staff at your service.*

Turning back he pressed his face against the window to peer past the thin shades which obscured everything except the vague outline and movements of the person within. He could not discern whom the person was but his heart thudded as he knocked energetically upon the door with his cane.

A voice called out – a female voice, but a voice that was not Julia's – "We are closed for today; come back tomorrow when we will be open for business and can help you with whatever you require."

"I am not come on business, madam; I must speak with you – whoever you are – it is of the utmost urgency. Please open the door; I am a friend of Mrs. Younge."

"I am sure you are, sir; Mrs. Younge has many friends but still, I shall not open the door to you or any other person after dark. If you would care to leave your name, I will let her know you called, sir."

Wickham, sick at heart, called out, his voice flat with disappointment:

"Tell her, her cousin George Wickham called. I hoped to speak with her, to see her at her house in Edward Street but she is entirely gone away. I saw the light on in the window here and my hopes rose, but obviously, in vain."

He turned away from the door in the ensuing silence, a beaten and despairing man with no place to go; no one to go to.

"Her cousin, Mr. *Wickham*? Good Lord, well I declare! I believe we have met once before, sir. A year or more ago when Mrs. Younge ran this business herself; I recall that you helped her with it in the past, have not you?"

He could hear the bolts being pulled back, and the door opened to reveal a stout motherly-looking woman with a shawl around her shoulders against the growing chill of the evening.

"It is you, indeed! Come inside, sir, although I cannot help you with your enquiry. Mrs. Younge is certainly not here, nor at Edward Street, as you say; she continues in America, you know. I am Mrs. Belmont, sir, if you do not remember me; although, I certainly do remember you. Such a distinguished-looking young gentleman, I used to say to Mrs. Younge. She was always so proud of you, sir, fairly blushed with embarrassment anytime I made a compliment about you. And what brings you to

London, sir? I did hear that you had made a fine match for yourself and moved North, but I did not hear very much else as Mrs. Younge then quickly took herself off to America and, apart from letters concerning what she sees there and enquiring about how this business fares, which I was proud to explain had been most profitable indeed – I have a certain knack with the clients who come here, you know - I have learnt nothing more."

She peered at Wickham's shocked expression and took his arm as if to steady him.

"My word! Are you feeling unwell, sir? You look all done in. Where are you staying? Shall I call a cab for you, sir? For truly you do not look well at all."

"I am sorry, Mrs. Belmont, but it is the sudden shock at your news; I can hardly believe it." He sat down heavily and shook his head slowly.

"*America*, you say? Julia is in *America*? But what does she do there? She married that Clemens person she was so taken with, I suppose? Oh! How could she? Tell me everything you know, for I know nothing at all, it would appear."

"Oh, dear, sir, I had no intention of shocking you; I imagined you knew, sir, being so close with Mrs. Younge as you were. But, yes; yes she did leave with Mr. Clemens but only as his housekeeper, not his wife. She would not have him before they left, although he was keenness itself, and she has told me she still will not have him now. I do not know her reasons for it but there it is; she always has been an independent lady and so probably cannot stomach the idea of giving it all up. But she does appear most taken with America, indeed she does, she fairly dotes upon the way of life over there."

Wickham felt a slight relief at his selfish thought that at least she had *not* married; at least she was still his Julia. He shook his head and managed a smile.

"Well, I thank you for informing me; clearly, I shall have to write and chide her for being so secretive and mysterious these past months. Perhaps I may trouble you for her address, Mrs. Belmont, before I leave you to lock up again. I have kept you long enough and I, too, must make some haste as I have just today arrived from the North and have spent the time re-visiting old haunts and remembering - foolishly, as it turns out. I have no arranged lodgings and am now going to have to search in the dark and damp for something reasonable in this part of London. Do you know of anywhere, Mrs. Belmont, before I waste too much time and effort?"

She looked at him curiously and then bustled off into the tiny back parlour where she kept the essentials for making tea for clients and brought back a steaming mug along with a wedge of bread and cheese.

"I apologise sir; this is all that I have to hand, but you are welcome to it. Sit down, sit down for a while." She seemed deep in thought as she watched Wickham devour the bread and slurp the hot tea.

"You have nothing arranged, you say, sir? No friends with a room, perhaps? Your club? It seems most irregular to have nowhere arranged, a man of your standing."

Wickham grimaced. "I am no longer the man of standing you remember, Mrs. Belmont. I confess to being in Town firstly as a seeker of employment and then of accommodation, in that order. Until I have the former, I cannot possibly achieve the latter."

"Oh, dear! That is most unfortunate. But I will not enquire too deeply into your affairs, private as they are. It is enough that you are the gentleman I remember. Good breeding never fails you even in the worst of situations.

"Come with me, sir. I believe this will be the best thing to do in the circumstances and I am absolutely certain that I will have Mrs. Younge's approbation regarding the care and well-being of her cousin."

Mrs. Belmont lit a lamp and, holding it high, she led the way down a small passage and then up some very steep and familiar stairs. Julia's old rooms were very much as she had always had them; the furniture had remained and the kitchen essentials still lodged conveniently in the cupboards. Looking around,

Wickham almost expected Julia to walk through the bedroom door to greet him as of old.

Mrs. Belmont smiled at him comfortingly. "This here apartment, small as it is, has been let, up until recently and I was about to let it again today except that the gentleman who wanted it did not return – I thought you was he, sir, tonight – and so his loss is your gain. It is at your disposal if you have no objections to it."

Wickham breathed a sigh of relief as he surveyed the room.

"No, indeed. I have no objections to it at all, and I thank you for your kindness. I will stay only as long as necessary, until I find something suitable; I shall start my search tomorrow. Although I hope Julia will not be angry at my taking advantage of her hospitality in her absence. As you know, we have not been in contact with each other since my marriage; she might think it presumptuous that I am once again relying upon her generous nature when she hears of it."

"Well! I am sure I do not know about that, sir, but if I know my friend at all, I know she would not wish for any relative of hers to be wandering the streets looking for accommodation in the dark and cold when there was a perfectly good place right here. Now, you make yourself at home, sir; I must be off now. I shall return in the morning and bring you some supplies. Good night, Mr. Wickham."

And so that good woman took herself off down the stairs; Wickham heard the shop door being firmly closed and the key clicking in the lock and then silence enveloped him. He went to the window and opened it for a while, listening to the street sounds and the general night noises of the city: the criers, the bells, the singing and shouting and laughter from the nearby clubs and taverns, the clip-clopping of hooves along the cobbles and the rattle of cart wheels, the vague murmurs of passers-by.

After a while, he closed the window tightly and unfolded the blankets laid in a neat pile upon the bed. He had not realised just how exhausted he was and felt his whole body relax as it slowly warmed through, not only from the warmth of the covers but also from the knowledge that the bed in which he lay had also served Julia for several years, and he took some comfort in the notion of her nearness. Wherever she was at that moment in actuality, she was here with him in his imagination as he floated away into a deep sleep with that happy thought playing in his mind.

Chapter 21

Wickham woke early the next morning, a delightful dream containing Julia still hanging in rags about his consciousness, refreshed and anxious to begin his new life in the City. Mrs. Belmont was as good as her word, arriving with a basket of edibles such as would provide for his needs for the next several days: bread, cheese, ham and some of her own fruit cake. He thanked her profusely and offered some payment - which she refused – claiming it all as a mere nothing and the least she could do to help a relative of her friend.

"But I will mention in my next letter that you are here, Mr. Wickham; Mrs. Younge will want to know who has rented the flat. I still must rent it out, sir, you understand, unless, of course you intend to stay here for some time and wish to do so?"

Wickham flushed and quickly rejected the offer.

"Well, of course you are welcome to stay in the meantime, but, as I say, it must bring in an income for Mrs. Younge. I would be remiss in my duties if I did not rent it out to the first suitable person as comes along."

"I understand completely, and I should not wish to interfere with your intentions of doing so. You have been more than kind, in Julia's absence, to allow me to stay this one night and I may need to trespass upon your good nature for perhaps another night or two before I am situated in a more permanent place. But, certainly, do not consider me in any of your plans; I shall vacate at a moment's notice if needs be."

Wickham smiled and closed the door as Mrs. Belmont descended the stairs to open the shades and begin her day. He turned his attention to making his toilette in as fastidious a manner as possible; he knew he would encounter fashionable crowds in the street below. At last, after taking the greatest care over the tying of his cravat and admiring the effect in the small mirror, he took up his cane and hat and made his way downstairs, bowing to Mrs. Belmont and her first client who were in deep discussion over the merits of a particular maid, and passing through the door into the already-bustling street.

For a moment he just stood, delighting in the scene before him and the knowledge that he was here, back in the place he loved so well, under his own direction and free to do just as he pleased. The depression of yesterday was entirely dismissed from his mind and after perusing left and right, he bowed to a passing couple and raised his hat to two servant girls who giggled delightedly, and then set off towards the area where the clubs were in close proximity to each other. He would know people there, he was sure, and he could at least begin to re-establish himself again amongst his fellow gentlemen and businessmen although he must just resist all urges to join them at the tables. Who knew what might develop from such meetings and conversations?

His walk was not long and his first port of call not promising. He recognised few and was recognised by even fewer. Not discouraged, he left and entered another establishment, an establishment further above his meagre means than the first had been but where, he knew, several acquaintances used to gather at just this time every day to discuss business and the events of the night before. Taking a deep breath and assuming an air of nonchalance, he nodded to the doorman and entered the dark and richly-furnished interior.

The smell of spirits and cigar smoke assailed him and the low rumble of laughter from some clustered chairs by the fire alerted him to the whereabouts of the occupants. Wickham made his way towards the group, alert for any overtures of friendliness that might be made in his direction. The man with his back towards Wickham, obscured from view in a high-winged chair, was regaling his listeners with an amusing account of his terrible losses the night before at another club, his confession almost a badge of honour. They all knew what it was to lose heavily, but they all knew what it was to win, also. That was what kept them returning to the tables night after night; the lure of the elusive win. But to lose was no shame. It was only a shame if one showed unnecessary concern about it, or if one could not afford to honour the debt. Then there was shame aplenty.

"And then, you know, Fredricks had entirely cleaned me out and he said, 'What else have you got hidden away? I will take whatever you care to offer.' And so I thought a while upon all that I could afford to lose - and some that I could not - and then I said ….

"Upon my word! *Wickham*! George *Wickham*! What on earth brings you here? Gentlemen: This is an old acquaintance of mine who should be in the North of this country, but is, it appears, right here in the City! What a pleasure, sir! Sit and join us. Here are some whom you remember, surely?"

Wickham was pulled into the midst of the group, nodding at those he knew whilst Jardine introduced him to all the others. He was handed a drink and a cigar, and Jardine continued interrogating the meaning of Wickham's presence for several more minutes. Eventually, Wickham laughed.

"No, Jardine; enough about me. Continue with your story that I so rudely interrupted, for it sounded as though it was to have a rather unpleasant ending for someone, and I know how you enjoy those!"

Jardine nodded, quickly finishing his story and then returned his attention to his guest; a guest, he noticed, who was looking rather the worse for wear, with black circles under his eyes and a certain drooping of his shoulders, quite unlike his assurance of old. This was a new, more chastened Wickham before him and he wished to know more of his friend's situation. Jardine returned to questioning Wickham as the other gentlemen drifted away into smaller groups to discuss other matters, one of which undoubtedly concerned the re-appearance of the infamous George Wickham in their midst, their recollections of why he left in the first place, and what the meaning of it could be.

"You are married, I heard?" Jardine prompted, "But not to Mrs. Younge. I was sorry to hear of it as I know how fond of each other you both were. You did not bring the new Mrs. Wickham with you so I might meet her?"

Wickham smiled slightly and shook his head, unsure how to begin his story in the face of such effusive interest and friendship.

"No, indeed; it seems Julia and I were never destined to be legally married. My wife, Lydia, is staying with her sister in Derbyshire for the moment and I am now tasked with the requirement to seek both lodging and employment before I am to be re-united with my wife. We have left the North for good, Jardine."

"*Employment*, Wickham? But I heard you were bought a commission in the regulars by Darcy only six months ago upon your marriage. Have they dispensed with your services already? Or did you behave so disgracefully that even *they* could not countenance it?" Jardine laughed, knowing as he did Wickham's propensity for gambling and enjoying other pleasures rather than focusing on hard work that did not suit him.

"No! Nothing as scurrilous as that, I assure you, Jardine. I found that the military life was not for me and so sold off my commission to the highest bidder – happily there are still some who believe it to be the way of life for them – and intend to use the proceeds to set myself up here in London somewhere, in some occupation or other. It is discovering what that occupation is to be that is the problem, but I hope time and experience has at least improved my abilities and worth."

"Well," Jardine looked at Wickham thoughtfully. He knew his friend's faults of old and had seen him overcome them once. He was wary but not unduly so. The trouble with Wickham was that he would never stick to anything for any great length of time; if anything of the slightest difficulty raised its head, he would immediately quit it. He would not trouble himself to undergo the pain and suffering that others understood they must endure when starting out in their various careers. Such was

Jardine's experience of Wickham's resolve but he could not believe that a man of almost thirty years had still not thought seriously about how he would support himself and his wife.

"It is a great pity that the military did not work out for you, Wickham. But Darcy must have laid out a great deal for that commission; I imagine he was not pleased to hear you had cashed it in so soon after his purchase of it. Indeed, he must have been displeased in the extreme – I know I should be if such a gift was rejected."

"Darcy – indeed everyone other than you – is unaware that I have done so. Just as you say, Darcy would not understand my failure to make something of his generosity, and so I thought it best to keep the news from him until I could prove I had made a sensible choice in doing so by finding other, more amenable employment elsewhere. You cannot fault me for leaving something that did not suit me, surely, Jardine?"

"That is for you to wrestle with Wickham, but I wonder what you *might* find more amenable; what it is that you have fixed your mind upon to do here in the City. For surely you cannot be here entirely without some idea."

As he spoke, Wickham fidgeted nervously in his chair and took a nip of his brandy.

"I hope to fall in with a businessman who can steer me into the path of some employment - whatever it might be - for I am willing to learn, to work hard, to put my brain behind such an endeavour, if only someone would see the potential in me. You know of my abilities, Jardine. What would you recommend I do, or with whom I should become acquainted?"

"Aah, yes; your abilities are certainly very great in certain areas, areas which have served me well in the past, Wickham. I will agree you are exceedingly good at making arrangements, letter-writing, dealing with servants and merchants - that cannot be denied - you could definitely return to being a personal assistant, as you were with me. On the other hand, there is the danger of your returning to your previous 'career' of playing the tables every night in the hope they will be kinder to you this time;

however, I should never recommend that as employment where none other is being attempted, least of all to one of my friends with responsibilities. Although there are some who claim to profit by it, they are certainly in the minority and are looked at askance wherever they go. Their stories never seem to equate to any others'."

Jardine looked at Wickham to see if his words had had any effect: Wickham's face was inscrutable. He tried another tack.

"But what does your new wife think you should do? I know how it is with ladies; they appear to be submissive, but in everything they do and everything they say there is the hint that they will overrule whatever you have decided upon because it is not quite what they expected. Is that how the new Mrs. Wickham behaves? But perhaps she is quite the opposite; perhaps I prejudge her unfairly. Perhaps she is more pragmatic and does not much care what you decide upon as long as it will provide an income and certain security."

Wickham laughed ruefully. "I do not think you could call my wife pragmatic but, you are right: Lydia does not care to think about anything unless it concerns new clothes, entertainment or gossip, and then she is indefatigable indeed. Her only expectation of me is to return with a general announcement of my success, assure her of being able to provide for her every whim and frippery, and bring her to London where she will expect, I have no doubt, to be housed somewhere very large and exclusive with servants at her beck and call. How or what I have done to earn these assurances is not her concern. As with any lady, she has great difficulty understanding the need for prudence and limiting her expenditures and so, I find myself looking seriously for something that will provide her with the security and some likeness of the life which she expects. She has been forced to throw her lot in with mine and I do feel the responsibility of my situation."

Jardine looked quizzically at his friend. "*Forced* to throw in her lot with you, Wickham? My word, you do not paint a picture of wedded bliss. It sounds less like a felicitous match and more like a business deal gone badly wrong, and after only six months, too. It would not do as an advertisement to induce someone like me to enter that state.

"I heard the rumours, of course, but hoped that at least there was some degree of affection involved on either side, or some extra quality that attracted you. You forsook your Mrs. Younge for her, after all; your plan was always to marry that lady and her security, was it not, now? But if there was no affection, and no security in marrying Miss Bennet, it would appear you have mismanaged for yourself the worst of both worlds, my friend, and I am sorry for it."

Wickham looked down at his boots and brushed some cigar ash from his trousers. He had not intended making confidences, he had intended keeping his life a secret, but in the face of such friendly interest he could not resist sharing his torment. He looked up at Jardine who waited with a concerned expression.

"I made a very foolish and costly error in judgment, Jardine, and it is one that I shall have cause to regret until my dying day," he admitted quietly. "It was a mistake that I was forced to pay for by marrying Lydia." He thought rapidly before continuing his tale.

"Lydia was in Brighton at the same time as was I last year, but after several weeks, wished to return to her family – I will not go into the particulars now other than she was very distressed – and convinced me to accompany her in her flight."

"But who was her chaperone? Who was her guardian? Surely she was not entirely without friends there? And why did not you return her immediately to her family if she was so distressed?"

"That was always my intention, of course it was; as soon as I could arrange it, we left Brighton and made our way to London where I was to return her to her aunt and uncle in Cheapside. Foolishly, I did not realise until too late that such a journey – over two days and nights of travelling with a young daughter of a gentleman – would automatically necessitate my marrying her. Darcy and her uncle insisted upon it and I certainly do not blame them; it was the honourable thing to do. Her reputation would otherwise have been ruined. But I cannot lay all of the blame at her door. She might have used her wiles but I should have resisted them with greater determination than I did. I knew of her feelings for me – she had made them plain enough for months - and she loves me still, I believe, so at least one of us is happy."

Jardine sat silent after Wickham had finished his confession. He drew on his cigar and considered. He had personally never been this close to disaster himself, prudent as he had always been both in his business and personal attachments, but he could see in his friend's face the regret and despair at being permanently attached to a woman he did not love, much less respect or care for.

"And what about Mrs. Younge, Wickham? Have you seen her since your arrival? Has she anything to say about your situation or should I surmise that she refused to have anything to do with you or your life – and one could not blame her for that - after everything she has endured at your hands, but you always held her opinion in high regard, I know."

Jardine looked long and hard at Wickham before he spoke again.

"Have you seen Mrs. Younge since your marriage, Wickham?"

"No, I have not, but, even though I have remained constant to Lydia in my actions, I confess Julia has been in my thoughts every single day of my marriage. I did call upon her the moment I arrived in London, foolish and hopeful as I was; I could not restrain myself."

"And what was her reaction to you?"

"There was none. I was sorely disappointed and shocked. She is in America, Jardine, as housekeeper to a most obnoxious American gentleman who had been a regular guest at her house the previous year. Apparently she has not married him – one piece of information I was selfishly glad to obtain – but she is still there with him and who knows what arrangements have been entered into. It makes me sick to think of it."

"Well, why should she not find herself another man, if that is what she has done? She is still quite young and attractive, as I recall, and financially well placed, as you told me. Why should she not carry on with her life and find herself some happiness?

"Mrs. Younge was always too smart for you, Wickham, out of your sphere, anyway. She loved you but also knew what you were and the danger you presented to her security. What have you done to restore her faith in you, Wickham? If she *had* opened the door, what would you have offered to prove to her that your love was still as strong as it ever was and your intentions and future were much improved?"

Wickham stood suddenly and walked away from Jardine. He had no answer because he had had no plan, just as he never had a plan. He had only imagined Julia's face wreathed in love and forgiveness, her calm voice setting his world to rights as she had always done, her gentle touch almost too much to bear. He had conveniently forgotten her angry reactions to his many failings, her refusal of him as a husband until he could prove his worth, and her pain the very last time he had seen her, that fateful night when he had turned up at her door with Lydia in tow, expecting her, once again, to solve his problem.

"I have no answer for those questions, Jardine. Perhaps it is as well that she is out of the country and so saved herself a most uncomfortable meeting. I was being selfish, that was all."

Jardine nodded. "Well; hard as it will be, the best thing for you to do is to stop thinking of Mrs. Younge – she is no longer available to you, nor you to her – and start thinking of the best way to organise your new life and make the best of it as many are forced to do.

"Marriage! The more I see and hear of it, the less likely it is that I shall ever trust another human being with my affections, estate or connections, and especially not a female. No, I believe I shall remain a bachelor rather than live to regret the mire into which I might inadvertently throw myself at the first instance of weakness.

"You are right in coming here, though; the City is certainly the place for you. You do not suit the confines and unvarying nature of country-life, I think, and we shall put our minds to solving the problem together. You must look forward with determination, not backwards with regret, and decide what is best to be done to ameliorate this unsatisfactory situation in which you find yourself. Where are you staying?"

"I am presently in a temporary situation until I can find something more permanent and suitable. There is, in truth, very little that I can afford, Jardine, given my present circumstances."

"Then you must come and stay with me, Wickham. No, no, I insist. It is no imposition at all and it will give you access to all of my friends and acquaintance, which will place you in the best possible situation to execute your plans.

"Come now, let us take a stroll in the Park to continue our discussions and see to whom you can be introduced. It is all a matter of whom you know and the impression you give; after that, everything relies upon your attitude and the level of your determination to succeed. That will make the best impression in the end. Come; before the rain spoils our plans, and then we shall take a cab to the Square and get you settled in. It will be just like old times!"

Chapter 22

Two weeks later found Wickham and Jardine on either side of the large desk in the library discussing a promising business venture that had been presented to Jardine that very morning; a business venture in which he had neither inclination nor time to invest but - they were both of the opinion - could prove to be something hopeful for Wickham. The question was how Jardine could transfer the offer to Wickham, without the other gentleman demanding too many assurances about Wickham, a character with whom he was entirely unacquainted.

Wickham was pressing his case most eloquently to Jardine as he was very interested in this venture. He could see it as something for which he was suited – liaising with merchants, and negotiating the buying and selling of goods were skills of which he was perfectly capable – when they heard the front doorbell clang and the sound of a deep voice requesting to see Jardine immediately. They both relaxed back into their chairs to continue their debate; Jardine had left orders he would see no one that afternoon.

However, there had been time for only one more word when the door to the library was thrust open.

"Mr. Darcy to see you sir; he would not be put off…" apologised the butler before hurriedly backing out of the room.

Darcy stalked in, quickly surveying the room. His expression changed from one of polite enquiry to grim satisfaction when his eyes flicked from Jardine - who had risen from his seat in surprise - to the other person in the room, and found himself looking upon exactly the man about whom he had come to seek information.

Wickham rose also, flushing at the intrusion. He had no time to wonder just how Darcy had found him, returning Darcy's stare with growing concern.

"Mr. Darcy; good day to you, sir. You are very welcome," Jardine bowed. "We have met briefly about Town in past years of course, but I am sure you do not recollect …"

"Mr. Jardine. I am delighted to have found you at home. Allow me to apologise for my unannounced visit. I have come to London in search of this exact person with whom you are currently engaged, as it would appear. I do not wish to appear ill-mannered, sir, but my business is with Wickham and is of the most pressing nature, I assure you."

"Well, of course; naturally you will wish to discuss your business in private. I will leave you to do so." Jardine left the room as abruptly as his visitor had entered, feeling rather stung by Darcy's high-handed manner.

Darcy, entirely oblivious to any affront given, turned to Wickham and fixed him with a fierce glare. Neither spoke for several seconds.

"I hope there is nothing amiss at Pemberley that drives you into Town in search of me with such haste, Darcy?" Wickham tried his most conciliatory tone. It was neither convincing nor conducive to soothing Darcy's temper.

"*You hope there is nothing amiss at Pemberley, do you, Wickham?* I thank you for your concern, sir but what makes you care, now, pray? Have you made any attempt since your departure to find out how your wife is faring without you, *at Pemberley?* What do you imagine such an extended silence from you conveyed to those of us who know you best? Those of us who know of what you are capable: your predilections, your irresponsibility?"

"I am sure I do not know at what you are hinting," blustered Wickham, "but whatever it is, you have entirely misunderstood, Darcy. I wrote to Lydia very recently, in fact, informing her of my progress here in Town with the hope of being happily situated very soon. I may have waited a little long, perhaps, before writing her of my news but there was little to report before that. I have been entirely focused on making connections and enquiries. I really have had no time to write letters."

Darcy glared at him and strode to the window, clearly trying to control his temper.

"Your ingenuousness does not convince me, Wickham. Let me explain how that disappearance and subsequent silence appeared to those of us tasked with her comfort and happiness in your absence. Three days after your departure, a reasonable person would expect a letter announcing your safe arrival in London, along with details of your new address: no such letter was forthcoming.

"We then anticipated a letter would arrive by the end of the first week informing your wife of your progress and desire to have her by your side as soon as could be arranged. But no; again all was silent on that topic. It appeared, Wickham - to us all, with the exception of your wife who seems to believe everything that you chose to tell her, truth or otherwise - that you have absconded with no intention of returning to her or your military post in Newcastle. Hence my hasty and inconvenient journey, forced away from those with whom I would rather spend my time, to find you and discover the truth."

He advanced upon Wickham. "What *is* the truth, sir? Have you abandoned your wife, as it appears?"

Wickham recoiled under Darcy's anger and blustered, "That is a shocking question indeed, Darcy, and one to which I shall not deign to respond. I am affronted that everyone immediately thinks the worst of me merely because of a slight lack of communication.

"But you may be satisfied on one point. I will tell you the truth regarding my current situation, and the truth of it is that my friend, Jardine - to whom you were so rude just now, and in his own house - has been putting himself at my disposal, introducing me to all of his business acquaintance, to improve my chances of beginning a career in the city. We were, as a matter of fact, just discussing the merits of one such venture when you broke in upon us."

Wickham adopted an injured air and looked away from Darcy.

Darcy looked scathing. "What business opportunities – what *businessman* – would attach themselves to someone like you? You, who have no experience, no connections, no backing, and certainly no good references for your character. I cannot believe that any sensible person would take a chance on you, Wickham: it is all a bluff.

"And why are you in search of another position? What has happened to your commission? Surely you have not been thrown out of the Regulars already?"

Wickham raised his eyebrows and shrugged his shoulders.

"I certainly was *not* thrown out: I have sold my commission, if you insist upon knowing every little detail. The proceeds are necessary to set up in business here – it is not easy without ready cash, you know."

Darcy's face was thunderous as he glared at Wickham and picked up his hat; he could not trust himself to speak any more on the matter.

"I shall return tomorrow when we may all be in a better frame of mind to discuss this reasonably. Expect me then, Wickham, and expect to prove your intentions to me then, too, including *every* consideration regarding Lydia in these so-called *plans* for your future."

He slammed out of the room and Wickham sank into the nearest chair, wiping his forehead in relief. Jardine re-entered and looked at Wickham.

"What has put Darcy in such a high dudgeon, pray? I realise that he is very rich and can afford to give offence wherever he chooses, but I draw the line at being dismissed from my own library; there had better be a good explanation for his discourteous behaviour."

"Darcy is convinced, it seems, that I intend abandoning my wife, leaving her to the charity of her family, and taking up my old life here in London. He has come to ascertain my real intentions and wants to see proof of it with his own eyes when he returns tomorrow."

"Or what?"

"I do not know he has thought that through, or if he has, he gave no hint of it to me, the temper he was in. He was, of course, shocked to see me here and was not armed against it, but his main concern appears to centre around my responsibility to Lydia and how I intend supporting her in this new venture. I believe he fears she will remain under his protection longer than he wishes."

Jardine thought for a moment. "Then you must impress upon him the advantage of this business proposition, Wickham, and prove his fears are unfounded. I shall enquire no more into the matter but you have convinced me, at any rate, and will endeavour to do the same for those who need convincing about your character and willingness to learn the business."

He stood and smiled down at Wickham. "Come, man; all is not so bad. You have a great deal to be thankful for, you know: you are not entirely friendless; you have a wife who you say loves you, even if you cannot return those feelings; and you have the prospect of a lucrative career if you can gain it. That is not a bad situation for any young man."

Chapter 23

"Lizzy! Listen to this!" Lydia shook her letter at her sister as she rushed into the parlour. "Wickham has written again! He writes: 'I am making constant progress towards my goals, my dear, but must entreat you to remain patient for a while longer and cannot agree with your expectation of joining me in London in the near future as you suggested in your letter.' Do you see, Lizzy? He is making a success of his endeavours in Town and has undoubtedly run into many of his former acquaintance who are only too happy to help him! Oh! How exciting it is to have a successful husband!"

Elizabeth looked up from her own missive that had arrived jointly with Lydia's and smiled at her sister's obvious delight and naiveté.

"I hope that it is so, Lydia, and I am happy for you both if it is the case. It is unfortunate, though, that he is uncertain when you will be able to join him, although I am sure he is as anxious for that event, as are you."

Lydia was quickly finishing the letter and let out a sigh of frustration. "Oh! He says that I am not to accompany you all into Kent, either; he does not wish for me to be away from home in case his situation changes and *can* arrange for me to join him in Town. Oh; that is most disappointing indeed. He says I must return to Longbourn and await word from him there: Ohh! He says that he has seen Darcy! Darcy has visited him at his friend's house – whose he does not say but I wager it is Denny of whom he speaks – dear Denny! Always a true and honest friend when one needs one. Excuse me, sister, but I must find Lady Catherine and tell her that I shall not be able to accept her kind offer of hospitality at Rosings."

Elizabeth watched her sister's speedy departure with misgiving; her own letter contained a more sobering account of that same meeting and it did not bode as well as that her sister had received. Darcy was clearly very upset at Wickham's situation in Town and very doubtful of any successes having been already made.

He had, he wrote, met with both Wickham and his friend Jardine, and while they assured him of Wickham's diligence in seeking employment, could not absolutely guarantee of any such thing materialising in the near future.

…for, even though I respect Jardine as a gentleman and as a businessman, I cannot but believe him to be hoodwinked by Wickham regarding both his imaginary plight and his intentions. It can only be a matter of time before he sees through the man for what he is and removes him from his company and protection. It would appear that Wickham has given up the idea of the military as a career entirely - which vexed me greatly - and intends using the proceeds from the commission I bought him to further these goals in Town. I will return there tomorrow after meeting with your father and uncle, and make Wickham a final offer. I hope he will take it as it is meant and thereby put an end to his nonsensical dreams which will all come to nothing.

Elizabeth smiled at his loving words which followed, as always astonished that such a reserved man could pen such thoughts of love and longing without embarrassment. She pressed the letter to her lips and then filed it secretly amongst the others received in the short course of their marriage.

Now to the decision about removing with Lady Catherine into Kent. Lady Catherine was most insistent and had brooked no opposition. Lydia, Elizabeth and Georgiana *must* accompany Anne and her back to Rosings Park and await Darcy and Fitzwilliam there. "For what purpose," she had demanded in various forms several times over dinner the previous evenings, "can you be expected to remain here alone until Darcy deigns to return, when he can just as easily travel into Kent from London when he has finished his business there?" She allowed herself a small glance at Lydia, "And travel a shorter distance? It would be a sensible and thoughtful thing to do; indeed you must consider it to be so."

Elizabeth readied her pen and looked thoughtfully out of the window. The grounds were already mantled in their Spring adornments and she longed to walk for miles, by herself, without the cares concerning her sister and guests and Darcy weighing upon her. She sighed and dipped the nib into the inkpot.

Pemberley
April 24rd 18~

My Darling,

I am relieved you have found Wickham, at least, with relatively little trouble, and have discovered the truth behind his situation. I am glad that you will allow those of your friends and relations who have offered support in this matter to be of assistance to you, now. There is no reason for you to bear it all on your own as you have done in the past. Permit my father, uncle and Bingley the chance to be of use in this situation, to help decide what the best plan of action must be. My father should be happy to assist considering what you have already done to secure his youngest daughter's happiness.

Lydia, of course, has received a letter regarding the same meeting but, unsurprisingly, it contained none of the reservations within your account. She is under the impression that Wickham is doing well but, as yet, not well enough for her to join him in London and so she has been instructed to return to Longbourn and await him there. Lydia was most disappointed, but not so much as I would have expected. She has already informed Lady Catherine that she cannot come into Kent with us and appears most sanguine about the reversal of her travel aspirations. It is most unlike her not to cause trouble about being thwarted in something she had set her heart upon, but perhaps this is a new, sensible Lydia we are experiencing; I pray it is so.

With that subject in mind, my dear, Lady Catherine intends to return to Rosings within days and proposes that we accompany her thence. We would be able to travel quite comfortably together, and Georgiana and Anne have become quite firm friends since they have known each other. It seems a sensible idea to me and would relieve you of any concerns you might have about me staying here alone; you would also be nearer to Rosings when your business in London is complete and you can join us there without the unnecessary return to Derbyshire in between. Of course, if you have any objection to this plan, then please convey your wishes immediately as I believe Lady Catherine has every intention of leaving as soon as I have word from you.

Although I would rather remain here and have you to myself upon your return, that happy situation is not to be for the immediate future, it would seem, and I do look forward to seeing Charlotte again. We must remain patient, my darling until ……..

The remainder of the letter contained those thoughts that are particular to those newly and deeply in love. She smiled as she sealed the letter and then started another to Charlotte, alerting her to the imminent return of perhaps not only her patroness and Georgiana, but also of her most intimate friend. She was, Lizzy wrote, most anxious to see her friend and son and could barely wait until they were together again.

Darcy was not long in responding. He thought it a splendid notion and was deeply grateful for the thoughtfulness of his wife. He also apprised her about his latest meeting with Wickham which had taken place the previous day under the auspices of not only Jardine but also of Bingley.

… I wished to make absolutely certain that there could be no misrepresentation of my words or actions; the other two gentlemen, although silent for the entirety of the meeting, were worthwhile as witnesses to the whole transaction, a transaction with which I hope you will agree.

I made an offer of a yearly sum which should be more than sufficient to support him if he chooses to live in a reasonable house in the country and constrains his household spending. Bingley assured me that it was a most generous sum, and was quite shocked at the cool manner in which it was received. But it was nothing unusual to me; I have experienced Wickham's avarice many times before and nothing I could have offered would have induced him to show gratefulness, I am sure of that. I await his consideration, for which I have allowed him three days: three days to decide if he can live with my regulations regarding his behaviour and responsibilities, or whether he still believes he can forge ahead with his own future under the guidance of his friend. I believe, however, that Jardine has already had his eyes opened to Wickham's actual reasons for being in Town and may be a little less anxious to continue with their plans after this. I would not wish him to feel he has been taken in, as have so many others in the past, by a winning story told by someone with all the appearance of goodness but having none.

I bid you a safe journey into Kent, my darling wife, and will write to you there with news of when Fitzwilliam and I shall be joining you.

My love is yours, always,

D.

Elizabeth smiled, folded the letter in amongst the others, and rising from her chair, made her way through to the servants' hall to inform them that a move was afoot, and soon. There were many preparations to be made: guests to be re-packed; sister to be organised; Georgiana and herself to be made ready along with a separate trunk for Darcy and his necessities.

Very soon, all was flurry and activity as servants were given their orders. Lady Catherine and Anne were the first ones ready and spent a deal of time assisting Lydia who, of course, could find none of her things discarded as they had been about the house and garden. Maids were dispatched in all directions to find missing books, combs, gloves, bags, and work. A busy day was spent in organisation and the following morning, very early, the ladies were boarding the Barouche box as the trunks were loaded in, settling themselves very comfortably on its wide seats.

"Ooh! How delightful, Lady Catherine. This is quite like sitting in a chair in the parlour, is not it?" sighed Lydia as she stroked the upholstery. "It is by far the most comfortable carriage I have ever ridden in, I assure you. For, of course, I have experienced many different types of equipages in my recent travels …."

"Thank you, Lydia. I do not believe we need reminding of your travels nor the reasons for them," Elizabeth cut in before her sister got carried away with her reminiscences.

"Well! I am sure I do not wish to relate stories that no one wishes to hear," Lydia pouted, "but it is going to be a tedious drive if we do not talk of something."

There was silence for about ten minutes while Pemberley Park rolled by and Elizabeth felt her old excitement mount at the prospect of travelling; first to pay a quick visit to Jane whom she had alerted and had delightedly offered them a bed for the second night, and then onwards, minus Lydia, to London and beyond, into Kent. Although her travelling companions were not all that she would desire – she felt sure that Lady Catherine and Lydia would quickly wear upon her nerves in such close quarters– she felt a kinship with the other two ladies and was glad to see Georgiana taking a quiet interest in the scenery passing by the window and talking quietly of what she saw with Anne.

However, even though the carriage was everything comfortable and supportive, and protected its occupants from the greater jolts along the road, it was not many hours before the ladies were silent and wishing for more to see and think of than the country passing before them. Even Lydia had given up on her former high spirits and was gazing blankly out of the window, thinking deep thoughts, when the carriage pulled into an inn yard and drew to a halt in front of the doorway.

All was a sudden bustle and busyness: servants ran to open the door and help the ladies down, others caught and carried the trunks inside and the owner himself came to greet his most honoured guest distinguishable by her mode of travel. Nothing was too much trouble for her ladyship, and before too much time had passed they were all relieved of their cloaks and shown to their rooms where they could take advantage of some privacy to restore the damages travelling had wrought upon their appearance.

Elizabeth was quickly finished with her toilette and, after discovering that her room overlooked the courtyard at the rear of the property, happily spent several minutes observing the noisy comings and goings below. A knock on her door revealed Georgiana, Lydia, and Anne who were, likewise, finished and ready to take some exercise through the small village before being confined to the inn all evening. They agreed to take a turn about the village green and along the small length of shops but without Lady Catherine, who, Anne explained, had developed a headache and would rest until dinner time. This was happy news indeed for all of the ladies and they set out to discover the delights on offer.

Lydia had quite regained her composure and amused her two newest acquaintances with a re-telling of her and Kitty's first adventure out on their own together a year previously, when they had gone to meet their sisters and Maria Lucas upon their return from visiting Kent.

"For you know, it was there that Lizzy was thrown much in the company of Mr. Darcy and Colonel Fitzwilliam; you were there, Anne, do tell us how the two of them got along amongst strangers!"

"Lydia! There is nothing to be told about that meeting, I assure you. Indeed, I was more concerned with spending as much time as possible with my friend than I was with making new acquaintance."

Anne smiled, remembering. "Ah, yes, but I do recall how Mamma was most put out with your pert opinions and at my cousin's attentions to you. Darcy had always been so silent and reserved whenever he was in Kent, but for the first time he showed an interest in the conversation and, in particular, your ability at the pianoforte and singing."

Elizabeth coloured slightly as she averted her gaze to the wares in a shop window. She, too, recalled Darcy's interest and what had happened in private between them; it was all too strange to hear it recounted by another person who had watched without any knowledge of the feelings engrossing them. She was sure that they had neither of them betrayed even the slightest hint of those feelings: hers of distaste and anger; his, unbeknownst to her, of real attraction and love. Her insides curled up anew remembering her harsh words to him, her downright refusal of those natural and just feelings which he had so openly expressed. How blinded she had been! How foolish to have believed the false words and appearance of Wickham over the truthful words of Darcy!

"I hardly think that Lady Catherine was so very much aggrieved by his attentions – such as they were at the time – Anne. She perhaps would have preferred to have her two nephews entirely to herself, and that is quite reasonable for a lady who has only limited contact with them to be so possessive when they do pay her a visit. But she will have to share her time with him this visit and for all succeeding ones, I am afraid. I shall engage my husband far more than I engaged the little-known Mr. Darcy then.

"Should we return to the inn, ladies? It is becoming quite cool now the sun has set and I am rather anxious to find a warm place in the parlour for the evening, if it is not too crowded."

Chapter 24

Two further days of travelling found the ladies rolling through the verdant woodlands surrounding Rosings Park. Lady Catherine and Anne were quietly delighted to be back amongst familiar surroundings and welcomed the gasps of pleasure emanating from their companions. Georgiana, the only one of the four to whom the scenery was a revelation, commented on everything upon which her eyes alighted: the beauty and depth of the woods; the height of the farmers' crops; the walls and fences, and when they at last arrived within sight of the house itself, Elizabeth nudged her sister and pointed it out, smiling at her reaction.

Rosings Park had been built with ostentation in mind and captured none of the quiet formality and elegance of Pemberley. It was very grand, to be sure, and imposing upon first view, and boasted of many windows of various sizes and shapes, but Elizabeth, knowing as she did that this excess of questionable taste continued throughout the interior, smiled encouragement at her sister's surprised first expression. There was little to become effusive about and Georgiana managed a non-committal, "Ah, delightful" before pretending to be quite overcome with emotion at the sight before her. Fortunately, Lady Catherine believed Georgiana's response and preened herself with satisfaction.

"Yes, yes, indeed, my dear. You are impressed by Rosings, I see, but why would you not be? Used as you are to Pemberley and its own particular attractions, to be faced with another of equal if not exceeding delights can only be a source of amazement to one such as yourself who has travelled very little and seen even less of the country's great architects' work.

"And now, here we are in good time for a rest before dinner. Perhaps you would like to visit your friend, Elizabeth, before that? I should not feel it an impertinence to me, I assure you, and Mrs. Collins would be glad to know of your safe arrival."

Elizabeth smiled and nodded happily at the suggestion, although she was absolutely certain that Charlotte would already know of their arrival through the very effective methods of observation employed by her husband. He would never have missed the arrival of her ladyship's carriage.

"If you are sure it is agreeable, Lady Catherine, I should certainly like to walk over to the Parsonage and visit my friend; it has been too long and we shall have much to discuss. I confess I am also most anxious to make the acquaintance of her son. I shall be back for dinner, you may be assured of that."

And so it was that, within the hour, Lizzy found herself walking along a very familiar path towards the house where she had spent many happy weeks the year previously. She smiled as she approached the door and saw her friend standing waiting with a small bundle in her arms. They embraced closely and Lizzy remarked upon the bundle which had started to wail; Charlotte ushered her friend inside so they could talk and comfort the child in private.

Lizzy watched her friend as she fed the baby, admiring the absolute serenity and happiness exuding from her every movement. How much she had wished to become a mother, and how well fulfilment of that wish suited her! Even the prospect of meeting with Mr. Collins faded into insignificance in the presence of such contentment.

"I see you are happy, Charlotte. You certainly have all the skills necessary for a mother; little William is fortunate indeed to have you watching over him. He will be a most beloved person and that is everything to a child, is it not now?"

Charlotte smiled down at her son and responded quietly, "Indeed it is, and more than you can imagine. I have learnt first-hand just how a negligent parent can badly affect their child. I cannot claim to be an expert in this but at least I know the value of nurturing and loving my child. He already knows he is very precious to both of us. William is quite the doting father; he has none of the stern extremes some men seem to think necessary in raising children, particularly male children, and for that I am grateful. There could be nothing harder for a mother to see her child being made miserable by a dogmatic father."

"I have no doubt that he takes his cues from you, my dear friend. He sees how you manage the baby and understands the effect of it. He is also a very fortunate man to have such a sensible and loving wife. But where is my cousin, pray? I am astounded that I have been here almost an hour and he has not come in to greet me."

Charlotte smiled and advised her husband had been called away early that morning to visit a dying parishioner and, much as he wished to be available to greet Lady Catherine and Anne upon their return, and welcome his cousin, Charlotte had convinced him that his duty lay with his parishioner.

"And so I have you all to myself this afternoon, Lizzy. I hope it will not be too tiresome for you?"

"Oh; I shall endure it as best I can, Charlotte, and hope the time will pass quickly enough admiring your son and garden and any other improvements that have been made in my year's absence! Give him to me, if you please, so he can begin to make my acquaintance all the sooner. And shall we walk a little? I confess to feeling rather stiff and lethargic after so many days travelling; a turn about your garden will soon put that to rights."

Lizzy stayed to tea and then excused herself for the grandeur and chill of dinner at Rosings Park. She would have preferred to stay and continue her conversation with her friend but, she consoled herself as she returned quickly along the path, she would visit every day, even with the dubious pleasure of regularly encountering her cousin, and for a while everything would be almost as it used to be in Meryton.

Chapter 25

Meanwhile, Wickham had had a great deal of thinking to do after Darcy had re-presented himself, along with Mr. Bingley, at four o'clock the afternoon following the day of his surprise visit. Darcy's manner had cooled to an icy politeness – perhaps Mr. Bingley had exerted some influence in the interim - and Jardine had accepted Darcy's curt apology for his earlier ill-manners with a polite nod of his head, more than happy to remain, as requested by Wickham, for the entirety of the meeting.

Jardine had not been without his suspicions, knowing as he did Wickham's behaviour in the past, including his reliance upon the Darcy name and fortune both of which, he understood, had more than once been pressed into service for the benefit of Wickham and the continuation of the good name of the Darcy family, and so was more than a little interested to know the meaning of Darcy's current disquiet.

It appeared to be an offer sincerely, if coldly delivered, and upon first reflection answered Wickham's every desire: a consistent amount to be paid quarterly, enough to survive comfortably in a small rented house in the country, with no other requirement to be made of him other than to act, if not be, the faithful husband to Lydia.

This last was the rub; of all the other constraints that would fall upon him by accepting the offer, this was the most egregious: the loss of his independence; being closeted in the country for ever and unable to live where he chose; the possible proximity to his mother-in-law; the loss of the excitements of London, or Bath, or Brighton (such a limited sum could never provide for travel) were nothing compared to the idea of being burdened by a wife he had never sought nor desired.

He had never loved Lydia. She had been a distraction perhaps, an amusing companion for a very short while in Brighton last Summer, but he knew now, absolutely, that he had been manoeuvred into running away with her from Brighton, and forced into marriage with her as a consequence. Of her affection for him, he had never been in doubt; indeed, he had tried to ward off her feelings from the first instance she had made them apparent in Meryton, even on the first day of their acquaintance. At that time he had been merely flattered to be the object of affection and interest from so many handsome young ladies - Lydia's sister, Elizabeth, had particularly sparked his interest until he learnt of the family's limited circumstances – but he had with absolute clarity on several occasions, spoken to Lydia about her behaviour towards him and his disinterest in it; to no avail. She had determined to have him and he, desperate fool that he had been at the time, had fallen into her trap.

Darcy had delivered his ultimatum, advised that he expected a reply within three days hence, collected his hat from the chair where he had lain it, and left with Bingley, who had said nothing for the entire meeting. Indeed, it was five minutes in which no other person in the room had spoken after the first introductions. Darcy had completed his task, making no attempt to hide his disgust at the unpleasantness of having so to do, and swept out as if desirous of shaking the very contamination of it all from every fibre of his being.

Jardine had remained silent, waiting for some response from Wickham who had dropped his head in mortification while silently contemplating the offer and its various merits compared to the path he was embarking upon with Jardine. He could live the life of a country gentleman – with very limited means, naturally – but he would have his leisure and be his own master; but master of what? The invisible leash would always be there, attached to Darcy as he would be, in his debt forever, unable to live life, unable to enjoy life as he imagined himself doing. It would be a miserable kind of leisure and he was sure that the restrictiveness of it would become irksome very quickly.

However, it would mean he need not labour for his bread; it would mean that he could support a family without lifting a finger to do so, merely wait for the money to be deposited each quarter in order to pay off the merchants' bills and the rent. He would have to confirm that the amount Darcy had offered would, indeed, be enough to cover all expenses, including rent and furnishings, but he believed it to be a generous offer.

Wickham raised his head and saw his friend watching him quizzically. He smiled ruefully and ran his fingers through his hair.

"That, since you have hardly met the man, was Darcy in all his glory, displaying every proud trait as becomes the master of Pemberley. I hope you were impressed, Jardine: for myself, I regret to say I have been in this situation more times than I can remember – being at his mercy; being informed how my life will be lived - it gets no easier, I assure you, and he certainly seems to enjoy it even less. It was quite an offer, though, do not you think?"

Jardine, perplexed, asked, "But surely you cannot even *begin* to think of accepting it, Wickham? This is not a loan, or a payment of a debt: a singular payment with the threat it had better not happen again. It is a *permanent* agreement to hold you in and control your behaviour for the rest of your life. You must live where he says; you must spend what he gives; and you must live with Lydia regardless of your attraction for her. There can be no escapes to Town for pleasure – you will not be allowed it, even if you could eke out enough from the payment to do so – and with what on earth do you propose to fill your time, hidden away in the depths of the country as you will be?

"I know your temperament, Wickham, and you will not last in such circumstances. And what should you do when the call of the tables – or Julia – become too much, as they inevitably will? Then what will happen to the agreement when you defy its very purpose? What revenge will Darcy take upon you then? For I can assure you he will take a *very* dim view of any reneging on your part. He was more temperate than I would be if you had already thrown away one method of supporting yourself which I had paid for at great expense, only to discover that you had responded similarly to my next solution.

"As generous as it is, Wickham, supposing you find yourself able to live within its parameters, it still means you will be a kept man with no autonomy of your own, unable to make the slightest decision without reference to your benefactor. You had much better taken the living you were offered so long ago; at least with that you would be honourably employed and enjoy some status through that employment, although I pity the poor parishioners under your auspices!"

Wickham listened to his friend's advice, a sickening feeling of dread starting through his stomach. While a life of leisure without any accompanying worries about money was certainly attractive, the life, as outlined by Jardine, was not.

He was torn indeed. He had always taken the easy way out of his problems, taken offers of money and employment without looking any further than escaping his current predicament by whatever means possible. This was an escape of sorts but one of more permanence, as Jardine had said.

"How certain are you of this business acquaintance's acceptance of me as his business manager? I cannot think of refusing Darcy's offer without having some certainty of employment elsewhere."

"Aspinall wishes to meet with you tomorrow. He was suitably impressed with my recommendation after I set out all that you were responsible for whilst in my employ, and added other areas at which I am certain you will excel. He is a reasonable type of fellow but not interested in the daily grind of business and, quite frankly, I would not recommend that he do so, for he is not a very personable individual and finds conversation, let alone buying and selling types of conversations, almost impossible; whereas you, my friend, I am sure, can sell anything, whether the buyer needs what you are selling or not!"

Wickham nodded, smiling slightly at the compliment.

"Then let us meet with Mr. Aspinall tomorrow, if you would be so good as to arrange it, and see what can be decided before I must give my reply to Darcy. I am of your mind, I think, that I should continue along the path I intended when I came to London and not be diverted from it by Darcy's low opinion of me."

Darcy was, therefore, rather astonished two days later, when Wickham was announced at ten o'clock in the morning and ushered into his study. Darcy eyed him warily whilst waving him to a chair opposite his desk. Wickham settled himself and withdrew a paper from his inside pocket and handed it to Darcy.

"I would have you read this Darcy, so that you can be satisfied that I am in earnest about pursuing a career here in Town. It is a formal offer of employment as business manager to a Mr. Aspinall: gentleman, importer and exporter of a growing company based here in London. He requires a person confident in management and overseeing staff, and at ease conversing with all levels of society. He offers a reasonable remuneration and a quarterly commission. The position will also enable me to travel frequently between London and other business centres, and, he expects, into America when he expands his business there. It is an exciting opportunity and one which I am not about to refuse. I thank you for your offer of support, but I must refuse it for the reasons stated."

Darcy was silent. He read the letter in his hand and could see nothing deceitful or underhand in it. He remained dubious, however, at Wickham's assertion of his talents and of just how much this Aspinall knew about him. He handed the letter back to Wickham.

"That is all very well, Wickham, and I hope for your sake that you are capable of everything you have claimed to Mr. Aspinall; you cannot fail Jardine who has, I presume, guaranteed your reliability and talents. I have heard of Aspinall, and the little that I know informs me he is no fool; he will not suffer laziness or incompetence or deceit. You will be at his beck and call, required to account for your time, your production, your successes and your failures. If you intend accepting his offer, as you say, then be absolutely certain that you know and understand everything you will be engaged to do.

"That said, I do wish you well and hope that this is the opportunity that finally sets you on the road to security and prosperity."

Darcy lent back in his chair and surveyed Wickham. The self-assured smile; the easy nonchalance; the debonair manner of his carriage and appearance had never faded and were there arrayed in front of him once again. Wickham could persuade and flatter anyone he chose and so, market transacting would be an easy employment for him. Unfortunately, it would also put him in the way of temptation every hour of every day, of that Darcy had no doubt. The people he would be mingling with would think nothing of spending entire evenings carousing and gambling until the early hours, and Wickham would relish just such company and entertainments to the detriment of his pocket, his career, and his marriage.

"Tell me, sir: how do you intend supporting yourself and Lydia whilst you are establishing this new career, may I ask? Presumably this position will entail living in Town and everything that goes along with doing so. You must have considered those expectations, surely?"

Wickham had *not* considered such mundanities in the excitement of proving himself to Darcy and Jardine. He hesitated slightly, quickly calculating.

"It is, after all, untenable for your wife to remain at Longbourn indefinitely, entirely dependent upon the goodwill of her family whilst you are here in London establishing yourself. You must see that, surely, Wickham?"

Wickham, stung, responded quickly. "And why should not they provide such support, Darcy? It is not unreasonable for her to spend some time amongst her sisters or parents, surely, whilst leaving me free to concentrate upon establishing myself? After all, it was you and her family who insisted upon our marriage, and now I am to be burdened from the very start of my new career because of it? All I ask is six months' reprieve after which I expect to be in a position for Lydia to join me."

Darcy glared at him, suddenly realising Wickham's ulterior motive: he would not only be establishing his career in London, but also himself again. A wife did not fit into the conception he had of himself as a man about Town.

He thought quickly. He still did not have the peace of mind that he would have if Wickham had accepted his offer of an annual sum and the accompanying restrictions: in the country there were limited temptations. Now, with this new freedom, at any time Wickham could abandon Lydia, disappear as he had done in the past, leaving his debts behind him. It could not be allowed to keep happening, it simply could not.

"I do not intend discussing the reasons regarding your marriage – they were clear enough to everyone concerned – or how badly you feel you have been treated. You are entitled to your opinion but I would advise you to put all thoughts of blaming any other person than yourself, aside.

"The fact of the matter is that Lydia cannot be left for six months alone without her husband, and you know it; it will cause a scandal wherever she is. However, if having your wife by your side is to be such a *burden*, as you call it, then I see no other alternative but for you to accept my offer for a limited time of, say, one year." Darcy paused as he calculated quickly.

"I will assume the costs involved in finding, renting for one year, furnishing and staffing a house in one of the newer areas on the outskirts of Town where rents are still reasonable, company will be entertaining for Lydia, and you will be able to travel easily between home and work. I am sure my manager will know of something suitable. I will also provide a small monthly allowance during that first year for general household expenses. It will require a firm hold on expenses – do not imagine me to be too generous; any over-spending will be your concern, and no one else's. After the year is complete, I will remove all material assistance in the expectation that you will be self-sufficient by that time.

"Is that an acceptable compromise, sir? If so, I will have my lawyer draw up an agreement to that end, effective immediately."

Wickham nodded his agreement. He could not refuse to have his wife to join him and Darcy knew it. But this was an offer which he could accept without any great humiliation on his part: one year's head-start and a position in which he believed he could succeed. He stood and reached out his hand, Darcy responded in kind.

"I am most grateful to you, Darcy. Firstly, for not deriding my sincere hopes for the future, and secondly, for assisting me in a manner that allows me the freedom I crave without the former threat of constant surveillance. I shall make every attempt to finally make a success of my life, for I realise, it is about time."

And with that uncharacteristically sensible announcement, he picked up his hat and left the room.

Chapter 26

Some reunions are special because of the length of time the individuals have been apart; some because of the circumstances of the separation; some because of the anticipation of shared memories; and some simply because one day without the company of that person is one day too long. Whatever the reason, whatever the understanding, whatever the necessity of it, all that good sense fades into senselessness without that person from whom you have been forced apart, and so it was for Elizabeth, forced apart for a second time from her husband of only a few months. After the distraction of the journey into Kent, after the happy reunion with Charlotte, she went about her days at Rosings with far less animation than she had the year prior. Every action seemed pointless; every letter was expected to bring news of Darcy's arrival, and was a dismal disappointment when it did not; even her frequent visits to the Parsonage were dimmed as though she participated through a gauze, her every thought and action occurring beneath a blanket of anticipation that today he would write, or, even better, arrive.

She had received a letter early on the first day of her arrival at Rosings containing information about Darcy's progress in London, but had heard nothing since and was beginning to regret ever setting foot in Kent without him. How she wished she had left the other ladies when the coach went through Town and sought him out. He would have been easy to find, after all; either at their house – which she had yet to visit – or at his club. But she had not thought that this second separation would wear upon her as greatly as it had; if anything, she had expected it to be a little less - she should be more accustomed to it, surely?

But by the fourth day, Lizzy was thoroughly distracted. She could settle to nothing, could listen to Lady Catherine for only a few moments together before excusing herself, and found only limited solace in visiting Charlotte who was always so busy with either the baby or her other occupations that frequently Lizzy felt to be in the way or taking up her time, and as soon as her cousin imposed himself upon their conversation, she immediately excused herself to wander the lanes and bridleways with which she had become so familiar last year.

Just this morning, Lady Catherine had announced that Colonel Fitzwilliam would be arriving within the next day or so — she held his letter to that effect in her hand as she made her announcement - and pontificated regarding the very great attachment the Colonel had to Rosings and what a pleasure it would be to have his company once again. She had glanced sharply at Elizabeth and continued:

"But I am sure he will have to diversify his attention rather more this year than he did last, since the object of it then is now a married woman." Not receiving any response from Elizabeth, she glared around at the other ladies and continued:

"It would seem that he has not heard from Darcy as he usually does and so intends to make his own way here without him. Have you heard from my nephew, Elizabeth?"

Lizzy re-focused her attention on the group who were all staring at her.

"I am sorry, Lady Catherine; what were you saying?"

Lady Catherine repeated her question with a fixed expression upon her face.

"Oh, no, I have nothing to add, I am afraid. Darcy has not written about his return as yet. I imagine he is still busy with his work in London and has not had time to plan his travel into Kent."

"Well, that is most remiss of him, I should say," opined Lady Catherine. "He knows he is due here to meet with the Colonel regarding the estate. What can he be doing that is taking up so much of his time, I wonder? He must have dealt with the other matter as soon as he arrived, surely? I presume he has found Mr. Wickham, has not he?"

Georgiana and Anne looked open-mouthed at Elizabeth.

"Is Mr. Wickham *lost*, Lizzy," asked Georgiana. "Has something happened to him in London? Is that why Lydia could not accompany us? Oh! It must be something terrible indeed if his wife cannot know about it."

Elizabeth smiled reassuringly. "It is nothing terrible, I promise you. And, yes, Darcy has *found* Wickham – who was not lost in the least – and is even now working with him towards an ending that will hopefully prove satisfactory for all parties concerned; it is merely taking longer than he expected, that is all, and accounts for his tardiness in joining us. But, I confess, I do wish he would come soon."

Elizabeth rose abruptly from her chair and announced her intention of visiting the Parsonage and then continuing around the Park. None of the other ladies wished to join her and so, once again, she donned her hat and jacket and made her way across the lane to her friend's house.

Elizabeth had apprised Charlotte of some of the facts regarding her sister and Wickham – enough to allow Charlotte to construct a fair simulation of the situation, and offer her opinion upon it. Today, however, seeing her friend so downcast, Charlotte decided to keep all conversation away from missing or absent husbands, London, and worrying sisters if it was at all possible. It left hardly anything of merit upon which to converse, but Charlotte valiantly decided to distract her friend as best she could.

She greeted Elizabeth warmly and rang for tea. Elizabeth settled herself and then smiled upon the baby who was sleeping soundly upon a rug in his little basket.

"How sweet he is, Charlotte, and he grows every day, I am almost certain of it! You could not ask for a more placid child than he – I do not believe I have heard him gripe more than twice since I have been here."

"Oh, he has his moments, let me assure you. But, in general, I would certainly agree with you, although I confess I rather like it when he needs soothing; I am content to comfort him and make his life as pleasant as I can. You will understand when you have a child, Lizzy, mark my words. I do not understand those women who have no affection for their children, who only wish for them to be out of their sight and so out of mind, also. I would not like having another person taking care of my child, not knowing just how his day has been, nor his night, for that matter. I do hope you will not have to give up your children to be raised in a far apartment at Pemberley, as so many of your rank do. I cannot imagine that you would, but you might be prevailed upon to do so, you know."

"I think you forget, Charlotte, just how little effect *prevailing* upon me has! Others have tried and failed, so I see no reason for such an idea to ever occur to those of my acquaintance; and for those who do not know me, well, they will learn it quickly enough, do not you think?"

Charlotte smiled as she poured the tea.

"Of course they will, and I am very happy to hear you talk as you are used to doing. I am glad that you have not forgotten your pert opinions and startling announcements quite yet, even though I am sure Lady Catherine has been working upon you."

"On the contrary; Lady Catherine has quite given up, so it would seem. She accepted the olive branch Darcy and I offered and behaved astonishingly well while staying with us. She was all gracious politeness and accommodation; it was rather unsettling.

"Darcy could not understand the change that had been wrought since his last encounter with her, when she was all accusations and vitriol. And, of course, then the expected battle between her and Lydia did not eventuate - after the first salvos were fired, of course – in fact, Lady Catherine rather took Lydia under her wing, taking her visiting local acquaintances, and we watched many a slow promenade about the garden with the two of them, as if they were old friends. It was very strange indeed."

"Her attention to your sister is not so strange, Lizzy. Lady Catherine is not as unfeeling as she first appears; I can attest to that. She has always treated William and me with the utmost consideration, and her attention to the comfort of her tenants has gained her quite a devoted following. She does, it is true, expect certain things to be done as she wishes; she expects certain attention to be paid to her opinions, and certain displays of gratitude and recognition when they are called for but, over it all, she continues to be a surprisingly accommodating benefactress and one whom I should not wish to lose. I am sure that Lydia gained a great deal from her interactions with her ladyship."

"I am sure you must be right, Charlotte," Elizabeth laughed, "but whatever you declare, I shall remain the most astonished at this new and more approachable person, someone who only last year struck me as the most opinionated and self-centred I had ever had the misfortune to meet, and who considered me to be an *upstart young woman* using my *allures* to tempt Darcy away from his obligations and her daughter!"

Elizabeth glanced about the room and then out of the window which gave out onto the vegetable garden where, very often, Mr. Collins could be seen digging vigorously: happily, today, he could not be seen.

"William is not at home this morning, Lizzy," said Charlotte, perfectly following her friend's train of thought. "He is again out visiting the further reaches of his parish; I do not anticipate his return for another hour at least. Did you need to ask him something, perhaps?" she asked with a twinkle starting in her eye.

Elizabeth started and then smiled. "No; indeed not, I thank you. But how do you stand it, Charlotte, to be left alone every day with only the servants and baby William for company? I confess to being quite forlorn without Darcy – quite ridiculous of me, I am sure you are thinking – but there it is; I cannot help it and I wish most fervently he would return from London."

Charlotte smiled at this – her own domestic arrangements were such that they ensured she spent as *little* time as possible in the company of her husband, improved as he indeed was, but even so, less was certainly more where his society was concerned.

"Oh, William and I need only meet once or twice during any day – our days are so similar that there is little new to discuss. William, of course, keeps me informed about all of his parishioners, and Lady Catherine, and I contribute any little information I can about my work about the village, or what our son has done which is only of the utmost interest to his parents and none other. I never feel the need for more society, although," as she recollected her friend counted as 'more society', "naturally, I am delighted when such company as yours is available and I confess to feeling the loss of it when it is removed. That is the only sadness I feel about your visits, Lizzy.

"But it is perfectly natural for you to feel such sadness at the absence of Darcy – you have not been married long enough for his company to pall and his opinions to have been heard before. I am glad you have such strength of feeling and I am sure he is suffering the same melancholy as are you. Absence certainly does make the heart grow fonder, does it not now?"

Lizzy looked up and nodded, then rose and put on her bonnet.

"I thank you for your kindness, Charlotte, you always were able to make me feel better, but I feel in desperate need of a brisk walk. Would you care to join me, perhaps? You might leave little William with the servant so we can enjoy ourselves together as we used to do."

Charlotte looked at her sleeping baby and was not in the least bit persuaded that a walk, even with her greatest friend, could possibly surpass waiting for the little chap to awake. How she loved that dewy, sleepy smell of him as he snuggled into her before opening his eyes. She smiled her refusal to her friend and walked with her to the front door. They embraced and Elizabeth stepped out alone down the lane and into the first bridleway leading through the woods, keeping to the edges for fear of riders who generally had no thought for walkers and considered it a great imposition to be forced to veer out of the way of some slow-moving person.

As she walked and noticed the varying vegetation, stopping occasionally to smell flowers or feel the softness of moss, Elizabeth let her mind wander over the last year and how much she had changed. She no longer felt as though her sole purpose in life was to argue against everything anyone said, as had been her wont, but now found she had greater consideration and patience with many people. She tried hard not to determine how others should lead their lives; although, she thought ruefully, she had not managed that with her sister. But that was another complexity entirely, and Lydia needed to be told for her own good.

She had tried not to make judgments upon first impressions, and believed that she was making great progress with that challenge. Where once she had instinctively decided a person's worth upon first glance, she now waited until she grew to know them better. Sometimes, her first instinct turned out to have been a good one, but just as often, if she persevered, she would find that there were other traits, better ones, that overshadowed those first instincts. She smiled as she thought back to her first impression of Darcy at the Assembly Rooms in Meryton. Oh, how proud he had been, all stiff and aloof, refusing to talk, let alone dance with any other lady than those with whom he had arrived. And her opinion had been verified once he had declared her merely *tolerable* but *not handsome enough to tempt him*. Now, she knew he was not proud, but cautious around strangers to a point of shyness, and his worst nightmare was to be thrust into a room full of such people and be expected to enter into conversation with them.

Her first opinions of the Bingley sisters, however, had only been increased against them; she had not been wrong in her estimation of them and their devious and spiteful ways. It was astonishing indeed that their brother had escaped similar traits and was such a charming and kind gentleman but she pitied Jane for having to tolerate such unpleasant sisters who would insist upon visiting more regularly than necessary and offering their advice unsought.

Another person whom she met for the first time last year was Mr. Collins. Oh, how they had all laughed at him: at his pompous formality, his appearance, his inflated ideas about his position and his eligibility as a suitor! But even he had caused her to reverse her first unkind opinion of him. He had made Charlotte very happy; he provided a comfortable home for his family; he was admired by his benefactress; and his work about the parish was to be applauded. His manner, to be sure, still irritated, but even that had certainly improved and Lizzy was in no doubt that such a change was the result of gentle encouragement from Charlotte. All in all, he had the makings of a pleasant man once he threw off his mantle of obsequiousness which he still believed essential.

Suddenly, her ears picked up the distant 'thud, thud; thud, thud' of the approaching hooves of a single horse, and her heart leapt.

Darcy?

She smoothed her dress and pinched her cheeks while trying to appear interested in a nondescript bush near her. The hooves grew louder and she could now hear the crackling of twigs and dry leaves as the horse trotted over them; then the sound of the horse's breath and the creak of saddle leather with each movement. She turned her eyes and bright smile upon the rider who was silhouetted against the sunlight, allowing her only a vague outline of his proportions and hat.

"Mrs. *Darcy*, I declare you are a sight for tired traveller's eyes! I have seen many a pretty view during my ride today, but none as welcome as this! Were you waiting for me, I wonder?"

Elizabeth swallowed her disappointment.

"Colonel Fitzwilliam! How fortunate: but we were only discussing your arrival this morning – Lady Catherine does not expect you for another day or so – of course we will all be very glad to have your company earlier than we expected. As you know, life at Rosings can be rather quiet."

Fitzwilliam laughed and dismounted, throwing the reins over the horse's head and leading it to a shaded patch of grass.

"Indeed; I am very well aware of the limitations of Rosings as a social venue, but, as I recall, it improved dramatically last year due to the addition of a certain guest!"

Elizabeth blushed. "Well, I am come again, and with Georgiana, but the company is not any better for our addition. I merely await my husband before that can be said." And then realising her rudeness added, "But your company will be greatly appreciated along with Darcy's when he decides to leave Town; when that shall be, I do not know, but I hope it to be very soon."

Fitzwilliam frowned. "I am unable to inform you about his whereabouts, I am sorry to say. I could not raise him by letter and he had not been seen at his club; when I called upon your house, he was not at home, and so I gave it all up as a lost cause and travelled here without him. But he has not written to you at all? It is unlike him to be so uncommunicative with those he loves."

"He is very busy dealing with a matter that concerns my sister. My father has already left, but Mr. Bingley still accompanies him, I believe – both brothers-in-law united in an effort to impress the third. Darcy wrote to say they had been partially successful, but there has been nothing since. I had very great hopes of you being he this morning."

"*Ah!* That explains the bright smile which I misinterpreted as being pleasure at *my* arrival. No matter; I will do my best to fill the gap with my sorry presence until my cousin returns. Tell me how you enjoy Pemberley, Mrs. Darcy. Is it everything you expected or does it rather alarm you?"

"Pemberley is a delight, Colonel, as you know very well. I have felt very welcome from the moment I set foot in the place. Georgiana is a delightful companion and we are making great improvements already about the village, visiting our neighbours and being as useful as we can. We try to get out every day and it is certainly improving Georgiana's ease amongst strangers. When I first arrived, she would not leave the house and had not done so for more than a year, unless forced."

"That is good news indeed; I know Darcy frequently commented upon just that situation and we spoke of possible solutions as joint guardians. But once you arrived, we knew it would not be long before she was encouraged into society again, and it has been done as we anticipated. I know I speak for my cousin when I say we are extremely grateful for your kindness to Georgiana; two males are not the equal of one female when it comes to empathy and sensible understanding.

"Shall we continue on back to the house? My horse appears to be cooling down nicely and needs to be quietly walked before going into the stable."

Lizzy nodded, smiling, and they both turned about towards the path that would take them the quickest way back to Rosings.

Chapter 27

Charlotte had not been alone for more than five minutes after Elizabeth left for her walk, when a knock upon the Parsonage door alerted her to another visitor – two in one day! – and, after glancing at the still-sleeping baby, settled herself by the table to greet her next guest.

She was delighted to see Miss de Bourgh enter the room, closely followed by another, taller and just as elegant young lady whom she presumed to be Miss Darcy. In this assumption she was correct, and after Anne made the required introductions, she bade them both be seated while enquiring if there was anything she could get for their refreshment.

"Oh, thank you, no, Mrs. Collins. Indeed, we have only just taken something at the house in anticipation of the long walk we can expect if we managed to catch up with Mrs. Darcy, but it seems we are already too late upon her heels. We rather thought she would be here still – has she been gone long?" asked Anne.

Charlotte confirmed that her friend had left a matter of minutes before and expressed her surprise that they had not met each other in the lane.

"Well, it is no real matter; she enquired if we would like to join her – which we refused – and now that we have changed our mind, we are too late, it seems. But I thought it prudent to leave the house; Mamma still attempts to engage me at every turn about my mysterious letter but I am determined not to let her force a confidence."

"That sounds rather secretive indeed, Miss de Bourgh!" laughed Charlotte, "but I assume since you have aired the subject,

I am allowed to enquire further, and that Miss Darcy is already your confidante?"

Georgiana smiled but remained silent while Anne sat forward in preparation of her news, only to be forestalled as, just then, the door to the parlour opened and admitted Mr. Collins, recently returned from his visit, who had observed the two young ladies as they made their way across the lane and, to his very great excitement, through his gate! He and his wife had not yet been invited to the house for dinner since Lady Catherine's return, as they usually were, and he was certainly not going to miss this opportunity of making the acquaintance of Mr. Darcy's sister.

He bowed deeply – once to each lady – and then looked to Charlotte who had immediately risen to make the introductions and interpose herself between her guests and her husband as well as she could. He smiled fawningly and began by welcoming Miss de Bourgh back into Hunsford – whose charms and ministrations, he assured her, had been sorely missed – and then brought his attention to bear upon Miss Darcy. He took a great breath before launching into a welcome speech befitting such an honoured guest.

Charlotte and Anne both looked away so as not to witness Georgiana's inevitable discomfort but quickly retrained their focus when they heard Georgiana pleasantly cutting through his verbosity.

"And how delightful to finally meet you and your wife, sir; I have heard a great deal of you both from my sister, and I feel that I know you almost as well as she. And, of course, Lady Catherine and Miss de Bourgh have praised your work highly; they are fortunate in your services, I am sure, as is the entire parish, Mr. Collins. But I suppose that we are trespassing upon your time with our visit - we certainly should not wish to keep *you* from your important work a moment longer, sir - and we shall not inconvenience Mrs. Collins longer than necessary, I assure you."

She smiled, and Mr. Collins, after trying to formulate a response, realising he had been dismissed, deeply bowed again to each lady and retreated with many wishes for a fortunate visit and happiness to be theirs.

Georgiana calmly re-seated herself without looking at either of the other ladies until they had done likewise.

"Now Anne, you were about to tell Mrs. Collins about your letter, were not you?"

Anne smiled and leant forward again. "You recall, Mrs. Collins, Mamma and my last visit to London? And how a certain gentleman had been so kind as to pay particular attention to me at several of the evening entertainments?"

Charlotte frowned, trying to remember the gentleman's name, a gentleman she had advised Anne to treat with very great caution: no man, gentleman or not, could escape the suspicion of being interested merely because of Anne's fortune.

"Ah, let me think a moment; a Mr. Sudbury, I believe you said his name was?"

Anne smiled at the name spoken aloud. "Yes, how well you remember details, Mrs. Collins! Well; Mr. Sudbury has *written* – a surprisingly lengthy letter for such a short acquaintance – expressing his hope that I shall soon be in London again that we may continue our discussions on literature and music."

Charlotte laughed. "I can hardly imagine how a letter can be so lengthy with such a specific goal to be transmitted, Miss de Bourgh; he must have approached the subject from every angle possible – 'tis a risk, as he might become dull after the third repetition!"

Anne blushed and looked at her hands; she still was not used to being teased. Georgiana saw her friend's discomfort and broke in.

"Ah, yes, well, that was his *main* purpose, but there were *other* ideas which he conveyed quite well I thought, too." She looked at Anne who had recovered enough to smile.

"He mentioned that he intended travelling into Kent on business in a week or two and enquired if he would be permitted to pay his respects to Mamma during his stay, as he did not have that pleasure whilst we were in Town. I believe he is quite in earnest about his interest in me, Mrs. Collins, and he is perfectly well-provided for, if you are still concerned about his motives."

"My dear; I am sorry for causing you discomfort. Sometimes I speak without realising the effect of my words. I am sure that when you broach this with her ladyship she will have no compunction whatever in cross-examining him within an inch of his life. And if he manages to withstand *that*, then he is certainly a man of great fortitude if nothing else and must, as you say, be entirely in earnest to subject himself to such scrutiny. But what is your question to me? It appears that you and Miss Darcy have decided between yourselves, or at least discussed it to both of your satisfaction."

"I confess, I do not know just how to ask Mamma for permission to have him call upon us. She does not know him – or of him – and she is already suspicious of his letter, never mind his person. I do not wish to enlarge everything out of all proportion – he is, after all, allowed to travel into Kent for whatever reason pleases him – but I do not know what to say to Mamma, what reason to give, Mrs. Collins, even though I would very much like him to call."

"At whose houses did you make his acquaintance?"

"At Lord and Lady Horesham's, and then another evening at the Grainger's."

"And these two families are known to Lady Catherine, and she thinks well of them?"

"Well, naturally! Mamma would never allow me to accept invitations unless she approved of the persons behind it – or she approved of their general situation."

Charlotte smiled and looked at Georgiana. "Have you thought how this might be managed, Miss Darcy?"

"I presume you are hinting that, if these are common acquaintances, then there should be little that Lady Catherine can object to: Mr. Sudbury has been approved by proxy."

"Exactly! All that you need mention is that an acquaintance made at the Horesham's and the Grainger's expressed regret at never having had the pleasure of being introduced to your Mamma, and you suggested that if ever he was in the county, then he should be confident of a welcome at Rosings Park. Your Mamma cannot refuse as you have already been polite enough to issue the invitation - not expecting it ever to be taken up, of course - but now that it has been, he must be received cordially."

Anne pressed her hands together in a silent clap and nodded her agreement. "Of course! How simple you make everything. But will you be there when I ask her in case I lose my nerve?"

Charlotte smiled. "I do not believe that will happen. You are not the retiring person you once were, just remember that, and you have Miss Darcy and Mrs. Darcy for support should you need it. My friend has far greater nerves than I have ever had. Ask her ladyship tonight – get it over with before you lose your nerve – and tell me all about it tomorrow."

Charlotte waved off her visitors with a smile and returned to her parlour where little William was stirring, but was again disturbed by the flurry of her husband's entrance and his obvious interest in what had transpired after his departure.

"There is nothing at all to tell, William. I was introduced to Miss Darcy, as were you, and Miss de Bourgh is anticipating the arrival of a visitor whom she met in London; that is all."

William bent down to pick up his son who was now flailing his arms about and gurgling to himself.

"There, there my little man. My goodness, how full of energy you are, to be sure! Is he in need of a feed, my dear?" he asked quickly.

Upon Charlotte's shake of her head, he then wrapped the baby up in his blanket and proposed a short walk outside around the garden beds and the hives, both of which were proceeding into their Spring-like forms and gave William great joy and satisfaction to share with whomever would listen.

"But it does concern me that it has been several days since their return and we have not received an invitation to dine from Lady Catherine; I thought certainly that was the purpose of Miss Anne's visit here today."

"You know very well that when there are guests aplenty, Lady Catherine has no need of our company; she has more than sufficient to divert her attention especially with the added promise of an entirely new person's visit. I, for one, do not miss being the sole focus of her attention and you should not either, my dear; you have many more important things with which to occupy your time other than worrying about invitations – or lack thereof – to dine. But go, take your son, teach him about your garden; there is nothing more precious than the time you can give him."

She kissed the baby on the forehead and tucked in the stray ends of the blanket, although the weather was not in the least cold, and then, upon impulse, also quickly kissed William upon his cheek – much to his pleased surprise – and then watched him go out towards the garden, smiling at the happy picture they made.

Much to her astonishment, while watching the slow promenade from her window, she heard the doorbell ring for the third time that morning. My goodness, the Parsonage was certainly a popular destination this morning! She settled herself in her chair and waited as she heard the deep tones of her visitor announcing himself to the maid. The door opened and Mr. Darcy was announced. He swept in and bowed, greeting her cordially while sweeping the room quickly with his eyes.

"Forgive the intrusion, Mrs. Collins, but I was informed that my wife had come to visit and I hoped to meet her here, but it seems I am too late."

"Indeed you are, Mr. Darcy, and you are not the only one this morning who has been disappointed by Elizabeth's elusive nature. Miss de Bourgh and your sister also hoped to catch up with her but she had already the advantage of them. She took herself off for a walk – I know not which one – more than an hour ago now. She was a little distracted and not expecting you today; but if I may say so, she will be very glad to see you. I am only sorry I cannot advise where to find her."

Darcy bowed stiffly and smiled one of his very rare smiles.

"She has had, at least, your friendship to sustain her since she has been in Kent. I know of none other with whom she prefers to spend time." He glanced out of the window and saw Mr. Collins, blissfully unaware of this latest guest.

"Your husband seems to be a doting father, Mrs. Collins. It is an unusual trait in a man to be so engaged with his child, but it is also very pleasing to see. The child appears healthy?"

"Yes, indeed. Baby William is very healthy – thank God – and Mr. Collins is, as you observe, the most doting father. I cannot say when he is happier than when he is tending William, and I promote it as much as I possibly can; it is good for them both, I believe, even if it is not the customary way of things."

Darcy watched for a moment longer and then said, "You are both very fortunate to have found each other, Mrs. Collins. I am happy to see it. But I must beg your forgiveness for the brevity of my visit; I must find my own wife before she walks into the next county!"

He bowed quickly and, picking up his hat, passed through the door and out into the sunshine. He followed the lane and then took the first path he came to – it was one he remembered had always led him to his not-so-accidental meetings with Elizabeth the year before and he hoped it would prove as fruitful this time. There was nothing more he wished for than to hold her in his arms, in private and peaceful surroundings away from the formalities of Rosings and the observations of his aunt.

The morning was growing warmer and the speed at which he was walking forced him to stop and remove his coat and loosen his collar. A little further on, he also undid several buttons and rolled up his sleeves.

There was still no sign of Elizabeth and he began to despair of coming across her. There were so many walks around the Park - she could be on any of them – or she could already be back at the house, or returned to the Parsonage. He laughed to himself – how ridiculous he was being! Chasing his wife through the undergrowth, along unknown paths where she may or may not have passed that morning, at every corner expecting her to be waiting for him in a clearing. What a foolish person he had become since his marriage! If any of his acquaintance could see him now, they would wonder where the Darcy they had always known had gone.

He shrugged and turned about to retrace his steps towards the house. He would look even more foolish if she had returned to Rosings and he was not there to greet her. This new anxiety propelled him forwards through the overhanging trees until he finally found himself in the open on the other side of the lake, the path of which approached the house. And there, frustratingly on the exact opposite side to him, sat Elizabeth, clearly deep in thought, staring into the depths of the water and unaware of her surroundings or his appearance. He smiled, suppressing the urge to announce his presence immediately, hugging the lakeshore while keeping his eyes fixed on the small figure that drew him with so many complex and inexplicable new emotions.

He managed to get within several yards of her before she broke out of her reflections and heard the crunch of gravel, becoming aware of the approaching figure. The utter joy that broke across her face said everything that needed to be said. It had been almost ten days of separation and they both had felt the pain of it.

After a while she moved back from his encircling arms and surveyed the man that was her husband, a man who was to all intents and purposes only half dressed in his rolled sleeves and flyaway collar, his jacket and hat lying in a pile at their feet.

She laughed, the joy of seeing him again overpowering in its intensity, causing her to introduce some levity to their meeting.

"My goodness! I begin to feel rather too *formally attired*, my dear! Would you prefer me to cast off one of *my* garments and bonnet so you are not so conspicuous in your dishabille? This is most instructive indeed: my first glimpse of you at Pemberley last year was of a similar state of undress; last month upon your return from Town I found you removing your boots in the servants' quarters, and now, you enter Kent in a similar shockingly casual manner!

"Am I to understand that this is the way you will always appear after a trip to London? Their fashions certainly seem a little different from ours. What will your aunt have to say? I hope she has not spied us from the long windows in the drawing room, for all our work convincing her of my good influence will be completely undone!"

Darcy efficiently silenced her for a while – on-looking aunt be damned - and they then stood locked in each other's arms, looking at the lake and the lilies that were beginning to form on its surface.

"I do not think anyone will dare comment on my state of undress, my dear, nor will I care if they do; and when did you become so concerned about the opinion of others, pray – especially those of my aunt? But perhaps I should improve my appearance before presenting myself. I wonder when Fitzwilliam will arrive. He mentioned he intended leaving several days ago but I did not see him in the house when I arrived; in fact it was almost devoid of any guests at all, and my aunt had not yet left her chamber, according to the butler. He was so good as to mention your intended whereabouts, though, and I called upon Mrs. Collins before she sent me hunting through the woods for you, my dear, to no avail. The Collins appear very content, are not they?"

"Yes, indeed they are. Charlotte is perfectly situated with her house and parish duties and her child. She can wish for nothing more to improve her happiness, and I am delighted to see it. And Colonel Fitzwilliam is certainly here – he arrived earlier this morning – but he was displeased with your singular lack of communication and hopes you have good reason for it. I explained your mission a little and he seemed satisfied but he will torment you with it, I'll wager, as soon as he sees you.

"But, tell me, my dear, what success did you have with Wickham and what has finally been decided?"

Darcy grimaced slightly, and they slowly made their way along the path - neither of them noticing that it was the one leading *away* from the approach to the house – arms intertwined, talking and listening intently each to the other in perfect harmony.

Chapter 28

It was a happy party that met for dinner in the opulent Rosings dining room that night. Everybody was there: Lady Catherine, Anne, Georgiana, Colonel Fitzwilliam, Darcy, Elizabeth, and, much to his gratification and relief, William Collins and Charlotte. To finally be included in such auspicious company fulfilled his greatest aspirations and, although he was not invited to sit at the head of the table, as was his distinction when the only male of the company, he happily settled for his position between Georgiana and Colonel Fitzwilliam which afforded him an easy hearing of most of the table's conversations.

The meal was served on elaborate silver and crystal which overcame the shortcomings of any culinary expectations of so grand an establishment. Candles were being lit later and later as the Spring sunlight lingered further into the evening, slanting off the tableware in a rosy glow, the last windows left open to admit the sweet smell of the early blossoms and the faint twitter of the nesting birds.

Lady Catherine was in her element. It had been quite some time since she had enjoyed such a large party at her table and she intended to make the most of it, beginning with her eldest nephew.

"You were very greatly missed, Darcy, this past fortnight. I hope your purpose was successful and, therefore, your absence, justified?"

Darcy paused, glancing at Elizabeth with a faint tightening of his lips.

"I believe so, Aunt. My purpose, at least, was accomplished; my success remains to be seen."

"Hmm." Lady Catherine stared at Darcy for a moment and then began again.

"But I hope that you put your case most strongly, Darcy. More than a few lives depend upon a favourable conclusion, and to be uncertain of that conclusion must be regarded as unsatisfactory, if not entirely unsuccessful."

There was silence at the table as everyone waited for Darcy's response. Elizabeth recognised the signs of irritation at such importunate questioning. She said quickly:

"Lady Catherine; perhaps this is a subject better left for another time, as so many of our company are unaware of the facts of the matter that it cannot be of interest to any of them."

Lady Catherine straightened herself even further and bent her eye upon Elizabeth, but Mr. Collins interjected before she could speak.

"Naturally, whatever her ladyship desires to discuss is always of interest to those of us who may, perhaps, not be *entirely* familiar with the subject matter, my dear cousin, - your thoughtfulness does you credit, I am sure - but that is occasionally the burden of the listener. I assure you, Lady Catherine, that we are *most* interested to learn of Mr. Darcy's travels into London and what was involved…"

Darcy had been staring long and hard at Mr. Collins as he spoke and broke in.

"And yet, sir, you shall not have that satisfaction. I have said all that I intend saying upon the matter, whether my aunt wishes to learn more or no."

Mr. Collins subsided meekly and returned to his dinner. Silence reigned for several minutes.

Lady Catherine tried again, but this time with her younger nephew.

"Fitzwilliam: how much longer are you intending to remain with the military, pray? There can be little need of your services now that the war with the French is all but finished."

"My contract will expire in July, Aunt. There are many of us who are exploring other avenues of employment; we all of us are second and third sons – a common complaint!"

Lady Catherine nodded. "We will speak further of this another time, Fitzwilliam, whilst you are here. An energetic and reliable gentleman cannot be underestimated in his usefulness, and you shall benefit from my contacts."

Fitzwilliam smiled and bowed his head in acknowledgment of his aunt's favour. In a much better humour, Lady Catherine then brought her attention to bear upon Georgiana, who flushed to be so singled out.

"And you, Georgiana, I suppose, anticipate being taken to London for The Season this year? It is an expectation of all young ladies to be amused in Town – until the heat and stench becomes unbearable, of course - and then you will wish to go to Brighton."

"I...I...do not presume anything of the sort, Lady Catherine. My brother is very busy and cannot afford the time to socialise in Town, I know, but ..."

"And hates the very thought of such tedious activities, do you not now, Darcy?" laughed Fitzwilliam. "Senseless chatter, endless dancing, dull shows, amateur card games – it all pales into insignificance compared with the quiet of Pemberley."

Elizabeth smiled at Georgiana's crestfallen expression showing she clearly *had* held secret hopes of some society this year, and was pleased at her sister's desire to engage in new activities.

"I am sure that even Darcy cannot refuse to stay in Town for a few weeks. After all, *I* still have to see our house there and would happily participate in some of those mindless entertainments you are so cavalier about, Colonel. And, of course, I should very much enjoy visiting with my aunt and uncle Gardiner in whose company we both take pleasure, do not we, my dear?"

Darcy looked from Elizabeth's smile to his sister's downcast gaze and sighed. He had been to Town twice now and had no desire to return if it could be avoided, but, it seemed, it could not. He was outnumbered by the two people whom he most wished to please.

"Naturally, we will stay in Town for a week or so as we pass through on our way back to Pemberley. You should certainly become familiar with our Town house, Elizabeth, and Georgiana must revisit some of the friends she made when last she was there. I am sure I shall manage to endure it again for a short while. Perhaps you might wish to write to your sister and encourage the Bingleys to join us – well, perhaps not *all* of them, although I am sure *they* will all come regardless of an invitation or not – and Fitzwilliam, you must come too. If we surround ourselves with familiar and agreeable company, I shall not complain too much."

"I should be delighted, Darcy. And I shall invite some of my own friends, if I may, those of whom I think you will approve, thereby constructing an enclave of our own and keep any undesirables out!"

Charlotte, who had remained silent throughout the meal, as was her wont, spoke quietly to Anne.

"Miss de Bourgh; do not you have any interest in being a member of this exclusive group about to descend upon London? I am sure you would enjoy such company and entertainments amongst friends with whom you are already acquainted and at ease?"

"Oh, yes; please say you will come, Anne!" gasped Georgiana. "We shall be as we have been: such good friends and confidantes. And you can expand our circle to include those with whom *you* are acquainted. And Aunt," she added, turning to Lady Catherine who was rather regretting the turn the conversation had taken, "you will not need to exert yourself if you would rather not travel into Town. Anne will be quite safe and happy with us."

"You assume, then, that I have no interest in visiting my own friends in London?" Lady Catherine drew herself up, indignant. "You presume that I should much prefer staying here by myself with the limited company that is available, whilst my daughter enjoys herself without me and my supervision?"

"No! No! That is not what I meant at all," Georgiana stammered, horrified at giving offence.

"My sister merely wished to relieve you of the necessity of having to go into Town, Aunt, should you not be so inclined, that is all," Darcy intervened calmly. "If such an arrangement were presented to *me*, I should accept it with alacrity, I assure you, but the offer remains, whether you choose to take it or not. Anne would be a very welcome guest at Darcy House and a happy companion for Georgiana."

"And, Mamma," added Anne slyly, "you know you soon tired of the constant visiting and gatherings the last time we were there. I had to rely upon Mrs. Jenkinson as my companion; otherwise I would have had no society at all. You know it is true."

"Yes, well," Lady Catherine was unwilling to concede the truth of the allegation. "I admit to feeling rather unwell last time and unable to withstand the rigours of constant comings and goings as is always the case in Town. I shall decide closer to the date of departure whether to accompany you this time."

"Well, that is settled, then," laughed the Colonel. "We are all to reconvene just as we are, in London in a week's time, with the very great intention of enjoying ourselves immensely, to see and be seen, to introduce the new Mrs. Darcy to London society who will, all of them, claim to be her dearest friend within an hour of meeting her, and the friend of any of those of her party within a minute after that!"

Darcy glanced at Fitzwilliam, and then at Elizabeth, both of them smiling happily at each other and revelling in the joke. Elizabeth's cheeks were flushed and her eyes sparkled brightly; she was the most attractive woman in the room and he could see that his cousin was entirely aware of it.

Darcy stood abruptly, almost tipping his chair.

"Come, Fitzwilliam, let us retire to the study. Lady Catherine; ladies; Mr. Collins, you will excuse us." And with that, he left the room, followed by a grinning Fitzwilliam who knew exactly what had vexed his cousin and intended teasing him about it rather vigorously.

The door closed on excited chattering between Anne, Georgina, Elizabeth and Charlotte, with Lady Catherine and Mr. Collins listening in and adding their opinions where they could. Plans were made; expectations aired, refuted or confirmed; discussions ensued regarding the shows known to be on in the theatres; the new pleasure park's attractions were examined. All increased the gaiety of the evening as the candles guttered in the slight breeze from the garden and flickered shadows against the mirrors and paintings upon the walls.

Privately, Georgiana was anticipating re-meeting with several of her acquaintances – the Stantons, Mr. Jardine, and, perhaps, if she had returned from America, Mrs. Younge – and she would show all of them just how much she had improved since her last visit, young and innocent as she had been then.

Anne also held very great hopes of meeting with a certain letter-writing gentleman, either very soon at Rosings, or certainly in Town where he resided. She would introduce him to all of her new companions and await their assessment of his qualities.

Elizabeth felt excitement at the prospect of entertaining her aunt and uncle in her own London home, just as they had done at the beginning of the year when they had been Darcy and her first visitors to Pemberley after their marriage. And if she could convince Jane to visit Town, too, then her happiness could not be marred by anything.

Perhaps, she mused, as she watched her sister and Anne make their plans, she might convince her father to send Kitty down: she was of age, and much less wayward now she did not have Lydia to imitate. That would be a treat for her, and teach her about proper behaviour and manners, something which had been severely lacking in her education at Longbourn.

And, as for Lydia, Darcy had assured her that all was arranged – not entirely to his satisfaction or peace of mind – but the fact that Wickham had insisted upon pursuing his desire for independence through working for his living had given Darcy some cause for hope that all would be well. Elizabeth certainly hoped so, and that her sister would settle down into her new life without the constant yearning to have what she could not afford, and Wickham would overcome his similar delusion of being a gentleman with a gentleman's income, and learn that he must earn it like everyone else.

End of Part One

Felicity in Marriage

Jane Austen's *Pride and Prejudice* continues…

Part Two

"The wife of Mr. Darcy must have such extraordinary sources of happiness necessarily attached to her situation that she could, upon the whole, have no cause to repine."

"His affection for her soon sunk into indifference; hers lasted a little longer ... and, consequently, after a moderate period of extravagant and wild admiration, her fancy for him gave way, and others who treated her with more distinction, again became her favourites."

Pride and Prejudice

Chapter 29

Good Lord, life in Meryton was certainly very dull; duller than ever she remembered, and in comparison to Newcastle? Well: there was simply no comparison to be made.

Kitty and Mamma were tolerable company, she supposed, but Mary could not be borne with her sermons and serious reading and mournful sonatas - which gained no level of improvement regardless of how much she tortured her instrument - and the parties at her aunt Philips' were a grave disappointment, certainly not as amusing as she remembered them.

Lydia sighed and drummed her fingers against the arm of the chair in which she was slumped. She had already written her daily letter to Wickham this morning, full of droll nonsense that belied little of her current ennui. She had hinted, for the third time this week alone, that she would be perfectly content with the very smallest of apartments, a very minimal number of servants, a very limited social calendar if only he would consent to have her join him in London. For what, she had enquired, could be taking so long that they must be separated for almost two months of their first year of marriage? And, she had complained, he had been most negligent in his correspondence; she had received only three letters from him, none of which had been the slightest bit encouraging with regards to his expectations for his business, nor his desire to have her by his side. Now here she was, stuck, waiting; an unwilling house guest in her family home after being her own mistress for so many months. It was intolerable indeed.

She levered herself from her chair and wandered to the window. There was nothing to be seen there, either, and she felt her enforced solitude weigh even more heavily. How had she *ever*

~ 229 ~

thought life here was entertaining? Even the few social engagements to be had were nothing to what she had become used to in the past six months. It was all too thoughtless and unkind of Wickham, it really was, and him there in London having a marvellous time, she had no doubt, visiting all of his friends and going to shows and parties every night without her.

She should be there too, enjoying society with him and making new acquaintances of her own. It was all so unfair. Perhaps she would ask her father to arrange for the carriage to take her into Town; if she arrived with all of her trunks and boxes, Wickham could hardly refuse to take her in, could he? And the address where he was staying was very fine indeed – a Mr. Jardine's establishment, apparently – Lydia had made enquiries and had it confirmed as being in one of the finest Squares on the fashionable side of Town. She wanted to be *there*, not here, tucked away in the country living the life of a sad spinster like her sisters, being watched over by her parents once again.

She yawned and leant her forehead on the smooth glass. Yes, that would be her plan. Perhaps she might falsely allude to a recent letter from Wickham claiming he was in torment without her by his side and desperately wished her to make haste to Town. Naturally, her father could not refuse such an ardent request, regardless that the horses might be needed on the farm – late Spring crop, or no late Spring crop – she would have her way.

Just as she had determined this and was about to approach her father, she noticed her sister, Jane's, carriage arriving. Aha! *She* would provide a moment's diversion on so dreary a morning.

Mrs. Bennet was already greeting Jane when Lydia sauntered into the back parlour.

"And, look, see; here is your sister too, Jane. I do not know where your other sisters are, but they will present themselves, by and by. Kitty certainly will wish to thank you again for her stay with you last month; she is quite the charming young lady, is not she, Lydia?"

"Oh, indeed she is. Quite fit to be presented at court, I should imagine, as long as she never opens her mouth and only smiles a great deal; her opinions are quite unsophisticated, but her appearance and deportment are much improved. You have done well with her, Jane."

Jane smiled placidly and sat where her mother motioned.

"It is about Kitty that I have come, Mamma. I have heard from Elizabeth - who is at Rosings Park at present - and she mentions that she and Mr. Darcy and several of their company – perhaps including Lady Catherine, although she could not be sure about that lady's participation - intend spending a short time in London before they return to Pemberley. Elizabeth suggested that Charles and I meet them there, and also to persuade Father to allow Kitty to accompany us. She would be well taken care of, I assure you, and we have no expectation of many great social affairs – Mr. Darcy, as you know abhors the very thought of them – but there will be enough to make her visit enjoyable and will further her instruction with which you have been so pleased."

Jane could hardly finish her request before her mother exclaimed,

"*London!* Oh! *Kitty?* To go to *London* and mingle with your fine friends and acquaintance? Oh, my dear, Jane! Well, naturally your father will agree; he agrees to everything that does not cause him any trouble, for he certainly would never bestir himself to do such a thing for any of his daughters. Let me go to him now, Jane, and convince him of the good sense of it all. *London!* Oh, I shall go distracted," and she rushed out of the parlour in a flurry of skirts and petticoats.

"*Kitty* is to go to London?" cried Lydia. "That is so *unfair!* But I cannot believe that Father will allow it – he never allowed *me* to do anything when he was asked – why should Kitty be given preference, I want to know? And here am I, stuck in Meryton, without so much as a word from my husband from one week's end to the next; a husband who happens to be *in London*, where I should be, with him, and she and you are to go in my stead? Oh! I am so angry, Jane; everything conspires against my happiness, everything."

"Calm yourself, Lydia," soothed Jane. "If there is unfairness in the world, you may not claim it all for yourself; unfairness is everywhere and must be tolerated as best one can. I may remind you that I have not yet had the opportunity to visit our sister at Pemberley – her absence is something that has most saddened me these past months – yet, you have had that pleasure, and you have met her new sister, and Lady Catherine and Anne de Bourgh, all of whom I know only through others' accounts. So do not make such comments that are more untrue than true; it does you no credit."

Lydia was prevented from retorting by the hurried re-entry of her mother followed closely by Kitty who positively glowed with happiness at her unexpected good fortune, her main object being to relay it to her friends as soon as may be and enjoy being the focus of their jealous questions.

"Lydia," Mrs. Bennet declared, clutching her bosom, and sinking into the nearest chaise, "you are to go to your father; he wants you immediately. Good news, Jane! He has agreed to your proposal, as I knew he must, and Kitty is to go with you to London. He started to itemize all the things she should *not* be allowed to do but I forestalled him by reminding him in whose company Kitty would be staying, and he soon agreed there was no need to over-exert himself regarding her safety."

She smiled from Jane to Kitty and then saw Lydia still in the room, gawping at the news that her sister had their father's blessing to go into Town.

"Why are you still here, Lydia? Did not I tell you to go straight to your father? I would not annoy him whilst he is in such a benevolent mood. Go! Go, now."

Lydia glared at Kitty as she passed her, a glare which had no effect whatsoever, as Kitty was now talking excitedly with Jane and her mother. Lydia knocked and immediately entered her father's book-room - a place she had hardly ever visited - and looked about her curiously as she walked towards the large desk behind which sat her father, watching her over his spectacles.

She raised her chin and said, "I think it most unfair that Kitty is to go to London, Father, when I know you stated categorically last year she would never be allowed to go anywhere before she married. You would not let *me* go to Brighton until Colonel Forster and his wife invited me. You have always preferred Kitty over me, I know you have."

"Are you quite finished, Mrs. Wickham?" He looked at her with irritation.

Lydia pouted and looked away.

"Sit down." He sighed deeply.

"It is true that I have agreed that Kitty may join Jane and her party going to London. I feel assured that she will be in no danger under both her sisters' watchful eyes."

Lydia began to speak but he silenced her with a wave.

"When I spoke about Kitty last year it was a reaction to *your* disgraceful actions and behaviour that almost brought this house and our good name into disrepute, not from any particular concern *she* had given me. I presume you recall the actions and behaviour to which I am alluding?"

Lydia glared at him but did not dare answer back. Her father's temper was not something she thought prudent to rouse any further.

"I have had a letter – actually two letters – and I wish to discuss the content of them with you as they pertain to your current situation. Both your sister, Elizabeth, and your uncle Gardiner have written to explain the agreements that have been entered into, and have asked that I, in turn, inform you of the same."

He reached into his desk drawer and pulled out several sheets of letter paper, both covered very closely on both sides with neat handwriting. He looked from the pages to Lydia and cleared his throat.

"What has Mr. Wickham relayed to you with regards to his sudden departure from Newcastle and his business prospects in Town, Lydia?"

"Why, only that he wished to explore a business prospect in London and so needed to leave Newcastle in order to do so, and has now found something which he believes will suit him very well. He intends to become very successful, as I am sure he will be, and I intend to enjoy that success with him as soon as travel to London can be arranged, Father. Indeed, I was about to request the carriage just before Jane arrived, to allow that journey."

Mr. Bennet again cleared his throat and glanced at the letters in front of him.

"While it is true that, apparently, Mr. Wickham *has* managed to procure for himself some sort of occupation in the marketing of goods, it is not the whole truth of the matter and I want you to listen to the truth which I have here from your uncle Gardiner and your sister Elizabeth, who writes on Mr. Darcy's behalf; Jane undoubtedly has had it from her husband who was also involved. I, too, you may recall, was in London recently with all of those gentlemen but had to leave before the solution had been arrived at, which was to bring the matter of Mr. Wickham's constant impecuniousness to a satisfactory conclusion and attempt to ensure some security for you.

"It would appear that your husband has left the military entirely, has *sold* his commission that was dearly bought for him only a very few months ago, and although, as I have said, it appears Mr. Wickham has indeed found a position, apparently it is not one that will yet support a wife let alone the cost of entertaining and those other household expenses that have an unfortunate habit of occurring with regularity. If it were left up to your husband, my dear, I believe you would be our permanent guest for another year, at least, before you would be able to live in Town, as you aspire to do."

Lydia pouted and flounced her head. "I am sure what you say is not right, Father. Wickham assured me of his success and I believe he wants me to join him as soon as possible. If he has sold his commission it is only to improve his circumstances. None of you like him - that is all - ..."

"You will not interrupt, Lydia, and you will not assume to know that about which you have no knowledge. Do not presume that such men as Mr. Darcy and your uncle are as easily fooled as are you. You will listen and heed my warning. For too long you have been allowed to speak and act wildly, but that will no longer be tolerated whilst you are in my house and under my protection.

"As I was saying; because of the nature of his new position and the lack of immediate resources, there has been a very generous offer of assistance made to your husband by the same person who has made very many generous offers to him, as I understand, in the past, and wishes nothing more in repayment than for you and your husband to finally settle down to a life that you can share whilst enjoying that hoped-for success.

"Mr. Darcy is the gentleman of whom I speak - if you do not understand my allusion, Lydia - and he has settled an amount to cover all expenses for your first year in Town. He again refused any help from those of us who should be allowed to help, but that is the man he is, and I cannot but judge him warmly for it, for he has already saved me a world of trouble and expense and, I have no doubt, will probably be expected to do so again in the future.

"Mr. Darcy has procured a year's lease on a modest, furnished house in Brompton – which by all accounts is a developing area on the outskirts of Town - along with the payment of wages for a servant girl and the stabling for a horse. My understanding is that after the year has expired, then no further assistance shall be forthcoming nor should it be expected. If I were Mr. Darcy, I should not be so free with my money a second time to such a profligate and ungrateful person, but I am not he and cannot presume to know his motivations, although I can guess at them."

He had been watching his daughter closely as he told her all of this shocking news but noticed with regret only her evident self-satisfaction and pleasure at the news that she was soon to live in London; that was her foremost and only concern. There was no shock, or embarrassment, or gratitude, or any indication that even one of those emotions had occurred to her. It was as if all of the other information had been entirely ignored.

"You have now been apprised of what has been arranged for you and your husband. You now know to what lengths Mr. Darcy has again gone for your and your husband's benefit. A little gratitude and an assurance that you will attempt to improve both of your behaviour would not go amiss, daughter, when so much has again been pledged for your future security."

"Yes, yes, of course; it is all very kind of Mr. Darcy, I am sure, and I will thank him when I get the opportunity to do so. But I am to go to London! I am to live in London with Wickham – finally; at last! Ooh! That is all I have wished for and nothing will make me cross again. I will leave tomorrow if I can!"

Lydia's face was wreathed in smiles, and she almost danced her way towards the door, her pique at her sister getting preferential treatment entirely forgot in the light of such wonderful news. She cared not one jot as to the extent of Mr. Darcy's involvement; she cared not one jot more for her father's stern warning. All she cared for was the knowledge that she would very soon be at her husband's side being squired to balls and parties galore. No more enduring dull country talk from the local farmers and landowners with their red hands and noses, and their wives with their pearls lost in the folds of their neck; no more of Mary's sonatas, her father's speeches or her mother's ailments. She could not wait to have her trunks packed and be on her way. As she passed through the doorway into the hall, she was interrupted as her father also rose from his chair.

"I will accompany you to your mother and sisters, Lydia, to ensure that they all hear the *correct* version of the news I just told you."

"Both Kitty *and Lydia* are to go to Town, Mr. Bennet?" his wife asked, astonished at the news carefully recounted by Lydia. "Are we to take Mary as well, then, thereby ensuring equal treatment for all of our daughters?"

"Indeed not, Mrs. Bennet. The mere thought of it causes me palpitations of the most serious kind. Let me be very clear upon this matter: there will be no more excursions to London with me as one of the party. One visit every ten years or so is as much as I can bear. I abhor the place, and you know Mary would not like it either." He turned away from his wife to allow her to prepare her next assault.

"Remember, Lydia: you have a great debt of gratitude to Mr. Darcy for what he has again brought about to ensure the security of your marriage. Do not abuse it again, and ensure that your husband does not either."

"Well!" Mrs. Bennet exploded, unable to contain herself. "And why should he not, the money he has? They were childhood friends, after all, and Darcy has used Wickham very ill, to my way of thinking …"

"Then *your* way of thinking is entirely without merit, Mrs. Bennet, and it would behove you not to take sides in this matter about which you know very little. They are both our sons-in-law, and I suppose we must try to be equally proud of both of them, whatever their successes or failures. They are our daughters' choices and we should not show nor speak of any preference."

Mrs. Bennet subsided into silence but tweaked the skirt of her dress with spiteful vehemence, clearly having much to say but recognising her husband's tone brooked no opposition.

Kitty had listened to everything with her head bowed, secretly vowing to ensure the man she chose to fall in love with was much more like Mr. Darcy than Mr. Wickham, so she would never have to submit to such censure from her father.

Jane broke the tense silence. "Charles suggested also that we take you with us to London when we go, Lydia. It will save expense for Father and make pleasant company on the journey. There is no great rush – although I am sure you would prefer to leave this very minute if it could be arranged – Charles and Elizabeth have both informed me that it will take Mr. Wickham until the end of next week before he can take possession of the property, and, of course, a servant must be found and other housekeeping taken care of. We thought it would be best for you to leave with our party in a week and stay with us until everything is in order."

Lydia looked about her: at her sister, Jane's, gentle smile, wanting to smooth everything over; at Kitty's broad grin, her excitement obvious; at her mother's self-satisfied nodding as she agreed with Jane's suggestion; and finally, at her father who remained inscrutable, but, she knew, would pounce on any indication of selfishness or ingratitude.

"I am sure I can wait a while longer, Jane; I thank you for your kindness. Although I would much prefer to be in London to oversee such arrangements to my new home, I quite understand the sensibility of your suggestion and will be happy to leave with you and Kitty in a week. Please excuse me; I must write some letters before the post leaves."

Chapter 30

George Wickham felt exceedingly pleased with his situation. His natural inclination to regard himself highly had been entirely restored upon receipt of the letter from Darcy's attorney informing him of the extent of the material assistance Darcy was prepared to offer as agreed at their meeting. This, coupled with his first days of employment with Mr. Aspinall, who had been most encouraging and complimentary, clearly tinged with relief at the prospect of handing over the more unpleasant aspects of business, had given Wickham every reason to believe that all boded well for his future.

How fortunate he had been to so quickly fall in with his old friend who had been instrumental in forging this new business acquaintance. How fortunate that Jardine had also been so kind as to provide him with lodgings for the past month in a superior house and neighbourhood which lent an air of distinction even to those who had not yet earned any distinction of their own. How fortunate that he had, through his superior connections, been able to fend off Darcy and others' bad opinion of him when they had come calling, expecting the worst.

In fact, the only unfortunate things to have happened recently to George Wickham centred around the women in his life, and the disagreeable reminder of one sat in his lap; a letter, hastily written, full of exclamation marks and under-linings, from Lydia, announcing her imminent arrival and her absolute joy at the prospect of being with him again, and of all the things she thought they should do to entertain themselves now they had London at their disposal.

He glanced through it again and his heart sank. It seemed there was no possibility of diverting her: she was to come with her sisters in a week, and was only restrained by his lack of accommodation – which, she hoped, he would see to as soon as possible – as she could not wait to be his 'proper wife' again after so long. Perhaps, she suggested, Mr. Jardine would offer to accommodate her until such time as their own house was ready?

Wickham pursed his lips, noticing upon this second perusal that not once had she enquired about his difficulties over the past month, his new position, nor offered to take on some of the tasks involved in preparing the house in Brompton. He was not surprised - he knew her character very well by now - but her self-absorption only served to remind him of what he could expect. Her silly notions and delusions of what they could afford would have to be firmly addressed once she was in front of him and could hear the truth of it in his voice. There would be no parties or assemblies; there would be no outings into the country; there would be no extravagant meals or ornaments.

He did not wish to live as far out as Brompton, but that was where Darcy's agent had found a house for which he was willing to pay, and so Brompton was where they would be living. In fact, today, after he had completed his business, Wickham intended to ride out to the new house to survey its possibilities and defects with an eye to any improvements that might be needed before taking up residence.

Jardine had advised him upon the matter the evening before over dinner.

"Indeed, you must inspect the place, Wickham. Darcy's agent is, I am sure, a very capable fellow but it is not he who is intending to spend the next year at least in it. I am sure Darcy would expect you to take an interest and report back with satisfaction or any problems. It is too late after you take the keys and move in, you know. Yes, go as soon as possible. It will be nice enough, I am sure, but you do not want to discover a damp and dark place in a questionable neighbourhood, do you? No. It is better to get the lay of the land immediately, set your mind at rest and know that it will be deemed suitable by your wife. Ladies have great expectations about their houses, I understand, and it will not be any different with yours."

And so that was Wickham's intention, much as his heart dreaded it. He would much prefer to stay in London, alone, in the smallest of rooms – dark and damp if need be – where he could hear the City and be in its hub, but he knew why Darcy had situated him outside of the City. For precisely that reason: to keep him away from the excitement and amusement the city offered, and force him to go home to his wife before it became too late and dangerous to travel.

How he hated the dreary thought of it already: working all day, and then riding home to be greeted by Lydia who would, he already knew, complain about her day, just as she had done in Newcastle; complain about her boredom, her lack of friends, her lack of amusements, her lack of everything she deemed necessary for her happiness. She would expect to have entertainments laid on every night now they were so close to Town, and would not understand that their still-straitened circumstances prohibited it.

It was all too dismal to contemplate, and so he re-directed his mind to more agreeable matters; those of the rest of the work he must finish by this afternoon, and the prospect of a pleasant ride on one of Jardine's horses out to Brompton. The fresh air would do him good and clear his head of the gloomy thoughts Lydia's letter had wrought.

He pulled out the letter sent by Darcy's attorney to verify the address of the house: *13 Yeoman's Row*, just off Brompton Road. He sighed, hoping that the name of the street did not signify the lowliest sort of premises. He could not imagine Darcy to be so mean-spirited as that, but one never knew, especially after the manner in which he had treated Darcy's generosity so often in the past. Darcy had every right to house him in the least sort of place considering the cost of it was being borne out of his own pocket.

And so it was with the smallest of expectations that Wickham trotted out of Town along the Knightsbridge Road towards Brompton. He felt the worm of anxiety build as he passed the type of house Darcy's agent had *not* thought suitable for him to start out in: large, spacious, and with land to spare all around. No; he had obviously dismissed these establishments as more than Wickham required - as they were - but they certainly were houses that would make his life very comfortable and please Lydia very well indeed.

Shortly, he had passed through most of Town and admired many of the squares and crescents with their elegant settings and outlooks, and he began to wonder if he had passed his destination without noticing - that it might even have been one of those dwellings he had coveted - when he finally came upon the sign for Yeoman's Row and entered it with not a little trepidation.

It was still quite light and the lowering sun gave a warm tint to the brickwork of the houses. He slowed the horse as he looked for the numbers. And there it was: a moderate cottage-style sturdy building in a row of ten others, all similarly built, of two storeys and wide frontage of three windows' width. The entrance was not large but boasted a pedimented door-hood giving it a modest air of elegance. It was a better first glimpse than he had been anticipating.

Wickham dismounted and tied his horse to the iron link embedded in the garden wall. He looked up and down the street to assess the company in which he was about to be thrown, but could see only a small child playing on the next-door path whilst the clash of metal and a cooking aroma from within declared that a meal was being prepared. He nodded at the child who had paused in his play to stare at Wickham's horse, and then opened the gate which led into a small front garden that clearly had not been tended for quite some time such was the state of the flower beds.

Wickham walked slowly up the path, stepping over fallen vegetation, and tried the front door: unsurprisingly, it was locked, and so he moved along to peer into the first windows to see what the inside held, cursing himself for not contacting the agent to gain access and enable a thorough survey. The room looked large enough with plain panelling on the walls. It seemed clean and dry, and this was enough to encourage him to proceed around to the rear of the property.

The large garden here was also overrun with weeds but he could see that it afforded a pleasant aspect over the field which separated this property from those across the way. He turned and surveyed the rear of the house and noticed steps leading down from the garden into a cellar-area. Without expectation, he made his way down the steps and tried the handle: it gave under his gentle twist, and he found himself inside what he now already felt to be *his* house.

A short tour revealed a very satisfactory abode. Darcy's agent had not scrimped at all; he had chosen a suitable and sensible dwelling for a person in Wickham's position. It had everything he and Lydia could need: three bedrooms, two reception rooms, a kitchen, and space to spare in the attic along with storage in the cellar. It would do very well indeed and he found himself smiling as he took his second tour to ensure he had not missed anything. It might even be possible to house a servant in one of the attic rooms, if they could manage the expense, which would please Lydia greatly to have a servant under her direction; but, if not, then they would have to make do as they had done in Newcastle with a maid coming every day to cook and clean for them.

He froze as a knock came upon the front door. What was he to do? Someone must have seen him enter, so he could not pretend there was no one home. Affecting an air of nonchalance, Wickham opened the door and greeted a middle-aged man standing there with his fist raised ready to knock again.

The man appeared surprised and stuttered, "Ah! Good afternoon, sir. My wife told me there was someone walking about the property and I thought I should check – thieves and vagrants, you understand – the house has been uninhabited for many months and a lure for those types of person. We do not want that kind of riff-raff hereabouts and so I have been keeping watch for the owner, d'you see. But naturally, as I told her, those types do not arrive on such an animal as you have tethered outside."

Wickham bent his head in grave acknowledgment of the man's tale.

"Indeed not. Good afternoon to you, sir. My name is George Wickham, former Captain of His Majesty's Army; now London businessman and new tenant of this house."

"Ah, yes. John Worthy, sir, at your service; carpenter for many of the better building merchants in London. We are to be neighbours, then, it would seem, sir."

"So it would seem; are you to my right or to my left, may I ask?"

Worthy pointed to where the child was still playing.

"There, sir, is my house. You must come and meet my wife; she is all agog to know who our new neighbours might be. As I mentioned, this house has been empty for several months now since the last tenants left and it makes her anxious to have it so, especially when I am away for periods of time, as I often must be for my work, d'you see, sir."

Wickham nodded, thinking that these were not the class of neighbours that would please *his* wife. "Well she must take comfort that my wife and I shall be in residence here within the week. We wait merely for the papers to be finalised, and for my wife to join me. It seems a pleasant street, is it not, Mr. Worthy? I hope there is not too much villainy goes on to make the feminine heart flutter with fear?"

"No, indeed; you are right, Mr. Wickham. We have our share of characters, of course, as does any neighbourhood, but mostly it is of the drunken variety from the inn, nothing vicious. You are very welcome, sir, and we shall look out for you next week, and then perhaps you and your wife would do us the honour of taking a meal with us to celebrate your arrival."

Wickham smiled non-committedly, making to close the door upon his talkative neighbour who turned away saying,

"Then we shall see you in a week, sir. Good luck to you," and John Worthy made his way back to his own house.

Wickham closed the door, relieved. He locked it and then took another tour around, then letting himself out the way he had entered, mounted his horse and rode off into the gathering twilight.

As he rode he mulled over the various jobs that needed completing before Lydia arrived and they could take up occupancy of the house. Darcy had, he knew, set up a modest account for them at one of the larger merchants in the city where necessary items such as furniture and tableware could be purchased, but he was loath to do any of that, presuming that Lydia would wish to procure many of those items herself. And he had enough to do with his own work without the added burden of household supplies. He determined to leave that job to Lydia as the rightful responsibility of lady of the house and one she should enjoy, never yet having had such an opportunity in their married life in Newcastle where they had lived in furnished rooms only. This was to be their first permanent home together, thanks to Darcy's generosity, and she should be made to see it as such and behave accordingly. It might also divert her nonsense about regular entertainments if she had household matters to occupy her.

Wickham nodded to himself in approval of his plan, deciding not to approach the merchant until Lydia was by his side. But with a sudden rush of excitement, he realised that there was one mission he would be *very* happy to execute: that of securing a daily servant. He knew exactly where such a person could be obtained and he would lose no time about it. He would call upon Mrs. Belmont that very evening – he knew she would not be closed for a while yet – and have her arrange it. He had not been back to the agency since he had moved in with Jardine, and he secretly hoped to hear some news of Julia during his conversation with Lucy Belmont.

Moving his horse into a faster trot, he made his way back through the streets with purpose and hope in his mind. The street lamps were just beginning to be lit as he approached the shop front but he could see there was light within and his heart began beating inexplicably faster. If only Julia had written to him – he would ask for nothing more than to see her writing again and to read her words – it would make him the happiest of men, even though he had made a bargain to remain faithful to Lydia, there could be no sin in receiving letters from an old friend, surely?

He tapped gently upon the door and turned the handle. Two ladies were sitting at the table, one with her back to the door and the other, facing him, was Mrs. Belmont who smiled when she saw who he was. She reached out and touched the other lady on the hand, who looked at her enquiringly and then turned about.

Wickham's blood froze in his veins; his heart stopped, as did his breathing. The silence was deafening. He became aware of the smallest detail: her hair was in a new style, and most becoming; her eyes were more deeply brown than he remembered, but had a strained look about them; her fingernails glowed softly pink as she reached up to smooth her hair. Her dress was adorned with a small pin inconspicuous but clearly expensive and, with a sudden rush of jealousy, he wondered who had given it to her.

Lucy Belmont looked from one to the other and broke the spell.

"Mrs. Younge has only just arrived back from her travels, Mr. Wickham. As you see, we have been discussing the business and it is long past closing time. I was not expecting her so soon, but, of course, I am delighted she is back safely and looking so well. Do not you agree, Mr. Wickham?"

Wickham roused himself but could not articulate what he agreed to. He merely nodded and stepped forward with his hands outstretched.

Chapter 31

The final week of their stay at Rosings passed quickly. Elizabeth found a renewed interest in her friend's life at the Parsonage and spent some of her empty hours in that home knowing with some certainty it would be several months, if not a year at least, before they would be together again and enjoy such intimacy. Darcy and Colonel Fitzwilliam were preoccupied with the affairs of the estate which took up the greater portion of their days - and an even greater portion of their restraint when advising Lady Catherine or making suggestions for improvements. But running throughout every person to differing degrees was the excitement of their impending removal to London and all it signified. Every person except one, that is.

Although Lady Catherine had, at first, relished the varied company that had descended upon her home, she began, towards the stay's end, to wish for nothing more than some peace and quiet; some time for reflection and rest. Guests invading every room of the house began to pall and did not support those wishes, and being a guest in another's house had not either.

She began to believe, as the imminent departure for London approached with all of its accompanying noise and excitement - the packing of bags and cleaning of gowns and gloves and polishing of jewels and the never-ending chatter and speculation - that she would *not* be one of the party, after all. She had been away from home enough already this year, she reasoned, and London would be teeming with people all of whom would make constant demands upon her time and attention. She rather disliked to be so pulled about and talked at. It would also become unpleasantly hot and malodourous the closer to mid-Summer they stayed, she knew from experience, and nothing could be more uncomfortable than having to walk about with a scented cloth held to her nose.

No: the longer she considered it, the more remaining at Rosings appeared favourable. She could begin to address herself to the needs of her tenants – some of which had already been detailed by her nephews – and she could be seen to be at home again, and not the absent mistress so abhorred by the masses. It would certainly be prudent to remain at home, she convinced herself. Anne could go, well-chaperoned as she would be, and enjoy herself. It was secretly rather pleasing the see the great improvements that had been wrought in her daughter in the year of her friendship with Mrs. Collins and now more recently with Georgiana, and Lady Catherine would not impose her wish of quietude upon this burgeoning socialite.

Her decision, announced at dinner ~~two~~ nights before the intended departure elicited only the expected platitudes from those who felt it incumbent upon them so to do, and which hid little regret.

"I am sure, Lady Catherine, that London will feel the loss of your company most severely; but the city is to be the loser, and we the beneficiaries. We shall endeavour to keep you entertained, as you deem it necessary – shall not we, Charlotte? – rest assured, your ladyship, you will have our complete attention so that you shall not suffer too much from the absence of all this company."

"Thank you, Mr. Collins for your concern, but I am sure I shall wish for nothing more than a week, at least, of peace and certainly no other entertainments for some considerable time after that." She turned to Anne who was speaking quietly with Georgiana.

"I shall, of course, expect very great correspondence from you, Anne, regarding your activities: whom you have seen, where you have been, and particularly about any new personages with whom you may make an acquaintance. I shall take a great deal of interest in anything of *that* nature, I assure you, and you," here she turned her eye upon Elizabeth who was sitting to one side of Charlotte, "will take on that responsibility, as her chaperone. I expect you to take your duties seriously, madam."

Elizabeth looked confused, close in conversation as she had been with her friend.

"I am sorry, Lady Catherine; to what serious duties are you assigning me?"

Lady Catherine tutted and repeated her demand. Elizabeth then smilingly assured her of having every intention of taking such duties most seriously indeed, along with those concerning her own sister and Georgiana.

"And so, you see, Lady Catherine, how expert I shall soon be at chaperoning young ladies about Town, even though I have not yet been there myself but those I am chaperoning, have. I do hope there shall be *some* opportunity to enjoy myself, that they will not commandeer all of my time. But I assure you, Anne will return to you a little more world-weary, perhaps, but none the worse for that because she will value the quiet life here at Rosings all the more!"

"Let that be the case; there are great temptations and dangers for innocent young ladies venturing into London and they must be carefully watched. I speak from experience, I assure you." Lady Catherine cast a stern glance upon each of the young women in question and made to rise. The gentlemen rose also.

"Colonel Fitzwilliam: a word, if you please; in the library."

Everyone looked questioningly at Fitzwilliam who followed his aunt from the room and then at Darcy for some kind of explanation. He shrugged: if he knew, he was not telling.

The ladies decided to repair to the drawing room. Darcy nodded at Mr. Collins as they passed through the door and then left the room without explanation nor invitation. Mr. Collins, therefore, was forced to join his wife and her friends in the drawing room, not entirely unhappy at escaping what would have been a tortuous silence with only Mr. Darcy for company.

Now that their departure was imminent, discussions about London continued for the next forty minutes. Georgiana and Anne compared homes they had visited, parties they could expect, acquaintance they hoped to encounter – and those they hoped were still in the country – musical delights, and theatres, the parks and shops and galleries. Oh! There was so much they had forgot and now happily recalled for the benefit of their friends. Elizabeth and Charlotte listened quietly, asking questions of the pair, and enjoying their excitement. Although both young ladies had stayed only short whiles on their respective visits, they seemed not to fear the terrible temptations and dangers Lady Catherine had predicted.

Mr. Collins busied himself with a book, feigning utter disinterest in the subject. His miserable upbringing in the lesser streets of London conveyed no such happy memories and could certainly not compare to the ladies' pleasant views of the place.

Eventually, Charlotte asked a question of Elizabeth unrelated to London, and the other two ladies separated themselves a little to continue talking of their plans.

"I shall miss your company, Elizabeth, as I always do when you leave me, but I shall be happy to think of you exploring your house in London and entertaining new friends and living the life Mrs. Darcy should live. You deserve such a life, Elizabeth; you have waited for it long enough."

"And you?" Elizabeth asked quietly. "Are you living the life you deserve, Charlotte? I believe you to be happy, but I would like to be certain of it."

Charlotte smiled. "I could ask for nothing to make my life more complete, I assure you. If this is everything my life is to hold, then it is more than I imagined it being and I am content. I have a comfortable home, a loving husband, a healthy child and a useful purpose. There is nothing more to be added to it, so you may be certain of my happiness, my dear friend."

She and Elizabeth smiled at each other, only to have their intimacy broken by the approach of Mr. Collins. If Lady

Catherine was to be closeted with her nephew for the duration of the evening, he could see no reason to remain.

"My dear? Do not you think it prudent we should return home to little William? Lady Catherine does not appear to require any more of our company this evening and I would not wish to overstay our welcome. She could be some time in discussion with the Colonel."

"I hardly think it prudent or polite to leave without saying farewell to Her Ladyship and the Colonel, my dear. I am sure they will return shortly and then, if you still wish to leave, I will be perfectly happy to do so, although I am sure William is fast asleep by now and is unaware of our absence."

Mr. Collins nodded and returned to his chair and book at which he stared without reading. All of this London talk had discomfited him. Unhappy memories intruded his thoughts, thoughts he had banished to the back confines of his mind and did not wish to re-examine: memories of his drunken father, memories of squalid rooms which he had escaped as often as possible, memories of want and need and hunger and desperation. No: London was not a place he cared to visit ever again, not even in his mind. What he wanted was to reclaim his happiness in his own pretty Parsonage, with his loving wife and child and a benefactress who thought highly of him. He wanted to leave, now, but, as Charlotte had said, it would be exceedingly ill-mannered, and so he must wait and remember and suffer.

A short while later Colonel Fitzwilliam returned in the wake of his aunt, both looking very pleased with themselves. Lady Catherine settled herself and accepted a glass of restorative wine from Mr. Collins.

"You will be wondering, I suppose, what topic of conversation could have delayed our joining you for so long? Ah, Darcy, I see you have also returned; just at the right moment."

Darcy had walked in the door as if waiting for his cousin before braving a room full of women and one parson and the attendant vacuous chatter.

"You may recall I have mentioned several times of my wish to be of some assistance to my nephew now he is leaving the military. I have now made him the beneficiary of my significant connections in London –he is quite astonished at the extent I am known – which will open many very important and useful doors to aid his search for employment. I could not have tolerated him going into Town without such contacts and wasting his time there. He will now have many avenues to pursue - to the detriment of his pursuit of pleasure, of course - but there must be sacrifices made if he is to be successful."

There was a surprised murmur of approval through the room and Darcy added,

"Of course, anything that I can assist you to, has only to be requested, you know that Fitzwilliam. My aunt is not the only person who has friends, it might surprise you to know."

Fitzwilliam bowed to his cousin and smiled at his aunt.

"You do me great kindness, Aunt, and I shall endeavour to use your kindness with discretion and care. I have high hopes of an opportunity presenting itself in the very near future because of it."

Lady Catherine preened herself with satisfaction and glanced about the room seeing the approval upon the faces of all of its inhabitants.

"It is something which I attempt to do for any of those whom I can assist; I have done it several times, you know. It is my duty to do so and I do it willingly with great hopes of being the means of effecting happy changes in a person's future."

At this, a great outpouring of gratitude flowed from Mr. Collins until stopped by Charlotte who rose and curtsied to Lady Catherine.

"Forgive us, Lady Catherine, but we must return to the Parsonage and baby William. The servants will quite think we have abandoned him for more agreeable company." Turning to Elizabeth she said quietly, "Please see us before you leave, even though I understand you will be busy tomorrow, preparing. I should like one last visit."

Elizabeth smiled her agreement and the Collins left.

Darcy watched the Colonel talking with Georgiana and Anne, with great animation, presumably about his plans for London and beyond, and said to Elizabeth,

"It is as well he will have other distractions in London. My impression of those whom he wished to introduce to us were eventually going to lead him into a restless existence – being not one thing nor the other – and he can now be focused entirely upon his future rather than trying to keep up with those who have no need for such direction. I cannot but wonder at the audacity of those younger sons who claim they can find nothing to do with themselves and so go on intentionally living off the good will of their families. It is insupportable. I think that my aunt recognised this possibility in Fitzwilliam and has firmly adjusted his expectations. One such young man is enough in any family and I am afraid Wickham claimed that position well before Fitzwilliam considered engaging with it."

"Oh, surely not!" expostulated Elizabeth, hating to hear such accusations being formed against a gentleman whom had always been her greatest supporter. "Although the Colonel did at one time remark to me that younger sons cannot marry where they like; that habits of expense make them too dependent and so they must marry with some attention to money. Perhaps he will turn his attention to finding a young, wealthy lady – he is charming and attentive enough and should not find such a task too arduous or lengthy. It might suit him more than earning a living."

Darcy looked at her coolly. "Yes; I have noticed that you are still quite taken with those talents he displays so readily. If he were not my cousin and friend, I might think there is something amiss with such an immediate defence of his character."

Elizabeth began to laugh and then stopped short.

"*Oh!* I see that you are in earnest! What nonsense, Darcy; am I not to speak and laugh with any man other than you, now? Am I not to defend those of whom I think well, without suspicion? I had thought you knew me better than that. I am your wife and it is you whom I love, never will there be any other, as you know very well, and I believe you have only accused me in order to hear those words spoken in public."

She looked over her shoulder where she could see that Anne and Georgiana at least, if not also Colonel Fitzwilliam had heard her response, and lowered her voice.

"And so in that, at least, you may say that you have the upper hand over me. But do not accuse me of such inconstant affections again, Darcy, it does not become you at all."

Darcy caught her hands, raising them to his lips and openly kissed them. Her heart melted and she had to drop her eyes to escape the desire that filled his gaze and which she knew was being returned through her own.

Chapter 32

Lydia could hardly contain herself; she read, over and over, the most recent missive from Wickham. It was true. A house! An entire house all of their very own! And, he hoped, a servant girl to *live in*. The house included sufficient room for that, at any rate, and she glowed with excitement at her sudden elevation in status. They had not had an entire house before: two rooms were what they had started with; two rooms – a bedroom and parlour - in a slightly run-down house in Newcastle. But that was before they had removed several times, and each removal had resulted in a reduction in the size of the rooms, the state of the house, and eventually, the number *and* size of the rooms.

Then they had left in a hurry, and Lydia knew why, although she would never own it. It was too humiliating to be so penniless that paying the rent owed to the landlord and the balance owed to the grocers was impossible; it had cut her to the quick that she could not meet tradesmen's eyes. So she had used some of the money she had won at the ladies' gaming tables along with some of what her sisters and mother had sent, to alleviate a portion of their debt. She had not told Wickham; it was none of his business. If he could not arrange their affairs honourably, then she was not necessarily going to stand by and be his accomplice.

But now he had written everything that was good and pleasant to read. A house – on the outskirts of the City, to be sure – but a house with several rooms and stairs and a garden; and neighbours, and close enough to the shopping and entertainments, and Wickham's business. And a live-in servant girl! Oh! She clutched the letter to her bosom and whirled about her bedroom. She sat down again determined to re-read the only part of the letter which caused her some dismay and not a little anxiety.

…Everything is quite taken care of - Darcy's agent has been more than thorough in the execution of his duties - except that you must understand we shall not be able to partake of many entertainments - parties, dinners, shows - until I am sufficiently secure in my position and we can afford such things once again. You will have to be patient and not expect them, or a great housekeeping budget either. I will explain everything more clearly when we meet.

Lydia marched downstairs to her father's book-room, letter in hand, knocked peremptorily upon the thick panels of the door and opened it before her father registered her presence. He started up from his desk pulling his spectacles from his nose.

"Where, pray, is the fire that you come unannounced into the one place in this house where I am permitted some peace and quiet? I am engaged at present with my accounts - as you see - kindly take whatever nonsense you bring, away."

She looked questioningly at him and seeing that he was not completely in earnest seated herself in front of his desk and smiled.

"Please, Father; do finish your accounts. I can wait."

"Finish my accounts! *Finish my* … oh! What it is that is so important? Speak to the point, Mrs. Wickham."

"I merely wish to know the distance between the centre of Town and Brompton, Father. Wickham has written to say it is too *far* from Town to allow us to visit easily and partake of the entertainments on offer there. But what am I to do, Father, without any such thing? Tell me, please do, that Wickham is in jest and that it is not so very far."

"Brompton? *Brompton!* I do not know, child. It is somewhere on the outskirts, I believe, and a very respectable, new and upcoming area, but as to its proximity to the City, I cannot tell you. I do not go into Town enough to be so familiar with it and its new suburbs, but you may be assured that Mr. Darcy will have chosen wisely and well. Do not be so ungrateful as to question his choices; you are very fortunate indeed that he has taken so much trouble over your comfort and well-being."

Lydia sighed. "Oh, well; I thought perhaps you might show *some* interest in your daughter's address but seemingly you care not one jot where I am to be discarded. But I am sure that if I do not like it, I shall leave immediately and knock upon either of my sisters' doors; they cannot refuse me. They will have to take pity upon me when they have so much and will be so happily situated." And with that she flounced out of the door and into the parlour where she found her mother and Kitty re-making Kitty's bonnet in an attempt at sophistication for her impending visit.

Her mother eyed her daughter out of the corner of her eye as she set the ribbons in place and held the bonnet up to Kitty's head.

"I see you have received a letter from London, Lydia. Has Mr. Wickham written any news? Oh! Kitty; have a care. I have not properly fixed them yet."

"Oh, yes, indeed he has, and such a delightful letter containing all manner of loving thoughts and wishes," Lydia fabricated wildly. "But he has mainly written to advise me that we have a *house*, Mamma! All ready for us to live in and big enough for entertaining and parties and all manner of things; and a live-in servant girl, too! What do you think of that, Mamma? Kitty?"

"Oh, let me see. Has he sent an artist's impression of it? Is it furnished? Because you know you may not like the choices that have been made and wish to change them. There is nothing so dreadful as drapes of a shocking colour or uncomfortable chairs with rickety legs. And what about linen and kitchen things? I will speak to your father about supplying you with the names of the best warehouses for you to visit and choose your supplies. I dare say he will be quite agreeable since he did none of it upon your marriage, and had no need to with either of your sisters. But if you are to shop, perhaps I should come with you to make sure you choose the right things, even though London plays havoc with my poor nerves. I know superior quality when I see it, and you have not that skill as yet." Mrs. Bennet nodded to herself in agreement with her thoughts before Lydia and Kitty widened their eyes in horror at each other.

"Oh, *no*, Mamma! There is no call for that," both cried out in unison.

"Lydia must choose her own furniture and supplies, surely, since she has been a married woman for quite some time and has certainly developed quite different tastes in such things than you," Kitty demurred, glancing at her sister. The very last thing either of them wanted was for their mother to suddenly decide she was well enough to accompany them into Town, and also knew that she, not Lydia, would be the one to bear the brunt of such unusual sociability in her mother. It was to be avoided at all costs.

"Kitty is right, Mamma; I could not imagine that anything I should choose would be even slightly similar to the furnishings here," Lydia wrinkled her nose slightly as she looked around. "Remember that I shall be in a much smaller house and so must decorate it accordingly. And you know how tiring upon your nerves you find any sort of shopping, even in Meryton; imagine how it will be in Town."

"Well," Mrs. Bennet was affronted. "I can see where I am not wanted; I am sorry for my interference, it was kindly-meant, but I should have liked the opportunity to visit with my brother and sister. I have not seen him for quite some time and none of us is getting any younger. However, just as you please; make your own mistakes. But you should ask your father about warehouses or you will be taken for a foolish young wife with no intelligence and pay three times as much as you should." And with that she thrust the half-finished bonnet at Kitty and sailed out of the room.

"Well; I daresay it was *kindly meant* but I do not want her poking about in my new home and finding fault with everything I have done to it and the way I have made my arrangements. She forgets that I have had plenty of opportunity to see other, grander homes than this, and have aligned my tastes to those examples. Lady Catherine was very kind, inviting me to visit a great many of her friends around Pemberley; they displayed very good taste, Kitty, both in dress and décor. I wish you could have seen them."

Kitty smiled uncertainly, "Oh, I am sure I shall see many new, tasteful and fashionable things whilst I am in Town. I can only hope not to be judged too harshly for *my* lack of it." She threw the bonnet on the table, bent her head and wept bitterly. Lydia, alarmed, rushed to comfort her.

"What is all this, Kitty? Surely Father has provided some extra funds to cover a new dress and accessories for your visit? Surely Mamma has insisted upon it? I have been so busy I have not noticed what arrangements have been made for you."

Kitty turned her tear-stained face to Lydia and nodded, wringing her handkerchief.

"Oh, yes, indeed; Mamma had Mrs. Smith in the village get to work immediately as soon as I was invited, but I fear that one new dress in a country style will be so very out of place in such grand society. It is a pretty dress, I like it very well and ordinarily I would be delighted with it, but I do not know if it is what I should be wearing. Mrs. Smith is not exactly a London seamstress, is she?"

"Well, Kitty; if it is not suitable, I have no doubt that both our sisters will engage themselves in ensuring your wardrobe *is* suitable. Elizabeth and Jane both will have to procure some fashionable dresses and ornaments, too, if they are not to be derided as country-folk. I foresee an extended and expensive visit to a London mantua-maker's establishment as soon as you arrive; a mantua-maker who will be excessively delighted to have at least three young ladies to dress and make beautiful, and who will show off her superior skills to society! Dry your eyes, Kitty. As long as you have one new gown which is serviceable enough to arrive in, then everything else will fall into place. It has never held me back, you know; with a few alterations, even a very dull dress can be re-made into something unusual and fashionable."

Kitty picked up the bonnet from the table and pulled at the ribbons, beginning to smile at her sister's words. "You are right, Lydia, thank you. I do hope you like your new house in Brompton; I hope I may come and stay with you when you are all settled in."

"I am sure you may; indeed I might insist upon it if I am to be thrust into the middle of the country without any means of entertaining myself, as it appears I am. It is the least my sisters could do, to allow me one friendly face to ease my way into whatever little society I find there. I shall insist upon it, indeed I shall, and you will be my companion just as you used to be!

"Oh! How I wish it were time to leave; I miss my dear Wickham so very much; just knowing we are soon to be reunited is a torment in itself. I must write back to him without delay and approve of everything, even the lack of entertainments, and advise him of our arrival date. I do wish Jane would call and tell us of her own arrangements, and then I can tell her of mine. How surprised she will be."

Jane was surprised indeed when she found her mother and sisters happily engaged in various tasks in the parlour later that morning, and was informed with great exaggeration and embellishment from all sources of the advances of Mr. Wickham and, therefore, his wife. Quietly, she allowed the gloating to continue, knowing of old the pointlessness of trying to break in upon the flood, until she heard the idea that Kitty would be accompanying her sister into Brompton as her companion. Firmly, she raised her voice above those of her mother and Lydia.

"Unfortunately, I do not anticipate that such an arrangement will be possible, Lydia. I suspect Father has not heard of these latest plans, and I am sure he will not agree to them when he does, as you very well know. Kitty is to enjoy the hospitality of the Bingley and Darcy households and will remain with either one of us for the duration of her visit to London.

And, I am sure you would not wish to limit her first experiences of Town society by keeping her in Brompton. It would not be appropriate for her to stay in a house that is unknown to us and surrounded by uncertain company. We will visit for a morning or afternoon to see how well you are settled."

"Well!" spluttered Mrs. Bennet. "And why should not Kitty enjoy a visit with Lydia and dear Mr. Wickham just as much as with you, pray? Lydia assures me that everything in her new home will be arranged and very comfortable. Poor Lydia needs some company and will not have any if you deny her of her sister's."

"That is all very well," broke in Lydia, "but are you Kitty's jailer that she may not decide for herself where it would best please her to stay? With whom she would have the most pleasant time without worrying about her clothing and manners? Truly, Kitty, you shall be far happier in Brompton with me; it will be much less grand and we shall train the new servant between us, and survey the shops and make great friends of the neighbours and encourage them to have parties! Oh, what fun we shall have!"

Kitty looked from one cross face to another and cringed. She loved her sisters very dearly, and with Lydia she had the most intimate understanding; there was nothing they had kept secret between them all the time they were growing up, even if they did quarrel mercilessly over ribbons and combs and bonnets. But she also wished to experience the society in which her elder sisters now moved; they could certainly offer her an opportunity to mingle with elegant and interesting people without her worrying she was being too demanding or costing too much in her board as might be the case at Lydia's new home.

"I would very much like to visit you - several times, Lydia - in your new home, just as soon as you feel it is ready for visitors; but meanwhile, I shall accept the kindness of my two sisters who have already undertaken to introduce me into society. Do not concern yourself, Lydia, Jane is right. It is fitting that you and Mr. Wickham are allowed your privacy and the opportunity to settle back into married life together without the added anxiety of a visiting sister."

"Just as you please," Lydia flounced her head. "I am sure you will have everything agreeable and do everything that is exciting and fun. I shall be too busy setting up my home, as you say, and taking care of my husband. But I must inform him of our date of departure: Jane, when do we intend to leave?"

"We leave on Thursday, Lydia. Charles has some matters to attend to on the estate and cannot leave until then. We shall be very early, so be prepared when our coach comes by to pick up you and Kitty."

Thursday! Only two days away, and so much to do! A great thrilling passed around the room as each lady present imagined how different their lives would be in such a short time.

Chapter 33

Elizabeth sighed with relief as the coach slowly turned the corner into an elegant square lined with trees in full leaf and smart front steps and porticos. Several times, as they had wound their way through the thronged London streets, she had feared the horses would startle and run away with them or overturn the carriage, injuring them all. London was so terribly busy; the streets packed with people and horses and carts and carriages, all thrusting themselves through seemingly impossible openings in streets too busy to admit any more traffic. The noise and smells assailed her at every moment and, where Georgiana and Anne appeared oblivious to it all, excitedly pointing out several sights with happy memories, she had felt a rising wave of panic and nausea.

No wonder Darcy and her father hated having to come here; she understood their unwillingness completely without yet setting foot upon the ground. She could see Darcy now, trotting alongside their carriage, his features set grimly, and her heart went out to him when she considered his thoughtfulness which had occasioned several such journeys already this year into a place he so abhorred.

She had seen several desperate-looking persons as they passed certain areas and had wondered at their destitution and filth; these were not the lower classes she was familiar with in Meryton and Lambton who, although poor, still had sufficient to eat and somewhere to live. No: these were dirty, starving people, many of them children, and women carrying children, and she had averted her eyes until forced to look out of the window again when the movement of the carriage intensified in her stomach, rolling and turning quite alarmingly. She was really quite ill when the carriage slowed to a stop outside a wide sweep of steps leading to an elegant double front door, painted dark blue, and could hardly wait for the coachman to open the door so Darcy could help her out.

"My dear?" he asked in alarm upon seeing her complexion. "You are quite pale. Are you unwell?" At her heavy dependence upon his arm, he immediately turned towards the house, lifting her with ease and leaving his sister and Anne to the Colonel's care.

The staff were all lined up to greet the arrivals but Darcy, barely acknowledging them, began issuing orders as soon as he had helped Elizabeth into a chair in the hallway.

"Mrs. Reynolds: kindly see to Mrs. Darcy. She is unwell, I think, from the journey and needs to go upstairs immediately to rest.

"Is everything else arranged, Grant? We will have no visitors today," he directed as he saw the enormous pile of visiting cards on the hall salver. "Say that we are indisposed and will need some days to recover.

"Hopefully, my dear," he turned back to Elizabeth, "we shall keep everyone at bay for the duration of our visit; that would certainly please me!"

Elizabeth struggled upright from the slump she had fallen into upon finding herself in a chair that was not swaying and jolting and smiled wanly, forestalling Darcy's intention of lifting her again.

"Darcy: please, do not fuss. While I do not feel very well at present, I am sure that now I am out of the carriage I shall recover perfectly and can certainly manage a flight of stairs. Please do not cancel anything that has already been arranged on my account.

"Mrs. Reynolds; how glad I am to see you! I would like to go to my room to refresh myself, as would the other ladies. We will partake of some refreshments in a little while."

"Of course, Mrs. Darcy: if you will follow me. Baxter is already arranging your room, ma'am, but she can wait a while until after you have rested." Mrs. Reynolds nodded and kept her opinions to herself. The mistress certainly did look awful peaky – no wonder the master was all a-jitter – but she wondered if it was only the carriage ride that had caused it. She would make sure some plain wafers were included in the refreshments, and a ginger syrup tea.

She smiled at the ladies and led the way up a grand marble staircase and along a balcony which led to another staircase – less ornate in structure this time – and finally into a wide hall where several doors were open along its length. She walked into the first doorway and looked about the room approvingly before nodding to Anne.

"Miss de Bourgh; this is to be your room. I do hope you find everything to your satisfaction. If there is anything you need, please ring the bell."

Anne smiled and walked over to the window whilst scanning the room with pleasure.

"Thank you, Mrs. Reynolds, this is very comfortable."

"If you will come this way, Mrs. Darcy: Miss Darcy, you remember your room, do not you? It has been a while since you were here but it remains the same, I assure you."

Georgiana smiled with anticipation and walked into the next room all painted white and pink and furnished in a very youthful style.

"Oh! Indeed it is! How lovely to be back in my own room again. But Elizabeth – please do not wait here – you need to rest. We shall see you later when you feel better."

Mrs. Reynolds led the way to the furthest end of the hallway where three doors faced them. She opened the left one and the middle one.

"This is your own room, madam, with a small room off it to use as your dressing room, and here beside it is Mr. Darcy's dressing room. The one to the right is Mr. Darcy's room. These are the largest rooms and face the rear of the house so as not to be disturbed by the street noise. It was always the arrangement when the late Mrs. Darcy was here and I hope I have arranged correctly for you, madam. The furnishings, as you can see, are the original but I am sure you will put that to rights whilst you are here."

Elizabeth, exhausted again and feeling the effect the two flights of stairs had on her general malaise, merely smiled weakly and entered her bedroom. Two large windows at the far end did, indeed, overlook the treetops that shaded the rear of the house. It was quite a pleasant aspect and she smiled with pleasure at the thought of waking to such greenery even in the centre of Town. Mrs. Reynolds watched her for a minute and then curtsied and closed the door behind her, descending several flights of stairs, stairs which became increasingly utilitarian the further she went, until she arrived in the servants' quarters and working areas in the basement. Mrs. Lewes, the cook, was anxiously awaiting her orders.

"Are there any plans for this evening, Mrs. Reynolds? I must send the boy out for supplies if so, and soon. I cannot make anything fancy with what is in the pantry here."

"No, indeed not, Mrs. Lewes. Do not expect an order for anything other than some simple refreshments in about an hour's time and then a small dinner for the house guests; something light and appetising if you can. They have travelled a distance and eaten much that has disagreed with them, I dare say. For the moment, do you have any plain wafers and ginger tea available?"

Mrs. Lewes scurried off after a quick questioning look at her friend and returned with a tin of wafers and the makings of the tea. She brought the kettle from its permanent state of simmering on the corner of the stove and filled a small teapot with the aromatic liquid.

"Thank you, Mrs. Lewes," said Mrs. Reynolds as she added a delicate cup and saucer to the tray. "I will take this up immediately. If you would have the remainder of the refreshments ready in an hour, as I said, that would be perfect."

Mrs. Lewes looked around and started organising her staff: two to begin preparations for dinner and one to lay out the cakes and small edibles for the tea. She sent the boy out to the grocer's armed with a list and strict instructions not to return unless it was filled in its entirety. The boy hesitated – he had not been to London before and did not know where to go – and after she grudgingly gave him his directions and the name of the grocer's he was to patronise, he left with a swagger in his step and swung the basket carelessly. He was to explore London and would be able to brag of his adventures to the girls!

An hour later found everyone assembled in the drawing room feeling rather less travel-weary, although Elizabeth, still not feeling her usual self, was quietly nibbling on the wafers Mrs. Reynolds had put at her elbow as a "great settler of uneasy stomachs." She noticed Darcy was already pacing, walking the entire length of the room several times before joining the ladies and Colonel Fitzwilliam, but then, unable to relax, set off again after only a few minutes. She recognised the symptoms – she had observed this behaviour before – and the next time he passed her chair, she reached out her hand to delay his pacing and whispered, "What is it, my dear?"

"I am sorry, Elizabeth, I confess my thoughts are elsewhere. My agent assures me that all is in order but I am concerned, that is all. I cannot be easy until I have checked up on Wickham and the arrangements that have been made. I can only imagine what he might have done in the name of obstruction to undo my work. Your sisters arrive tomorrow from Hertfordshire and Lydia will wish to go straight to their house. Wickham must be prepared to meet her and take her there without fail."

"Then go, my dear, if you are not too tired. You are imagining things, I hope, but I know you will not rest until you have seen with your own eyes that all is in order. You take too much upon yourself for those who are certainly the most undeserving of your attention, but that is why I love you so dearly." She smiled at him and he bent to bestow a kiss before pleading the company's patience.

"I shall return for dinner, but I have some matters that must be attended to without delay." Darcy refused the Colonel's offer of company, and left a room full of people confused at what could possibly be so important that it required his immediate attention only an hour after arriving in Town.

"Oh, my brother is ever thus," Georgiana laughed easily. "He is a rule unto himself and invariably becomes edgy when in Town; London society certainly tells on his nerves. The whole place makes him anxious for no particular reason other than he would much prefer to stay his whole life at Pemberley. Just wait until the Bingleys arrive tomorrow! Not that I refer at all to *your* sisters, Elizabeth," she rushed on with rising colour, "it is more the Bingley sisters and the dreadful Mr. Hurst with whom my brother cannot abide to spend time. If you would see him frequently leave a room, it will occur whilst they are visiting. I believe it is the only way he manages to keep a civil tongue in his head."

"*Georgiana!*" laughed Elizabeth, "*that* is a shocking observation indeed, but perceptive also as I, too, have felt a similar urge to leave any room which includes their company. But it is a two-edged sword: I cannot wait to see my sisters again – Jane in particular as we have been apart for so long and have so much to discuss and relate – but with them come the sisters *Bingley*. I wonder how they will treat me, now I am not the lowly Miss Eliza Bennet! It will be an extreme test of their good breeding and manners. Oh! I wonder if they have all come in the same carriage. Imagine: Mrs. Hurst, Caroline Bingley, Jane, Kitty and Lydia? Surely not! They would be uncomfortably cramped and their patience tested over such a length of time and in such close proximity. Oh; poor Jane! I had not considered her journey and all it would entail." The idea and her amusement in it quite made Elizabeth forget her sickness.

"I, for one, will be pleased to make the acquaintance of your other sisters, Mrs. Darcy," said Anne breaking into the ladies' amused laughter. "Mrs. Bingley must be a delightful person from your credit of her, and I am sure your youngest sister will also be very charming. It will be a great excitement for her to be so exposed to society and I hope I can be of some assistance to her, small experience though I may have to offer, but whatever I can do to make her stay more enjoyable, I am willing to try. I know what it is to be thrust under the eyes of others without proper preparation for such attention. I have always struggled with it myself and, were it not for Mrs. Collins and her encouragement, I should still be the retiring person I once was. Your friend, Mrs. Darcy, is a wonderful person, as you know very well."

Elizabeth smiled with fondness at such praise for one of the few people in the world she most loved.

"I am sure she only encouraged that of which you were already capable, Miss de Bourgh, but she is, as you say, a very dear person to me and one I am honoured to have always had as a friend. And I thank you, on my sister's behalf for your kind offer; she will enjoy your and Georgiana's company much more than mine. We shall have a very happy time here, I think, the sisters Bingley notwithstanding."

Georgiana had walked over to the table which now held the cards accumulated in the last few days once word of their imminent arrival had spread. She sifted through them and picked out some names she knew, and one that made her smile as she carefully placed it beneath the others separated by her little finger; here was one that she would keep for later.

"Here, Elizabeth, you should sort through these; it is your role. When I was here last, Mrs. Younge was very efficient with these and I never saw them until she had sorted out the suitable ones from the others. I see now what a great many cards arrive just in the hope of being invited or visited. These are ones I recognise and can recommend as interesting company, or the owners of delightful houses. We are here for so short a time that we must be careful with apportioning our time, must not we?"

"But *I* wish more than anything to spend most of my time with Jane and Kitty, whilst I have the chance, not conversing politely with those about whom I care not one jot," responded Elizabeth as she looked through the names. She glanced sideways at Georgiana's hand – she had seen the fumbling of the cards by the table – and held out her hand for the secreted card. "What have you there, my dear?"

Georgiana blushed and gave up the card. Elizabeth read the name: *Frederick Jardine Esq.*, and frowned. She looked up at her sister questioningly.

"Is not this person already known to your brother, Georgiana? He is a close friend of Mr. Wickham, as I recall. You are not intending to pursue any unsuitable friendship you might have formed from your last visit, are you? I do not believe your brother would approve of such a connection."

At Georgiana's continued silence, she sighed, feeling the return of her nausea and exhaustion.

"We will discuss this tomorrow once we are all rested; your brother will decide which of your former acquaintance are suitable. But I must leave you all for the evening as I feel a headache coming on and do not require anything to eat. Please tell Darcy not to worry when he returns; I am tired, that is all."

She rang the bell for Grant, and then requested Baxter to accompany her to her room. Once the door had closed, Georgiana looked at Anne and smiled quietly.

"It would appear that a much tighter rein is to be held on me than last time, even though I thought Mrs. Younge was quite strict enough then, but I shall not fight against it. I will not cause my brother one more second of concern than I have already caused him; he is too good to be treated badly.

"But I would like to see Mr. Jardine again. He, of all of the people I met was the most interesting and interested in me too, I believe; although, of course, Caroline and Louisa saw nothing remarkable or suitable in him and tried to warn me from his attentions. But I am older now and not so easily charmed. I have learnt my lesson, I hope, and will prove it by being the perfect sister!"

"I am sure your brother will decide whatever is in your best interests, Georgiana. I have always wished my older brothers had lived so I could have known them better, so I am very jealous that you have a brother who takes such an interest in you.

"I wonder; might I have a quick glance through the cards in case anyone known to me has called?"

"Oh! Of course; how rude of me: please do, Anne. I hope there are several whom you are eager to see. You must not spend all of your time being dreary with me."

She watched as Anne quickly read the names on the cards until, suddenly, she quietly paused over one in particular, and then laid it aside.

"What? Whose is it? Do tell!" cried Georgiana, moving beside Anne on the couch and picking up the card.

"I *knew* it; he has found you out already! How keen he is, Anne, your Mr. Sudbury; he is quite determined is not he? *Well!* We both have some convincing to do if we are to see those whom we really wish. Come; let us consider how we might manage my sister and brother. Two heads are better than one for such devices."

Chapter 34

Lydia twitched the drawing room drapes, peering into the increasing gloom of the London square.

Oh! Where was he? Why had not he come already?

She had sent word the second she had arrived at the Bingley residence: before she had taken off her bonnet, before she had taken any restorative drink or morsel, before she had visited her room - a room she sincerely hoped never to inhabit. She had so impressed upon the boy the urgency of the task she was assigning him, he had run off as if Lucifer himself was at his heels.

She turned back into the room and frowned. The Bingley sisters were, as always, whispering together on the sofa while sifting through the large stack of calling cards. How tiresome they were.

Should not Jane be doing that, as mistress, now?

She shrugged. Jane would not insist upon preserving her rightful place and its associated duties. But the more she watched, and the more she worried about her husband's non-appearance, something within her snapped. Two days' travelling with these harpies had stretched her nerves to breaking point.

She approached the sofa.

"I believe those usually are all addressed to the lady and gentleman of the house, are not they?" she enquired sweetly, noticing their rising colour with pleasure. "Surely my sister and your brother should be allowed to sort through them first and decide whom they shall visit whilst they are in Town?"

"Yes, well," huffed Caroline, quickly replacing those in her hand, "it has long been my duty to decide such things;

Charles has never cared to choose his society. If it were up to him, he would be run off his feet every night, and eaten out of house and home. And your sister, dear kind person that she is, has no understanding of such things, either. We merely wish to see who has called, and save them both an onerous task."

"I am sure my sister is more interested and capable than you give her credit, Miss Bingley, and she certainly will not improve in her abilities if she is not given the chance to do so."

"Mr. Wickham has not yet arrived, I see," cooed Mrs. Hurst. "How *unfortunate* to be left waiting after such a long separation. I cannot think what could be keeping him from his young bride."

"My husband is a working gentleman; he has responsibilities to his employer and cannot just absent himself as he pleases."

"A working *gentleman* with an employer? *Indeed!* I had no idea there was such a person, but I am sure you know best. I do hope his *employer* will not keep him over time, for your sake. You might wish to stay away from the drapes; I would rather not have the neighbours imagine we are spying upon them."

Lydia sent a vicious glance at Caroline and made a point of moving the drapes more than necessary to again peer into the gathering darkness.

Where was he?

Jane and Kitty entered the room, followed by Mr. Bingley. His sisters smiled adoringly at their brother, entreating him to sit with them and share in the perusal of the cards, whilst entirely ignoring their sister-in-law. Although Charles was long used to their questionable manners, it pained him to observe his darling wife still being excluded, but whenever he had brought attention to their rudeness, they, each time, had feigned ignorance of his accusations and proclaimed themselves utterly *distraught* that they were being less than solicitous to their new *favourite* sister. For a while, they would pay Jane all manner of attention and ply her with so many questions and choices that she would feel it very greatly and beg him, privately, to allow them their own amusements as long as they did not include her. This time, however, he believed – as had Lydia - that they had overlooked the politeness due to Jane as lady of the house.

"Louisa; Caroline; Thank you, but Jane and I will perform that role from now on. You must decide on your especial favourites and, of course, invite all those whom you choose. We shall have at least one party, shall not we, Jane?"

Lydia smiled with great satisfaction and silently approved her brother-in-law's new firmness against his sisters; they had ruled his life for long enough. Caroline dropped the remaining cards immediately, her face turned away to cover her embarrassment. Louisa glanced at her brother to see if he was in earnest and then at her husband to see if he had aught to say about the manner in which she was being spoken. His heavy breathing and almost-closed eyes confirmed that there was no place to look for support.

She cast her cards back in the dish and, fixing a smile upon her face, carried it to Jane who asked her to sit and account for each name written upon them. Louisa glanced back at Caroline, raising her eyebrows but, receiving no response, sat by Jane and began offering a family history and an example of the type of guest each person would make. Her caricatures were so vivid, and her stories so amusing that even Caroline and Lydia were drawn into the conversation, laughing and adding comments.

They were so caught up in their discussions and denigrations that their surprise was great indeed when the butler announced, "a Mr. Wickham, sir," and stood back to allow George Wickham, dressed every bit the gentleman, to sweep past him as if perfectly at home. He bowed deeply to the company but was almost knocked off his feet as Lydia swooped upon him and wrapped her arms about his frame in ecstasy.

"*Wickham!* Where have you *been*? What has taken you so long? I had almost given up all hope of seeing you this evening. Oh! How have I missed you!" and she planted a great kiss upon him, much to his and every other person's discomfort.

He put her away from him, straightening his jacket.

"My dear; I am glad to see you so well. And Mrs. Bingley, Mrs. Hurst, Miss Bingley; and sister Kitty! How delightful that *you* are come to sample the delights of Town. I am sure there will be many parties improved by your attendance.

"Mr. Bingley, sir; I thank you for your every kindness to my wife. Knowing she was in such safe and familiar surroundings with all her family allowed me to fully immerse myself in business these past weeks. But, now I must relieve you of her care; we must leave immediately and direct ourselves towards Brompton. I hope we shall be able to reciprocate your hospitality very soon once we are settled in our new home. It is quite near and most comfortable. You are all very welcome, I am sure."

"Oh! Yes, please do come and visit, Kitty; Jane! I shall be delighted to entertain you all – Mrs Hurst; Miss Bingley, too – I am so happy, I could burst. Come, Wickham! Take me to our new home, *immediately*!"

With a last flurry of her skirts as she picked up her bonnet where she had cast it, Lydia departed without a backward glance, attached firmly to Wickham's right arm.

"Well!" declared Caroline after a significant silence had developed. "I hope she finds everything as she envisions in *Brompton*! Although I imagine there would need to be very little necessary for that state to be felt by Mrs. Wickham. Mr. Wickham certainly fills very well the role to which he aspires; I congratulate him on his dedication."

"My sister is generally pleased with most things, Caroline. To be happy with the smallest thing is not a crime, and to her, the arrival of her husband and the prospect of a home of their own is a very great thing indeed. It will be as exciting for her as for any new bride entering her own home for the first time.

"I shall certainly visit her very soon to confirm her happiness, as will Kitty. Whether you find you have the time is, of course, entirely up to you, Caroline; Louisa."

"And I, too, will accompany my wife. I could not rest easily without seeing for myself that Lydia is at last comfortably settled. I hope this will be a new beginning for both of them," declared Bingley in a stout effort to support his wife.

"Well; let us decide who is available *in* Town before we are forced to travel out to the fringes of it," demurred Caroline as she returned her attention to the pile of cards yet waiting to be sifted through.

"Oh, look, Louisa: the Denbeighs! How delightful."

Lydia snuggled up against Wickham as the cab carried them through the darkening streets, past Hyde Park where the lights were beginning to be lit for the amusements that would follow. Oh, how she had missed him, and how elegant he was – she had quite forgot how well he wore his jacket and breeches! His head was turned to the window and she caught his chin with her hand, turning it towards her for a kiss. He evaded her and the kiss fell upon the side of his face.

She sat up.

"Kiss me, Wickham! Why do not you want to kiss me after all this time apart?"

He looked at her coolly and smiled as if from a distance.

"A cab is no place to kiss one's wife, Lydia. I have a reputation to uphold now; I am a man of business. What would my partners say if they should see such an exhibition? Wait until we are alone in our new home before showing your affection, if you please."

"Exhibition? *Exhibition?* What nonsense are you talking now, Wickham? If that is the case, then Jane and Bingley make a *constant* exhibition of themselves! And there was once, in a cab not unlike this one, travelling from Brighton – fleeing from Brighton, I should say – when you had no such qualms. Kissing me was all you had on your mind. Kiss me, *now,* or I shall think you have kissed someone else recently, thus explaining you lack of desire for *me.*" Tears had sprung unbidden and she wiped them away angrily.

Wickham sucked in his breath; things had come to a head rather more quickly than he had anticipated. Lydia's accusation hit more closely to home than she realised.

It was a kiss, that was all she wanted; a kiss.

He bent his head and bestowed a long, lingering kiss upon her, successfully rendering her speechless until they had passed Knightsbridge and had entered Brompton Road. He pointed out the landmark and Lydia sat looking out as the houses and establishments passed by. She was very pleased with what she saw.

After a short while, the cab turned down Grove Place and pulled up at the Red Lion. Wickham jumped down and helped Lydia as she looked about her in confusion.

"But we are not living *here*, are we Wickham? I thought you said we had a house, all of our own?"

"No; of course not, my dear. We must walk a little way down this street – see here? *Yeoman's Row* – it is not large enough to admit a carriage of any size but you see that the houses are quite spacious and new. It is very close now, I assure you. This inn is where I stable my horse; it is convenient and serves delicious food also, should we ever need to avail ourselves of their hospitality. Come with me: the stable boy will bring your luggage on a cart."

Tired now, Lydia could do no more than follow her husband down the street with the boy following at a discreet distance. This was not how she had envisioned her arrival at all. Wickham turned into one of the larger house's gate and opened the front door. He stood aside as Lydia passed through and into her new home.

Much had changed since the first furtive view Wickham had taken of it. Some serviceable furniture and furnishings had been sourced by Darcy's agent from various vendors, accompanied by some lesser pieces from Darcy House's attic. It was not grand but it was clean and comfortable and Lydia span about the living areas and kitchen, opening doors and peering into cupboards, and then ran lightly up the stairs; her own stairs!

She opened the first door to see nothing other than some trunks and other boxes. She moved to the next which pleased her greatly: a high and wide bed almost filled it and was the most luxurious item she had seen since leaving Pemberley. Its fluffy eiderdown and cream sheets and plump pillows enticed her to bounce down upon it in ecstasy, patting beside her for Wickham to do likewise.

"Oh, but this is quite a bed, my dear! Where did you find it, and how much did it cost, pray? You must be doing very well *indeed* to have furnished everything so well for us. Should you like to try it out right now, my dearest husband?"

Wickham moved quickly to the chest of drawers on the other wall.

"Here, you see, is plenty of space for your smaller items, my dear. Darcy's agent certainly thought of everything; he is the one you should ask about the cost and location of what you have seen. I had no input at all, I assure you, but I rather think this bed is from your sister, Elizabeth's, London house; we have several items donated from their surplus furniture, all of exceptional quality of course, but they do not look too out of place here.

"I am glad you are pleased with it all, Lydia. I shall leave you now in peace, exhausted as you must be from traveling. No, do not argue against it," he drew away as she began to protest. "I have my own bedroom – not as comfortable as this one but certainly better than any I have experienced whilst with the army – and should not wish to wake you when I rise early tomorrow to get into the City. The servant has her own key." He bowed formally and left the room, closing the door quietly behind him.

Lydia stared at the closed door in confusion. This, again, was not at all how she had imagined their reunion. She frowned and made to follow him until the remembrance of how passionate his kiss in the carriage had been, stopped her.

She sat down again and removed her bonnet. He was right: she was very tired and quite cold and the bed was very soft and warm. Tomorrow she would feel better and not imagine things that were not there; feelings that were still lacking. She eventually climbed into bed, pulling the covers up to her chin and smiled at the thoughtfulness of her husband.

He would want her even more desperately tomorrow when she would be rested and have had time to spend on her appearance. Things would be better now they were together again.

Chapter 35

It was with great joy that Elizabeth and Jane finally were re-united the following day after both had recovered sufficiently from their journeys. Earlier that morning, Mrs. Reynolds had given Elizabeth a tour of her house, being especially careful to show her new mistress every nook and cranny, even into the lower servants' quarters to see the state of the rooms and facilities there. Elizabeth made notes in her little book as she walked with her housekeeper and saw several areas in dire need of repair or replacement. Naturally, the house had not been used a great deal since the passing of the elder Mr. Darcy, who, apparently, had very much enjoyed passing time with his friends in the London clubs and parks, unlike his son who spent as little time there as possible.

Between them, Mrs. Reynolds and Elizabeth discussed and agreed upon a great number of improvements; each of the main rooms was scrutinized and, although proclaimed very elegant and charming, some notations were also included in the book. Mrs. Reynolds assured her that the lower entertaining rooms had been restored very recently – within the last ten years or so – and could withstand a longer wait before requiring attention.

The bedrooms were gauged as being in the greatest need of improvement and Elizabeth rather thought that they should be the ones attempted first. They certainly appeared to have been overlooked for the longest time: the colours were out of date, the paper peeling in places, and several of the window coverings beginning to crumble after being grasped too hastily by unwary servants.

Elizabeth breathed a sigh of relief. She was not at all confident in her ability to re-decorate such a house in the current style, fearing that any visitors, while quite sanguine about the older furnishings, elegant and expensive as they were, would not show the same respect for any mistakes *she* might make in replacing them. To make a design *faux-pas* was something to be avoided at all costs and she determined to take notice of the current vogue when she made calls upon her neighbours. Elizabeth relaxed in the knowledge that her first attempts at decorating would be hidden from public view; any mistakes in the bedrooms could be ignored or amended without any public condemnation.

She had just finished with Mrs. Reynolds when Jane and Kitty were announced. The sisters' delight was great and they embraced for a long time, pausing in between to ask questions, or answer, before re-embracing each other. Finally, they all settled themselves and in response to Jane's question about the house, Elizabeth answered:

"I like it very well indeed, although having just finished my tour with Mrs. Reynolds, Darcy will believe me to hate it, the number of things that must be done. What about your house, Jane? Is it in desperate need, too?"

Jane laughed, "Oh, no! My sisters have seen to that, I assure you; they have kept up with the fashion quite admirably. It is stylish, I suppose, although not quite to my taste – too stiff and formal – but perhaps it is that my taste is too countrified and comfortable for London. I shall not dare to mention it for several years, I do not suppose; although, I hardly care in what colour or fabric my settee and chairs are covered, as long as they meet the expectations of society – which I am assured they do – and do not fail in their primary use under any of our larger visitors!

"If you like," she added slyly, "I could ask Caroline and Louisa to call and give their fashionable opinion on Darcy House. I am sure they would be delighted to afford you their expertise!"

Elizabeth shuddered, shaking her head. "I do not know how you stand them always about you, Jane. Why must they be with you every minute, especially the Hursts who should have their own lives to lead? I feel quite jealous of them."

"Do not be, I pray you," laughed Jane. "I can do nothing about their constant presence; it has always been so and until Caroline deigns to marry someone worthy of her, she will stay with us. The Hursts do have their own home, it is true, but it is much more pleasant for them at Netherfield or the London house; why would they stay away and suffer the inconvenience?"

"Well, I am glad they did not feel the need to accompany you here, today, dear Jane, and Kitty. I wanted to have you all to myself for an hour or two." Elizabeth smiled at her sisters warmly and then continued.

"Georgiana and Anne will be back shortly; I am very anxious for you all finally to meet. Georgiana, especially, has long been wishing to make both of your acquaintance. We shall be a happy party, I think, and become great friends. We must plan several gay events for us all whilst we are here."

Kitty joined in the general agreement before clearing her throat and speaking what was uppermost on her mind.

"Elizabeth; Jane; would it be possible, do you think, for us to see what the fashions are here in Town before we attend any such gatherings? I am quite sure that this dress will not do other than for family visits and daytime wear, from what I noticed coming through Town yesterday. I would not wish to embarrass either of you with a sister who is inappropriately dressed."

Elizabeth looked at her sister and then down at her own gown which was an older one she had had since before she was married. It was comfortable and relatively new compared to others she still owned, but now realised that since her marriage she had not bothered at all with improving her wardrobe, settled in the country as she had been and quite content with what she had. Her sister's words jolted her. She looked quizzically at Jane who had already amended her wardrobe with the assistance of her new sisters and looked every bit the fashionable lady about Town.

"Of course! That is the first thing we must do; this afternoon if possible! Jane: perhaps you would be so good as to give us the name of your mantua-maker in London so we shall not embarrass ourselves?

"Ah; here is my sister and Miss de Bourgh."

Georgiana and Anne, newly returned from a ride around the Park, greeted the new-comers with the greatest affection; they had both been anxious to meet the sisters of Elizabeth about whom they had heard so much. After the introductions were made, Anne enquired as to any plans that might have been made in their absence, declaring herself agreeable to anything. Georgiana nodded her agreement.

"Well!" laughed Elizabeth, "I would not say that we have made much progress in that area and are willing to have you both advise us with some suggestions for our entertainment. What we *have* realised is that both Kitty and I are in desperate need of new gowns if we are not to disgrace ourselves. We were just discussing the need for a mantua-maker in possession of the best skills but with the speed of lightning. We cannot wait weeks before we are acceptably dressed to venture out in company, and we cannot venture out – Kitty insists – until we are fit to be seen. Can you advise us?"

Anne nodded; this was something with which she was more than familiar, as her mother updated her own and Anne's wardrobe every time they came into Town.

"Madame Blanche is the person Mamma entrusts with our dresses. I do not believe she is actually French for I caught her once shouting at one of her poor seamstresses in a very broad Northern accent, but she runs a very efficient establishment and knows all of the latest cuts and arrangements. She also provides every accessory you might require and can arrange for a milliner to be part of the consultation. I will send a note to her immediately and advise her to expect a party tomorrow of – how many shall I say? - " she looked enquiringly up from her note.

"Kitty and I, most definitely: Georgiana? I expect you would wish for at least one new gown in the latest style? Jane?

You must come and advise us – please do – it will be just like old times going to be fitted in Meryton."

It was agreed that they all would call upon the person whose skill would transform them into ladies of Town as quickly as possible. Once that note was dispatched, the ladies fell to discussing other items of interest, namely whose party they should attend that evening, bearing in mind that they would not be dressed elaborately enough for many. Both Jane and Elizabeth had received similar cards and invitations, and with Georgiana and Anne's help, decided that the very best place for their first foray into London society would be a small gathering and musical soiree at the Thornton's. They were an older couple who had known the Darcy family for many years and deserved the distinction of being amongst the first to entertain the new Darcys and their party.

Georgiana took Kitty away to see which of her own dresses might do as a temporary solution and Jane, after perusing her sister's wardrobe in vain, convinced Lizzy to accompany her back to Bingley House to see if any of her own gowns could be made to fit with some quick adjustments. Fortunately, Jane being slightly larger than her sister, one gown needed only some discreet tucks before it would do for a quiet evening of sitting and listening: for a dance, it would never withstand being pulled about. Jane smiled when she saw the dress pinned against her sister.

"It suits you very well, Lizzy. It is such a delightful silk but I believe I had it made too small, so I am glad it will fit you. I have not been able to wear it recently without feeling it strain; I fear I have put on some weight since I have been married, although Charles says not, but a dress never lies! Here; try this shawl about it." She stepped away to admire the effect while the maid made the final adjustments before taking it away to be stitched.

The sisters walked about the house and Jane showed Lizzy all the rooms and their different decorative styles – those which she could tolerate and those which she intended changing just as soon as she thought it prudent – before opening a final door at the front of the house which gave into the drawing room with a warning raise of her eyebrows. The sisters Bingley were in residence, waiting to be called upon, and greeted Lizzy with their usual malevolence, and Jane, their feigned affection.

"Mrs. *Darcy!* How delightful that you could find time to call upon us so soon after your arrival in Town; I would have thought you to be entirely taken over with managing that lovely house for a week, at the least. I am sure it is in some need of attention, is not it? And what a pity you were not able to see Mrs. Wickham before she was whisked away last night to the far reaches of Brompton; we are already missing her company this morning, are not we, Louisa?"

"I have every intention of visiting my sister once she is quite settled, Miss Bingley. I hope to find her perfectly satisfied with her situation."

"Yes, well; let us hope she is. I expect it is difficult for her being attached to a man such as Mr. Wickham, but he appears to have found himself a fortuitous position in the City – so dear Jane tells us – and will, perhaps, finally allow others to rest easy about him.

"But is not Georgiana with you, Mrs. Darcy? How I do so long to see her again; you know, we were her constant companions the last time she was in London, and would be most happy to be so again, would not we, Louisa? Such a charming and accomplished young lady, who has, I am sure, improved even further in the last year, but, I hope, she has also improved in her judgment of strangers. She had an alarming propensity to make such *interesting* alliances – your brother-in-law being one of them, Mrs. Darcy – that we had to be quite plain with her. But she left London very soon after that, and we have not seen much of her since. I believe the last time was a year ago when we were all at Pemberley and you visited with your relations. Is she much grown?"

"Almost, Miss Bingley; it was July last year when I was travelling with my aunt and uncle, and I was first introduced to

Georgiana. She has, I believe, not grown much since then, or perhaps it is that I see so much of her that I have not noticed. But she is, as you say, a most delightful companion and one with whom I anticipate spending a great deal of time whilst we are in London, but I am sure that you shall see each other at many gatherings during our stay."

"We were discussing our plans for this evening, Mrs. Darcy. There is a large party to be held after the opera at the Denbeigh's; will you be joining us?" Caroline smirked as she looked Lizzy's dress up and down.

Lizzy stared at her, completely understanding the meaning of her perusal but controlled her temper; rising to the bait would only encourage the woman and give her something to build upon.

"I think not, Miss Bingley. We are to attend at the Thornton's tonight; they are old family friends and Darcy and I believe in attending those events hosted by such acquaintance before trying to impress those whom we hardly know. Jane and Charles will also be attending, as will all of our party. We have Miss Anne de Bourgh as our guest, you know. I fear the Denbeighs must wait until we have paid the proper respect to our personal friends and relations, for I shall insist upon several private family parties whilst we are here. We see so little of our aunt and uncle."

"Ah, yes, of course; the Thorntons are very great friends of the Bingley family, too, but if our brother and dear sister are to attend, then I believe it is perfectly acceptable for the Hursts and me to continue with our previous plans; it would be most inappropriate to cancel now. How unfortunate we shall not see each other tonight. I am devastated, are not you, Louisa?"

Louisa confirmed herself to be at least, if not more devastated than her sister, and then they rose, announcing their intention to call upon some friends.

Elizabeth breathed a sigh of relief upon their departure: arrogant, vain women! How unfortunate for Jane that she had to endure them every day. Jane, entirely unperturbed, took Lizzy's hands in hers and smiled.

"You must not let them vex you, Lizzy. They are difficult to bear a great deal of the time, I admit, but they are what they are and cannot be changed now. We must endure them as best we can, for Charles' sake, and mine. But your plan is an excellent one! Let me send word to Cheapside and invite our aunt and uncle to dinner for tomorrow evening. Everybody must come and we shall have a wonderful, private dinner. How I long to see them again."

"Let us take the message ourselves, Jane! We have nothing more to do today until this evening. Georgiana, Kitty and Anne will be perfectly happy without us for a while longer, I have no doubt, and no one expects to visit me today. Oh! Do let us visit aunt Gardiner; what a surprise she will get!"

Mrs. Gardiner was indeed surprised and delighted to be her nieces' first call in London and she listened excitedly to all of their news, agreeing immediately to the proposed dinner the following evening.

"I can accept for both of us, as I know your uncle has left several evenings free this week on the chance that just such an invitation would be forthcoming."

Their visit was long and touched upon all things familiar and whatever gave them all pleasure to discuss and remember. Mrs. Gardiner was quietly impressed by both her nieces: their assurance and sensibility in their new situations was everything an aunt could wish for and she silently hoped their happiness would always be thus.

Chapter 36

Several days later found Elizabeth sitting quite contentedly at her writing desk finishing a letter to Charlotte:

…and so, it would appear that my youngest sister is very busy and quite content with the arrangements that have been made on her behalf in Brompton, if her silence is anything by which to judge. I have not yet seen her, although we have been here a week, and my notes of the past two days have not garnered a response of any kind. Although I know I must call upon her in her new situation before we leave Town, I also wonder if it is for the best that she is left to her own devices for now, without interference. It is difficult to know what to do.

Kitty is having the best of visits, as you can imagine, and is now intimate friends with both Georgiana and Anne. Both of those ladies are having a very good effect upon her manners and behaviour; it is a pleasure to watch them together. We have had many pleasant evenings spent amongst friends and family, and my heart has been overflowing with happiness at my constant contact with Jane after such a long separation, and also with our aunt and uncle. They shall all be sorely missed once we are gone. Why must we always leave those of whom we are the fondest?

There are some secrets to tell - some to which you are already a party, I understand - so breaking my promise is not so shocking. A Mr. Sudbury has visited already and seems a very pleasant young man indeed, and quite well placed. His interest in Anne is very plain, although he attempts to hide it behind his attentions to me, and she seems to find him not entirely abhorrent. I believe you have already been apprised of his significance, have not you? Perhaps you should prepare Lady

Catherine, as I am sure Mr. Sudbury has every intention of calling at Rosings Park when Anne returns. It might be prudent to warn her ladyship in whatever way you think suitable before she is surprised to learn that not everybody sees her daughter as an unappealing invalid. Darcy has discovered a little about the gentleman; his fortune is such that his attachment is disinterested from that perspective at least.

We are to go to the theatre tonight, finally! Kitty and I have received our new gowns; Madame Blanche must have had every girl in her shop sewing through the night, the speed at which they were completed. We are still awaiting the delivery of another one each, but one is all we need to be able to show ourselves in public without shame! I feel rather too fine – quite unlike myself – but 'clothes maketh the lady' and mine certainly does that. Not even Caroline Bingley will be able to sneer at it.

We are all very well and I hope that you and baby William are, too. I expect he is growing apace, along with your happiness, and I am delighted for you. Please do write soon; your letters are always a great treat for me, as well you know.

With greatest affection
Elizabeth

Elizabeth smiled and pressed her new seal into the wax on the folded papers, looking out of the window as she waited for it to dry. It was a fine, sunny day and Kitty, Anne and Georgiana had already taken themselves for a carriage ride in the Park to see whom they could, and likewise be seen. Elizabeth had no qualms about such diversions. She and Darcy had agreed that a certain amount of freedom could be permitted to the young ladies as they were a tightknit threesome and interested in each other's safety. A carriage ride in the morning sunshine could hold few terrors and even fewer chances of impropriety.

The doorbell clanged heavily and Lizzie sighed. She took no enjoyment in the social round of calls; it all seemed rather pointless and boring. She would much rather take herself for a walk in the Park than sit and entertain ladies with whom she had very little in common and even less to talk about.

But it must be done - it was her duty, after all - and she smoothed her hair, waiting for Grant's inevitable knock on the door. She heard the murmur of voices in the vestibule and then the door opened, admitting Colonel Fitzwilliam. She smiled delightedly and made a quick curtsey to answer his bow, waving him to a chair on the other side of the fireplace and sat herself opposite.

"What a nice surprise, Fitzwilliam; we have seen so very little of you since we have been here. Have you been quite overtaken by Lady Catherine's connections?"

"Indeed," he laughed. "Lady Catherine's connections are no less imperious than she, I assure you, but they are proving useful, which is what she wanted and I am grateful to her for that."

"Then I am glad to hear we have not been deprived of your company without good reason," Elizabeth responded. "But have you had no entertainment since your arrival? Come now; I cannot believe such a thing possible!"

"If I cannot be entertained by my cousin and his beautiful new bride, why should I wish to be elsewhere, pray? I intend yours being the first engagement that I accept, and since a formal invitation has not been forthcoming thus far, I conclude I am to never to be entertained!"

"Not invited?" Elizabeth gasped. "Surely Darcy has given you an open invitation to dine with us at any time, and if he has not then, accept one from me. I would not have you stand on ceremony with us."

Fitzwilliam smiled at her distress, secretly pleased to have aroused her colour in such an attractive manner.

"Do not distress yourself, Elizabeth, I merely tease you. Of course I know I am welcome here, but now I have it from your own lips, it is a more enticing offer than ever, and one I am determined to accept very soon."

Lizzy looked away whilst working to regain her composure. The Colonel certainly had an overpowering effect when he wished; it was astonishing indeed he was still unattached.

"Yes; please do accept it very soon, Fitzwilliam. We are to go to the theatre this evening but we will return here for a late supper, if you would care to join us then?"

Colonel Fitzwilliam nodded his acceptance and said he believed he might be able to free himself from a previous engagement. He looked about the room and asked,

"I expect you have been planning the complete refurbishment of this house, Elizabeth. It has long been in need of a lady's expertise and you must have given Darcy a lengthy list of requirements!"

"There are many things needing attention, it is true," Elizabeth agreed, "but mainly in the nether regions of the house. I dare not embark upon the public rooms until I am more confident. These furnishings will suffice for a while yet. I do not entirely dislike any of them, and remember, I have much to set in motion at Pemberley, too. I would not have Darcy thinking his wife dissatisfied, spoilt and demanding."

"I cannot imagine such thoughts would ever enter his head, it is so full of love and admiration for you. I believe if you were to demand the entire estate razed he would not disagree. I know, were I in his enviable position, I would deny you nothing. You ladies hold us in your sway more than you know."

Elizabeth blushed again; really, Fitzwilliam was a far worse flirt than she remembered.

"Oh; I am quite sure that he would not agree to *that*, and I would certainly never ask for any unreasonable thing. I am quite delighted with both houses and very conscious of the trust he has placed in my limited abilities to run them both well. I only hope I do not disappoint him."

Fitzwilliam smiled gently and then changed the subject, seeing her increasing distress.

"I am sure whatever you do will be elegant and charming, Elizabeth; and speaking of such qualities, are not Kitty,

Georgiana and Miss de Bourgh yet risen, and on such a pleasant morning, too?"

"You find me all alone here this morning, Colonel. They are already abroad, riding in the Park along with all the others who find pleasure in such activities. I prefer to remain here and attend to some household matters. Darcy also left very early this morning on some private errand of his own. Do not ask me for particulars; he did not say where or what it was about."

"O-ho! That is a very bad sign indeed. Secret excursions into Town so early in the morning and so new to marriage! If I did not know my cousin better, I should be raising my eyebrows and arranging to meet him at dawn tomorrow. Damn fool; leaving his wife to her own devices and deductions. Disgraceful, indeed!" He chuckled at a sketch so unlike Darcy that it was laughable. Elizabeth joined in as she, too, imagined Darcy on some underhand mission.

In the middle of this jollity, the door opened and the cause of their humour strode into the room. Darcy came to an immediate halt and glanced quickly from his smiling wife and laughing cousin, their ease with each other, disconcerting.

"Fitzwilliam! You have been quite a stranger since we left Kent. I thought you promised to be one of our party whilst in Town? We have certainly been lacking evidence of that promise. But I see Elizabeth has been entertaining you in my absence. What brings you here today?"

"Yes, she has and in her usual admirable style. As she will inform you, I have been much taken up with planning and plotting my future with our aunt's acquaintance and I would discuss some ideas I have with you, if you have the time. I can come back, if now is not convenient."

Darcy looked irritated for a second and looked to Elizabeth with raised brows.

"Can you spare me for another half an hour, my dear? It cannot be longer than that as I have made arrangements with a merchant to call upon us, as you requested, and I suspect you would want me there? Not that I have any knowledge or expertise to offer, of course, and the decisions will be yours alone."

At Lizzy's smiling nod, he and Fitzwilliam left for the study and she once again fell to her correspondence. A short while later, after ringing the bell for Grant to take away her mail, the sound of raised voices filtered through the closed door, and increased in volume as Grant quickly opened and closed it. Elizabeth frowned and, after handing over the letters, followed him out into the hallway, with a sickening realisation that the voices were emanating from the study. Darcy's voice seemed loudly urgent with Fitzwilliam's a quieter but firm counterpoint.

She stood dithering for a moment – their conversation had nothing to do with her, after all, and listening to others' conversation was an abhorrent thing to do – but at another, now angry exclamation from her husband, she walked quickly down the hallway and paused outside the door.

"You will do no such thing, Fitzwilliam! It is insupportable that you should even broach such a subject. Am I forever to be surrounded by men who can neither weigh their actions against the future nor see the foolishness of their ideas?"

There was a quieter moment in which the Colonel obviously answered, but Elizabeth could not hear clearly, and then Darcy again:

"You will mark my words, Fitzwilliam. Superiority in one sister does not automatically transfer itself to any others. The one is of quite a different mould than *any* of her sisters; do not suppose that your – and I will say this – untoward and open affection for *her* can be translated into equal affection for her sister. You cannot afford to choose where you will, and you know it. Focus on your occupation; forget about marriage until you are in a position to consider it – to anyone."

Elizabeth had heard enough and quickly climbed the stairs to her room, her head spinning with what she had heard. She had never heard Darcy so angry with his cousin before; they had always seen things the same way, but now here was the Colonel, apparently intent upon some lady without a fortune merely because he found the sister agreeable. Why, then, did he not follow his affection for the sister? What resistance could a young unmarried lady have against such charm such as he possessed? Had not she, a happily married lady, just been flattered by his attention?

She sat in her chair, mulling over what she had heard, satisfied that her suspicions were correct. One thing was for certain: the Colonel had *not* been entirely taken up with boring acquaintances of Lady Catherine this past week as he had claimed. At least there was only good in the Colonel, unlike Wickham, and any lady who managed to attract his attention and good opinion would be fortunate indeed. But who could she be? And why had the Colonel decided on the sister rather than the one he clearly preferred? It was all most tantalising indeed.

She heard the front door slam and left her room to regain her place in the parlour where she found Darcy pacing up and down the length of the rug, slapping his thigh as he paced with clenched jaw and faraway gaze. She paused at the threshold, uncertain of her welcome; he noticed her upon his return up the room and smiled thinly.

"The Colonel has gone already?" she enquired innocently. "Were you able to assist him in his decisions at all, my dear?"

"Fitzwilliam has turned into a fool, Elizabeth. I never thought I would have to say such a thing about him, brave soldier and sensible gentleman as he has always been, but I believe his head has been turned and he is on a path to ruination if he continues with it."

"Oh; I thought you were discussing his *employment* prospects, not his love life," she smiled gently. "Surely if he does well with the one, he may do as he chooses with the other, cannot he?"

"He has yet to embark upon any type of serious employment, let alone do well at it, and his choice in the other is not made with good sense; it is not based on knowledge, only fantastical assumption.

"How long did we know each other, my dear, before we were confident in our regard? Months? A year? Yet he thinks that because he is acquainted with *one* sister, then the *other* whom he has his eye upon, will turn out just like her. And I did not like his comments on the first sister at all. He made my blood boil even though there is nothing in it, he assured me."

Elizabeth hesitated. "I presume the first sister – the object of his actual affection - is unavailable and so he transfers it to the next sister in the hope of duplicating his feelings?

"How absurd, as you say! The last man who tried such an approach to felicity was my cousin: he preferred Jane at first sight – because, of course she is the most beautiful and the eldest – and then he transferred his imaginary affections from her to me after being told Jane was very likely engaged; and then, when I absolutely refused him and Mamma attempted to influence his feelings again towards Mary – who would have been the most suitable in temperament and interest – he refused completely and fixed himself upon Charlotte. They were engaged within two days! But I cannot believe that a man of the Colonel's charm and eligibility should behave in such a foolish manner. Why; there must be many very suitable young ladies who would be flattered to be the object of his admiration."

Darcy glanced at her suspiciously. "And why would they? Although it seems you are always flattered by his company – every time you are together you revert back to your first meeting - all flirtation and secret laughter and convenient walks. It will not do, Elizabeth. I have told the Colonel – cousin or no – he is not to visit you alone again. It is not appropriate and I will not tolerate it."

Elizabeth gasped.

"You cannot be serious in your accusation, Darcy! There is nothing untoward in our encounters, nor has there ever been. He has always been a pleasant friend and easy conversationalist, nothing more. He must have been greatly insulted by your insinuations, as now am I.

"I do not understand your sudden attack against his and my character but I expect you will soon come to your senses and apologise, to me, and most certainly to him. Such unfounded accusations are not to be tolerated. It is humiliating indeed."

She flared out of the room whilst uttering her final words, appalled by her sudden inclination to burst into angry tears, but determined not to give him that satisfaction.

The joy had been extinguished from her day, a day that had started so happily and with such anticipation for the evening ahead. Darcy did not re-appear to speak with the merchant as he had promised, and Elizabeth found herself dealing with swatches of fabric and leather and designs for chairs and tables with only Georgiana and Anne for guidance, but between the three of them they made sufficient progress to have decided upon all of the necessary changes to be made for the bedrooms. Georgiana, especially, was delighted to have her say about her own decorations.

Upon completing the order, the merchant assured Mrs. Darcy that everything would be completed to her specifications and delivered and fitted within the month. After warning him that she likely would no longer be in residence, and that he would need to contact the caretaker whose name he could get from Mrs. Reynolds, he hurried away to place the orders with his suppliers.

Lizzy had just rung for refreshments when Grant announced another merchant for her. Elizabeth frowned; she had not expected any other person.

Grant admitted a very elegant older gentleman, quite debonair in coat and breeches cut in an old-fashioned style. He carried a large bag under his arm from which he withdrew a strongbox whilst looking around the room, presumably for a place upon which to deposit it. Georgiana, Kitty and Anne all strained their heads to see what could be inside, and looked at Lizzy for an explanation. Elizabeth read the man's card – *M. Freschet, Esq.* – and raised her eyebrows.

"Madame Darcy," he murmured, bowing low, "your 'usband, 'e called on me this morning and choosed several pieces from my collection, and requested my presence 'ere at this hour. "E is 'ere, perhaps?" He looked around dubiously at the other ladies and returned his gaze to Elizabeth. "I do not think … that is … er, I belief that 'e wished for him to be 'ere pendant que vous faites votre choix; I am very sorry, I do not know what I should be doing now. I fear I 'ave made a mistake."

The man hitched the box further under his arm – it appeared to be quite heavy – and furtively dabbed at his brow with a large handkerchief.

"Monsieur Freschet," Elizabeth smiled gently, "please do not concern yourself about my husband's absence. Even though your appearance is of a surprise to me, as he did not tell me to expect you, I am sure you are right: he most certainly would prefer to be here, to explain the reason for it, and I would like that much better, too. My husband is generally known for his attention to time and appointments. You may rest assured that if he has made an appointment, then he will soon be here.

"Please; will not you take a seat and some tea with us whilst we wait for him? Leave your box there on the table."

It was as she suspected, and hoped. Just as she had convinced M. Freschet to take a seat and accept a cup of tea, Darcy made his appearance. One sweep of the room told him everything he needed to know. He bowed to their visitor, glanced at his wife and then requested that the other ladies leave them for a half hour.

Elizabeth sat very coolly, waiting for some explanation from the man who had so incensed her only two hours earlier; however, his demeanour conveyed no indication that anything had ever been amiss between them. He came to sit beside her, taking her hand, and motioned to M. Freschet to continue.

M. Freschet, much relieved, eagerly withdrew a large iron key from his inside pocket and opened the box. Inside lay several smaller boxes, in various shades of leather, and he looked enquiringly at Darcy for instructions. Darcy leapt up and brought over the small table holding the box, pointing, as he placed it in front of Elizabeth, to a particular long, slender box of green leather.

"That one first, if you please," and the box was opened with alacrity to display, nestled in a pale blue satin bed, deep blue sapphires and diamonds set in a filigree gold lacework. Darcy lifted it out and handed it to Elizabeth who was too astonished to speak.

"This, I think, will suit you very well, my dear. It is less heavy and more delicate than my mother's but it is very suitable for evening wear, M. Freschet assures me. Apparently, this openwork style is quite the fashion at the moment."

M. Freschet smiled. "Indeed it is as I said, Monsieur Darcy. And Madame Darcy's complexion will set it off *parfaitement*, si vous me permettez l'observation, Monsieur."

Elizabeth fingered the beautiful piece and demurred.

"I have no need of such a precious thing, Darcy. I hardly have had occasion to wear your mother's; I would hate to have two such beautiful objects hidden away in the safe, never to see the light of day but twice a year. You know I would prefer a simple adornment, something I can enjoy and wear everyday as a token of our love."

Darcy smiled in satisfaction and nodded at the jeweller. M. Freschet drew out another smaller box and opened it, placing it upon the table. Elizabeth gasped and reached forward instinctively to take it up. Here was something she *could* wear every day very happily: a thin rope of coral intertwined with the occasional diamond and ending in a pendant gold cross set off with one diamond in the centre. This she could wear! She smiled delightedly at Darcy, immediately handing it to him to fasten around her neck.

"You realise that this one is but a fifth the price of the other, do not you, my dear?" he murmured as he bent close to her ear to fasten the catch. "It is hardly a significant show of my adoration; I should be ashamed to admit this is all I bought you to celebrate our wedding!"

"Nonsense!" she kissed him impulsively, as M. Freschet coloured and looked away. "This is exactly the symbol of our love and happiness. We are not ostentatious people, my dear, and should never attempt to become so. No, this is by far the better choice, although this other is certainly very beautiful."

"But Madame!" interrupted the jeweller, glancing at the unopened cases still lying in his box, "there are others for you to see. Monsieur Darcy was most thorough in 'is assessment of my pieces; I should not wish for you to choose without seeing them all."

Elizabeth laughed and took Darcy's hand. "Then I shall look at everything, my dear, as you have taken so much trouble. But when did you arrange this, pray? It is all so unexpected."

"We shall discuss that and other matters in private very soon, my dear. But please do as M. Freschet suggests, and view everything that I wished you to see. I would like it confirmed that I am capable of choosing well, so that in future I can make these decisions alone, if necessary."

And so Elizabeth spent the next half an hour trying on the different necklaces and one brooch, admiring the effect in the long mirror at the back of the room, and discussing each one's merits and flaws. All were eminently suitable indeed, and she felt her husband's consideration in each piece, but at the end of it all, it was the coral necklace she decided upon for herself and insisted on wearing immediately.

Darcy, however, was not to be satisfied with such a piece, and retained the sapphire necklace against her objections, assuring her that he was willing to withstand several more evenings in society to ensure it being worn very frequently.

After the jeweller had gone, they sat together and she took his hands in hers.

"Thank you for such precious gifts, my dearest, I shall treasure them always. But we must discuss this morning's difference of opinion, do not you think? Not even gifts of this magnitude can erase your accusations of me and your cruel treatment of the Colonel. Why were you so angry and unreasonable, pray?"

"Because," he shifted his position, slightly discomfited, "I had just returned from M. Freschet's establishment, having spent considerable time choosing those pieces for the woman I love very deeply, only to find her laughing and sharing intimate stories with the Colonel, on her own, upon my return. I expected to find you alone so we could spend the day together choosing, first, the furnishings for our house, and then the surprise I had set about. It was not as I planned, that is all, and I was angry at you, unreasonably so, I see that in hindsight. Please forgive me."

Elizabeth silenced his words with a kiss and then sat back, considering.

"But that does not quite fit with your accusations of the Colonel being foolish – I think you called him – in his manner of choosing his future wife. There must have been something more to the conversation than just your disappointment in seeing him with me and ruining your carefully-laid plans."

Darcy sighed, rose from the chair and walked to the window where he stood looking blankly out, immersed in his own thoughts until Elizabeth approached and put her arms around him. She could feel his tension through his coat and she longed to make it disappear.

"Tell me what it is that is causing you so much concern and antipathy against a man whom you have always held in the greatest regard, my dear."

Still facing the window but covering her clasped hands with his own, Darcy said,

"I vowed never to interfere again in others' love lives after my arrogant behaviour with Bingley and your sister, but I cannot ignore it when something is brought to my attention and I am even asked for my opinion of it. I cannot be so restrained, Elizabeth, I cannot!"

"And nor should I, or any other person wish for you to be so, my dear. Everything you have ever done has been only out of concern for the welfare of the parties involved - I know that -

even if sometimes you might misunderstand the depth of feeling those parties have, one for the other. But where there is true attachment and affection, nothing anyone can do will separate them.

"You mentioned a sister admired by the Colonel – is she someone we know, perhaps? Someone of whom you do not think highly, I suspect; someone about whom you believe the Colonel to be mistaken in his attentions? Tell me her name and I will do all that I can to discover her situation and worthiness as his prospective bride."

Darcy grimaced, turned and took Elizabeth's face in his hands, gently kissing her cheeks and forehead.

"On the contrary: I have learnt to think *very* highly of this lady whose sister's name is Catherine, a young lady whom you already know well enough to judge her character. Believe me when I say that no further investigation is necessary. The sister upon whom Fitzwilliam is basing his assumptions that one sister will be the copy of the other is named Elizabeth.

"Yes," he smiled grimly at her shocked face, "yes, my dearest Elizabeth; he has fastened his affections upon *your* younger sister in the belief that she will turn out just like you. I should, I suppose, have taken it as a compliment to my wife that another man finds her so attractive he would believe such a thing, but I lost my temper, accusing him of covetousness and all manner of other hideous failings. I do not think what I have said in the shock of the moment can be undone."

Elizabeth stood stunned at his words: that the Colonel had made such a declaration, and to her husband, was foolishness indeed, and he deserved any and all anger directed his way. She could certainly see why Darcy had been so angry and ordered her to stay away from seeing the Colonel alone. Clearly the Colonel's affections for her ran deeper than she ever imagined, but to project those feelings onto *Kitty*? Kitty was no more eligible to marry him than she, herself, had been, and he had been very clear to *her* last year that younger sons could not always marry where they chose, but rather where they must.

"That is strange indeed; to be so fixed upon a person he has never met, for when has he seen Kitty, pray? Towards me he has always been a true gentleman and friend, I assure you, but now I see that, if what he has claimed is true, then being friendly towards me has somehow translated into a desire for my sister! How bizarre! I can hardly think the Colonel capable of such strange fantasies; is he in his right mind, do you think?"

"Apparently, it is not all based upon his interactions with you, slight and innocent though I know those have been. He has made a point of being in the Park each morning to chaperone – as he puts it - your sister and mine, and Anne. Evidently, he claims they have all become well known to each other this past week."

Elizabeth gasped in horror. Oh! And she had been so complacent about allowing the girls a small freedom each day; to be each other's companions and chaperones. Who else; which other young men had been taking advantage of her absence? Her heart dropped painfully as she realised her mistaken laxity. She pulled away from Darcy's arms and walked unsteadily towards the door.

"This is not to be tolerated! I shall call the girls down at once and we shall hear what they have to say about their outings in the Park before we condemn them, but I must say I will be disappointed indeed to learn they have been encouraging the attentions of other young men, as well as those of the Colonel."

Darcy watched as she sailed out of the door, her spirit entirely restored and her determination to get to the bottom of the problem very clear. He did not know how he would deal with the Colonel but he felt fully assured that any feelings that gentleman held for his wife were entirely one-sided, and he silently berated himself for ever thinking otherwise.

Chapter 37

Julia yawned as she closed the shutters on her front room window in the flat above the agency. The street below was becoming quiet and other merchants had already left for the day. She had had the shutters affixed very recently as a preventative measure against thieves and other terrors that were reputedly roaming the streets of London at night; she had no wish to become one of their statistics and a sensational headline in the evening paper.

She pulled the drapes across and moved into the kitchen area to prepare the food she had bought earlier in the market: fresh bread, vegetables, cheese and a cooked chicken. She did not have the facilities to cook anything elaborate in the flat, and as it was only her to provide for, she had found this sort of meal to be more than sufficient. Her friend, the good Lucy Belmont, frequently remembered her, bringing slices of cake and other delicacies from her own kitchen to supplement Julia's meagre diet. Occasionally, she would visit a local inn but found the awkwardness of eating alone outweighed the variety of the food on offer.

However, hunger had been of little concern recently for Julia; her swirling thoughts after her meeting with George a week ago had decreased her appetite. His appearance on her doorstep had been a shock - Lucy having assured her that he had taken himself off to his friend's house and had not been seen since - and every day for the past seven days, Julia had been in a fever of anxious waiting. Her nerves were on edge; she knew absolutely that George would return, it was only a matter of when, and that certain uncertainty was creating havoc with her usually calm and sensible demeanour.

His object in being at her agency had all but been forgotten in the charged atmosphere that had followed his unexpected arrival that evening, and it was not until their mutual shock, surprise, delight and questions had been addressed that she enquired of him his purpose.

He was in need of a maid-of-all-work for his new house out in Brompton, he had explained wonderingly, and he had wasted no time before patronising the one place he knew where he could obtain such a person. Julia had nodded, regaining her sense of business with difficulty. She searched for words that would reinstate some prosaic discussion into the situation.

"It is not a large house, then, George? I could not send out only a single maid if it would be too much for her to cope with on her own."

"It is a moderate-sized house, my dear, nothing that one woman cannot manage by herself; indeed the wife next door manages admirably on her own and with a young child to care for besides. Lydia, of course, has neither experience nor ability to manage that kind of work as she displayed very clearly during our life in Newcastle; even the most simple of household tasks are either beyond or beneath her, which makes the acquisition of a maid an absolute necessity."

Julia winced slightly at the mention of her rival's name but steadied herself before asking,

"And how is it that she is not here to arrange such things for herself? Is she not in London with you, George?"

"Not at present, my dear. I find it eminently easier to manage things by myself, although much has been taken care of by Darcy's agent; he has been most thorough. And, naturally, I have been much taken up with my new position in Town. Having Lydia here would have interfered with my concentration in these beginning weeks. She has been quite content living in the lap of luxury with her family in Hertfordshire awaiting my letter to call her to Town, but I confess to leaving the writing of that letter until the latest possible moment. Now, it is unavoidable; I have settled into my work, and the house is ready for our occupation. All it lacks is a maid and a mistress."

Julia looked down at the note Wickham had made of his new home's address.

"Then I shall send someone suitable as soon as possible to this address. If you would be so kind as to describe her responsibilities, I will be able to calculate her rate, which would be payable in advance."

"In advance, Julia?" Wickham looked disconcerted for a moment. "Surely it is usual to pay quarterly for such services?"

Julia fixed him with a knowing stare and smiled slightly.

"Yes, indeed; that is still usually the case, but I make my decisions based upon experience, and change my terms to fit each customer, George."

Nothing more needed to be said.

Wickham coloured faintly and fumbled with his gloves as he rose from the chair. Julia could see her remark had stung, but she was not about to offer credit to someone whose mode of living she knew so well, and so remained silent as he raised her hand to his lips and kissed them as he was used to doing, not quite as certain, as he had first supposed, that her feelings for him were unchanged.

"As you wish, my dear. Please make your calculations and the fee will be disbursed tomorrow before I start work."

He hesitated.

"Would you care to take dinner with me, Julia, for old times' sake? It is becoming very late and I am rather hungry, as I am sure are you. I believe we still have a great deal to discuss now that we have recovered from our surprise at seeing one another again."

Julia considered for only a moment her scant supplies in the flat and nodded quietly.

"I should like that, George; for old times' sake, as you say."

The evening had been delightful, just as it had always been when life was being good to George. He was attentive, charming, sympathetic, and listened assiduously to her views of America and how business was run there and her ideas for her businesses here and, perhaps, there in the future. Nothing was too expensive for her to order: nothing too dull for her to discuss. Julia was almost beguiled into her former state of attachment, so effective was his assault of attention.

But that had been the extent of their intimacy. The knowledge of Lydia now being his wife was too much for Julia to ignore, and she now feared, a week later, that her coolness towards his advances explained his prolonged absence.

She slowly prepared her small meal, all the while telling herself to concentrate upon matters which she *could* control. Now she was back in London, her first matter of urgency must be to find herself somewhere to live; she could not receive friends and guests in this small flat, convenient as it was.

Lucy had intimated in one of their first conversations that the lady to whom Julia had sold the lease of her Edward Street house was not entirely delighted with the transaction. Lucy had met her accidentally in the market and been forced to listen to a great discourse of disappointment regarding said property: being a landlady was not to her liking, she had discovered; the business had never been anywhere near as brisk as Mrs. Younge had assured her of it being; many of the regulars had fallen away and the occasional traveller could not be counted upon against the upkeep of such a large house.

"In short, my dear friend, I believe the lady would be very eager to return the house and its problems back to you, should you wish it, and look about for a more interesting and profitable business to pursue."

Julia had smiled noncommittally - it had been an early conversation after her return from America and she had not as yet thought much about her future plans - but now that future was beginning to fall into place with alarming clarity, she felt a sudden rush of panic as she realised that she had wasted an entire *week* waiting for a knock on her door. She drew her notebook towards her and began one of her lists:

> *Write to Mr. Brown to advise of my intention to visit Cambridge properties*
> *Visit Edward Street <u>tomorrow</u> to assess situation and availability*
> *Go over the accounts for all businesses – assess financial position*

She glanced at her pile of correspondence and added,

> *Deal with all letters – <u>tomorrow</u>, without fail*
> *Resist all temptations re. G*

After double underlining the items that required her immediate attention the next day, she lifted the account book onto the desk and began re-acquainting herself with the success of the agency.

Lucy had certainly been an active manager and had taken a great deal of pride in expanding both the number of clients and available employees. Julia added a note to her list to increase her friend's commission, before returning to the precise notations and accounting.

While she worked, other thoughts were also quietly revolving in her head; unformed ideas and plans that were slowly fermenting and coalescing.

Her recent travels to America with Mr. Clemens had impressed and delighted her and, although he had not fulfilled *his* wish to convince her to become Mrs. Clemens, she was grateful to have been given the opportunity to see his world and the opportunities it offered. Everything seemed to be possible there, nothing was beyond being attempted, and the relaxed rules and regulations compared to those of London made it seem as though ideas were merely one thought away from becoming reality. When she looked down at her list she found she had written *America?* several times at the very bottom of the page and she smiled to herself. Clearly her mind was not entirely engaged with her London concerns.

It was with a great sense of relief that Julia set out the next day in the direction of Edward Street after consigning her two letters to the mails – one to Mr. Brown and the other to Mr. Clemens advising him of her safe return to England – and informing her delighted friend of her increased circumstances. It was liberating to once again be taking matters into her own hands, making decisions and acting immediately upon them, not mooning about the agency waiting for a certain person to re-appear.

She alighted at the familiar front door in a very spirited frame of mind, noticing with distaste the grime on the windows and weeds in the small pots. The house appeared to be in a doubtful state of maintenance, not something prospective guests would wish to greet them upon arrival.

She rang the bell, proffered her card, and was admitted by an indifferent maid into the front parlour – which brought the recollection of several still-painful scenes to Julia. As she waited, Julia ran her finger along the mantelpiece and re-arranged the cushions thrown in disarray on the sofa, while calculating the possible state of the other rooms.

"Mrs. Younge! How are you? What brings you back to London, pray? America did not suit you, is that it?" Mrs. Smith entered, all cheerful friendliness with not a hint of dissatisfaction regarding her current situation, inviting Julia to sit and take some tea, which Julia refused.

"I am very well, I thank you. Yes, I have only recently returned from my visit, and, on the contrary, America suited me very well indeed; it is a new land of great opportunity and has planted several interesting ideas in my head, I assure you.

"But I thought to call to enquire about our arrangement of last year and your satisfaction with it. I know it was entered into with some speed and without much instruction from me, for which I now apologise. I understand the challenges of such a business if one is not familiar with it, and I wish to amend my neglect of you, even at this late stage should you require it, although I am sure you do not."

Mrs. Smith drew herself up haughtily, her assumed manner dropping as her irritation increased.

"Indeed you are correct, Mrs. Younge. Generally, I would 'ave no need of any advice from you or any other person with reference to my ability to run this 'ere establishment, although I 'ave found - not due to any failin' on my part, mind you - that some of the assurances you made 'ave not been quite true. We 'ave not been as busy as what you claimed we would be, we 'ave all but lost our long-term guests and cannot rely upon the 'casional traveller to fill every room each night. No; business is not what you led me to believe, Mrs. Younge, I 'ave to say that. I 'ad to release several of the servants, leavin' me with the bulk of the work to do myself."

Julia nodded sympathetically: all was exactly as Lucy had reported.

"I am sorry for that, Mrs. Smith, indeed I am, and I take the responsibility for your troubles upon myself. I should have been more attentive and foreseen the pitfalls you might encounter upon entering a new business and advised you better. But I truly believed I was selling the lease of a profitable business to you, a lease that still has another year to run, does not it?" she enquired innocently with a concerned frown.

"Well, yes, it does but if business continues as it 'as done, then there will not be any point in considerin' the lease; all of my money will be gone, with nothin' to show for it. If things do not soon improve, my investment will have been a very poor one. I should like to know what you intend doin' about it since now you say you accept some responsibility in the failin's of it."

Julia bowed her head as if in deep thought, all the while containing her excitement at the prospect of regaining her house before the lease expired. It was all nonsense, this claim that business had fallen off. Mrs. Smith simply lacked the ability and diligence required to run a successful boarding house; the evidence of that was abundantly clear even within this room. None of these thoughts were reflected in Julia's face as she raised it to meet the indignant gaze of the landlady.

"You are right, Mrs. Smith, something must be done. I would not have you suffer any more losses on the back of those you have already. I should hate for you to be left with nothing after my claims of being provided with a decent income have been disproved so promptly. Would you, perhaps, be willing to sign the lease back over to me? I, in return, am willing to reimburse you three-quarters of your original payment, which is more than fair, and would allow you to explore other business options."

Julia rose from her chair, noticing the greedy gleam starting in the woman's eyes.

"You must understand, however, the amount stated is not negotiable, Mrs. Smith. I am not able to pay any more than that, nor should you expect it. It is a very generous offer for a failing business, as you claim, but I, as I have said, do feel obliged to relieve you of your current situation.

"I shall leave you to consider the offer. Please contact me at the address on my card within the next two days, after which the offer will be withdrawn and the lease will continue unchanged for the next year.

"Good day to you, Mrs. Smith."

The following morning, early, Mrs. Smith appeared at the agency, agreed to all terms and walked away certain in the knowledge that she had secured a very propitious solution to an unsolvable situation, feeling even a little niggle of guilt to have taken Julia's money for a business proven to be so unprofitable.

Julia, however, was in no such need of consideration. Within a fortnight she had spruced up the house, re-hired maids and cooks, advertised and booked out all rooms except two, re-established contact with her neighbours, and moved herself and her stored belongings back into her old room and private parlour.

The fact that George Wickham had not called in that time had barely crossed her mind and once she did think about it, smiled to herself in satisfaction: immersing herself in work had always been her solace and solution.

Next on her list was Cambridge, and she lost no time in securing herself a seat on the next day's stage.

Chapter 38

Elizabeth sat silently at her desk, working her way through the tortuous allegations and assumptions being made in her mother's latest letter enumerating everybody's delight and happiness at being in London without her: how, she was sure, not one single person was giving the slightest consideration to her exclusion; that very few neighbours had been to call in the weeks since both Kitty and Lydia had been gone; how Mr. Bennet remained as always within his book-room and refused, absolutely, to take her to Town for the smallest of visits, which she felt was the least he should do to rest her mind regarding the concern she was experiencing for the comfort and happiness of her girls; that it was becoming too hot, the sun would insist upon shining relentlessly every day, there was not a shady aspect to be found, &c., &c. Of Mary there was no mention.

Elizabeth sighed as she turned the page, knowing as she did, the querulous nature of their mother when fancying herself slighted, and the difficulty Mary would be experiencing in assuring her that the lack of visitors was not a conspiracy nor the effect of her daughters leaving.

Elizabeth, in fact, had no doubt that Lady Lucas, Mrs. Phillips and others would be visiting regularly, just as they always had and discounted her mother's vexations as the result of being too much alone without any interest or occupation with which to divert herself now she had three daughters married.

She scanned the rest of the page and, seeing it contained nothing more of interest, placed it under her blotter; she would respond to it later when she had something conciliatory and uplifting to say. Truth to tell, Lizzy had not been feeling entirely well each morning and had finally made an appointment with the doctor about her queasiness. She had taken Mrs. Reynolds' advice and certainly found that the ginger tea and dry toast relieved the symptoms but her concern was that they continued which was surely a sign of a greater problem.

Lizzy heard the girls out in the foyer preparing for their morning drive and rose to intercept them before they left. They all looked so handsome in their Summer dresses and light pelisses, bonnets and parasols, no wonder they attracted the attention of young gentlemen wherever they went. She smiled and called them into the parlour, waving for them to sit. The girls looked at each other and silently did as they were bidden.

"My dears, I want to remind you of our discussion yesterday, although I am sure you are all still sensible of it. You were good enough to inform me about the gentlemen who have been paying attention to you, who have been acting as your chaperones, and certainly I have no reason as yet to doubt any of their intentions. However, a woman's virtue is her most prized possession and any indication of allowing that distance between you and the gentlemen to be breached will have dire consequences for you all; the perceived contamination will affect you all by association. Being too friendly with one gentleman will set the gossips' tongues afire and once they are lit, it will be almost impossible to dampen the blaze of disgust that will be set against you.

"No, do not interrupt, Kitty," she added severely as her sister sought to interject. "It matters very little whether these gentlemen are new acquaintance of good standing, or even," she looked at Georgiana, "your guardian whom you have known all your life. What matters is that they are all unattached *young* men and your responsibility is to act in a demure and ladylike manner whenever they try to accompany you. There is no reason for them to do so; you are perfectly safe in the carriage, are not you? And if you have the need of a chaperone, I have said I am perfectly willing to drive out with you. Well, except this morning as I confess to feeling a little unwell.

"But I have given it some thought, and I think the most sensible plan is to invite all three gentlemen for dinner this week, so that their intentions and manners can be assessed by those of us who have been assigned the task of safe-guarding your security and happiness. The Colonel, of course, is well-known to us, but Mr. Jardine and Mr. Sudbury are not, although they are understood to be gentleman, but until Mr. Darcy and I have become better acquainted with them, you are to preserve a discreet distance. Do I make myself clear?"

The girls, secretly delighted that the objects of their affection who had afforded them many amusing mornings, would now be brought openly into their family circle, all nodded with eyes downcast.

"Then I will trust you to continue your rides unchaperoned, but do not break that trust or it will be the worse for you all, I assure you. Mr. Darcy will not require much encouragement before packing us all up back into the country before the month is out."

She nodded at them as they rose and filed silently out, holding her breath as another wave of nausea swept over her. She was to see the doctor this afternoon and she could hardly wait for the appointment. She rang the bell and asked for another pot of the tea. It was odd, but again, Mrs. Reynolds smiled more broadly than required for such a simple request and suggested that she might like to take a short turn about the Square; fresh air was often quite beneficial, she mentioned, as she closed the door behind her.

Elizabeth frowned at the door and rested her head on her hand. A walk about the Square, indeed! It was as much as she could do to sit still and control her churning stomach. She dabbed her forehead with a lavender-scented handkerchief and took several deep breaths.

A knock on the front door alerted her to the imminent arrival of some unnecessarily-early caller, and she brushed her hand over her hair and eyes, swallowing deeply, and pinching her cheeks to regain their lost colour - really, she did feel dreadful -

and moved over to the couch recently vacated by the girls, leaning back against the cushions.

A second quiet knock preceded the entrance of Jane. Oh; what a relief and a joy! Jane took one look at her sister and felt her forehead.

"My dear Lizzy, you are quite pale and your skin is damp. Are you sickening for something, perhaps? Let me call Mrs. Reynolds and have her bring you a little wine or a powder. Really, you are not well."

"No, no, I will be better soon. I have these turns almost every morning; a little tea and toast seems to be the remedy. Mrs. Reynolds has already been dispatched, I assure you."

Jane looked at her quizzically.

"Do you know, Lizzy: Lady Charlton, with whom I have become quite friendly since she is our neighbour here in London, complained of the exact same symptoms a while ago; exactly the same symptoms, Lizzy!"

Mrs. Reynolds entered with a steaming pot of tea and plate of thin toast, and placed it beside Lizzy with a smile.

"There you are madam; everything will come right in a few weeks, I am sure of it. Do not you worry yourself."

Lizzy looked from her housekeeper to her sister and frowned.

"Wait, Mrs. Reynolds, if you please. My sister is telling me of another lady with the same symptoms as I have; I fear there is an epidemic of sickness in London. Is anyone else ill in the same way, do you know? For if so, I will return immediately to Pemberley. Perhaps it is the water or the food that is contaminated – I would not be at all surprised."

Mrs. Reynolds smiled at her mistress and asked enquiringly of Jane,

"Is it Lady Charlton of whom you speak, madam? For if it is, then I believe the cause of that lady's symptoms could be very similar to Mrs. Darcy's, do not you?"

Jane returned Mrs. Reynolds' smile and nodded, her face beaming more brightly with each movement of her head.

"*What?* What is wrong with Lady Charlton, and what illness do I share with her, pray? Jane! Tell me, I insist on knowing the truth."

Mrs. Reynolds excused herself and closed the door quietly. Jane sat beside her sister and took her hands.

"It is no great *illness*, Lizzy! Lady Charlton told me she is expecting her first *child*! She felt quite unwell for many weeks – months even, and we were all terribly concerned for her – but now all is improved. I think it is one of the many secret trials we married women must endure with grace and dignity, but I am sure the blessing of a baby outweighs any discomfort you may be suffering at the moment, does it not, now?"

Elizabeth looked at her sister in disbelief. *With child?*

"What, sister dear?" Jane laughed at Lizzy's shocked expression. "Do not you believe me? 'Tis entirely fact, I assure you, and I thank my new friend for her intelligence as we were never advised by our own mother on the subject. And, I am sure, Mrs. Reynolds has known of your condition all this time, ensuring your comfort with tea and toast! You are a very lucky woman, Lizzy, to be so blessed and so quickly. I wish I were in your situation; it would make Charles and me very happy indeed. I would endure any amount of sickness for such a joyful prospect, I assure you."

"No, no!" gasped Elizabeth. "It is entirely possible, as you say, and expected, and very happy news indeed! If I did not feel so ill I would be far more enthusiastic, believe me. I just had no idea, and to think I have made an appointment for this afternoon with the doctor to discover what ails me. I must cancel it; how mortifying! What a fool he would think me."

"There!" laughed Jane. "Rest here until you feel better and I will stay with you. Oh, happy news! How delighted Mr. Darcy will be, and everyone– especially Mamma!"

But at the mention of their mother, Elizabeth demurred, preferring to wait for that predictable inundation of joy until she felt better able to endure it. Jane reluctantly agreed to keep the news a secret, apart from Charles, of course, until Elizabeth decided that the general populace could be informed.

Once all aspects of the happy situation had been discussed, and Lizzy's discomfort had receded, Jane brought up something that had been preying on her kind heart for a while.

"Perhaps we should discuss visiting our poor sister whom we have neglected since our arrival and her immediate departure into the outskirts of London. I think we should go to her very soon, when you feel strong enough for it. I do not like her silence; it is not like Lydia to keep any news to herself and I heard from Mamma this morning, who also has heard nothing, which is very unusual, and bade me to find out everything. Has Kitty had any word, do you know?"

"No, indeed not. It seems no one has heard anything from Brompton these past weeks and we have been so busy, we have not noticed. Truth to tell, I have rather enjoyed the lack of her company and the ever-present anxiety about her behaviour. But what concerns you, Jane? What do you imagine is keeping her away? I, too, thought she would have called before this, but perhaps she feels uneasy, or perhaps she has already found new company and has no need of ours. You know how thoughtless she is when life is going her way. And she has Wickham's undivided attention finally, so perhaps we should not invade their privacy so soon."

The sisters quietly talked about the best thing to do - Lizzy's arguments losing out to Jane's quiet determination - and decided to set out that very morning now Elizabeth's nausea had abated. Jane claimed she could not be confident until she had visited their sister in her new home and knew all was well.

"And, after all, Lizzy; Lydia may well feel unable to call upon us knowing as she does the antipathy in which her husband is held. She could not expect to be invited to any of our family gatherings and she will feel it sorely, knowing as she does that we will be seeing so many people including our aunt and uncle. No, I think we must make the first visit and be favourably impressed with her situation, whatever that turns out to be. I think we must, Lizzy."

And so, after the girls had returned from their morning drive and discussed their conversations and sightings and the news they had gathered, Elizabeth asked Kitty if she would care to accompany her and Jane to visit Lydia; Kitty was delighted at the chance to see her sister again and pressed her hands together in happiness. She had been worried, she had felt guilty, even, as she had enjoyed her many and varied experiences whilst she had been in London because she knew her sister was out there somewhere but unable to join in her happiness and excitement, detached from the family as she now was as a married woman, and married to such a man as Mr. Wickham.

Kitty was no longer the foolish young girl she had once been under Lydia's governance; she now recognised the impropriety of her sister's behaviour and choice, and understood the discomfort caused by Lydia's change in situation. Lydia had altered during her time in Newcastle; she was not the free spirit she once was, and Kitty felt she was the only one to recognise her sister's pain. Her letters had dwindled to a trickle and her confidences had, by virtue of her status, had become almost none. So Kitty donned her jacket and bonnet with alacrity, in contrast to her two older sisters who felt no such joy at the prospect before them. But until they had made the visit, their minds could not conceive the manner of Lydia's life or her level of satisfaction with it.

They were pleasantly surprised, therefore, when the carriage drew up outside an inn, the driver explaining that this was as far as he could take them as the house was a little further down to the right.

The sisters alighted and, side-stepping mud and puddles, followed the man's arm pointing to Yeoman's Row, number 13. They looked at the house from the street and saw it was neat and tidy with a small garden, two storeys with windows winking in the sunlight.

Elizabeth knocked at the door and looked around at her sisters; there was no indication that anyone was at home. She knocked again and this time could hear, quite clearly, Lydia's voice shouting: "Mary! Get the door."

Mary appeared: a little mouse of a girl, hardly older than fourteen, thin and already worn-looking for one so young. She held the door slightly ajar and stared at the visitors with wide eyes.

Elizabeth smiled. "We are come to call upon Mrs. Wickham; is she at home?"

Mary nodded dumbly and closed the door, leaving the sisters on the doorstep. Elizabeth was outraged.

"*Well!* I should think Lydia could have bestirred herself enough to train her servant in the correct manners required of her situation. This is intolerable, to be left on the doorstep!"

"Calm yourself, Lizzy; I am sure it will not be long. Do not blame the poor girl for not having the benefit of a conscientious employer."

The door was re-opened and Mary whispered,

"My mistress says she ain't receivin' visitors this mornin' and you may leave your card, if you like."

Kitty gasped, Jane opened her mouth to explain who they were, but Elizabeth merely brushed Mary aside and marched right into the hallway. Her sisters followed, looking around at the scant furnishings in the dim light, smelling the odour of unaired rooms, stale cooking smells, and mildew.

"I think our sister will see us regardless," Elizabeth announced in a loud voice which carried throughout the entire house, "unless she is very unwell, in which case our presence will be even more acceptable. Where can we find Mrs. Wickham, pray?"

Mary silently pointed up the stairs and watched as the three ladies – ladies dressed so fine, Mary could not remember when she had seen such gowns – ascended to the floor above and disappeared into the bedroom. Fearing she had entirely failed in her duties and would be dismissed on the instant, Mary betook herself down into the cellar and hid in the farthest corner awaiting her fate.

Elizabeth was the first to enter the room, the dimness from the drawn curtains preventing her from seeing her sister immediately. Lydia, therefore, having already heard her sister's voice below and the advantage from lying in the gloom for the entire morning, had quickly affected an invalid manner, leaning back against her pillow and resting her hand upon her brow as if in severe pain. Kitty and Jane followed their sister into the room and also stopped to bring their eyes into focus. Elizabeth, now recovered, moved over to the window and drew back the curtains to Lydia's accompanying groan.

"*Oh!* The light is too bright; close them again, I beg you. I cannot stand it!"

Kitty rushed to Lydia's side and bent to kiss her forehead.

"What is the matter, Lydia? Ohh; you do feel rather damp and hot. Are you quite unwell?" She looked around at Elizabeth who was also regarding Lydia but with a wrinkled nose and disgusted expression.

"What do you think, Lizzy? Should we call a doctor, perhaps? Feel her forehead; she is quite ill, I believe."

"You believe that, Kitty, as you should, my dear; your sincerity does you credit. But I believe that Lydia understands from what her indisposition stems, if my sense of smell is anything to be a judge. Run downstairs and have Mary bring up a powder and some strong coffee, as quickly as you can, if you please."

Kitty took off to do her sister's bidding while Jane and Elizabeth sat one on each side of their sister's bed. Lydia closed her eyes against their scrutiny and refused to open them. Elizabeth waited and then nodded at Jane; they each took hold of the covers and pulled them off their sister, exposing her half-dressed self, accompanied by screams of outrage.

"How *dare you?* How dare you come into *my* house and treat me as you were used to doing when we were at Longbourn? How dare you...."

"How dare *you?* How dare you lie there long past noon, pretending illness when it is as clear as day that you are merely suffering the ill-effects of an evening's over-indulgence? Why should we not treat you as we always have as it would appear your behaviour has not improved any since that time? Get up this minute, and make yourself presentable. We have come to visit since we have heard nothing of you since you left Jane's, and I refuse to be entertained in your bedroom. Our mother might take to her bed at the slightest trouble or imagined illness but it is not an affectation to emulate, I assure you. Where is Mr. Wickham? I presume *he* is not lounging still in his room?"

"No; of course he is not. He is at work, where he always is." Lydia replied moodily as she reached for her dress and waited whilst Jane did up the laces. "He is always working early and late; I have hardly seen him. It is so unfair. He is as inattentive as he was in Newcastle - if not even worse - so I have to console myself as I can."

"And how, exactly, are you consoling yourself, Lydia? Does he know what you are doing in his absence? And with whom are you consoling yourself? It is disgraceful for a married woman, Lydia, to be so dissatisfied with her situation, so quickly."

Lydia sat as Jane picked up the hairbrush and attempted to tease Lydia's rich curls into some semblance of order, ignoring her protestations of how it was hurting her head.

"*With whom?* I do not go out with anybody, Lizzy; how could I? I know no one here. I am invited nowhere. There are not even the officers' wives to amuse myself with. And if I help myself to the brandy wine, then who is to stop me or complain about it? I must do something to improve my situation or I shall go quite mad with boredom.

"Oh! Jane; enough, thank you. I believe you have relieved me of enough hairs for one day."

She cautiously rose and donned her shawl; Elizabeth stepped aside and waved Lydia out of the door, following her and Jane into the parlour where Kitty was waiting for Mary to boil the kettle. Kitty held a glass jar in her hand which contained the restorative powders and Elizabeth raised her eyebrows when she saw the emptiness of it. The sisters sat in silence and waited for one or other of them to break it.

It was Mary who finally broke it by bringing in the coffee pot, almost dropping it when she saw the ladies all assembled around her mistress.

"Thank you, Mary," Jane said gently. "Would you be so kind as to bring us all a cup?"

Mary scuttled away and Elizabeth turned to Lydia.

"And so; how are you settling into your new home, Lydia? It appears to be perfectly adequate, quite comfortable if you cared to take some interest in making it into a home, that is. That is something with which you could be occupying yourself, instead of feeling sorry for yourself and wishing for entertainments elsewhere. I understood it was furnished a little when you moved in, was it not now? But I am sure that either Jane or I could find some more small articles to soften the severity of the lines; some vases, perhaps, and some books, and a clock or two. I know there are several in our box room going unused. You could bring in some of the roses from your front garden to brighten it up."

Lydia glared at her sister, taking a cautious sip of the coffee.

"Mary! *Mary!* Bring me something to eat for I am famished; I have eaten nothing all day," she moaned as if suddenly realising. "I do, indeed, feel quite unwell."

"Oh! Poor Lydia!" sympathised Kitty. "I am so glad we have come to make you feel better. But why did not you send word before? We should have come at once, you know."

At this Elizabeth rolled her eyes and Jane pursed her lips. Nothing would have been further from the truth and each could not imagine the efficacy of a note from their sister allowing she had over-indulged the night before and wished to be taken care of.

"No, no! I am quite alright, I assure you, Kitty; do not fuss. It is merely a small attack of indigestion and a headache. 'Tis nothing at all and is already passing. But I am glad you have come to see me. I was telling our sisters how I have been so alone and lonely here, separated from everything. There is very little that is amusing, and the neighbours – although very good people, I suppose – are not quite what I would like to have as friends. It is not one quarter as amusing as Newcastle was with all of the officers, you know, and if it were not for Denny's visits, I am sure I should already have died of boredom."

"Oh! *Captain* Denny from the Militia, Lydia? What is he doing here?" Kitty was all excited delight at hearing about their old friend. "Is he in business with Mr. Wickham; is that why you have seen him?"

"No, naturally not; *he* is still in the military - I cannot recall where he is stationed - but he assures me it is even worse than being consigned to Brompton, although I cannot imagine how that could possibly be, but I am sure he only tries to improve my spirits by saying so. He came home with Wickham a week or so ago – they had come across each other in Town quite by accident - and it was just like old times, even Wickham was more attentive for a while. Denny has called several times since, but always Wickham has been working, and so, Denny has taken me to dinner or for a walk about the Park or for a drive or to the library. He has seen how despondent I have become and takes it upon himself to amuse me in Wickham's absence. At least someone cares about me."

"How kind of the Captain!" Kitty smiled. "He always was very attentive to you, was not he, Lydia? I always thought he preferred your company to that of any other lady's."

"*Kitty*! Think of what you are saying!" Jane gasped. "It is *not* kind of Captain Denny, not at all; he should not be paying visits to a married lady without her husband's knowledge or approval. It is most indiscreet, indeed."

"Oh, la, Jane!" scoffed Lydia, the coffee finally easing its way through her consciousness. "There is nothing indiscreet about Denny's visits as Wickham is perfectly aware of them; would that he were even the slightest bit jealous or interested, but he is not. All he cares about is his business and being in London doing whatever it is he does there. I would be better off returning to the country with one of you when you leave, for he would not miss me, and being so close to London does me no good at all if I am never to visit it." She looked at each of her elder sisters as she spoke but neither picked up on her hint.

"I have been missing your company, Kitty; what have you been doing to amuse yourself since I left? Do you have many suitors beating a path to your door and is Mr. Darcy beating them back just as determinedly? Oh, would that I were you, Kitty, with not a care in the world and men dancing attention upon me as they used to. A married woman has not the allure, it would seem, of a single woman; not even to her husband. But you must stay with me now you are here; we shall have such fun just as we used to."

Elizabeth drew a deep breath but Jane quickly intervened.

"That is very kind of you, Lydia, but Kitty has many engagements in Town and cannot put them off." She raised her eyebrows at Lizzy who nodded.

"Yes, indeed; we must make our way back, now we have assured ourselves that all is well with you, Lydia, as I am sure it will be once you decide to make it so. Please give our regards to Mr. Wickham and Captain Denny when next you see them."

"Well, I am sure I would not want to detain you from your amusing lives; I quite understand. There will not be an invitation for me to join in any of your parties or dances, I do not suppose? Even my aunt and uncle have not had the grace to call upon me, and after all the time I stayed with them last year. You have all cast me off; you are all punishing me because of Wickham. Even Lady Catherine was more considerate than my own family is being; at least she had no horror of being seen with me in public."

Jane looked at Lizzy in distress. Lizzy moved across and held Lydia's hands in hers, speaking gently but firmly.

"You have chosen this life, Lydia. You were determined to have Wickham despite all that you knew about him, despite his lack of status and his questionable lifestyle. You were captivated by his outside charms, were not you? But now you have been forced to understand the man behind that charming exterior, and if that is a punishment for you, then it comes not from us. *You* may call upon me or Jane whenever you might manage to arrange it, and we would both be happy to see you, but where Darcy is present, Wickham cannot be received. Therefore, you must understand and accept that family dinners and parties cannot possibly include you because, as a married woman, you should attend such gatherings with your husband. And, I believe, if you were to come across Lady Catherine at home in Kent, she might not be so willing to be so sociable with you."

"Yes, well; I do not see why I have to moulder away here by myself without the slightest distraction whilst you are only miles away having the most marvellous time. It is unfair; you know how much I enjoy parties!"

"Then you should mention that to your husband when he comes home tonight. Tell him of your feelings and your sadness. He is not unkind, and must have made some amusing acquaintances to whom he could introduce you. He perhaps merely has not thought of your happiness due to his attention being elsewhere. I am sure life will improve soon, if you try to make it so, Lydia."

"And I would advise you to dissuade Captain Denny from his visits; it does you no good and will eventually anger your husband," added Jane as she moved towards the door with Kitty. "I cannot think that any husband would condone such behaviour no matter how close the friend is. Take Lizzy's advice and speak with Mr. Wickham before things go badly wrong."

The three sisters left Lydia standing forlorn on the doorstep and re-traced their steps back to the carriage. Not a word was said until they were rolling through the square leading to Bingley House where Kitty was to stay with Jane for the rest of the day and evening's entertainments. Each was filled with their own thoughts about their poor sister, for each truly did feel for Lydia, and the contrast with her former carefree self was shocking to behold. That she was unhappy, they all agreed, gave them no pleasure even though they knew she had brought that unhappiness upon herself and it had been dearly bought. They only hoped Wickham was truly making a success of himself, and his hard work would soon materialise in having more time for leisure and attention to his wife.

Chapter 39

Lydia turned back from watching her sisters disappear down the street, to survey her front parlour from the front doorway. Their visit had not improved her spirits and their advice rang in her ears. The room was comfortable enough, certainly; Wickham and Mr. Darcy had seen to it that they would be sufficiently comfortable: the old but elegant chairs and settee were still in reasonable condition, barring some wear around the cushions and arms, giving the impression of having spent their earlier life in far grander surroundings than those in which they now found themselves; the small tables and candlesticks upon them were glowing in the afternoon light from the vigorous polishing they had suffered at the hands of Mary that very morning; the rugs and floor also both bore witness to her ministrations. But as Lydia glanced about, she realised the truth in her sisters' advice; nowhere had she imprinted that indelible mark all her own showing a pride of the ownership she had long desired. There were no flowers to brighten the surfaces, no prints framed upon the walls, no work in progress as was always seen at Longbourn, resting upon a footstool. It was, indeed, very bare and as Lydia saw her home through her sisters' eyes and compared it to what she knew they were accustomed to, she felt disappointment.

This was her own home, something she had long hankered after, and she was not appreciating it, was not making it her own, was not showing how well she could manage and create. Her bonnets had always been the talk of Meryton; everybody had admired her creative spirit, and her addition of ribbons and lace to old dresses was legendary. But that was before she had the running of a house to see to and to somehow rekindle the affection of an absent and disinterested husband. Life had become unbearably dull and pedestrian. Not only had she to concern herself with ordering supplies and seeing that jobs were done by Mary, but she also no longer enjoyed the excitement of being young and carefree, of being the object of every man's attention and desire. She no longer enjoyed the company of friends and family, and as shown by her sisters, could not expect to be invited to enjoy those things with them.

She sighed and walked slowly back to the kitchen where Mary was preparing some vegetables for the dinner. Lydia would order some cooked meat from the inn to go with them as she had still not discovered a good reason to exert herself and learn how to cook any more than the few vegetables; buying meat already prepared was almost as cheap as cooking it herself, she reasoned, and a good deal less arduous. And, besides, her sisters were none of them cooking their own meals, so why should she?

The kitchen was clean enough, and with the fire banked up and a kettle sighing quietly on the back corner it was the most welcoming room of the house. Mary looked up from her task with a concerned frown, already knowing her mistress' volatile temper and wondering at the meaning of the visit. Lydia sat down at the table and watched the peeling and chopping without showing any inclination to assist or turn her own hand to something.

"Are you happy here with us, Mary?" she asked suddenly as she picked out a carrot and chewed thoughtfully on it. "You are not very old, are you? Is this your first position?"

"Oh, no, Mrs. Wickham; I 'av been a scullery maid in a bigger 'ouse afore this which was nowhere near as nice. I 'ad ter be washin' dishes all the day and most of the night, I 'ad, and 'ell to pay - beggin' your pardon, ma'am - if I was so clumsy as to break anythin'."

"So you prefer to clean rooms and prepare meals and bake compared to that, do you?"

"Oh yes, indeed. I 'ope you ain't got no complaints, ma'am. Mrs Younge would not like for you to be displeased wi' me. Not after all she done for me."

Lydia's attention was arrested by that name which she had not heard for many months.

"Mrs. *Younge,* you say? I did not know that you knew her; what has she done for you, pray?"

"Why; Mrs. Younge is ever so nice an' kind an' thoughtful an' all, ma'am. She took me from my old job and trained me right up so as I could come 'ere and work at a nicer job wi' better wages and hours. She said it was … appallin' … yes, that was it, the way my last employer was treatin' me; said she could get me much better elsewhere, and jus' swept me away from there like as if she was my guardian angel, indeed she did, an' then a few weeks later she introduced me to Mr. Wickham an' assured him I would do very well for 'im an' he agreed an' 'ere I am. But don' say to 'er I ain't suitable Mrs. Wickham, please; I am doin' my best."

Lydia sat in shock for a moment.

"You mean Mr. Wickham was with Mrs. Younge when you were interviewed and taken on? I thought you had been sent from some agency, a Mrs. Belmont's agency, I was told, sight unseen, to prove your worth. I did not realise that you had been specially selected by my husband and Mrs. Younge."

"Oh, yes; Mrs. Belmont is also a very kind lady. She was lookin' after the agency while Mrs. Younge was in America, an' is managin' it still, I believe. Mrs. Younge is a very independent lady too, I think, and they are great friends."

"Yes, I am sure they are. No, no; your work is above reproach. It is my husband with whom I wish to discuss the matter although, given his persistent absence, I shall have to bide my time to make my enquiries, but make them I shall; without a doubt, I shall," she muttered to herself as she rose from the table.

"Thank you, Mary, you are doing very well."

"Thank you ma'am. Them ladies was very fine today, ma'am; very determined though. I am sorry I could not stop them from enterin' at all an' botherin' you since you was so tired."

"Yes, Mary; they are fine and determined. Those were three of my sisters, two of whom are now very grand indeed, and living in Town for this month in rather more salubrious surroundings and enjoying all that is on offer in London. I should not anticipate a return visit any time soon, though, such is the extent of their social whirl; a social whirl I should dearly like to enjoy, too, but, it seems, is not to be extended to include their poor sister."

Mary, who had absolutely no concept of a social whirl, merely nodded and returned to her chopping, murmuring, "They'se gowns was very fine, indeed; I did see that much."

Lydia wandered out into the rear garden where a few sorry shrubs were attempting a show of colour against a thicket of weeds and brambles, chewing her lip and thinking about what she had just heard. Wickham had not mentioned anything more about his "friend" after they had been turned away from that lady's door on the evening of their arrival in London after eloping from Brighton last year, when she had refused to help them; refused to give them shelter.

She had been altogether unpleasant and unfriendly, not what Wickham had expected at all. Lydia had noticed that at least: his white face, the tightening of his jaw, his curt behaviour towards her when they eventually found somewhere else to stay, his unloving manner so different from the previous evenings whilst travelling. When he had refused to answer just how well he knew Mrs. Younge - because from her reception of him, one would imagine he did *not* know her very well at all, so icy and angry had it been - Lydia had accused him of all manner of deceits and strategies, flying into an uncontrollable fit of sobbing and despair which had left him just as unmoved and uncommunicative as before, and ever since, Lydia had refrained from mentioning the woman's name even in jest.

In truth, Lydia had convinced herself that there had been some falling out between them and that accounted for the silence on the matter, and so did not pursue it. And after they went to Newcastle, there had been no need for jealous rages or insecurities - for a while, anyway. But now, Mary's news that Wickham had been with Mrs. Younge here in London while she, Lydia, had been ensconced at her parent's house far away with no threat of her breaking in upon their happy intimacy, started an icy dread in the pit of her stomach.

Where *did* Wickham spend his days away from her? Was he really busy every night or was he meeting that woman in secret at her convenient house? Did that explain his lack of affection towards her when she tried to be loving towards him; his insistence upon separate rooms as befitting their marital status, as he claimed?

Lydia pulled a leaf from a shrub and stripped it from its stem as she thought. Surely not! Surely he would not go against Darcy and all that he had provided him; surely he would not humiliate *her* to such a degree already. Did not such behaviour in husbands only happen to older wives? Wives who had lost their looks, their figure, their sense of fun? Wives who were so taken up with duties of household and maternity that there was little attention left for husbands?

Well, she was not such a wife. She still had her looks and her youthful figure and her sense of fun, if only he would notice and take advantage of them.

She threw away the shredded leaf and picked another, deep in the most miserable of thoughts, which now turned on the fact that she now no longer had the opportunities she had enjoyed in Newcastle, including the very real opportunity of improving her situation through the playing of cards for small wagers. There was nowhere in Brompton that she could see, for ladies anyway, that offered such distractions. The nearest possibility was the inn and although a most useful place to purchase slices of meat for dinner, did not appear to be the place to enquire about card games.

She looked up as the sound of hooves came along the street and, through the gap between the houses, saw to her delight, Captain Denny approaching. She blushed faintly and rushed indoors through the kitchen and into the parlour, scooping up a basket of ribbons and lace and ripping her bonnet from the hook in the hall, managing to settle herself in a chair just in time for Mary to announce, "A gentleman, ma'am."

"Mrs. Wickham; Lydia; I am glad to find you at home."

"Denny! I am sure it is no great surprise to find me here; you always do, do not you? There is nowhere for me to go and no one with whom to go if there was. I am confined to barracks, as you army men like to say, without friends or family who care about my happiness. All except you, dear Denny; you are my most constant visitor these past weeks. Lord, I see more of you than I do of Wickham! Would you care for some refreshment?"

"No, indeed, I thank you, for I am come to offer you the same, only to take it in Town, if you are agreeable, that is. I thought a trip away from Brompton might raise your spirits a little. I cannot bear to have you feeling low just because Wickham insists upon working all hours. I have not seen sight nor heard report of him in Town for days now."

"I believe he is working very hard, it is true, but I am not angry at him for doing so, I assure you; he must learn and progress in his profession and I am not a wife who nags and moans, Denny. I only hope he does not overwork and make himself ill. But, you are right; it is hard to be left so much alone and your offer is a very tempting one. I am sure my husband could have no objection to the pleasure of an afternoon's entertainment in Town, and, anyway, I cannot ask him as he will certainly not be home until much later this evening."

"Then fetch your cloak and bonnet and we will be off for a visit, my dear. You do not mind if I call you that?" he asked upon seeing her blush. "It feels so strange to have to call you Mrs. Wickham when we have known each other for so long and been such good friends all that time."

"No! No, of course you must call me as you always have. All this nonsense, *Mrs. Wickham*, makes us too formal and only leaves me feeling old. Come; I am quite ready. Where have you in mind, I wonder?"

Lydia spent the rest of the day and early evening enjoying herself on the arm, once again, of a handsome, attentive young man in uniform, seeing and being seen, looking in shop windows and eating small cakes in an elegant coffee shop. To be in Town was a delight and she wished it would never end; her seclusion had never been so apparent to her as it was now she had escaped it.

As they strolled about the Park in the late afternoon sunshine, commenting upon the dresses and waistcoats and bonnets they passed, she cautiously brought up the lady uppermost in her mind and enquired of Denny what he knew about Mrs. Younge and her situation.

He claimed no recent knowledge at all; he had not seen that lady in perhaps two years or more. Not wishing to pursue it further and appear too interested, Lydia then changed topic to first deplore the lack of entertainments close by her in Brompton and then to remind him of her talent at cards which he had witnessed in Meryton and Brighton. This line of conversation led quite seamlessly into enquiring about polite card games suitable for ladies in London.

"For surely," she argued with a laugh, "there are many other ladies who enjoy the excitement of the turn of a card?"

After thinking for a moment, Denny declared that this was a subject about which he did have some knowledge.

"Allow me to introduce you, tomorrow, perhaps, to some ladies of my acquaintance who are of a similar mind as you. They are all very pleasant young ladies and are always happy to make new friends. But perhaps you should request Wickham's permission before I do so? I would not like to be presumptuous in exposing his wife to people or situations he does not approve."

This was very satisfying news indeed and she smiled with great affection into his eyes, gently pressing his arm.

"Oh, dear, kind Denny! I knew I could count on you to relieve my boredom. You are such a great friend, and have always been of course, and if Wickham had not claimed me first, why, I think you can guess what might have been between us, then! How strange life is, is not it?"

Denny covered her hand with his own and returned the pressure, drawing his finger along the seams of her glove.

"Wickham is a most fortunate fellow indeed, and a foolish one, too, to leave you so much alone. If I had a wife, I would not allow another man to pay her attention. I believe she would be more tired of my company than pining for it, and I am sorry that my friend prefers to spend all of his time upon work than with you. Or, perhaps I am not so sorry; if he were more attentive, then I would not be allowed the pleasure your company, and that I would regret."

"I would regret that too, although you should not hint at such things to me, Denny; Wickham is your friend and my husband, and I do love him most dearly. La! How funny! My sister, Jane, warned me about just such overtures from you this morning when she visited; she warned that I should not encourage you. But, then what am I to do every day? How should I endure a life in Brompton with only Mary for company? I do not think we are doing anything too wrong in our meetings, are we?" She took her hand away and looked anxiously at Denny to see if she had offended or hurt him - both of which she rather hoped she had.

"Naturally we are not, my dear; we shall remain simply as good friends who rely upon each other for relief from our everyday lives; although, I regret it shall not be for much longer that I will be able to entertain you, so your sister can rest easy. I must re-join my regiment in a month when we return to Brighton. Even though the necessity of training has rather worn off recently, we still must be prepared for every eventuality. We cannot trust that the French are entirely done with us yet."

"Ah, yes; Brighton! Oh, how I enjoyed my time there. The shops and the sea and the parties; it was all so exciting and interesting. I can hardly believe it has been almost a year since we were all there having such a gay time.

"What a great deal has happened since then: I have married; lived in Newcastle; stayed with both my sisters; met Lady Catherine and her daughter, and now I live in my own house in Brompton with my own servant! Which, perhaps, is not the most interesting part of the story but has been greatly improved with your help, and I have every expectation it will be even more so when I make some new friends."

Denny smiled at her sudden change of mood. Here was the young girl he remembered and he delighted in watching her laugh as she teased him about who his lady friends could be and how he knew they played cards and what they would think if he brought a married lady to their game. Suddenly, everything was amusing and exciting again, and he happily joined in with her suppositions as he guided her through the Park and back onto the street towards home.

Chapter 40

Elizabeth sank thankfully into the chair in front of the parlour fireplace currently filled with a large floral arrangement, and loosened her Spencer jacket.

It had been an eventful day. She was extremely glad not to have any engagements planned for the evening and eagerly anticipated some peace and quiet. She rubbed her hands over her stomach and realised with satisfaction that the events of the afternoon had quite taken her mind off her recurring sickness; she had not had a single queasy moment since this morning.

How foolish she had been! How ignorant indeed not to have worked out the reason for it and she smiled with relief that it had been her sister to dispel her fears. If having their first child was the reason for it, then, as Jane had said, any amount of sickness could be borne and she allowed herself to imagine, first Darcy's joy at the news, and then herself as a mother to a child who would bear a resemblance to him. This would be a child who would not, however, inherit its parent's predisposition to judge everyone upon the strength of a first meeting, she would see to that.

Considering that determination, she thought further about her advice to Kitty and Anne and Georgiana only that very morning: that a dinner party would be arranged to include their new gentlemen friends so that she and Darcy could ascertain their intentions and suitability. Even Colonel Fitzwilliam must be invited, against Darcy's wishes - she had no doubt it would be a struggle to make him see the sense of it - but to see if there was any true attraction between her sister and him.

How uncomfortable it was to think the Colonel had been doting upon her, Lizzy, all this time! And no wonder Darcy had become furious at the thought of it. Lizzy smiled despite herself. It was certainly charming to have two gentlemen vying for her attention, and the thought that Darcy could be so moved, further proved the depth of his love for her and she cherished that knowledge.

But she could not waste time idly sitting and daydreaming whilst there were parties and dinners to be organised. She reluctantly rose to see if Darcy was yet returned from his business to acquaint him with her varied news of the day. With which detail she was not sure she would start, but believed it would necessarily be the most momentous one of all, which would guarantee his immediate acquiescence to all the others, particularly the notion of a dinner party.

She found him, just returned and opening the afternoon's mail in his study. He smiled warmly as she entered and rose to greet her. It was fortunate indeed that no servant or guest needed to speak with the master for the next ten minutes, so engrossed was he with his wife and her delightful news. He put her away from him at last and gazed into her eyes.

"You cannot imagine the happiness you have caused, Elizabeth. To have a child of my own is something I have longed for. Tell me; when is it expected? Should we return immediately to Pemberley? I am quite certain the London air must be unhealthy for you. Yes; I think we must return as soon as maybe - well, perhaps you must - I will have to remain until I have concluded my business here in a few more days. Would you like Jane to accompany you? Does she know? Perhaps your Mamma should come to stay?"

"*No*! No, indeed not, my darling man! There is no need for you to worry or fuss. There are many women in my condition in London and I am sure being here does little harm to their unborn babies. And you may rest assured that Mamma is the *last* person I should wish to have as a companion; she would require more attention from me than she would give. Father would make a better one.

"Yes; Jane does know but only because she guessed first, as did Mrs. Reynolds. Indeed, I believe Mrs. Reynolds knew as soon as I arrived. We will remain here just as we planned until the beginning of June and then we will return to Pemberley. By then all of my furnishings and improvements here should be in process and I shall be happy to enjoy some country air and peace and quiet once again.

"But I would broach another subject or two with you, if you are not too busy?"

"Come and sit here, my dear. What have you to *broach* so formally with me, pray?"

"Merely that I believe we must host a small dinner party and invite all the young gentlemen who have recently made the acquaintance of our sisters and Anne: including, I am afraid, Colonel Fitzwilliam."

She rushed on as she saw Darcy's colour rising and the thinning of his mouth.

"It would be negligent indeed to your aunt and my parents if we should know nothing more of them when we are asked for our opinion, would it not? After all, the girls have been under our care this visit and we should make an attempt to understand their attachments if any have been made. We would invite Bingley and Jane for their opinion also, of course, and my aunt and uncle. It would relieve my father of an onerous task regarding Kitty, and one or other of the gentlemen of having to deal with my mother until absolutely necessary." She smiled at Darcy who was beginning to relax as he saw the reasonableness of her concerns.

He took her hands in his and kissed the fingertips, looking down as he spoke.

"You are, of course, correct and I agree with your summation. It will be difficult to have Fitzwilliam in the same room with you but I am sure he will not disgrace himself nor cause you any embarrassment. After all, it is Kitty upon whom he intends to direct his attention, even though I doubt very much he will be in a position to marry within the next five years, you know, and Kitty is a charming young lady, one who will attract many suitable men very soon. But, as you say, we do not know the level of feeling involved and an evening should discover it, should it not? I shall leave that to you and Jane to fathom whilst I remain at the edges as I am used to doing. I will observe as you and my unborn child mingle and chatter nonsense, and consider myself the luckiest of men, will that do?"

Elizabeth reached up to kiss him. "That will do very well, my dear; as I recall, you became rather adept at observing me not so long ago, and commenting upon my abilities and attractiveness to whomever would hear it! You must try to keep whatever opinions you may have to yourself this time, though; the young ladies will not thank you to be too condemnatory of their choices."

Her expression grew serious as she thought of another choice that had been made.

"We went into Brompton to visit Lydia, today."

Darcy raised his eyebrows. "Indeed? And how did you find her?"

"Very ill-tempered and disagreeable. Lonely, I think; she has no friends as yet, and she sees very little of Wickham as he is so busy. She feels abandoned by everyone and terribly bored. She was still in bed when we arrived, and it was all we could do to get her dressed and downstairs. I have never seen her so low."

Darcy looked concerned. "Did she say that Wickham was at work or back to his old tricks?"

"Oh! She believes he is at work, building his business, but I can see how she would feel alone without the Army wives as constant companions as she had in Newcastle, or her family and friends as she was used to having in Meryton.

"We assured her that she could visit us if she could arrange it during the day, without Wickham, of course, but I am sure it would not be easy for her without a carriage or horse at her disposal. On the other hand, it would be unfair to introduce her to our social circle of which she cannot ever be a part. It is unfortunate indeed; even our aunt and uncle have not invited her to visit them in Cheapside. She seems much worse off here than ever before, even though she has a house of her own and a servant."

"You must not worry too much about her, Elizabeth. Lydia is not one to wallow in gloominess. You came upon her in a bad hour, that is all, and I'll wager she is already out and about enjoying herself with no notion that you would still be so concerned. She will make the best of her very fortunate situation - you mark my words - once she comes around to it and feels more at home in Brompton. Change is always a challenge, but everyone must do it if they are to improve themselves. It is what she chooses to do with the newness of it all that will define her future. Do not worry one more second; truly you are the most sympathetic of creatures, even after all she has put you and your family through."

"Oh? And you are not to be accused of kindness and sympathy regarding her and Wickham, I suppose? After all they have put *you* through and all you have done for *him* in particular? And you call me unduly concerned!"

"We both do not wish them harm: we wish them the happiness we have found, is not that right? Then we are sympathetic to a fault and should be whipped soundly for our softness of feelings for those less fortunate than ourselves. There; will that do?"

"Well, it will do for now as I must leave you and your nonsense to see Mrs. Reynolds to arrange a very important dinner party. Then I shall sit down with the girls and, as we write the invitations, I shall endeavour to learn something of their conquests and the seriousness of them all."

Darcy caught her as she stood up and pulled her back down into his lap.

"And may I ask one more favour, Mamma-to-be?" he murmured into her neck. "That we do not make our news generally known just yet? I would hold it private and precious for a while longer and keep it only between us."

Elizabeth laughed as she released herself. "And Jane and Bingley and Mrs. Reynolds, of course. We shall keep the secret, we five!"

The girls were delighted at the chance to mingle openly with their new gentlemen friends and eagerly supplied Elizabeth with their addresses. Elizabeth raised her eyebrows at their intimate knowledge and wondered to herself just how much had transpired on those public travels through the Park each morning. Colonel Fitzwilliam's inclusion on the list did not seem to be of any interest to Kitty, she noticed; indeed, Kitty merely referred to him in a very neutral manner when his name was brought up.

"Oh; Georgiana's guardian, whom we have come across several times, well, almost every day, I suppose. He is a very charming gentleman and always asks after you, Lizzy, most particularly." Which only served to confuse Elizabeth even further as to that gentleman's intentions.

Mr. Jardine's address was already known to Georgiana and Darcy from several years ago, and so being immediately known was not of any great surprise, but Anne knowing the address of Mr. Sudbury by heart gave great clues as to the extent of their familiarity. Elizabeth gave no indication, but made a note to watch those two very carefully indeed. Lady Catherine would not be inclined to be in the slightest bit forgiving if anything untoward should happen to her daughter.

By return of post, Jane and Charles assured her of their attendance and swore their secrecy as to the "other delightful and exciting matter," and the Gardiners declared themselves entirely at her disposal to help her in any way that she deemed necessary.

The girls decided that a shopping trip was certainly called for and when Elizabeth announced herself to be too busy overseeing preparations, inveigled Jane to accompany them to buy extra frills and lace and other fripperies necessary for such an evening.

"Oh; it is a shame that Lydia is not able to come out with us as she used to do. She always knows which is the very best in style and colour," mourned Kitty as she held several spools of ribbon, her eyes flicking indecisively between them, "and now I am afraid to choose. I can hear her voice in my ear saying, '*good gracious, Kitty, surely not that one!*' but I cannot decide to which one she is referring. Oh, bother! I shall not buy anything; that is the safest way, for I do not know why I am even thinking of doing so. No one is expecting to be delighted with what I am wearing, I am sure, and just as well, too."

Jane walked over to her sister and held the ribbons thoughtfully.

"Is there not, my dear? Are you quite sure of that? How about this one? It will match your new dress perfectly, and if you get extra, you could put some around your bonnet. It is very pretty."

Kitty looked at her sister in astonishment.

"Yes, I *am* quite sure of that, and I do not think I want any ribbon; I cannot be bothered with sewing, anyway. Who is to be coming other than Anne's friend, and Georgiana's friend and her guardian who is also Darcy and Elizabeth's friend, pray? Unless there are other guests Lizzy has not mentioned, I find your questions to be rather peculiar, Jane."

Jane merely smiled and ordered several yards of the offending ribbon, adding it to the growing pile of packages on the counter. She then went over to where Georgiana was trying on some lace shawls and Anne was looking at a very pretty hair pin which she placed in her hair, twisting her head to see the effect in the small mirror. She smiled quietly as Jane complimented her choice, and nodded to the saleslady that she would take it.

Jane looked about her before asking, "Does Colonel Fitzwilliam appear much when you are out, Anne? More than usual, I mean?"

"More than usual, Jane?" laughed Anne. "I could not say what *that* might be but he does seem always to appear and wish us good morning just as we arrive. I believe he likes to see Georgiana and me enjoying ourselves out and about, feels a brotherly care for both of us. He never stays long, only enough to greet us and ask after our families and any news, and then he makes his excuses and leaves for toil and drudgery, he claims. He is such a delightful man; we are the envy of several other ladies, I assure you!"

Jane smiled and nodded, treasuring up her morsels of information to discuss with her sister later.

And there were plenty more titbits on the evening itself once the guests were all assembled and introduced. Darcy was on his best behaviour and made an excellent performance of the hospitable host such as had not been seen since Pemberley. He was all charm and ease and more than once did Elizabeth have occasion to smile behind her fan at his manner.

She noticed everything: Fitzwilliam - who studiously avoided her - paid her sister only a little attention and then remained beside aunt Gardiner for most of the evening; Sudbury's admiration for Anne was evident enough, which gave Elizabeth great joy to see, especially since it would seem his affection was returned in full by that lady; and Jardine, who spoke at length with Darcy and then uncle Gardiner, before remaining with Georgiana for most of the evening and insisted upon escorting her into dinner. Jane, she noticed, was also paying attention as was she, and she looked forward to having a long discussion as they were used to having at Longbourn after an evening's entertainment.

Aunt Gardiner moved across to stand beside her niece, a line of worry between her eyes.

"I have heard some alarming news just now, Lizzy, from your uncle who has been speaking with that rather pleasant Mr. Jardine. He meant nothing by it, I am sure, but as he is such a close acquaintance of Wickham he says he is surprised at how little of him he has seen recently, new business venture notwithstanding. He says it is almost as if Wickham has gone into seclusion, but did not you say that Lydia has seen barely anything of Wickham, either?"

"Yes; she certainly is missing his company. Well, aunt; let us decide that perhaps, for once, Wickham is actually working every hour of the day as he claims, and therefore has been seen by no one recently. Is not that a reasonable assumption?"

Her aunt nodded doubtfully, looking around at the guests and then turned again to Lizzy.

"But that is not the most worrying piece of information, Lizzy. I do not think that Lydia *is* missing her husband's company too terribly, as she claims. Mr. Jardine also mentioned that he has observed *her* in Town twice recently. The first in a coffee shop and the second at an evening of cards at a friend's house, and both times she was in the company of a Captain Denny, who, he discovered, is a long-time friend of both Wickham and Lydia. He said he did not know who Lydia was, at the time, not having been introduced, but was informed by a friend who mentioned the long-standing friendship of the two men and how kind it was that Lydia was being entertained so well in the absence of her husband."

Jane came to join their conversation and her happy demeanour dimmed as she was apprised of the news.

"Oh! But this is shocking indeed, and after our warnings to her only a few days ago. But perhaps it is all in innocence and Wickham is fully aware and has given his blessing for such excursions in his absence. He has, perhaps, realised that Lydia cannot remain isolated for long and is showing some concern for her welfare, which does him credit."

"You may think that, Jane, if it gives you comfort, but I must visit my niece very soon; I have been remiss in my duties. She shall be brought to her senses and must realise that such behaviour is merely grist for the scandal-mongers' mill. Has she learnt nothing in the past year, I wonder?"

Aunt Gardiner walked off to converse with her husband and Darcy, her cheeks flaming with indignation.

But now, Lizzy thought, *I must sit down*. Her nausea had returned with a vengeance and the smell of food wafting in from the dining room was quite revolting. She reeled slightly, enough for Jane to catch her elbow and lower her into a nearby chair, returning immediately with a small glass of wine and a plain biscuit, blocking the rest of the room with her skirts.

Elizabeth smiled her thanks but could take no more than a sip before clutching her stomach, desperately trying to restrain herself from crying out as bands of pain gripped her. A black fog surrounded her and the last thing she knew she was falling into it; but it had no bottom, this fog, she just kept falling and falling and falling.

Chapter 41

Julia Younge smiled to herself, quickly turning her face to the window of the coach before any other passenger noticed. A week spent in Cambridge had clarified several unasked questions held at bay since she had left that town for London early one morning many years ago in the company of George Wickham for their supposed new life together.

Her face grew serious as she reflected upon the events which had followed; events which had affected their relationship and her trust in him. Their life had certainly not developed as either of them had anticipated that happy morning. Now, finally, she had made a decision that would set in motion a new series of events which would further shape her future without reference to George Wickham, or any other person.

Her eyes left the passing scenery only to meet the enquiring gaze of the gentleman sitting opposite her. She met his frankness with calm detachment and returned to her perusal of the scenery. She was not unused to the admiration of men; Julia knew she was still an attractive woman - even though she was past thirty years of age - and that attraction had proved useful over the years. It had enticed many to her side - her late husband, George Wickham, Mr. Clemens - and she quietly revelled in her power still to be able to command such attention.

But it did not mean she encouraged it: she simply no longer had need of it and, after her recent negotiations in Cambridge, she believed she could probably meet this gentleman's worth and beat it. The thought brought a smile again to her lips which she compressed firmly so as not to give him any false ideas.

The evening was drawing in and the entire company enclosed within the coach was relieved to hear a change in the tempo of the horses' hooves as they slowed down to enter the inn yard. Suddenly, all was relief, activity and excitement.

Julia smiled her thanks to the coachman as he handed her down from the carriage, and stretched slightly to ease her stiffness as she waited for her trunk and small bag to be off-loaded. Just as she was easing her shoulders, she felt a presence and a quiet voice spoke just behind her.

"I understand your discomfort, madam, and I share it, I assure you. Would you perhaps do me the honour of accompanying me for a turn about the village green, here? It is not much to look at but should give us the advantage of relieving our cramps from the hours of sitting and bumping over the many potholes and lumps we have encountered on the roads today."

Julia looked up to see her observer smiling down at her; he was certainly much more imposing when not at eye level, but, just at that moment, her trunk and bag were handed down and the coachman looked at her enquiringly.

"Kindly take them into the inn. I shall need both this evening."

She turned back to the young man and looked at him with detachment.

"I thank you for your kind offer, sir, but I assure you, should I wish to take a turn about the village, I am perfectly able to manage it by myself. It has never been a weakness of mine to require or expect the assistance of any gentleman. Good evening to you."

She felt his gaze upon her as she followed the coachman into the inn but then thought of him no longer in the flurry of activity and the happy prospect of a clean and comfortable bed for the night. She completed her toilette and hastened downstairs to enquire about dinner. There was almost an hour to wait, she was informed, and so decided to take herself for a walk down the main street and amuse herself with the sights undoubtedly on offer in the shop windows there. She felt no concern at walking alone; it was something she did almost every day in London and that was certainly a far more hazardous place than this.

As she paused to admire a blue bonnet beautifully displayed in a window, and to wonder at the cost of the ribbons attached to it, she again felt a presence at her elbow and drew in her breath in annoyance. Really, this was intolerable! She had been quite clear; she could not have been less encouraging, and now here he was again. Julia turned about and met his arrogant smile with another cool flick of her eyes and continued walking along the high street. His boots crunched along behind her and, after several steps, she finally stopped and faced him again.

"Is there a particular reason that you walk so closely behind me, sir? Should I be concerned at your determination after I explicitly told you I had no need of your assistance? Is there something you wish to say, perhaps? I can only assume it must be of a most urgent nature, if so."

He smiled and bowed very formally.

"Madam; please forgive the intrusion upon your privacy but I saw you walking alone and could not, in all good conscience, allow you to continue so unprotected, even though you insist you have no need of such protection. Please allow me to offer you my arm so we can continue together and enjoy each other's company. If you would permit it, I would be interested to learn more about you; although, it seems rather an overdue notion, I know, as we have spent the whole day together in the close confines of the coach.

"My name, madam, is Henry Winslow, at your service." And again he bowed low, his quiet charm and assurance exuding from his every movement.

Julia, peeved, felt she had no alternative other than to accept his irritating arm and even more annoying thoughtful action without causing a small scene in front of the other walkers from the coach, several of whom, she knew, she would have to face the following morning. Gritting her teeth, she laid her hand with the lightest possible touch upon his arm and allowed herself to be propelled along the rest of the street.

There was a period of silence broken only by their breathing and the scuff of their shoes upon the hard mud of the street. The shop windows had lost all of their pleasure for Julia. All she wished for was to return as soon as possible to the inn and so rid herself of an unwelcome but very attentive admirer.

Mr. Winslow was the first to break the silence. He coughed and then, after a quick look at Julia's face, commented,

"You appeared very pleased about something today, madam, if you will excuse the observation. I could not help but notice your very charming smile: when others of us were merely enduring the journey as best we could, you appeared to be unaware of it and thoroughly immersed in thoughts concerning something much more pleasant."

"Yes, indeed, sir. My visit to Cambridge was a successful one."

Silence again fell between them like a thick blanket; she could feel his interest and also his reticence. She hoped the reticence would win. It did.

Nothing more was uttered until he bade her a pleasant evening as he deposited her at the dining room door with a quick bow and turned to make his way upstairs. Julia watched his back moving away and, surprising herself, called out,

"Mr. Winslow: the evening meal is about to be served. Do not you intend partaking?"

He turned around and now she noticed a slight vulnerability in his expression. All traces of assurance and arrogance had gone, if they had ever been other than in her angry imagination.

"I think not, madam; I have some edibles in my luggage which will sustain me until London. A good evening to you."

He turned and mounted the stairs leaving Julia feeling strangely bereft as she opened the door to the dining room and took a seat at an empty table. A young man with impeccable manners and of limited means, but one who knew how to live within those means; an unusual person indeed! Suddenly, she could think of nothing else other than whom he was and what his situation could possibly be and silently berated herself for her grudging behaviour towards him. She called over the servant and instructed him to deliver a message to Mr. Winslow.

Within minutes the servant was back with another message, thanking the lady for her kindness but refusing her offer of dinner. The gentleman was, the servant assured her, perfectly content with his own provisions in his room.

Well, that was that. She had done what she should and had been treated in the same manner in which he had been treated by her. Julia shrugged her shoulders and started her meal. What did she care? After tomorrow, they would never see each other again.

That evening, Julia spent some time in her room re-reading the letters and documents Mr. Brown had prepared regarding the sale of her properties in Cambridge. These had been her security ever since the demise of her husband and had served her well over the years, providing her with a regular income and enough for investing elsewhere.

It had been a difficult decision to sell her houses, particularly the gambling house which she had worked so hard to build up into a place where affluent young men would choose to spend time and part with their money. It was also the place where she had first met George Wickham, already in trouble, but her attraction to him had been so immediate and deep that even she, sensible businesswoman that she was, had fallen for him without a second thought for her own security in attaching herself to such a man as she already knew him to be.

But those thoughts belonged in the past. Julia now understood you could never go back, only forwards. She had moved forwards in her life further than she had realised, a fact brought home to her when visiting the house after such a long absence. She knew she would never again live above that gaming house or work long hours behind the bar there. It was a sad realisation, but also a freeing one.

Mr. Brown had assured her that it would take no time at all to find a buyer who would offer what she wanted for the business, and she had felt not a little surprise at the ease with which she had agreed to release it. Mr. Brown had, however, been very concerned at what he considered to be a reckless abandonment of all that her late husband had built up - he worried over her as the widow of one of his oldest clients - and so she had accepted his advice to retain one house in Cambridge; she did not need all of her money released and he had assured her that he would oversee the property himself.

Julia had determined to use her investments to fund her newest venture. Ever since her return from her visit to America, she had been mulling it over as she had checked through her London affairs and set her boarding house back up and running. The things she had seen there, the business opportunities on offer, the energy of such a young and booming country had impressed her deeply and she knew she could not stay in London and wonder what might have happened if she had tried her luck elsewhere.

She would keep the boarding house on Edward Street and the staffing agency - both of which she could leave in Lucy Belmont's capable hands - as her security in London, whilst developing a business in the New World. Just thinking it made Julia's skin tingle with excitement.

Julia closed her trunk and bag in preparation for the early morning start and climbed into bed. She felt content and excited and certain about her future. She had decided not to defer all of her decisions against the possibility of a certain person either re-entering her life or confusing her plans with his presence. George Wickham would no longer be a consideration in her future and she felt as though a great weight had been lifted from her shoulders.

Chapter 42

Elizabeth slowly adjusted her eyes to the gloom.

Where was she? What time was it?

She frowned, trying to remember why she was in bed.

Had not there been a dinner party?

The small chink of grey light through the drapes eventually informed her that, at least, she was in her own bed chamber and it was daytime, but she felt very ill indeed: bruised and hurt and thirsty, very thirsty. She let out a small croak and a shape at the end of the bed unfolded itself and moved to her side: Jane!

"My dear, do not try to sit up. Here; take a sip of water." Jane held Lizzy's head as she drank and then gratefully sank back down into the pillows.

"Jane? Why are you here? What has happened? I feel so weak; my body hurts, my legs ache."

"Shh, now. Try to rest while I fetch Darcy. He has been on alert all night and absolutely refused to sleep even though I assured him I would tell him the moment you awoke."

Jane disappeared only to be replaced by a rush of air surrounding Darcy as he flew into the room and halted by the bed, uncertain of what to do next. Lizzy held out her arms and he sank down, gently holding her as if she were fragile china.

"My darling! It has been such a long night; such a long wait. After the doctor gave you the sleeping draught, he could not estimate how soon you would awake and what would happen when you did. But Jane says you are in pain? He has prescribed some drops for that; he said it might be so. Allow me to measure some into a glass of water."

Elizabeth watched as Darcy's hands shook so badly, his first attempts only deposited the drops onto the bedclothes. He swore and tried again. Elizabeth reached out and held his hands still.

"Stop for a moment, my dear. Tell me what has happened. I cannot remember and you are frightening me with your concern and all this talk of drops and draughts and doctors. Why am I in bed? Why is Jane here taking care of me? Darcy? Answer me."

Darcy carefully placed the bottle onto the cabinet and took her hands in his and kissed them as if trying to stretch out time.

"Darcy? *Tell me.*"

"It appears, my dearest Elizabeth that our child is not to be. I am so sorry, my dear; I am so sorry."

Elizabeth was silent as she digested this horror.

Her hands released from Darcy's and passed over her stomach, feeling the dull ache of the muscles around the soft mound that still promised their child. Now she remembered the pains squeezing like iron bands during the party; however, although she had been told the truth of the matter, she felt no other difference.

"But, are you quite sure the baby is lost, my dear? I do not recall any of it, and I do not notice any reduction here, although I do feel pain and quite ill."

Darcy sighed and looked away.

"The doctor says it is merely a matter of time before the baby is lost, and so we must brace ourselves against it. He says he has seen this many times before. You must be strong and we must wait together."

Elizabeth felt her anger rise along with a glimmer of hopefulness.

"So; the baby is not actually lost? I thought so. I should know it, should feel it, if that was the case. Well; I refuse to give in to the doctor's mournful predictions. I care not how many times he has seen it; our baby will survive this, I assure you, my darling. I shall do nothing to distract it from its purpose and everything I can to encourage it. Perhaps it is only too much activity and excitement on my part that has caused this weakness in me. It is a warning to take things slowly; that is all." She smiled bravely into his eyes.

"Please do not concern yourself any further; all will be well."

She kissed him and once he was comforted, she requested Jane be sent to her immediately. After discussing the events of the previous evening, which were slowly coming back to Lizzy, and the events of the days before that and what had occupied them and all of their accompanying concerns, Lizzy felt justification in her determination, reiterating she would rest for as long as necessary to bring about a healthy infant.

Jane merely smiled hopefully and agreed with her sister's plan as being very sensible both for Lizzy and also the baby, but refused to project any of her own hopes upon the matter. As far as she was concerned, the doctor had spoken and knew more than any other person, including her sister, about the general prognosis in cases such as these.

And so it was with great delight and satisfaction, after a week spent entirely upon her back, propped up by pillows and attended by the doctor, her sisters and very frequently, Darcy, Elizabeth was eventually able to state one morning as she ate her breakfast with him, that she intended to rise and dress and spend some time downstairs. Darcy immediately started to remonstrate but Lizzy held her ground.

"No, I insist, Darcy. I have lasted longer than the doctor said I would; I feel no pain, there have been no further complications and I feel I have regained sufficient strength to allow this. I do not propose to do anything more than walk downstairs and sit in the drawing room quietly, but I assure you that if I have to look at these four walls any longer, I shall go mad. A little stroll about the house cannot hurt me or the baby."

Seeing she was in earnest, Darcy immediately went to call for Mrs. Reynolds and Baxter to help Mrs. Darcy dress. She found him an hour later pacing the length of the drawing room, which he interrupted to help her to a seat in front of a great fire he had clearly ordered be built. As it was a rather warm day, the room was already hotter than her bedroom had been. Elizabeth laughed as she settled herself on the chaise and absolutely refused the wrap with which he was threatening her.

"Darcy! Please stop! I shall expire from heat stroke if you are not careful. I thank you for your kind concern but you must stop worrying and go about your business; I have held you up for too long. I will see Georgiana and Kitty and Anne, and probably, Jane this morning and they will take very good care of me. Please, take yourself to the club, or to Parliament, or wherever others have need of you. I shall be quite comfortable here just as soon as I can get Mrs. Reynolds to damp down that fire and open the windows."

Darcy embraced her with great tenderness and, after whispering secret admonishments in her ear, which merely served to make her laugh, smiled and left the room. Elizabeth ran her hands over her stomach. She had managed it against the solemn looks of the doctor and Jane and Darcy. The baby was safe and no more bleeding or fainting had occurred since that night one week ago. In fact, the baby had made itself very visible in such a short time and it gave her great pleasure to see the obvious bulge under her dress.

They had had a scare; that was all. Nothing more than that, but she determined to take more care of herself and not allow worries about her sisters to overwhelm her.

Georgiana and Kitty and Anne all came into the room with quiet solicitude and delight at seeing her amongst them again. They called Mrs. Reynolds and ordered tea whilst the fire was reduced and the drapes and windows opened to allow the air in from the bright day. Lizzy felt tired but very happy to be in her usual place again as she listened to the other ladies who soon lost their reticence, regaining their usual brightness and cheeriness of manner, laughing about the play they had seen and the sights in the park that morning.

"And have you seen anything of Mr. Sudbury and Mr. Jardine again since the party and my rather dramatic exit?" enquired Lizzy. "I do hope you have apologised on my behalf as I have been unable to do so."

Anne rose and went over to the salver on the bureau, returning with several cards which she handed to Elizabeth.

"Here, you see, both gentlemen and the Colonel have been regular visitors enquiring after your health and progress. Indeed, we were becoming quite jealous of the attention you were receiving, even if you had no notion of it."

"But what nonsense!" exclaimed Elizabeth as she examined those and several other cards from new acquaintance who had heard of her illness.

"Why was not I given these earlier so I could reply to them? They will think me very ill indeed if I cannot even respond to gestures of kindness from my sick bed."

The girls looked at each other and then Georgiana explained.

"My brother was quite determined that you were not to be disturbed by anything at all. Nothing was to reach you and certainly nothing that might upset you." She bit her lip as she realised she had allowed something to escape.

"*Upset me?* What has happened this past week that might upset me, pray? Kitty? Georgiana? Tell me."

Again the girls looked at each other but refused to elaborate any further, pleading fear of telling too much and an angry response from Mr. Darcy for having done so. To their great relief, at that moment Jane arrived and was a welcome distraction. Jane had, of course, been a constant visitor at her sister's bedside and a source of much gentle care and conversation but now, Lizzy realised, that conversation had been purposefully bland and amusing. She had been told nothing for the entire time.

Jane's unalloyed joy when she saw her sister so recovered and looking so well diminished quickly once she understood that Lizzy's active imagination had taken over and was conjuring up all manner of terrible things that had happened behind her back.

She looked at the other ladies and nodded to them; they were more than happy to leave with waves and kisses blown through the air. Jane settled herself beside her sister and smiled warmly.

"It is so good to see you out of bed again, Lizzy. I knew it would not be long and told Darcy to expect a revolt once you felt stronger. Did he put up much of an argument?"

"Oh; he tried, unsuccessfully. And now he is gone to carry on with his interrupted business although he promised to return within the hour. He is too concerned and kind and patient – indeed, as you all have been. Thank you, Jane. I do not know what I would have done without your calm presence and unselfish dedication."

"Well, there is little enough to do in London, after all," Jane laughed. "One has to engage in *something* so as not to allow the boredom to take hold. It was fortunate indeed that you fell ill and so gave me some employment!"

"But, Jane; now I am better, tell me what has been happening recently. Georgiana hinted that Darcy has been keeping things from me and I would prefer to know the truth rather than imagine the worst. And, what of the purpose of the party - the suitors? Has anything transpired with any of them? Please Jane, do tell everything. I am well, truly I am, and can take anything you wish to tell me."

"Well, other than your attention-seeking collapse which rather ruined any romance in the air that night - well done, by the way - I understand that Darcy and Bingley have cautiously approved the two gentlemen previously unknown to them: Messrs. Sudbury and Jardine. They both appear eligible and have good connections and fortunes; although, of course, both of them are *in trade* and I hear about that *constantly* from my sisters at home. It is interesting, is it not, that the Bingley family's wealth comes also from trade? But such details are easily forgot, particularly when I happen to mention that our father's income does not. It works as an effective gag upon Caroline's contempt of those she considers beneath her."

Lizzy laughed. "My goodness, Jane, you are becoming quite pert in your opinions. You had better take care or you will make everyone uncomfortable and you know how you would hate that! What has come over you, to be so outspoken against the great Caroline Bingley? Tell me: has she condescended to marry anyone yet, I wonder? I pity the poor gentleman who chances his future with her; he will well deserve any improved lifestyle to suffer her."

"Lizzy! That is cruel and I cannot have you saying such things about my husband's sister!" Jane smiled in agreement. "But there is one gentleman who keeps calling and whom she manages to tolerate for about five minutes per day. Perhaps he will wear her down and next year, if he is very fortunate, he will gain an audience with her for ten minutes together!"

They both laughed at the thought of the poor gentleman enduring an endless, painful courtship with Caroline only to discover the prize as not being so attractive once won. Eventually, Elizabeth returned to seriousness.

"And what of our own sister and her situation in Brompton? Have you heard anything from her? I recall being told at the party she had been seen in London in the company of an officer and some unsavoury ladies. Is that so?"

"I am afraid it is, my dear, and that is what your husband has been keeping from you. It was after you had been told that news at the party that you collapsed and he thinks you should not be worried about it again."

"Nonsense, Jane. You should know enough of my desire for frankness by now, as should Darcy. I will hear everything. It is not reasonable that you should bear the brunt of it alone as you have been forced to do in the past. Tell me what is amiss with our sister."

"Well, I have nothing to add particularly. I have not yet been back to visit Lydia, nor has she been to see me, so I cannot confirm the rumour absolutely but, she has been seen about Town, several times recently but never in the company of Wickham."

"Then we must presume Captain Denny is still a constant visitor? Or has she already another suitor? Unsurprisingly, she has not heeded our advice at all. And do we know how she amuses herself in the company of these ladies and gentleman?"

"She is a great favourite, apparently, at the large gaming parties about Town. There are some very important and influential people who attend them and I do not know how Lydia, of all people, can afford to be there. But these are all rumours, you understand, Lizzy; I have none of this on good authority."

"Yes, Jane, your reticence does you credit as always, but I am astonished that Darcy and Bingley have not attempted to discover the truth and remove her from the situation. Why have not they, Jane? Surely they can see how much trouble she is exposing herself to? And why has not Wickham intervened, either? Where is he, I would like to know? Regardless of his feelings for Lydia, she is his wife and should be behaving as such, not running about Town in dubious company. Oh! It is all going very badly indeed."

"Calm yourself, Lizzy, or Darcy will hold me responsible for upsetting you. But you are wrong to accuse our husbands of disinterest, Lizzy, for what should they do? As you rightly point out, she is Wickham's problem and responsibility now, after all, and he must be the one to step in and put an end to it. Our husbands have no jurisdiction over the behaviour of another man's wife."

Lizzy looked at her sister, considering. Jane was right. It was no longer a problem of Wickham's possible mistreatment of his wife; if anything, it was now quite the opposite. This was now a matter to be resolved between man and wife, but, still, it made her blood boil.

"Foolish, imprudent, thoughtless girl! Again, she refuses to control her behaviour and happily pulls all of us down with her as she seeks excitement and entertainment. What should *we* do, Jane since our husbands can do nothing? Something must be done."

Chapter 43

"George!" Julia started up from her desk, dropping her pen onto the accounts book where it left a small lake of ink, obliterating her last few entries. She raised her hands to smooth her hair back from her forehead, and then clasped them in front of her skirts.

"Why…what brings you here? I had not expected to see you – I am just returned from Cambridge and busy as you see" – she gestured to the desk – "reviewing accounts and business and …."

Whatever else she had intended to say was lost as Wickham moved swiftly to silence her with a long, languorous kiss; a kiss so deeply intimate, filled with such emotion, its message could not be misunderstood. She melted against him as she had so many times before. There was nothing to be done against such passion, and she had no real desire to fight it. All her good intentions of the past days dissolved in an instant.

Eventually, George put her away from him and led her to the settee, settling himself right beside her and taking her hands in both of his.

"My dearest, darling, Julia. I cannot bear it. I have tried to do the right thing; I have struggled, but my feelings for you cannot be repressed. This separation is unbearable. My future is worth nothing if I am to live it without you.

"No, do not interrupt to remind me that I am a married man and the reasons why I must accept my fate," he hastened as she struggled to object.

"My marriage, as you very well know, is a sham: a cruel joke, a miscarriage of justice, perdition the Devil himself would not be so cruel as to cast upon me. My life with Lydia is meaningless. I have no feelings for her: I cannot bear to be in the same room as her. And this is not recent, not only since I knew of your return. Very soon after our marriage, I found it impossible to keep up the pretence which, of course, she quickly realised and it hurt her feelings greatly, but such a one-sided attraction cannot last.

"You know, perhaps, that in retaliation for my lack of attention to her, Lydia has already taken another lover after only a few weeks in town? No; of course you cannot. She disports herself all over Town with my oldest friend, Denny, who takes her to parties and dinners and plays. Not that I care with whom she amuses herself, do not imagine for a moment that I do. I consider it more a thoughtful service to me on Denny's part.

"She accuses me of neglect; insists I am to blame for forcing her to look elsewhere for her entertainment and attention. And she is right. I cannot play the required role while my longing for you still rages, and your response just now gives me cause to hope that your feelings remain unchanged, too. Tell me it is so, Julia, my dearest."

How easy, thought Julia, to be so seduced. How comforting, familiar, desirable. All her good intentions of only days before were mere bravado. Far from forgetting George Wickham, she had been longing for this moment for almost a year, but suppressing it, knowing it to be the foolish and futile desires of a weak woman. She had thought she would be strong against his applications, against his attacks, against his ardour, but she had thought wrongly and she did not care. She leaned towards him to once again seek out the contour of his lips with her own, to feel the beat of his heart under the soft cloth of his shirt, and she felt finally at home again, at one with another person, no longer alone and lonely; at peace.

Finally, they pulled slightly apart; Wickham leaving his arms about her, she resting her head upon his shoulder as they had sat many times in the past. Their silence was familiar, close, intimate. No conversation was necessary.

"What are we to do?" she murmured after a while. "What *can* we do, George, without causing a terrible disgrace and heartache through our selfishness?"

"We are not so important, my dear, that any persons other than those of our closest acquaintance will know or care. If the Prince Regent and all those of his court are allowed such freedoms with impunity, then, I believe we should be quite safe from the gossips' tongues. Of course, my agreement with Darcy will be cancelled the moment he hears rumours about us and, I have no doubt, will cause his wrath to be brought to bear upon me once again, but I shall not care if you are with me."

"But it is not only Darcy whom you must consider now, George," Julia remonstrated. "Lydia will be sadly affected by our reconciliation when she learns of it, regardless of her current teasing behaviour; behaviour which, I am sure, she uses only to regain your attention. She will not take kindly to you taking a mistress within the first year of your marriage: no new wife would. And I am not sure I wish to be labelled as such, either. Our position is so much more precarious than it has ever been, you must see that."

"I would have taken you as my lawful wife years ago, Julia, you know that. My feelings for you have never diminished even though my behaviour has not matched them in integrity, I am sorry to say. I have been a foolish, thoughtless, arrogant being and I do not blame you for refusing me - several times - and I understand, understood, entirely your reasons for doing so.

"But now I am committed to making something of myself, to be accountable only to you. Do not you think we have wasted too much time, Julia, and we should make up that wasted time as quickly as possible? That we should start being happy together as we used to be, not unhappy, apart, as we are now? Tell me you agree, my darling."

Julia sighed with desire for it to be so again, all the while knowing they had moved far beyond that seemingly achievable object now. George was married, an inescapable fact, and his responsibility was to his wife and their life together no matter how much she or he might wish it otherwise; no matter how unhappy the situation might make them for the rest of their lives.

She could not put her own happiness above that of a girl of not yet seventeen, a girl who still needed all the protection and guidance she could get. Lydia could no more take care of herself as Mrs. Wickham than she could as Miss Bennet; she had no fortune, no skills, no education. If she was left, abandoned, a discarded wife, she would be shunned, her life reduced to grave limitations and seclusions, inevitably forcing her return to her father's protection: whereas, she, Julia, was a respectable widow, also alone but with property and the intelligence to improve her situation in life. She was more than capable of fending for herself and making her own way just as she had always done.

Julia gently kissed George again and then rose to sit in a single armchair by the empty grate. She needed room to collect her thoughts and steel her nerves for what she was about to say.

"You say we should live life and be happy again, George, that we have wasted too much time, and we have. You are quite right. But it has never been the right time for us, never the right situation, never enough trust, and I fear it still is not.

"We cannot simply reclaim the past and pretend it is our future without regard to those whom we would affect by such actions. I would never be easy knowing what we had ruined, whom we had hurt to accomplish our own happiness.

"You are right: it does seem a severe sentence for a two-night mistake made by you last year, to be permanently tied to someone for whom you have no affection, but that fact makes you no different from several, let us say, many, husbands and wives who discover the truth about the person to whom they are married. Felicity in marriage is a matter of chance, after all, and once that step has been taken it is irreversible."

"*No!* Do not be so definite, my darling!" George leapt from the settee and tried to gather Julia back into his arms as if he could smother her words and thoughts. She resisted and put him away from her with determination.

"Do not make this harder than it is already, George. God forgive me, I want you back as desperately as you want me, but it cannot be – you must see that, my dear. It is not only Lydia and the suffering to which we will condemn her I cannot countenance, but also that of Mr. Darcy who has done so much to assist you - far more than he needed to - and his family, and that of the Bennet family, all of whom have done nothing to deserve having their good name dragged down by our actions.

"Therefore, it is impossible for me to agree with your proposal, my dear, as dearly as I might wish it."

"But we are miserable, Julia!" Wickham cried out. "We are both utterly *miserable* without each other! Why do not *we* count for something in all of this? Why does not *our* happiness count for anything? Why do I have to be punished, why do *you* have to be punished so severely for a single error of judgment? Why cannot we seek comfort against the disappointment that my folly and imprudence have brought on? It is unfair; it is unreasonable; it is cruel indeed and I cannot live a life of such despair. Give me something to hope for, my darling - *something* - a very little will suffice."

Julia felt her resolve weakening; his anguish was tearing her heart into shreds. It was worse than any separation they had before faced because it had the certainty of being the last they would ever suffer through. She knew this would be the encounter to end their relationship for ever.

And, truth be told, she could not let him go; she could not let that happen, that was the problem. The idea of such finality chilled her to the bone. High morals, sensible words and good character counted very little against her feelings for this man.

"What would you have me say, George?" she asked softly. "You know what I feel and what I think about the position we are in. I can see no solution that will satisfy everybody and that is the only solution we should consider."

They both fell into a long silence, then she asked, remembering.

~ 365 ~

"Tell me what you hoped for in coming here today, George, for surely you know me well enough by now to know strong words and feelings would do little to sway me. What was your true purpose?"

Wickham stared at her, his look a mixture of dismay and desire.

"There are two things that are going well in my life, that cause me to hope, however faintly: your return from America, and my new position. Both give me a reason to build my future in the way *I* want it rather than having it shaped by others or merely accepting it as fate has ordained as I have in the past. I know you are sceptical, my dear, that you have heard me say such things before, but I hope I have proven the one aspect - of my love being entirely yours - and can prove the other part of what I say is true. All I ask is that you not be so final in your rejection of me, of us, Julia. I cannot bear it. It is not until a prize is almost lost that its value is appreciated. I came here today to begin that process of proving my intention to you."

Wickham reached into his breast pocket and pulled out a wad of notes. Julia gasped: she had seen him produce such amounts of money before and knew from whence they came.

"*No*, George! You will *not* win my approval by showing how well you have done at the tables in one night. I will not return to that foolishness again. If you are gambling away your wages, then our relationship is entirely over, there is no more to be discussed."

Wickham smiled quietly, looking at the money.

"I do not blame you for such suppositions; they are perfectly understandable given my history, but, on the contrary, this is evidence of my new stability and success, Julia.

"As Darcy has covered my living costs for the year, I have very few expenses, and my reason for coming here was to ask you to keep my accounts along with those of your own; I can think of nowhere safer. I would have you take charge of my earnings such as are extra to my needs, as proof of my success; to build your trust in me again and regain your good opinion."

"But this is most irregular, George; why would not you keep your own account, pray? I have no need for such evidence; I have no reason to expect it. Your wife, on the other hand, is the one upon whom you should be bestowing your generosity and proving your success. *She* expects it and has real need of it, I am sure. Perhaps if you tried harder with her, you would not be so unhappy," she ended weakly.

"I have no wish to try harder with Lydia. If she scented any excess money, it would not be banked in a sensible manner: it would vanish on frivolous fripperies without a moment's thought. No; please allow me this mode of safekeeping for I intend building up a contingency with your help. Enough, I hope, to provide for our future when something can be arranged. I cannot rely upon Darcy for everything. I finally see that now, and only regret it has taken me so long to realise. Please say you will not deny me this request, my dearest Julia."

"This I cannot deny you, George. I am delighted to learn of your sensible provisions for your future and am perfectly willing to help you attain them. However, for the rest, we must wait and see how that future develops."

She smiled at him and walked over to her desk where the ledger lay, the blob of ink now dried and wrinkled over the last entries. Sitting, she picked up the pen and dipped it into the pot. She turned to a new page and looked at George enquiringly.

"What shall I enter as your business name, my dear, to account for all of these entries?"

George smiled and bent over her, kissing her neck as he murmured in her ear,

"It cannot be my name, I suppose? That would be too flagrant of our attachment. Perhaps a coded business name that only we will understand?"

Julia nodded after thinking for a moment, and wrote: *Youngham Enterprises, London.*

Wickham laughed quietly. Without fail, Julia would always come up with the neatest answer to a problem. He handed over the notes and, after counting them, Julia entered the amount into the ledger. They both looked at her neat writing for a moment. It was as if they were starting their lives together again, joined by a similar interest, but heading out on a seemingly impossible journey into the unknown that is the future; a future that they both hoped might be kinder to them than their past had been, if they could only manage it better.

Chapter 44

Spring was quickly giving way to Summer and London was beginning to empty of its denizens who had the option of country residences or seaside towns to remove to before the weather became intolerable and the stench even worse. The Season had all but wound down and there was nothing to keep them any longer.

Jane had already announced their intention of returning to Netherfield within the fortnight and was especially eager for Elizabeth and the other ladies to return with her.

"For," she had argued, "you have not stayed more than one night in Meryton since you left, Lizzy, and Mamma, Mary, and Father would enjoy a visit, and I am selfish enough to wish not to lose your company so soon, either. It could be of the shortest nature, a rest period, if you like, in consideration of your recent illness, before facing the journey further North."

Lizzy had laughed at the idea that anything that involved Longbourn and its inhabitants could ever be considered a 'rest period', but she, too, was reluctant to leave Jane again, now their accustomed intimacy had been restored. Although, it would mean being without Darcy - he would refuse outright to detour from his homeward path even for an hour, especially if the reason was to spend time with his mother-in-law - and she was not sure she wished to endure any more of his absences.

Her health over the past few weeks had steadily improved; so much so, that she had been able to attend many of the final gatherings and musical evenings, and several times had accompanied the girls on their morning rides through the Park, allowing her further opportunities to become more closely acquainted with the gentlemen who took it upon themselves, for an half hour at least, to entertain the ladies and walk them through the various glades and gardens.

Mr. Jardine appeared to be very taken with Georgiana but Lizzy did not notice any particular preferment on her sister's part, and had already advised she should not allow herself to be pressured into feelings of affection which are imaginary or fleeting at best.

"Because," Lizzy had cautioned, "even if Mr. Jardine is the most pleasant gentleman whom you have met thus far, you have as yet met very few with whom to make comparison, and there is no great rush on your part, even if there might be on his. I cannot fault him for his choice, of course, but marriage is not to be taken lightly and it is best to know as much as possible about your partner before entering that state. If he is truly serious, he will pursue you even into the wilds of Derbyshire!"

Georgiana had reluctantly agreed that her feelings had not been greatly affected, although the attention was something to be flattered by and she did enjoy his company. Lizzy had laughed wryly at her own memory of being flattered by a man's attention and her enjoyment of his company. She doubted that if she had married George Wickham she would be as pleased with him now, and she reflected on her own sister in the exact predicament she had avoided and was warning against.

Mr. Sudbury and Anne, in contrast, were both very affected by each other and at Lizzy's urging, Darcy had sought out that gentleman several times in order to further ascertain his intentions and character. Both had apparently passed muster and Darcy had pronounced Sudbury to be a sensible, intelligent sort of fellow with his own income, who spoke well and was highly regarded amongst the London set. He did not gamble, or entertain ostentatiously, and Darcy had been unable to discover any whiff of gossip about him. All of this information he passed on to Lizzy, but to Anne all he said was,

"He has my approval, at least; however, it is Lady Catherine's that he needs to secure. I would suggest that you write to your mother and request permission for him to be a guest at Rosings as soon as we leave here. It does not do to extend these things beyond what is reasonable and necessary."

Anne had looked shocked, delighted and terrified all at once and had immediately gone to Georgiana to discuss the matter and seek her advice.

Darcy had also discovered other, less favourable news which he imparted to Lizzy one afternoon when they were alone. He was reluctant to burden her but knew she must be told.

"I met Aspinall at the club today - Wickham's employer - and he is quite delighted with him and the work he is doing. Apparently, Wickham is very efficient and enthusiastic and well worth the wages he is being paid. I said nothing other than congratulating him on his choice and hoped that the arrangement would continue thus for as long as they both wanted."

"Well, my dear, that was very restrained and sensible of you! It is entirely certain then, that he is changed and determined to make something of himself. I am glad to hear it, for Lydia's sake. I must go to her soon, before we leave, and make sure she is happier now with her situation."

Darcy looked at her and then started his usual pacing to the far windows and back. Lizzy watched him and waited. She knew his moods and mannerisms by now: there was something else to be told.

Darcy stood looking out of the window, his hands behind his back, and spoke softly.

"Oh, I believe she is happier now but not, perhaps, in the way you imagine."

Lizzy sat up straight, dread starting in her heart.

"Tell me, Darcy, whatever it is that you know about my sister. Has she been seen in Town again? Jane warned me there were rumours."

Darcy turned and faced her, tapping his hand against his thigh, seeking the most suitable words.

"It would seem that she has found herself a set of *friends*, not all of whom are suitable I understand, and is frequenting the gaming houses and private parties that enable ladies to gamble each evening with them. Apparently, she is admired for her skill in various games and is the centre of attention wherever she goes. Parties, night-time strolls through the Park, and theatre visits have also been mentioned in connection with her name. Some acquaintance thought to warn me as she is a relative of mine; I could not deny it, obviously."

"Oh! *Gambling!* It is worse than we thought. She has reverted to her activities in Newcastle about which she hinted and was so proud. Of course, she must be entertained and make friends where she can, and they will not always be to our standard, but I had hoped she would show more propriety than this. What does Wickham do, have you heard? Is he also returned to his gambling ways along with my sister?"

Darcy looked at the floor and cleared his throat.

"Wickham is not part of the group, Elizabeth. In fact he has been conspicuous by his absence; it has been commented upon. Lydia is, apparently, always with this group of friends, or arrives later with Captain Denny. They are more a couple than Lydia and Wickham have ever been, it seems. Many people understand it to be so, never having seen Wickham in the same room as your sister."

"*Oh!*" Elizabeth exhaled. "It is true, then. Is there any scandalous talk about her and Denny, did you hear?"

"Not at the moment; it is clearly understood the state of their friendship is merely that of companions and undertaken with Wickham's approbation - so Lydia tells those who wish to know - and at the moment it seems to be believed and not questioned. I dare not gauge for how long such an arrangement can continue before the gossips' tongues do start to wag, but it cannot be for too much longer. I am sure Lydia thinks she has fooled them all and cares not one jot for her sisters' or parents' opinion, as much fun as she is having."

"Well, naturally she does not. Fun and flirtation has always been her object; she needs only the smallest encouragement to attach herself to anybody. Her affections have always continually fluctuated and, as we regularly observed in Meryton, sometimes one officer, sometimes another was her favourite, as their attentions to her raised them in her opinion. And now that Wickham has withdrawn his attention through work or otherwise, she happily reverts to her old behaviour and finds attention elsewhere. Thoughtless, thoughtless, Lydia!"

Darcy rushed to her side and held her in his arms, almost regretting his decision to tell but knowing that to keep such news from her would have been inexcusable.

"My dear Elizabeth, please calm yourself; there is no benefit in becoming upset and it might cause harm to the baby. None of this is surprising to those who know your sister; it is merely an unfortunate reminder of her absolute disregard for propriety.

"But I do confess to being unsure as to what intervention I should attempt when it seems that everything I have attempted in the past has only made the situation worse. I do not know what to do, but I feel that something must be done, do not you?"

Elizabeth nodded, thinking of what best *could* be done and why it *should* be done without delay, but with every thought she came against the fact that Lydia and Wickham were simply two careless people, people who cared nothing for family or even their own reputation. They saw no reason to abide by rules which offered them nothing in return, rules which restricted their amusement and enjoyment of life.

Lydia wanted attention: attention she got, even if it was of the most mortifying kind for everyone associated with her. Lydia wanted to be married: married she became, wildly proud of her success no matter how she had come by that success and what it cost others to avert a disaster. Now Lydia found that the London home and marriage she had craved was not as exciting as anticipated and so was adjusting her life to suit her wild need for excitement and attention by playing cards and trying to imitate the Ton.

But, in the end, as Jane and she had discussed and agreed, Wickham now had governance over his wife's behaviour: not Darcy, not Father, not Lizzy or Jane, and if he did not feel the need to rein her in and insist upon proper behaviour, then who should? It was concerning indeed and Lizzy could not immediately think how to advise her husband.

"Has anyone seen Wickham at all?" she asked eventually, "or Mr. Jardine, perhaps, or even Mrs. Younge? Any other person than Mr. Aspinall, with whom you obviously cannot discuss such a delicate matter, but someone who can shed some light on what Wickham has to say about Lydia's behaviour as her husband and, therefore, the most affected by it? For surely he cannot be entirely sanguine; even *he* must understand the implications not only to Lydia - which he clearly does not care about - but also to his own name and standing in his new business world, which he should. He has charm enough for anything but it can only shield him for so long before he is found out and caught up in the scandal that his own wife is creating.

"I think Wickham must be spoken to, Darcy, he must be warned of the consequences at least. You must talk with uncle Gardiner and Father and decide the best way to proceed, even with the knowledge that neither Wickham nor Lydia will appreciate your interference. It is difficult indeed, but they must be made to see the error of their ways."

They sat together, folded in each other's arms, silent for quite some time, each mulling over the best way of dealing with the situation, but finding no satisfactory option.

Darcy considered what Elizabeth had said and it rang unpleasantly true: Lydia and Wickham could behave just as they pleased. They did not have to consider any others if they chose not to, and they had already proved they cared nothing for others' opinions of their behaviour, and indeed, appeared almost unaware of how it could affect anyone else. At last he roused himself and sighed.

"I will write to your father and uncle and we will see what can be done but, as you say, there is little we can do about your sister if her husband does not object to her behaviour. This is an entirely different matter than when he appeared to be refusing to honour his obligations to her and she required protection. Now it seems almost as if *he* is requiring protection from *her* before her conduct ruins any chance he might have."

"And I shall make that visit to Lydia tomorrow; it is long overdue. She must understand our concerns about her conduct and its implications for everyone. What she chooses to do with those concerns will, unfortunately, be entirely up to her but I must at least try to prevent an inevitable scandal."

Chapter 45

"Mary! *Mary.* Bring me my breakfast, and a powder; *now!*"

Over the past months, young Mary had become very accustomed to her new mistress' routines and expectations but her unpredictable temper was still a terrifying prospect; some days were pleasantly peaceful, but others more often found Mary shaking in her boots down in the cellar. Mrs. Wickham was always very contrite afterwards, blaming her temper on worry or tiredness or loneliness, but it made for a rather uncomfortable time. At least in her last position there had been other, more senior servants to hide behind if her actions had even been noticed - up to her arms in soap suds as she was all day and night - and sometimes, she reflected, perhaps that lowly position had not been so bad, after all.

She quickly poured water into the coffee pot and gathered up the tray which had already been set for hours, awaiting the call from upstairs. Mrs. Wickham required nothing much in the morning other than her coffee, her powder and a muffin spread with preserves. It would be much more complicated if she required a cooked meal; that would involve a wait and Mrs. Wickham did not like to be kept waiting.

Mr. Wickham, on the other hand, was all ease and charm itself, if she ever saw him, that is. He did not require anything. He left the house very early just as Mary was cleaning the grate in the kitchen, and never returned until late in the evening by which time Mary had retired for the night up to her little garret room. Sometimes she noticed he had eaten the meal she had prepared for them both, but more frequently he had not and so Mary happily ate it either at breakfast or lunch. She had never been so well-fed in her life.

Mary climbed the stairs and knocked gently on the door with the tip of her boot.

"Yes, yes, Mary; come in for goodness' sake. I know it is you; there is no need to knock all the time. Who else would there be in here?"

Mary placed the tray on the bedside table whilst Lydia groaned as she pulled herself upwards and leant forward so Mary could lift the pillows behind her. She watched impatiently as Mary poured the coffee and stirred the powder into the glass of water.

"Very good; that will do – give it to me now." Lydia gulped the water thirstily and then turned to her muffin and smiled slightly.

"Mary: bring me my reticule from the chair and I will show you something you will never have seen before!"

Mary looked at the heap of clothing tumbling off the chair and scattered at the foot of it. Just poking out from under the confusion was Lydia's beaded bag and Mary retrieved it, handing it to Lydia before turning back to the clothes to fold or hang them neatly, or gather for washing.

"No! Leave that, Mary. Come here and see!" Lydia was as excited as a child with a great secret or new toy. From her reticule she produced a velvet bag, which she opened to reveal rather a large stash of notes and a pair of earrings and a necklace. She beamed expectantly at Mary who was so astonished, as her employer had predicted, that she could say nothing.

"*Well?* What do you think of that?" Lydia laughed. "What a night I had last night. Every card went my way and never failed me. It was truly the best night of my life. No one could believe it; the other ladies would not give up because they know luck never lasts, but it did! And so they lost not only their money but also their jewellery, too! The gentlemen there were very impressed and consoled their wives as well as they could but nothing could beat me! And, as I said to the general company, it is not possible I could be cheating, for inspect the limits of my dress, if you please!

And I paraded my dress for all to see, and they all laughed for, you know, we ladies have no sleeves, no long boots, no coat pockets to hide anything in.

"Oh! It was a wonderful evening! Wickham would have been so proud had he been there to see it. But, of course, he was not. Has he left already, Mary?"

Mary paused in her admiration of the earrings and looked sideways at Lydia: his evening meal had not been touched and his bed not slept in.

"Oh, yes, indeed, madam. I 'eard 'im leave as I was wakin' this mornin'. He certainly works 'ard, don' he, ma'am?"

The light fell from Lydia's eyes as she scooped everything back into her bag and returned to her muffin.

"Yes, indeed he does work hard, Mary. I fear for his health if he continues in this way. It is not sensible to spend so much time away from his home and his wife."

"But it is good that you 'ave found yerself some new friends, madam," Mary consoled. She knew this quick change of mood in her mistress boded ill for the rest of the day. "It is good that you can amuse yourself, jus' like las' night without always needin' 'is company.

"Now which dress shall I prepare for you this mornin', madam? It is a very fine day, but it will be hot, I believe. How about the sprigged muslin, madam?"

Lydia did not answer. Mary removed the clothes for washing and laid out the new dress in silence before leaving the room. It was a shame that such newly-married people should spend so much time apart. It was clearly upsetting her mistress no matter how hard she tried to cover it up; how the master was affected, she could not gauge.

Meanwhile, Lydia laid out her winnings upon the eiderdown and stared at them whilst finishing her breakfast. If she could manage this regularly without many losses, she could certainly do far better for herself here than she had done in Newcastle.

But the excitement of her achievement paled as she thought of the scarcity of people she had to discuss it with. She could not gloat openly with any of her new friends - they would consider it in very bad taste - and she wanted above everything to remain in their good opinion, and Mary had to be impressed, as her maid.

Oh! Where was Kitty? Why could not she be here? She would be everything that Lydia needed: a friend, a supporter, an admirer. Even Harriet Forster would understand the enormity of her success and be excited for her, although that friendship had been all but broken since Brighton.

Once reminded of the lonely truth of her life, she gloomily stuffed the money back into the bag and hid it under her mattress, its euphoric effect on her entirely dispelled; she would hide it more securely in her little box under the floorboard, later. The earrings and necklace she put in her reticule, ready for trade with the jeweller down the high street. Beautiful as they were, she could never wear them in public and she could never use them as surety in another game, either.

There! She smiled to herself at the thought. She now had something with which to occupy her day before Denny called later that afternoon. She slowly completed her toilette, spending a great deal of time on her hair - she was becoming proficient in doing it herself as Mary had proved herself entirely incapable - and finally, taking up her bag, descended the stairs, the picture of restored confidence and youthful beauty.

There was a knock on the door: a caller? This early? Mary came from the kitchen and looked enquiringly at Lydia who shrugged and shook her head. She was not expecting anybody.

"Take your time, Mary. I will be in the parlour, whoever it is."

"Thank you; I know the way." Lydia heard her sister's voice and grimaced. *Elizabeth!* What did she want?

"Lizzy! How kind of you to call, and so early, too! You must have left before your breakfast; may I offer you anything?"

'No, indeed; I thank you, Lydia. I do not require anything at present. I am glad to see you downstairs this time; it is an improvement on our last visit. How have you been, Lydia? How is Mr. Wickham?"

"We are both very well, Lizzy, although exceedingly busy with our lives, as, I am sure, are you. How are you faring with your new responsibilities? Have you entirely refurbished Darcy House yet? As you see, I took up your and Jane's suggestions and have improved this room at least." She pointed to the lone vase of wilted flowers and then wished she had not bothered; her sister looked less inclined to be approving than her last visit.

"I understand you have been busy making new acquaintances, at last, Lydia. Darcy has heard from several sources that you have been seen out in Town with them?"

Lydia smiled with satisfaction at her celebrity.

"Oh, yes, indeed. I have been having a most enjoyable month since your last visit. I have been fortunate to be introduced by a mutual acquaintance to many other ladies and gentlemen who enjoy similar entertainments to me – we go to the Park and the theatre and clubs - they have unreservedly welcomed me into their groups and houses. I have had such an exciting time and made ever-so-many new friends; they are all so clever and amusing…"

"And encourage your desire to play at card games, too, I understand? I hope you are not playing beyond your or Mr. Wickham's means, Lydia. It is very difficult to limit yourself when in more affluent company. I am surprised Mr. Wickham has not warned you about dangers he is so familiar with, himself."

"It is not all card games, Lizzy, and your immediate assumption that it is does you no credit. There are the other activities I mentioned, and Denny is very attentive; when he has concerns, he advises me to leave the game and take my winnings. For, Lizzy, I almost always win something, you know. Why especially last night I …"

"I have no wish to know what happened last night or any other night for that matter, Lydia. But you have now confirmed the other concern which prompted my visit. Captain Denny is still calling, is he? Even though Jane and I seriously advised against any encouragement of that gentleman's attentions?

"There is talk, Lydia, already, about your behaviour as a married woman going about Town without her husband, in the company of dubious acquaintance and another man. I am glad you have made some friends, and socialising with them during the day is one thing, but in the evening it is quite another, I assure you. It will not do, Lydia; surely you can see that?"

"No; I do *not* see that: why *should* I see that? For what do you propose I do, Lizzy?" Lydia stormed. "What *exactly* do you propose I do? Here am I, left alone every single day, as I told you last month, and no one to call upon or to call upon me - not even my own *family* who are a mere four miles away - and you *presume* to come here and preach to me about what I should and should not do to improve my isolated state?

"What can you know of it, happily situated as you are with friends and family at your beck and call, parties every evening if you want them, money enough for anything? You have not any idea of my life since I married Wickham other than what I have disclosed and what you have guessed at, when you could find the time to think of me at all.

"I told you in January of my misery, of the already failure of my marriage, of Wickham's detachment from me. Well, it has only deteriorated since being in Town. He has no feelings for me; I know that now very well. He has left me entirely alone since we have been in this house. He does not come home in the evening, and he leaves, if he does come home, very early the next morning. I do not think I have spoken to him for the last eight days, at least.

"Everyone says how hard he is working, and I pretend to agree and be understanding, but I *am not*, Lizzy; I most *certainly* am not! It is not natural for a man to so ignore his wife, to treat her with such disinterest and I will not have you tell me to endure it, to work on it, to accept it. I will *not* accept it, Lizzy; *never*!

"And why should I, indeed? I am too young to be tethered to a man who shows me no affection, no love, no emotion, no respect. It is as if I were his sister, and a sister he does not particularly like, at that."

Lydia's anger evaporated and she broke down into wild crying, the weeks of isolation and inattention overflowing and breaking through the wall of bravado and denial she had built against it. She felt hurt, humiliated, depressed and unloved. She could feel no worse.

Elizabeth rose and went to her sister, taking her shuddering body into her arms and just held her until the sobs subsided. She was shocked. She had never seen her sister so distressed, so unhappy and she felt dismay at her own neglect of her.

When Lydia finally raised her head, Lizzy saw through the redness and the swelling of her eyes to the deep unhappiness that lay there.

"I am sorry Lydia that I have not understood your situation properly, nor have I tried to help you with it. I have been too judgmental and focused only on improving your behaviour so that it will not affect our family's name without any consideration of how you are coping or feeling.

"Of course you must be unhappy; any woman would to be so ignored by her husband, and that must be brought to Wickham's attention without delay. Regardless of his feelings for you, he has no right to make you feel this way, to abandon you, to leave you to your own devices in a strange town. He may be working hard and he may have supplied you with somewhere to live but he is not providing the support and friendship that is the least a marriage should offer, and I am sure that much of your current behaviour is merely an attempt to regain his interest, is it not, now?"

Lydia sniffed and wiped her eyes.

"What else can I do? He is never here so I cannot impress him any other way than by making him angry or jealous; but it has not had any effect thus far.

"And now, I begin to think, Lizzy, that if he does not want me, then I do not want him: it would be the best solution for us both. I believe he has another from whom he is receiving affection - in fact, I know it is so - therefore, why should not I also look elsewhere for someone who admires me, who wants to spend time with me? Why should he have all the freedom in the world to do as he pleases and I, none?"

"Because, my dear, that is the way it has always been, and probably always will be. A woman's reputation is far more fragile than that of a man; the slightest question about her behaviour, her friendships, her opinions, will always lead to gossip and condemnation. You saw how Lady Haveringham has been treated and how she must live such a retired life due to her decision to divorce her husband. Perhaps that was what motivated Lady Catherine to introduce you to her – to show the consequence for women who rebel against a man's world. None of the issues were of her making other than she found herself married to a man who did not wish to be married to her. Her fault, in the eyes of society, was that she had the bad manners to expose her troubles publicly. That was her crime and for that she was punished. Her husband, on the other hand, continues with his philandering, business, and general life as if nothing happened.

"This is what you must consider, Lydia: any decision you make will hurt you the most; your family, less; Wickham, hardly at all. He will continue as he is now with little censure from society: you, inevitably, will be condemned and discarded by all those whom you imagine to be friends.

"This is what I fear for you, should you make a hasty decision, but I do now see more clearly your reason for considering doing so."

"Well, it is unfair to be treated in such a manner, and I shall not retire quietly to the country when I have done nothing wrong."

"Then what shall you do, Lydia? Remembering your family and your own reputation?"

"Oh! I shall be discreet, just as Wickham is being discreet, do not worry on that score. But what is acceptable behaviour for him, will be acceptable for me. I shall remain as *Mrs. Wickham* and feign interest in his work and good health - which, of course, I have good reason to do since he is required to provide for me, is not he? I have no intention of emulating Lady Haveringham's so-called disgrace just yet, but I refuse to sit here alone and miserable when there are other enticements available to me."

Lizzy looked at her now-calm sister and shuddered inwardly at her nonchalant appraisal of her situation and prospects. At least she had promised to be discreet, although Lizzy doubted very much Lydia had even a vague concept of what such behaviour entailed, but she appeared to understand that to break everything with Wickham would have very ill consequences for her future security. It seemed that Lydia's impetuous acquaintance with adulthood and all of its accompanying responsibilities was beginning to make an impression upon her; Lizzy only hoped that the impression would protect her sister from making an irreversible mistake that would close the door to society on her, forever.

"Then there is nothing more for me to say. I shall take my leave of you, Lydia and convey your decision to my husband. I will advise him that you wish to manage your own affairs without his assistance - is that correct?"

"Yes. Thank you, Lizzy. Please thank Mr. Darcy for all of his trouble on my behalf for I know he has done much and only out of interest in helping me. Please tell him I am perfectly content with my life as it is, and it is a life which Wickham and I shall fashion for ourselves without compromising any of our relations or friends. You have my word on that."

Lizzy nodded sadly. "Then I wish you well, Lydia, and sincerely hope you are able to manage a life that will make you happy. We are to return to Pemberley the day after tomorrow by way of Longbourn. Is there anything you wish me to relate to Mamma or Father?"

Lydia smiled ruefully. "No, indeed. I believe I shall leave it up to your discretion, Lizzy. Say what you think they would most wish to hear; there is no need or benefit in worrying them unduly, surely. They are so removed, there is little prospect of them hearing anything untoward, if I do not wish them to."

The sisters embraced and Lizzy left with a new-found, if not respect, then a higher opinion of her sister than she had ever before held. She believed her sister to be in earnest about her future and her marriage, and hoped, most sincerely, that Lydia and Wickham would eventually broker some agreement and happiness within that marriage. But she feared for the future and what it might bring down upon all of their heads.

Chapter 46

Lydia sat staring at her hands lying in her lap, trying to regain the sense of control and happiness with which she had started her day. Lizzy's visit had disturbed facts and truths which Lydia preferred to remain buried and ignored. Her position, she knew, was certainly precarious. Should Wickham decide not to honour their marriage, he could remove all assistance and disappear in a moment; and with what consequence for her? He had had little remorse about breaking many other commitments in the past, not repaying debts, fleeing from creditors in the middle of the night, so why should his marriage vows be any different? She had assured Lizzy that she and Wickham would fashion their future for themselves – but what did that mean, exactly?

She looked about the parlour and realised that everything could so easily be taken from her if she did not begin to make sure it would not. Her talent at the gaming tables was small comfort; it assured her of some increase in her meagre allowance from her family and Wickham, but it could not be regularly relied upon, especially now that everybody was about to leave Town for the rest of the Summer, rendering such opportunities limited, at best, until their return.

And then what? With no parties, no friends, no Denny?

Denny! Oh! He, too, was about to leave: for Brighton. She was not sure she could bear the loss of his regular visits and concerned attention. What would she do with herself, alone again in Brompton, until everyone returned next year?

She could go to the country, too, she supposed: to Longbourn, or Netherfield, or Pemberley; perhaps, even Rosings Park. She could make the rounds until she wanted to scream with boredom. No, that would not do. She was tired of the country and all its provincial problems and never-ending scenery.

So what *should* she do? Lydia sat thinking and planning and casting aside each idea until Mary knocked on the door, thinking to clean the grate.

"Beg pardon, ma'am; I thought you might 'ave already gone out. Is there anythin' you need, ma'am?"

Lydia straightened up and smiled briefly.

"No; thank you, Mary. I am on my way and will be gone until later this afternoon. Just leave me a cold plate for when I return."

Lydia donned her walking jacket and boots, checked the contents of her bag, admired her reflection in the mirror - relieved her eyes had quickly recovered after her crying outburst - and let herself out into the street. She would walk - how Lizzy would be surprised! - and settle some business that she should have dealt with long before this.

Meanwhile, Lizzy had returned to Darcy House in a sombre frame of mind, deeply troubled about her sister and the implications her intended behaviour had for everyone even slightly connected to the marriage. Not only the pair involved, but also each family member's importance and respectability in the world would be adversely affected by the couple's behaviour and included in their inevitable disgrace.

She quailed at the thought of telling Darcy about the content of their talk but knew she must apprise him immediately, before he set forth to attack Wickham once again. Certainly, it was not Lydia's wish for him to do so - she had made that clear enough - and, as Darcy had himself reflected, it was not anyone's business now other than the two involved: if Wickham and Lydia could agree on terms of behaviour for their marriage, who else had the authority to contradict them? Who else should intervene if they both were satisfied with the solution to what had turned into an unpleasant problem?

But Darcy would not be pleased. He would want to interfere even though he had vowed never to do so again; he would want to impress his own standard of behaviour upon them. Unfortunately, Lydia and Wickham would never behave to Darcy's, or anyone's standard. They never could, being the type of people they both were: selfish, opportunistic, unabashed, and profligate. They never would consider restraint or the feelings of others. With such people the usual expectations of polite society did not apply, and Lizzy grieved for them both. She knew how it would eventuate, foreseeing a never-ending procession of visits from Lydia seeking relief from the effects of such reckless living.

Lizzy imagined every kind of horror raining down upon Pemberley and Longbourn - this was too great a price for Darcy to have paid, indeed it was! - but he must be told the news without delay. She rose and went to his study, knocking gently before entering.

Lydia finished her business with the jeweller, very pleased with the price she had garnered for the necklace and earrings, and continued along past the Park towards Town. Walking had calmed and clarified her thoughts; her initial notion of confronting Wickham at his place of work had faded in favour of another, more effective attack.

She hailed a passing cab and instructed the driver before she had time to doubt herself.

"Take me to Edward Street, if you please."

"What number Edward Street, madam?" the driver enquired.

"Just take me to the end of the street; I will find my way from there."

She thought, hoped, she *would* be able to recognise the house she had visited in the dark of night last year, but could not be certain. It had not been her main object that evening to indelibly memorise all of the details of their visit, particularly not the details of the house, but hoped her memory would not entirely fail her when she arrived.

The cab drew up at the far end of the street and Lydia climbed down, feeling nervous now, not recognising it at all. Taking a deep breath, Lydia nodded to the cabbie and began a slow promenade along the street, surreptitiously glancing this way and that trying to remember just how far along she and Wickham had been when the cab had stopped.

Had it been this far? Or a bit further?

All the houses looked very similar and she realised she could not even remember what colour the front door was, or how many storeys there had been, or what had been in the front garden.

Oh! It was hopeless!

Lydia arrived at the end of the street and began her slow procession along the other side, feeling more and more uncomfortable with every step she took, absolutely convinced she was the object of interest to every person observing her from behind their drapes. She straightened her shoulders and steadied her breath.

Think! Where had the cab stopped that night?

There had been a streetlight directly in front of the door; that was certain, as Wickham had been very visible, even in the dark. She closed her eyes momentarily and reviewed the scene.

The maid opening the door ... a smart, blue door? No, dark green, that was it ... well kept, well painted; steps, yes; three steps to the door.

She looked around and saw what she had envisioned just a little further along from her. Nervously, she climbed the steps and pulled the bell. The loud clanging rang deeply within the house. Footsteps approached. The door opened and a smiling maid greeted her.

"Ah," Lydia stalled as she glanced past the maid's shoulder into the hallway and recognised the interior. *It was the right house!*

"Good morning. Is Mrs. Younge at home?"

"I will find out, madam. Please come this way. Whom shall I say is calling?"

"Miss Maria Lucas, of Bromley."

Lydia was shown into the same room she and Wickham had been hurriedly ushered into, although it was a great deal cheerier today than she remembered. But she had been so upset at the time, all she could focus on then was the couch, her tiredness, and Wickham and Mrs. Younge arguing.

The maid left and Lydia sat for a second, but sprang up immediately to prowl about the room, moving the objects on the mantelpiece and twitching the curtains.

What was she doing here? Wickham would never forgive her for this. It was a terrible idea. What could she possibly achieve? She should leave before Mrs. Younge arrived.

Lydia started for the door and had her hand almost upon it when it opened and …

… *Wickham* entered!

They both stared in astonishment at each other. Wickham looked behind him as Mrs. Younge followed, and the three of them waited for someone to break the shocked silence.

"Miss Maria *Lucas*, indeed!" Wickham eventually laughed under his breath, staring hard at Lydia.

"I told Polly she must have the lady's address wrong, even though I was confused as to why and how Miss Lucas had arrived on this doorstep in this part of London, and on her own. I thought it highly improbable it could be the same lady but wished to ensure her safety.

"But, instead, Julia, it is my wife who has come calling upon you, using her friend as a disguise. Perhaps we should enquire why."

Lydia's shock had not worn off as quickly as her husband's and she stood, rooted to the spot, her mind blank and a loud ringing in her ears. She could feel the colour had drained from her face and began to realise her hands were shaking. She felt sick.

What was Wickham doing here? He should be at work; he worked during the day. Is this where he came in the evenings, too?

Julia, at once seeing Lydia's distress, moved quickly and led her to the couch, arranging the cushions behind her, and ringing a small bell for the maid.

"Polly; bring a glass of water, as quickly as you can."

She removed Lydia's gloves and rubbed her wrists vigorously, anxiously watching for Lydia's colour to return.

She was so young - too young, no more than a girl - to be forced to deal with such a situation. This is what she had feared, had warned George about. It was too cruel, indeed.

Wickham watched with distaste and a growing unease.

What had Lydia intended to say to Julia in a private meeting? To warn her? To threaten her? And how had she found out about them?

Lydia sipped the water and began to regain some of her colour; the ringing reduced to a faint buzzing and her faintness subsided for the moment.

She immediately removed her hands from the ministrations of Julia, who retreated to the doorway.

"You want to ask *me* why, *Wickham*?" she hissed, "when you stand here yourself, in *her* house, as if you belong in it more than in your own? But perhaps I mistake your reasons for being here; perhaps we are in need of another *servant* already, are we, and you and your *friend* are arranging it, as you arranged for Mary? For I cannot imagine what other errand could *possibly* bring you back here after the way she treated us the last time."

Ah! So that is how she became aware. Wickham grimaced.

Julia felt her own colour draining away and opened the door.

"I shall leave you to discuss this in private." She left the room without a backward glance, closing the door quietly behind her and instructing the servants not to enter for any reason.

Wickham and Lydia glared at each other, neither wishing to speak the truth that was uppermost in their mind; to do so would open too many old wounds and force the re-examination of blame.

Eventually, Wickham moved across the room and stood by the window. Lydia watched him in silence, finding herself surprisingly calm and unmoved by being in his presence again, now she was over the shock.

"Yes, Wickham. I recently learnt from Mary that you had been one of the party who interviewed her; that you and *that woman* had agreed about her suitability and placement with us, and suddenly everything about your behaviour became unpleasantly clear. I have always suspected that she was more than a friend to you, and now I find my suspicions to be correct."

"So what was your purpose in hunting down Mrs. Younge, Lydia, since you claim to already know the truth? What was your intention, today, in coming here?"

"To confront her, to remind her that you are a *married man* with responsibilities and connections; that I had won you and she had lost and must leave you alone.

"I tried to believe that your disinterest in me and our marriage was a result of your full attention being given to your new position; that you were making a new start; that you fully intended trying to make our marriage work, until I heard that you were, once again, in the company of *that woman.*

"I *have* been working hard, Lydia, to make you comfortable, to ensure that you have more security than you had in Newcastle…"

"Then where is all of this *security* you have been earning for *my* comfort, as you claim? Why should I believe anything you say? I have seen nothing more than my usual allowance in all these months and enjoyed even less of your attention.

"And now I know why. Now I fully understand why I have been left to my own devices out in Brompton, why you have only very rarely spent time in your own house when I find you here, appearing as the gentleman of *this* house. It is unspeakably cruel to treat me this way, Wickham."

She had thought she had missed him, had wanted him back at home, but his sudden re-appearance here merely inflamed old animosities against his treatment of her since their marriage.

"I see now how foolish I was, was not I, Wickham, to believe that you could ever change? That I could make you love me as I loved you? That you would ever honour a commitment that did not suit you or that interfered with something that suited you more? Why should I expect it when I have seen abundant proof of your carelessness for every other thing, and every other person?

"But I have always foolishly chosen to ignore the truth, believing that eventually you would see the error of your ways; that my love would soften you and you would learn to love me, too. And you did seem to manage such an alteration, for a while at least, in Newcastle, where we were happy for a time, were not we, Wickham?"

Wickham nodded reluctantly.

"But now it is abundantly clear I am the unwanted and inconvenient wife for whom you have never felt any affection …" she broke off as her emotions overwhelmed her.

Wickham watched from the safety of the window and spoke quietly.

"Let us not re-write history, Lydia. You may have won me in marriage, as you say, but Julia never lost my love and affection. Remember, please, the reason we left together from Brighton. It might have been in your mind that it was for affection - love even - or that it was within your power to make it so, but we both know the reason for our flight and the reason for our marriage. Neither had anything to do with love on my part, and you knew it perfectly well at the time; but, as you say, you wished it to be so, and so it eventuated. Marriage to you was never what I intended."

"*Oh!* You cannot blame everything upon *me* and *my* choices, Wickham. You say you had - have - no feelings for me; therefore, you used me abominably for your own pleasure. Why should not I have thought there was some affection involved after our first night together? You are contemptible, *despicable*, to make use of a young girl and pretend something that was not true." Lydia broke down entirely and sobbed without restraint.

Wickham remained where he was, in fear of any sign of compassion or remorse being misconstrued. He felt anguish at Lydia's pain but knew the matter, for so long buried and ignored, must be resolved.

Eventually Lydia regained a modicum of composure; she drew a few juddering breaths and wiped her eyes. There was a long silence broken only by the distant noises in the street and at the back of the house. The effect was dreamlike: such high emotions being played out against such everyday sounds. Lydia imagined she had only to walk across to Wickham and he would laugh and take her in his arms as he once had been pleased to do, claiming it all a joke and how foolish she was being to be so taken in. She could not really believe that their year together had been such a lie, that everything they had spoken, everything they had endured had been an act, an act for which he had the entire script and she only her very limited part; that he had only been waiting to return to this place, this house, this woman whom he had loved all the time.

She glared at Wickham, hating him for his aloofness.

"So what are we to do about this situation, Wickham? For I cannot continue, knowing how you feel about me and our marriage. I have assured my sister of our discretion, but something must be decided upon."

"You have discussed this with your sister? To what purpose, other than to cast aspersions upon me?"

Lydia shook her head at his selfish concern. "A persistently absent husband is a difficult thing to explain away with any degree of success. My sister has twice now found me alone in Brompton and been apprised that my most constant companion in Town is not my husband. What is she supposed to think or ask in such a situation as it pertains to her sister's welfare?"

"I have no intention of leaving you without support, Lydia, you have my word on that. My work will provide sufficient funds for your comfort if you agree to live in a modest manner, but anything more intimate cannot be expected of me, as you have surmised. I agree with you that there is no benefit in prolonging this situation and pretending what is not true.

"It is not unusual, no longer shocking, that a husband and wife who do not share similar interests find them elsewhere. Indeed, if you consider it, there are probably a great many more who do not, than do get along with each other.

"I believe we must become one of those couples, Lydia, and manufacture a marriage that will not shock the general populace but will afford us some freedom to follow our own hearts and minds. We have been forced into a situation which will not work, and therefore, we must work around it as best we can to both our satisfaction."

After the first loud outbursts, Julia, who was lingering in the hallway desperate to know what was being said and decided in her parlour, heard nothing more troubling in the next hour than the murmur of voices and the occasional sound of boots crossing the floor.

At least they were managing to be civil to each other, she thought, but her heart really did go out to Lydia; she had forgotten just how young and immature the girl was and knew she would have a very hard life if left alone to fend for herself. But she and George had already discussed what should be done to assure Lydia's security and reputation, and if she agreed to the terms, then they would all be able to live their separate lives amicably enough.

But would George manage to persuade her? And would her family countenance such an arrangement? It was a nervous wait, indeed.

Chapter 47

Elizabeth had found Darcy in his study upon her return from Brompton, immediately apprising him of the extent of her sister's situation and intentions. After assuring him again that Lydia had promised to be as discreet as she could manage, Lizzy finally became aware that Darcy's attention was not entirely focused upon her tale. Unusually, he was not already striding the length of the room, grim of feature, plotting such actions as would make some impression upon the couple in question about the seriousness of their situation. Upon her news he bestowed only the slightest grimace and actually *shrugged*. Lizzy was astonished.

"My dear? You have heard what I said? That Lydia intends upon continuing with her activities and refuses to bow before society's rules? You did hear me, did not you?"

Darcy sighed and nodded.

"Yes, my dear, I heard." He thought a moment as he fingered a paper on his desk, and then continued.

"And, really, why should she not, Elizabeth, married as she is to such an ungrateful scoundrel? She is still very young; she has been married for less than a year and is already unhappy with her situation. Why should she suffer, when he does not intend to?

"It seems that such behaviour being exhibited by at least one member of one's family is almost common-place, almost a requirement these days – I have seen and heard the evidence amongst many of my acquaintance here in Town – it is no longer shocking to anyone. If you require any further proof, look to our own royal family. Perhaps we should embrace being included in the growing fashion of endorsing disgraceful behaviour in one's relatives.

"But it seems there is nothing more for us to do, as I have already said. I have spoken to Wickham many times about his behaviour: you have spoken to your sister, also. She is Wickham's problem now and he, hers. It is a waste of time trying to convince them to behave otherwise, as we have both discovered, and I, for one, wash my hands of the matter. As long as he maintains his side of the agreement we struck, continues to provide for her security as he should, there can be little actual damage done to us and our respectability from their actions. They must be endured as a minor disturbance on the distant periphery of our world. Trouble yourself no longer about the situation, my love, for neither of them will do so."

He changed his tone as he waved a letter before Elizabeth's astonished face and then replaced it upon his desk.

"Unfortunately, as you can tell, Wickham and your sister's behaviour is the least of my worries right now, as you shall soon understand."

Lizzy leant forward, recognising the determined stroke of pen that had written it.

"Lady Catherine?"

"Lady Catherine," he nodded.

"And what displeases her now, might I enquire?"

Darcy pursed his lips and scanned the page once again.

"Oh, merely that she is incredulous that I should have entertained such a notion as approving any person with the name of *Sudbury* as a sensible choice for her daughter, and a person in *trade*, as well – she underlines that word, as you can see. She accuses me of interference, as well as, confusingly, *negligence*, by encouraging Anne to make an alliance which she never would have made if she, Lady Catherine, had been here to prevent it."

"Well! I thought she had improved her attitude towards those who must work for their living. Colonel Fitzwilliam will soon be one of their number, assisted by contacts *she* provided. She cannot consider him and his kind an inferior alliance, surely?

"Poor Anne! But her claim is true in part: if Lady Catherine *were* here, Anne certainly would not have been allowed out of her sight, never mind make *unsavoury* new acquaintances. But pray, continue: of what else does your aunt accuse you?"

"Well, that is the general substance of the letter but she also declares she will never agree to receiving Sudbury at Rosings however much Anne may press for it, or however much I might approve of him. I fear she has regressed back to her previous character. Anne and Sudbury must fight their own battle and prove her wrong, themselves." He rubbed his face wearily.

"But what else does she have against him, other than being shocked by the news her daughter might actually be the object of attraction for a gentleman, in business or otherwise? Surely Lady Catherine cannot wish Anne to remain alone all her life? Such an outright refusal rather gives the impression of jealousy or fear of being left alone on your aunt's part, and it does not become her to be so self-absorbed. I hope she re-examines her reasons carefully and considers her daughter's happiness before her own selfishness."

"You are right, of course, and I, too, hope she will reconsider her stance, but this letter is also not my most pressing concern at the moment, either. There is an even greater problem than this which reared its head only this morning. I tell you, Elizabeth; our return to Pemberley tomorrow cannot come quickly enough for me. Town has far too many difficulties and dramas which never occur in the country."

Elizabeth smiled archly at him.

"Really, my dear? *Never?* Are you quite sure of that?"

He returned her smile. "Well; perhaps sometimes drama occurs in the country, too, but far less frequently. I feel positively besieged today by matters of the heart and its complications."

"That is unfortunate indeed, and you so experienced in that capacity! Tell me; what else concerns you, my dear? It is hard to believe that there can be something more worrying than my sister's imminent disgrace and your aunt's displeasure. You are besieged, indeed!"

Darcy smiled for a moment and then shook his head.

"No, Elizabeth; I assure you, you will not laugh at this. Fitzwilliam called upon me this morning."

"Oh!" Elizabeth searched his face to divine what had taken place. That gentleman had been conspicuous by his absence since her illness. His re-appearance and Darcy's grim reaction to it could only bode trouble.

"He requested my permission in the absence of your father, to call upon Kitty to improve her opinion of him. He claims they have met several times in the Park and believes himself to be favourably regarded already by your sister."

Elizabeth leant back in the chair and emitted a most unladylike "Pah!"

"The last I heard of *that* matter was from Jane who assured me Kitty showed no interest in him other than as a friend of the family. I believe I can state without error that she has *not* encouraged his attentions or even particularly noticed them. Is he quite sensible, do you think, to continue with this one-sided pursuit? She is barely seventeen, and has experienced nothing of life as yet. I will not have her dazzled by the first attention she gets, believe herself in love, and then live to regret it. But what of his prospects? Surely he cannot already be settled and able to think of taking a wife?"

"I think not; but he assures me he is on the verge of something - although I could not induce him to be explicit – and believes he will be in a position in a few years to provide a decent life for Kitty."

"And why would she have any reason to wait that long for his future to develop into something? As you have already said, my dear, she is an attractive young lady and there will be many other opportunities. Let me speak with her and discover whether I am right in my estimation, Darcy. There is no need for you to concern yourself with this.

"How did you respond to his request, by the way?"

"I said I would enquire into the state of her affections – which I have now done; and inform your father – which I shall leave for you to do when you get to Longbourn, as he is the one whose approval must be obtained if Fitzwilliam is in earnest. I also informed Fitzwilliam of our departure tomorrow and he seemed to regret the immediate loss of her company. But I have seen him like this before, which is what worries me if there is any feeling on Kitty's side. The separation from his object will soon cause *him* to recover and forget as he has done in the past.

"I would not make any great enquiries, my dear; I suspect all will blow away once she is removed from his sight and mind and others have taken her place. And if I am wrong, then, fortunately, your father must deal with it."

Lizzy found Kitty carefully folding her new dresses into tissue paper in preparation for their descent into the trunk standing at the foot of her bed. Her sister appeared slightly melancholy, merely lifting her eyes to Lizzy before returning to her task. Elizabeth smiled at her and took a seat on the bed. She waited for Kitty to say something, but the silence continued.

"Are you looking forward to seeing Mamma and Father and Mary again, Kitty? How much you shall have to tell them!"

"Yes, I shall. Mamma will be interested but neither Mary nor Father will bother to listen for long; no one gives me the slightest attention there. I fear Longbourn will be very quiet after all that I have seen and done these past months. I am not sure I shall like the solitude again very much, Lizzy. I wish I could continue on to Pemberley with you and stay. Jane and Mr. Bingley are very kind when I visit Netherfield but the sisters terrify me; I never know what to say or do. They make me very uncomfortable."

"That is something upon only you can work, my dear. But I should not concern yourself with their manners or attitude now you have seen how true gentlemen and ladies behave. However, I shall be staying for a week's visit, as you know, long enough to see you settled back comfortably into your own life.

"It does not do to stay away too long, you know, or you shall forget where you belong, Kitty. Remember: all your friends and family are there and have missed you – aunt Phillips will be delighted to have you home again and will certainly pay great attention to your stories, as will Maria Lucas, you know they will. And then, before you know it, you will have the Assembly Rooms open again and other house parties and you shall be as gay as ever before. We do not have such easy access to company at Pemberley, I can assure you. We are a great deal quieter than Meryton and you should feel it after a very short while and wish you were home again."

Kitty gathered together a glimmer of a smile which disappeared immediately as she turned away.

"Kitty? Kitty, my dear, what troubles you? Tell me? There is something more than concern about leaving the excitements of London."

Kitty reached into her trunk and pulled out a letter which she carefully unfolded but refused to pass to her sister. She found the passage and read:

"You have been too cruel and selfish, Kitty, ignoring my needs in favour of your own amusements. You know how I have wanted your company, how alone I have become here in Brompton, but never a word or a visit other than that first one, which I could have done without, as all that brought was the attack from my sisters. And using our sisters' rules as an excuse for never visiting is merely a device so you did not have to consider my feelings or your conscience. And now, of course, you are to return to Longbourn and our old friends and I shall be left here with nothing and no one. Well, we shall see what I shall do since my whole family refuses to help me. I shall do as I please and not care about any of you, either. Then see how you all shall feel."

Kitty refolded the letter. "You see, Lizzy, I should have been allowed to visit her – I wanted to visit her, for a day or so perhaps – and now she thinks I no longer care about her. But it is also true that I was perfectly happy not to go, preferring others' company and the amusements offered by them, than having to agree with Lydia's ideas and plans as I always have. But now she is angry and sad that I am leaving without having paid a proper visit. I do not know what to do; she seems so unhappy."

Elizabeth fought down the urge to relay everything she knew about Lydia's state of mind and marriage: instead, she stood before Kitty and held the hand still twisting the folded paper.

"You must remember Lydia's nature, Kitty. You know very well that she says things in an unguarded manner: what she thinks, she speaks or writes in the next moment. She has no concept of hurting your feelings, merely that she wished to make *hers* known. There was no reason for you to visit regularly, and to have done so would have constricted *her* enjoyment of life as well as your own. Please believe me when I tell you that Lydia, contrary to what is stated in her letter, has already begun forging a new and amusing life for herself, a life she would not have been able to embrace if she had had you as her constant guest. She certainly has no interest in returning to the country any time soon, of that I am certain, regardless of her protestations. And when she threatens to do as she pleases; well, tell me: when has she not?

"Now: no more worrying or feeling guilty about Lydia. Lydia is very well where she is and will always make the most of her situation once she works out how. Come; let me help you with this dress. Is not it the one you wore to our dinner party last month? The one Colonel Fitzwilliam admired so much?"

Kitty flushed and turned away.

"Oh, do not say such a thing, Lizzy. He is a very charming gentleman, to be sure, but he is very old is not he? Eight-and-twenty at least, and without any proper business behind him. He would keep mentioning his business interests in the City and how they were progressing, as if any of it were of concern to me! I tried to show some interest and understanding, but I am sure he would have been better off discussing such things with Mr. Darcy. And he was always appearing in the Park on our drives - to ensure our safety I suppose - but Mr. Jardine or

Mr. Sudbury were already there and so his attention was quite unnecessary, I thought. Anne believed his interest to be for Georgiana and her enjoyment in London this time. I understand, although I was not completely apprised, that her previous visit was not as pleasant for one reason or another."

Lizzy hugged her sister tightly, delighted at her innocence and disinterestedness.

"I am sure he was, Kitty. He is her guardian, after all, and should take her happiness seriously. And I am glad you tried to show an interest in his business ventures; gentlemen like to be able to discuss matters that are important to them with ladies they admire. Perhaps he found an encouraging listener in you, my dear?"

"I doubt that very much and I certainly did not *encourage* him, and he does not admire me, Lizzy, or I should hope not anyway. I am much too young for him and he, too old for me. I am sure no such idea ever entered his head."

"No, no, indeed not. You are quite right, Kitty. There! Is that everything? My goodness, your trunk is quite overflowing! How fortunate you have been. Mamma will be quite green when she sees your new dresses and how well they all become you."

Lizzy walked away from that meeting happy in the knowledge that she could inform both her husband and father that any idea of a romantic attachment between the Colonel and Kitty was a figment of that gentleman's imagination only; that Kitty would not be devastated by the loss of a lover she had no notion of having, and it would be a sensible idea never to mention his feelings to her. The Colonel - Lizzy agreed with Darcy's prediction - would very soon recover from his imagined feelings and quite probably immediately direct them elsewhere, and that would put an end to the uncomfortable situation he had created through his foolishness.

Chapter 48

It was with a distinct sense of relief that Elizabeth followed Georgiana and Kitty down the front steps and into the waiting carriage. Darcy was already there watching the final packages and bags being brought out, his horse tied to the front railing. Mrs. Reynolds and Grant were scurrying about ordering this and that be put here and there, and the coachman and driver checking the ropes were knotted securely about the trunks on the roof.

The morning was still cool but had the threat of unpleasant heat as had been endured for the last several days and everyone was glad to be leaving it behind. London was no place to be in the middle of Summer.

Elizabeth settled herself in a corner seat and leant back against the cushions; she still had to become accustomed to having everything done for her and felt slightly uncomfortable in her role as lady of the house: the instigator of events but not the contributor to their implementation. But how pleased she was to be leaving London, the heat and smell notwithstanding, for although there had been many pleasant occasions, there had been just as many, if not more, unpleasant ones and she relished the notion that once back in the country, her life would revert to its former orderly tranquillity.

It was nonsense, of course, as many of the troubling matters of their London stay would easily follow them wherever they went, country or no, but the idea was very appealing to someone who had had her fill of excitement and novelty. The anticipation of taking a long walk through Pemberley Woods was almost unbearable, knowing as she did that more than a week should have to pass before she could allow herself that pleasure again.

Longbourn loomed and cast its mood over hers. How should she find it, returning there after so long away? How should she manage her mother's garrulousness after living without it for so long?

Fortunately, Darcy, who had intended leaving her and Georgiana and continuing North alone rather than withstand the onslaught of his mother-in-law, had agreed to keep them company after Bingley's invitation to be their guests at Netherfield; he believed he would be able to manage the minimum of meetings if spaced widely enough for recovery after each attack. Lizzy was very glad, for his kindness and his presence; they had been apart too much and she wished to keep him close for as long as possible.

Finally, the coach lurched out into the street and, with the quick clip-clopping of the horses' hooves, Lizzy felt her heart immediately begin to rise. She leant forward to watch the now-familiar streets and houses and early walkers pass by and then sat back with a smile of satisfaction.

The girls were equally quiet, watching the passing scenes, but not with as great satisfaction as was she, she knew. They did not have any great delight in returning to the quiet of the country, family or no, and they would miss the excitement and freedom they had enjoyed the past months. They had said very fond farewells to Anne the previous day once she had been packed into the Barouche box that was to carry her back into Kent, all promising to write and voicing the hope they would meet again very soon. Those friendships, at least, had been a great success for all concerned; each young lady had benefitted from them in their own way and improved themselves as a result. Kitty, in particular, seemed to have grown in elegant composure in response to her companions' example and Lizzy hoped the effect would remain with her sister and not be weakened once she was again under the influence of her mother.

But *Lydia!* Oh! Lizzy cast her mind over her youngest sister's unhappy circumstances and sighed. It troubled her to know that despite everything Lydia had desperately tried to attain, she had been foolish enough to believe that love could be stolen or forced. She had certainly learnt at a very young age that life and expectations can turn out very differently from what you imagined or hoped for. But, as Darcy had said, there was nothing more to be done about it, and she determinedly turned her mind to other, more pleasant prospects.

By the time the carriage entered Meryton, Elizabeth was so uncomfortable with sitting and being jogged about that she knocked on the roof to stop the driver. Darcy drew up alongside and looked in.

"My dear? We are almost there, surely you can see that?"

"Well, naturally I can," she answered as she opened the door and climbed stiffly out. "I need some exercise and fresh air. I will walk from here, as I have done many times."

Darcy looked perplexed for a moment and then asked, "Would you like some company on this walk, or would you prefer to be alone, my dear?"

She smiled at him and planted a quick kiss on his cheek.

"I have no objection to company if it is someone whom I adore and will offer me his arm when the path becomes steep or slippery!"

Darcy handed the reins to one of the coachmen and offered his arm to Elizabeth, much to the astonishment of every other person in the party, and many on the street. Kitty and Georgiana laughed together as the carriage continued onwards and they looked back to see their brother and sister in the most intimate embrace before turning towards the lane that led to Netherfield.

Jane's astonishment was the equal to everyone's when the carriage arrived without her sister and Darcy but she understood the reason easily enough; in Lizzy's condition, a long journey would be very uncomfortable and exercise the best remedy. While they waited for their dilatory guests, she showed Georgiana to her room and left her happily settling into it, and then spoke to Kitty.

"I have not had a room prepared for you, Kitty, as Mamma is expecting you at Longbourn at any minute. I had enough trouble convincing her that Lizzy would stay here but she insists that you return home immediately. Charles has arranged a carriage to take you as soon as you feel rested enough."

Kitty looked downcast for a moment and then recovered herself.

"I shall wait until I know Lizzy has arrived and then say my goodbyes for today. But I shall be here every day, Jane, whilst they are here. I have had such a wonderful time in London, I do not want it to end. But everything must, I suppose."

"You should be very grateful that you have so many experiences at such a young age, Kitty. Other than Lydia, none of us have had the advantage of such entertainments and new acquaintance so far outside our limited sphere. Yes, indeed; all good things must come to an end or how else should we appreciate them?

"But I have arranged for a dinner party tomorrow night once everyone has recovered from their travels, and all of our friends will be there. You shall have Maria Lucas to impress with your stories, Kitty, so do not be too down-hearted; life in the country is not as unvarying as you fear. There shall be some amusements."

And the conversation around the dinner table that evening was of the type as can only be enjoyed when true friends and close siblings are gathered, people who have many interests in common and a clear understanding of each other's character.

Elizabeth and Jane were delighted to have each other under the same roof once again, allowing them their old intimacy which, even in London where they had seen each other regularly, had not been entirely possible. Darcy and Bingley also felt the pleasant companionship of long acquaintance and talked long into the night about their lives, loves, responsibilities, and hopes for the future.

The next morning, Lizzy pulled on her boots and light jacket and, with slippers in a bag, set out for Longbourn. Again, she had refused all offers of a carriage, preferring to re-trace her old paths and enjoy the familiarity of her surroundings. She approached the front door of Longbourn and noticed an unusual quiet where there had always been loud laughter, shouts, and the banging of doors emanating from its interior. Pulling the bell, she wondered if anyone was at home. Immediately, a beaming Hill ushered her into the parlour where her mother rose with dramatic effusion to greet her.

"My dear, *dear*, daughter! Oh, *Lizzy*, how I have missed you, and how annoyed I was with Jane when she quite insisted upon your staying at Netherfield as if we have not enough room here, but she would not be moved. Her determination to get her own way has certainly increased and I am not sure I like such a change in her. But I suppose she must be strict now as mistress of Netherfield, as must you be, although not many would try to cheat you, Lizzy, of that I am certain. But have not you brought *dear* Mr. Darcy and his sister to visit?" She looked at Lizzy's bag and then down at her feet.

"Surely you did not *walk* all the way here, Lizzy? What will Mr. Darcy think if his wife insists upon walking everywhere, getting all dusty and over-heated? Surely he cannot approve? You must stop this perverse nonsense, Lizzy, and behave as your situation demands."

"Mamma!" Lizzy kissed her mother and took a seat. "I am glad to find you well. Please do not concern yourself. Darcy has no complaint about me walking – indeed, he accompanied me last evening from Meryton to Netherfield when I wished for some exercise. It is not unladylike to walk, you know, and sitting tires me far more than any long walk ever could.

"Mary; you look very well. How does your music improve? I look forward to hearing it this evening at Jane's, if you would be so kind."

Mary blushed. "I should hope I have improved somewhat from what you might remember, Lizzy, merely due to the fact that our life here is so quiet that I must do something to occupy my time. I have also expanded my reading, upon Father's advice, which adds to my daily routine. And, of course, Mamma and I have many hours together doing our work, as you see."

Lizzy suffered a momentary pang of guilt at her sister's words; how dreadful to only have those three things to look forward to every day, and one of them enduring their mother's company and complaints. But Mary had always been a solitary creature, never making friends, preferring her music and books to society, and so Lizzy presumed that her lot was not as onerous as first feared. Mary's situation as a companion was a sensible choice for someone who wanted nothing more than to educate herself in her own way, and feel she was doing good by offering her companionship.

"Oh, indeed, yes. Mary is quite right: we have been very quiet here without Lydia and you and Kitty, of course. Tell me; how is my *dear* girl? Is she making the most of being in Town? I am sure she is; and a house all of her own, too! Quite grown-up and sophisticated; I dare say we should not recognise her. And dear Mr. Wickham? Is he happy in his new position? Does he make a success of it? Well, naturally, we were very surprised to learn he had left the military, but he is much better than that, so charming and genteel, much better suited to life in the City rather than hidden away up North. I told Mr. Bennet, there was no need to send him so far away and deprive us of our daughter's company – not that I accuse Mr. Darcy of any bad intentions, you understand – but both of them are much happier in lively company and I am sure there was none of that in Newcastle. But now they are in Town, and there they are to stay, are not they? How happy Lydia must be. I do wish she would write more often – we have heard only twice since she has been there, you know –

I am desperate to hear her news. I get so little of it now, there is barely enough to interest me."

Elizabeth allowed her mother to run on until she had exhausted all of her complaints and then smiled. "Lydia is quite happy in her new situation, I believe, Mamma. It is, perhaps, not everything she imagined it to be, but as she always manages to do, she has begun to fashion her own life there, one that pleases her and her interests."

Kitty had quietly entered as Lizzy was speaking and she darted a questioning look at her words. Lizzy calmly gazed back at her sister, impressing her with that gaze that this was the story to be told about their sister, and Kitty imperceptibly nodded her agreement.

"Oh!" Mrs. Bennet sighed in delight at her imagination of Lydia's happiness. "Well, naturally, not everything can turn out as one expects but Lydia will always manage to make the best of things, to turn things to her advantage. She gets that talent from me, you know; I always manage to do so and it is a trait worth developing for there is no use in complaining if one makes no attempt to improve one's situation."

Her daughters all managed to suppress their smiles at their mother's interesting view of her capabilities to live her life without complaint. Mary rang the bell for tea while her mother continued on another tangent.

"Does Jane appear to have gained a little weight, to you, Lizzy? I certainly noticed it when she called yesterday; her jacket seemed strained and her face much rounder since she has been in Town. She has not mentioned anything but I sincerely hope it portends my first grandchild! What do you think? I know she must have spoken with you about it, intimate as you always are. I do not like to ask before she wishes to tell but I believe I can always guess at such a condition; I am never wrong." She smiled, nodding happily at the prospect as she glanced about the room at her daughters.

"*Mamma!* I am glad you have not enquired. Jane would be mortified if she knew you were discussing such things in public."

"Oh, la, Lizzy! Where is this *public*, might I enquire? We are her family; we are not *public*. I should hope I know enough not to discuss such things *in public*. But, answer my question, Lizzy; is Jane with child or not? I am sure I am right."

Elizabeth drew breath whilst hoping her mother had not noticed her own weight gain.

"That is a question for Jane, in private, Mamma, and I refuse to speculate on so personal a matter. If she wishes to tell anything, she will tell of it in her own good time. But I would advise against broaching this with her; she will not like to be pressed as you should know."

"Oh well; if she does not care about her mother's feelings, then I suppose I must keep my suspicions to myself."

"And you, young lady," she turned her eye upon Kitty who had donned one of her new day dresses, "need not imagine that you may keep up your London ways here. Why are you wearing that dress, pray? It is far too good for daytime use; go and put on something less pretentious, if you please. No one needs your fancy outfits here, or is impressed by them. One of your old dresses will do very well."

Kitty flushed to the roots of her hair and began to rise when Lizzy interrupted.

"Nonsense, Mamma, Kitty looks very well in her dress and it was bought for just such use. It would be a waste to leave it in the closet and then find she had outgrown it. She must make good use of it while she can, for next year the fashions will have changed as will her size. Sit down, Kitty; Mamma will become accustomed to your new wardrobe soon enough."

"*Well!* I see I am to be over-ruled in my own house, now. I am not one of your servants, Lizzy, to whom you give orders and expect your every instruction to be carried out without complaint. There is no need for Kitty to make such a show of herself, and Mary here, still in her old gown of several years' wearing. I merely wish to treat all my daughters with equality, without favouritism, that is all."

"Really, Mamma? Is this a new trait you have developed in my absence? I am glad to learn of it but your favourite daughter of times past might not approve of having to share your affection, *equally*. It is as well that she is happily ensconced in her new life and unaware of your transition of feelings, and the dilution of them amongst her four siblings."

Mrs. Bennet worked to calculate her daughter's meaning before giving it up, fortunately being interrupted by the tea-tray's arrival.

"I do not know to what specifically you are referring, but I insist that Kitty not make her sister feel inferior. Mary has been my sole comfort since you all have left me and I will not have her made to feel self-conscious."

"Well, I am glad you think so highly of Mary's company, as you should. Perhaps Kitty should return with me to Netherfield? That would solve all of your concerns and I know Jane would be more than happy to have her, new dresses and all."

"*No!* I see no call for that; what nonsense. Kitty will remain here, with us, where she belongs, but she must remember her place, too." Mrs. Bennet pouted.

There was silence as the tea was poured and handed around, which continued far longer than ever Lizzy could remember her mother managing. Kitty kept her eyes downcast, and Lizzy knew how much she wanted to return with her to Jane's, but it was not to be; not yet anyway. Kitty must learn to endure what she and Jane had long endured. It would be instructive at least in reminding her of better manners and conversation to be had elsewhere.

Finally, Mrs. Bennet put down her cup and eyed Lizzy with disapproval.

"Marriage appears to suit you, at any rate, Lizzy. You appear to be quite content. I suppose all is very *easy* in the Darcy household, is not it? Your father mentioned how pleasant Pemberley is, and your aunt Gardiner *sings* its praises every time she writes. I am sure I should enjoy it just as much, should I ever be given the opportunity to do so."

"Yes, Mamma," Lizzy smiled. "Marriage is certainly everything I wished and hoped for, and much more. I consider myself the luckiest woman in the world to be loved by a man such as my husband. We understand each other perfectly already and he is the kindest, most endearing man I have ever met. I could not wish for a better partner in life."

"Yes, well," her mother stared at her and sniffed, "let us hope that such felicity continues a while longer, for it cannot last as long as you might wish it to; it never does. But if you understand each other, then everything will fall into place to the satisfaction of you both."

Lizzy merely smiled and asked to be excused to go to her father with whom she wished to speak. Kitty looked desperate at being left alone with her mother and sister but Lizzy ignored her mute pleas and went to the book-room. She knocked gently and entered.

"Lizzy! My dear. I had no idea you were here, so engrossed am I in this latest addition to my library." He embraced her with vigour and asked after everyone with more than his usual interest.

After the preliminaries were dealt with, and she had warned against her father accepting any advances towards Kitty by Colonel Fitzwilliam, Lizzy then turned to the troubling news about Lydia and Wickham. Her father had a right to know and would not over-dramatize it, as would her mother. He listened carefully and at the end put several questions to her to clarify some points. Then he leant back in his chair, finger tips together; a familiar pose when thinking hard about some problem or other.

"And it is Mr. Darcy's opinion that nothing should be done, you say?"

"It is all our opinions, including Lydia, that nothing should nor can be attempted. She and Wickham will decide on an arrangement to allow them both the freedom they require within the boundaries of their marriage. If he continues to support her, there is nothing with which we can argue, surely? It is a private arrangement between man and wife and not for others to interfere with."

"Well," Mr. Bennet shook his head sadly. "You mother must never know of it; she would not understand, she would not rest until I had done something, probably have brought Lydia home. I presume Lydia has no intention of spreading the news with her usual lack of restraint?"

'No, Father; I believe she has no intentions of that sort. She understands the damage it could cause, but, more importantly, does not wish anyone to consider her to have failed; she is sufficiently mortified upon that point at least to ensure her silence. She instructed me to relay a message that would most impress our mother and set her mind at rest, and that I have done, without any great falsehoods on my part."

"Then we shall leave it for now, Lizzy. But I will wish to discuss it with your husband and Mr. Phillips when next I get the opportunity."

Lizzy rose to leave and kissed him fondly.

"You will get that opportunity tonight, Father, after dinner at Jane's. But I am sure it will all work out for the best without our intervention."

Chapter 49

Wickham walked slowly back from Brompton, head down, oblivious to the evening crowds swirling around him. He had returned Lydia home in a cab and seen her safely to bed, instructing Mary to take great care of her mistress as she had had a terrible shock and needed a long rest. He had then packed a few more of his clothes into a bag before letting himself out into the warm evening. The moon was rising and a slight wind carried the faraway noises of the revellers in the Park as he passed by.

But to all of this he was unaware.

His heart was heavy; he had not wished to hurt Lydia, but as Julia had frequently advised, the agony was merely prolonged by not confronting her. Leaving her to guess, to become miserable and lonely was far worse than knowing the truth, and made him a coward. At least now she had no doubt about the truth of her situation, even though he felt like a cad of the highest order.

Once the shock had abated and the recriminations reduced to resignation, Lydia had grudgingly acknowledged her circumstances. Far from being able to intimidate Julia and rekindle Wickham's feelings back towards herself, Lydia now knew he was entirely lost to her in every sense other than in name and the purely monetary, an issue he had immediately addressed and increased to such a generous amount both of them privately wondered if he should be able to sustain it.

She had asked what she should say when enquiries were made about him; she had asked if he would ever come to visit her; she had asked if her freedom was the equal of his. To all of her questions he had answered with good will, expressing the hope she would endeavour to make a life of her own which she could enjoy and prosper in.

She had mentioned Denny and Wickham had conveyed his delight mingled with relief in knowing she had someone who took such a friendly interest in her. She had asked about her current living arrangements and he had assured her that everything would remain the same, for this year at least while Darcy was paying the expenses, and he hoped to be able to continue with it into the future, depending upon his circumstances.

She had vehemently voiced her opposition to being removed to a convenient cottage in the country: he was confident such an arrangement would not be necessary as long as she did not over-spend her allowance or bring unwanted attention to their situation. They had had the most intimate and instructive discussion of their marriage and it had been, revealingly, concerned only with continuing the façade of that marriage.

The carriage ride to Brompton had been silent. Lydia was utterly exhausted and Wickham no less tired, but it had been a silence of understanding, of acceptance of things as they were. He did not know how well the future would progress, but at least now the framework was established and he no longer had to live in fear of being discovered.

The worst had happened and they had both survived the ordeal.

However, the idea of her family's displeasure, of *Darcy's* displeasure was a constant worry: that they would insist he respect his marriage vows; that Darcy would immediately remove his assistance; that the law would somehow be invoked and brought against him for desertion, or worse, all created obstacles to their future plans. But Lydia had assured him that she meant to keep their new situation to herself and not reveal it to anyone as long as he stood by the bargain they had struck.

As long as you stand by the bargain we have struck, Wickham.

He had seen the glimmer of a challenge in Lydia's eye as she had said that and he knew she understood, perhaps, his future plans with Julia, of fleeing to another country, and wished to warn him against such a decision, leaving her without support. If she found out such a plan, he had no doubt she would bring the entire wrath of her whole family upon him.

But Wickham was not a man to dwell for too long on possibilities in the future over which he had no real control. He was free for the next year at least – the time Julia was planning to either return to America or expand her London businesses. He could relax a little until then and just enjoy being with the woman he loved once more without the accompanying guilt of avoiding and lying to Lydia.

By the time he had reached Edward Street, he was in a much more sanguine frame of mind and found himself able to impart the various issues discussed with Lydia in a very unemotional manner, assuring Julia of their complete security for the time being and his continued intent to improve in business and worth in her eyes.

Lydia, although completely drained emotionally from her distressing encounters with, first, her sister and then both Wickham and Julia, could not sleep. Her mind whirled, spinning from one statement to another, from one look or action to another, from one assurance to another. Upon whom could she rely, now? In whom could she place her trust? Not that she had ever entirely trusted Wickham, not even from the very beginning, but he had always appeared to have been hers alone. Now she knew with absolute certainty that he would choose Julia over her in any confrontation, in any disagreement. He would do what pleased *them* both and nothing that would interfere with *their* felicity. She could no longer pretend to have his support and must adjust her expectations accordingly.

She lay on her bed, their bed, a bed she had been so thrilled to see in their new home, and tossed and turned, casting about for her best next move. She could not gauge just how genuine Wickham had been in his assertions that she should have nothing with which to concern herself, financially; he had been quite adamant that she should be secure but, knowing him of old, she knew his words spoken in the moment to be a foolish illusion. Her only security was that he wished to keep their situation from Darcy, although that gentleman and her father would know already just from what Lizzy would have communicated to them upon her arrival at Longbourn. But Lydia hoped that all her family would respect her wishes, which Lizzy had also agreed to communicate, that they should not interfere with the decisions between husband and wife. Of course, that was before she had learnt the extent of her isolation and the prospect before her; that was when she imagined still having some sort of influence over Wickham.

Now, all that imagined power had evaporated in the space of an hour. There was nothing left.

The evening turned into night. She could hear the noises of the street, the shouts of laughter from the inn, the calls of friends, the cries of children and she lay there in the gathering gloom, lonely, afraid, and miserable. Even Mary had already gone to bed, otherwise Lydia would have called for something to drink; she could eat nothing, but thought she could manage some of the remaining wine.

She stumbled downstairs and lit a candle, hunting about for the bottle and a glass. One glass would restore her spirits and then, perhaps, she would be able to consider her next move. Fortunately, being young in body and mind, after taking only a few sips of the wine, she realised she had eaten nothing since breakfast and was ravenous. She then remembered leaving instructions for Mary to prepare her a cold plate which, to Lydia's great delight, that diligent girl had done.

There is nothing as soothing to the troubled soul as having access to the simplest and most ordinary of things, and Lydia found the modest meal satisfied more than her hunger. It reminded her that all was not as bleak as she had been thinking in her turmoil of the evening. She was still mistress of this house; she still had the protection of Wickham's name; she still had her income and the extra she could make from her games; she still had the affection of Denny, even though he had now left for Brighton, and his affection was not questioned by her husband – he had made that perfectly clear – and could continue without restriction if she so chose. The only thing that had changed in her life to date was that she now had irrefutable proof that she was on her own, rather than fearing it, fearing that Wickham loved another. While a bitter pill to swallow, it also brought relief as such pills often do, once the effect of their administration has been absorbed.

She pushed away the plate and poured herself another glass of wine. The food and wine were beginning to have the desired effect upon her active mind and she lay her head upon the table to rest, falling asleep right there, the candle burning low, flickering, guttering, then coughing itself out.

Silence and a modicum of peace finally reigned in the little house on Yeoman's Row.

Mary did her best not to disturb her mistress the next morning – she really did - believing her to have over-indulged once again judging by the half-empty bottle on the table. She tiptoed about the kitchen, easing the catch on the back door to go for the water and firewood.

Lydia slept on and Mary breathed a sigh of relief.

But upon her return, she realised that laying and starting the fire was going to be an impossible task, never mind the inevitable clanging and whistling of the kettle, and she reluctantly decided that her mistress must be awoken and sent to her proper bed immediately.

"Madam; Mrs. Wickham. You mus' go to your bed. You will be all over aches if you do not. Oh! Come now, madam. I will bring you some brea'fast when you call, and a powder. Now, off you go and le' me get on." She watched Lydia drag herself up the stairs and, shaking her head, set about her morning duties.

It was more than two hours before Mary heard anything from her mistress and she hurriedly poured the boiling water into the coffee pot and toasted the muffin she had waiting. She carried the tray upstairs and went straight into the bedroom.

To her surprise, Lydia was sitting up in bed, still fully dressed as she had been downstairs, and counting the contents of her little bag. She looked up as Mary entered and waved at her to bring the tray over.

"Mary," Lydia began as she took a great draught of the powder, "how should you like to become my lady's maid for a while? No cooking or cleaning, but taking care of my clothes as you already do, and being my companion when I should have need of one?"

"Well, I don' know, madam; I 'aven't been trained for such a position. I should not know what to do as a companion. An' I do ever'thin' else anyway. Why do you ask, madam?"

"Ah; because, Mary, I have an idea to leave London for the Summer and join my friends in Brighton. Unfortunately, Mr. Wickham will not be able to accompany me, busy as he is, but I cannot go alone. I should need someone to act as my maid-companion. There would be nothing terribly demanding for you to do; it is for appearances' sake only, you understand. But I should like it to be you as we know each other so well already, do not we? We could have such fun, just as I did last year; I could show you the sea and all the sights."

"*Brighton*, madam?" breathed Mary, her eyes shining. She had never been further than this corner of London in her entire life but understood that such foreign places were very exciting – even royalty went there to holiday.

Lydia smiled at the girl's enthusiasm and wished she could manage half as much on her own behalf. She recalled her own excitement last year when faced with a similar prospect; how innocent she had been, how easily amused, how eager to become part of it all. But this was no pleasure trip as had been the case last year: this was to be a working holiday, if it could be arranged.

But first she had visits to make to those of her new acquaintance whom she knew intended leaving soon, and see which one would be kind enough to include her in their party. She had no particular preference, there were several who would suit, who were wealthy enough to admit another person into their party without expecting remuneration of any kind other than amusing companionship, and that she was more than capable of providing.

She also rather thought she might write to Harriet Forster who still resided in Brighton. The last correspondence she had received from Harriet had been the news of the birth of the Forster's baby. Perhaps the Colonel would not be as against a visit from Lydia now that his wife had provided him with an heir; he might be inclined to show some gratitude by allowing Harriet to resume her old friendship, just a little.

She finished her breakfast and jumped off the bed.

"Come, Mary, get me ready for some important visits; my hair must be perfect, my clothes without fault. We have serious work to do, for our happiness and success this Summer depends upon it, I assure you!"

Chapter 50

"My darling," Darcy whispered in Lizzy's ear as he brushed a stray hair away from her cheek. "Elizabeth, dearest, wake up. I must leave soon." He kissed her forehead as she stirred and opened her eyes. They looked contentedly at one another and everything else disappeared for a while.

"Oh, why must you go, now? We were going to travel together, you promised, but there is Jane to consider, and Kitty who still holds great hopes of our relenting and taking her with us on to Pemberley. Why cannot you stay another day?"

"I have some business to attend to in Leicestershire and I can travel faster than the carriage. It is a minor separation, my dear, and one we must endure occasionally. You must stay and say goodbye to all your family and friends today and follow me tomorrow; indeed, it is entirely possible that we might arrive at Pemberley at the same time. I believe I have enjoyed more than my fair share of hospitality at Longbourn; it would be unseemly to take more and overstay my welcome." He smiled into her eyes and she laughed.

He had certainly been on his best behaviour: no caustic comments, no scowls across the dinner table, no abrupt departures, indeed nothing that could have caused her Mamma or aunt Phillips to consider their behaviour or opinions as unworthy of being shared in such company.

Of course, much of his time had been spent in the company of either Bingley, walking about Netherfield and giving him advice as requested or escaped with her father in the book-room at Longbourn where they both appeared to be improving their opinion of one another at a very pleasing rate. Elizabeth was delighted that her two favourite gentlemen had found shared interests and ideals.

"*Leicestershire*? Whom do you know in that county?" she yawned and reached for her shawl.

"No one, as yet, but I hope we *shall* know at least two people already very dear to us who will live not thirty miles away from Pemberley, if our business is successful today. Bingley comes with me – I forgot to mention."

"*Bingley* is going with you?" Elizabeth felt stupid with sleep. "But why, my dear?"

"We are going to see a house, an estate, actually – I caught wind of it in London – some men were discussing that the owner had fallen on hard times and was planning to put it out for lease. I made some enquiries, discovered which house and knew it immediately as something worthy of Bingley buying for his family estate, and have been discussing it with him these past days. He is determined to have it, if he is pleased with it and the owner can be persuaded to sell outright."

"*Oh!* Jane will be so happy if he can, and, of course, Caroline will be satisfied that at last her family will have a country seat. What house is it, my dear?"

"Brightwell Park: an estate comprising a fine well-proportioned building of fairly recent build with several farms, woods and a village. It is something of which Bingley could be rightly proud and I shall encourage him in the purchase if he likes it."

"And when shall we, Jane and I, be allowed to visit and offer our own opinion on its suitability, I wonder? I am sure Jane is as equally interested as Bingley and more practical. She will see things that two gentlemen would never notice. And I could certainly make a comment or two to help in the decision. Oh, why did not you mention this before? We could have been ready to go today."

"For those very reasons, my dear! Bingley and I shall make the preliminary investigation but nothing shall be final until Jane and you have both approved of it; there, will that pacify you?

Bingley might not like it, he might dismiss it out of hand and there will be an end to it for it has been some time since I have seen the property and it could be entirely run-down.

"You will see it soon enough, Elizabeth. Now go back to sleep and I will see you at home." He leant over her and kissed her gently but firmly, tucked the sheet around her shoulders and left the room.

She could hear his footsteps fading away down the hallway and a little later watched from the window as he and Bingley mounted their horses and trotted off down the drive. How she hated seeing him leaving her, but she had the entire Summer to keep him all to herself at Pemberley and she meant to do it, too.

"Well, Lizzy; leaving your poor father once again for the delights of Derbyshire, I suppose," mourned Mr. Bennet as he watched the preparations for the next day's travel progress under Elizabeth's eagle eye.

"I understand I might be losing Jane's company soon, too, if what Darcy tells me is correct. Never mind, I have no doubt that I am quite capable of manufacturing urgent reasons to draw me away from home into the North Country very soon and shall expect great hospitality from both of your houses, although I believe I shall retain my greater affection for Pemberley; this other estate in Leicestershire might not prove as pleasant."

"Father!" laughed Lizzy. "You know very well you are to visit as often as you please, and I know Jane will agree with me. But I believe you must allow Mamma to accompany you, at least once this year; she is all over jealous of her sister and you for your visits without her. She insists she will visit this Summer, just as soon as it can be arranged."

Her father looked at her with a grimace and retreated to his book-room while Elizabeth, smiling, continued with her preparations, checking all of her mother's orders and adjusting them accordingly.

Kitty watched the proceedings from the stairwell with a mournful eye, refusing to participate in anything.

"Well, do not just stand there, my girl," snapped Mrs. Bennet as she came through to check on the servants. "No one needs your pained expressions here. Go and visit Maria Lucas if you insist on being in the way."

"I am not in the way, Mamma," argued Kitty. "I am as far *out* of the way as is possible, if you notice. And Maria has a cold and does not wish for any visitors."

"Then go and see what Mary is doing and help her; make yourself useful at least. You will have to adjust to being back at home, dull as it may seem, I am sure, after your exciting life in London and all of the indulging that has gone on there. You need a touch of the everyday to bring you back to reality, I believe." She bustled out into the kitchen to check on the food being readied for the journey.

Lizzy watched her mother leave and then looked up at Kitty, but she had left the landing, probably to go and sulk in her bedroom. Lizzy shrugged and continued with her work. Their mother was right for once: Kitty could not expect her life always to be exciting and full of new experiences. And, she had no doubt, Kitty would soon be back at Netherfield, terrifying sisters notwithstanding, and would be one of the party when her parents chose to visit Pemberley, as had been threatened. Kitty's life thus far had certainly been a great deal more interesting than either Lizzy or Jane's had been at her age, and so Lizzy did not feel too much remorse at leaving her to her own devices in Meryton.

"In the way, indeed!" Kitty slumped into her chair and glared at a letter that had arrived for her only that morning, and, fortunately, due to the activity around the house which had completely engrossed her mother and sister, had been unnoticed by them. Lydia's sprawling handwriting blared out from the page but Kitty need not read it again - she had quickly understood its contents and its tone - but the question was: should she tell? Whom should she tell? Her sister's letter was alarming, alerting

Kitty to the possibility that all still was not quite as it should be with her sister's marriage.

...you must not be angry with me for my cruelty in my last letter, Kitty. I was upset and did not mean what I said, at all, and I am no longer angry at you or bored or lonely, you will be happy to hear. I have made lots of new and exciting acquaintance now and have been invited to go with one of them as her special friend to Brighton for the Summer! Wickham is so busy he rather thinks he will not be able to visit, even for the smallest time but is very pleased that I shall again be able to enjoy the sea air and all the entertainments on offer there, as London has become very quiet recently. But perhaps our family will not care to hear about my travels, disinterested as they all were while I was in Brompton, and so I should not bother them with the news unless you think it might be of interest as I know there are so few amusing topics to discuss at Longbourn...

Kitty tutted crossly and folded the letter into her book; she would say nothing unless Lydia was brought up in conversation. She was tired of her always being the centre of attention, even from afar, with her escapades and outrageous stories. No, Kitty would not broach the subject of her sister's whereabouts unless severely pressed to do so.

There is nothing quite as delightful as returning home after a prolonged stay away. As the carriage rolled through the green countryside and Lizzy started to recognise certain landmarks, her heart began to lift with happiness. The sun shone on the villages as they drove through, glancing off the ponds and roofs, and lighting up the hills. The sheer expanse of woodlands and meadows took her breath away after so many weeks of built-up streets and bustling city thoroughfares. She opened the window and listened to the bird song over the clatter of the carriage wheels, feeling the warm breeze on her face and smiled with anticipation. How wonderful it would be to wake every morning and know that the whole day lay ahead of her with its small demands and huge gifts. She smiled at Georgiana who was also viewing the scenery with satisfaction.

"And when did Mr. Jardine mention he was returning to the country?"

"Next week, I think he said. He had several calls on his time before then in Town but I believe he was rather anxious to leave as soon as possible."

"And shall we have the pleasure of his company at Pemberley this Summer, do you think?"

Georgiana blushed. "He asked if he might continue our friendship and I did not discourage him entirely; he is a pleasant companion and has taken a prodigious amount of interest in my entertainment whilst in Town both times I have visited. It would have been ungenerous to refuse him, would not it?"

"Indeed it would," Lizzy laughed. "But I was under the impression you had decided to wait a while before being interested in the qualities of various gentlemen. Has there been a change of heart, I wonder?"

Georgiana's colour rose even further and she merely smiled and looked away from her persistent sister's gaze.

Lizzy sank back into the comfortable upholstery of the carriage and allowed her mind to wander with general satisfaction over the various events that had occurred in the past six months, and to wonder what the next six would bring. If only Jane could be as close as thirty miles away from Pemberley, that would bring her the greatest joy. It had not been until their close proximity again in Town that she had realised just how much she had missed her sister's gentle advice and company.

The carriage entered the Park and Lizzy's spirits were in a high flutter as recalled her first ride along this same densely-wooded road in the company of her aunt and uncle only a year ago; how far away that memory seemed. She and Georgiana eagerly looked out to catch the first glimpse of the house and both sighed in unison as it came into view: the handsome stone building basking in the afternoon sunshine with the stream in front of the house already running low, and the windows all winking a welcome to the tired ladies. Of any human habitation, there was none to be seen and Lizzy's heart began to sink knowing that Darcy was still in Leicestershire or was following along the road some miles and hours behind them.

The carriage rolled over the small bridge and the front door opened. Mrs. Reynolds and Grant appeared, smiling and nodding as they waited. Lizzy fixed a smile on her face, allowing Georgiana to alight first, while gathering up her small bag and bonnet before accepting the hand of the driver and stepping from the carriage.

"Thank you," she murmured as she smiled ahead at Mrs. Reynolds, but glanced behind when her hand continued to be held in a firm grip.

"Welcome home, Mrs. Darcy!"

Darcy! How had he managed to evade being seen? Her happiness, relief, joy, contentment at his presence was obvious to all, and they were immediately left to their own devices as the rest of the servants and Georgiana went inside the house.

"Welcome home, my darling wife. I have been counting the hours, calculating the very minute your carriage should appear on the drive. It has been a tortuous day, I assure you!"

"Well, that was a torment of your own making, my darling man, and a just punishment for insisting on leaving me alone in favour of business. Were you at least successful in convincing Bingley about Brightwell? Please say you were. I cannot think of a greater gift than knowing my sister will be so close to us."

"Bingley approved of it, just as I knew he would. Not to say he is so complying that he has no opinion, but after my recommendation he was already pre-disposed to like it. He remains there still, in discussion with the owner, whom, I believe, will be more than happy to negotiate terms of sale, including some very fine furniture and paintings."

"Then Jane and I must view it very soon, my dear, just as you promised and before Bingley agrees entirely to take it. We must go there this week, perhaps? Oh! How delightful that will be.

"But we are here now, home again safe and sound, and other than a quick journey to Brightwell, here we shall remain. There is so much to do in the house, so much to prepare for the baby, that I cannot think but we shall have to remain here for the next year at least. I am afraid we shall be forced to content ourselves with the country's confined and unvarying company for which I know you have stated an aversion in the past."

"Surely not, my dear; I believe you quote me entirely out of context. You know well enough by now that I consider the country to be superior by far to the city, especially now you are one of the company.

"And, I understand, your mother is intent upon visiting this Summer. I think we shall have variation enough to suit us both."

They both laughed and walked happily, arm in arm, into their home.

While this work is entirely of the author's imagination, she would like to acknowledge the memorable characters created by Jane Austen as being the inspiration for writing this continuation of *Pride and Prejudice.*

Grateful thanks are also due to her primary proof-readers, Elyse Hill and Leigh Meggison, whose encouragement and detailed, thoughtful suggestions were warmly appreciated.

C. J. Hill is a high school English teacher and great admirer of Jane Austen's wit and social commentary. She has lived in England and Northern California, and now resides in New Zealand

Further information about the author can be found at:
http://amazon.com/author/cjhill
https://www.facebook.com/CJHillauthor
http://goodreads.com/CJHill
https://cjhillauthor.wordpress.com/

Readers interested in characters introduced in this novel such as Mr. Jardine and Julia Younge might want to read *Wickham's Wife* which explains the backstory of that gentleman and several of the encounters and conversations contained in *Felicity in Marriage.* The first chapter follows here for your enjoyment.

Prologue

"Stay here!" commanded Wickham as the carriage slowed to a stop in front of a nondescript front door in a street of similar doors. "Do not allow anyone to see your face. I must see what can be done. Be patient."

He leapt from the cab and disappeared for a moment into the inky blackness of a London street meagrely lit by the occasional lamp, reappearing at the top of a short flight of steps. She watched as he rapped impatiently on the door with his cane.

A maid answered, pulling her cap into place as though called from her evening's activities, and, after a short interaction, Wickham was left to wait upon the step staring at the closed door. He turned to look back at the cab and saw to his horror that she was clambering down, clutching her hat against the gusty wind.

"Get back in the cab, this instant! I said to wait there for me."

"Oh, la! What nonsense, Wickham! No one knows me here. It is too lonely waiting by myself. But why have not you been invited inside? I thought you were friends with the owner?"

"Perhaps the fact that we are calling far outside usual visiting hours may be of concern, do not you think? It is nearly eleven o'clock; people do not willingly open their doors to knocks so late in the evening. I was lucky mine was not ignored. Now go back to the cab, I will deal with this."

"I shall not! I shall stay here and meet your friend. I do hope he has room for us; I do not think I could endure any more travelling tonight." She slid her hand under his elbow and leaned her head limply against his arm. "I am entirely worn out!"

The door was again opened partway and a lady looked around it; an elegant, handsome lady wrapped in a shawl and carrying a lamp which she held up, gasping when she saw Wickham.

"George! It is indeed you! What in the world do you do here, and at this time of night?"

Her face fell.

"Whatever it is, it cannot be good - very rarely of late have you arrived on my doorstep with good news - but come in and warm yourself."

Her gaze then fell upon his companion who had pushed her way into the hallway in front of Wickham, unnoticed until now in the shock at seeing Wickham.

"Good evening?" she queried as she looked from the girl to Wickham for an explanation.

"Oh! Good evening," the girl giggled. "I was not expecting Wickham's friend to be a *woman*! How interesting! I am Lydia Bennet, soon to be Lydia *Wickham* - is not that a great surprise? Wickham says we will be married very soon, is that not so, my dear?"

Wickham, seeing the reaction upon the lady's face, hastened to intervene, colour flooding his own.

"Mrs. Younge: Allow me to introduce Miss Lydia Bennet … of Longbourn … in Meryton. Miss Bennet: This is a very great friend of mine, Mrs. Julia Younge, who has been the one person in my life upon whom I have known I could always depend and trust."

"*Well*," Mrs. Younge managed a very thin smile. "To be married at last, George. This is most *unexpected*, as you say. Quite a surprise for everyone concerned, indeed. What *good* fortune to have secured a beautiful young bride. But why are not you married already, pray? Travelling together as you are, and at this time of night, can only cast doubt upon the young lady's reputation, surely even you can see that? It is most inappropriate."

"Mrs. Younge; Julia! My dear! *Please*! I know that this looks very damning to you; I will explain, but I cannot at this moment. At this moment I must fall once again upon your mercy and good nature and beg you to offer Miss Bennet a bed for the next few nights whilst I sort out what is to be done."

Mrs. Younge looked astonished and then shocked at Wickham; he had the grace to redden again, unable to meet her gaze. She moved across the passage and opened the door closest to her.

"Come with me into the guest parlour; this must be discussed away from the prying ears of my guests and servants," she hissed as she ushered them through in hurried secrecy before closing it firmly behind her.

CPSIA information can be obtained
at www.ICGtesting.com
Printed in the USA
FFHW021305130519
52454931-57849FF